ON THE BRINK

For my parents, John and Dee Kelly, who always believed I could do this.

ON THE BRINK

RB Kelly

NewCon Press
England

This edition first published in May 2022 by NewCon Press,
41 Wheatsheaf Road, Alconbury Weston, Cambs, PE28 4LF

NCP273 (limited edition hardback)
NCP274 (softback)

10 9 8 7 6 5 4 3 2 1

ISBN:

978-1-914953-16-3 (hardback)
978-1-914953-17-0 (softback)

Cover by Ian Whates,
utilising an image sourced on Pixabay

Text edited by Ian Whates
Typesetting and layout by Ian Whates

Chapter One

Adam

In my dreams, I'm always running. I was born running. And I'll probably be running when I die.

Smoke hangs thickly on the air and the chant is a howl at the back of my skull. It started almost two hours ago, and I've been running for seventy-one minutes. In my dreams, I'm a younger man, but I'm not exactly young, and I'm not built for this. My heart thunders in my chest and my lungs feel like they're on fire, and the only thing that's keeping me going, upright and moving forward, is the fact that I know who the chant is for. There are no names on the datastream, but I don't need a name. I know who the chant is for.

Crowds scatter like frightened fish, heads bowed and covered. Rubble litters the ground. An explosion in the middle distance rattles windows and someone near me screams. I'm no longer trying to pinpoint the blasts; they're everywhere. All directions. Nowhere is safe. I feel the shock wave ratchet through my leg muscles and a blanket of cement dust scatters the air. I know this city by smell and footfall and touch and I have no idea where I am. This is not my city. I don't know it any more.

My feet slap scarred tarmac, and I run, staggering over unfamiliar breaks in the pavement. Gunfire echoes around the high buildings that reach up into the hidden skies above me and I barely break my stride. As I take a corner hard, losing my footing on debris, I collide with three young men carrying a fourth, face bloodied from an open wound on his forehead, eyes seared shut and swollen with the unmistakable marks of tear gas. They barely notice me and I don't stop for them. I'm moving again before I've even finished falling, stealing the momentum from the collision and turning it into an ungainly, loose-legged sprint across scattered chunks of masonry. A whine, a pop, the hiss of CS canisters releasing. I run.

The chant is like an aneurysm. It's like vomiting blood. It's like a full-body heart attack. Someone told me once, many years ago, that it's always stronger when it's someone you know. I've known a lot of people, and the chant has ripped the stream apart more times than I can count, but it has never been like this. It has never felt as though it's trying to saw its way out of my skull. It has never felt as though it's trying to wear my skin as a cape.

I know who the chant is for.

And so I run. I keep running, though I know, in my dream, that I can't run fast enough.

1.2 Adam

I wake up to total darkness, and I realise I've gone blind again.

Fucking *perfect*. I've got places I need to be today and it's going to be 100% harder to get to them if I can't see.

Luca, of course, is no help. I wasn't really expecting him to be, but I feel there are more productive things he could be doing than sitting in the corner of the room sniggering at me. I'm ready to go, my bags are packed, and I need to be out of here by 7, before the next guy arrives. What I really could have done without right now is a full-scale optical hang.

I sit up, carefully. My bones don't creak but my joints protest and my uplink fizzes and stutters as it moves from *background* to *booting*. I can feel my eyesight trying to come online, but it's not in any kind of hurry. There's a glass of water on my bedside table. I find it by memory. The iodine tablets are in the pocket of my coat, which hangs over the rail at the base of the bed. I don't need to see Luca's face to know that he's rolling his eyes as I pop one from its blister and let it plop into the water, fizzing and spitting as it dissolves. I don't need him to tell me I'm a fussy old woman. I know he's thinking it, and I grin in his general direction and answer anyway. "Honey, I was born old. Maybe you could un-piss yourself laughing for five minutes and help me find my shoes?"

I've stayed just long enough for this bed and this room to become familiar. I've plotted the cracks in the low ceiling and the pattern of night noises as the old house settles into sleep, but it's never been my home. The only memories that I've kept here, I'll be taking with me when I go, but knowing that I'm unlikely to ever see this place again after today is unexpectedly moving. I'm getting sentimental in my old age, as Luca never hesitates to point out, but at least he finds my shoes for me. My vision skitters and spurts as I bend down to pull them on, strobing violently in the way that it does when I'm about to spend the day buried beneath a pounding headache, and when I close my eyes to shut out the madness, the uplink hangs again and I'm back to darkness.

Oh well. Better than the other thing.

The truth is, I'm pretty sure that the only thing keeping me alive these days is stubbornness. The lag time on my motor pathways gets a little more noticeable with every passing week, and sometimes, in the mornings, they snarl up if I try to move too quickly and my hands or feet cramp into claws. There's constant, low-level pain in my knee joints where they're starting to degrade and in my spine where structural fatigue is beginning to settle in. My mouth lubricates less efficiently and I have to take on water every few hours or so or else the filtration barrier will fail, which is fine during the day, but less exciting at night. The extra water sluices my system, but my blood is less efficient at recognising waste from nutrients and so I lose calories unnecessarily. I'm tired, tired in my bones, and I know that this body is failing. It's just that I'm not prepared to die until I finish what I started.

"Ready?" I ask Luca, but I already know the answer. Everything I own is in the duffel bag on the floor at the foot of my bed. I haven't carved my name into the wall above the sink, as somebody called Marco has done, who saw fit to crosshatch the passage of days and weeks and months. When I leave this room, it will close over me and it will be like I was never here. This is how it's supposed to be and Luca knows this, but I think he'd like to leave a record of sorts: something to say that we were here, once upon a time, so that there will be something to remember when I'm gone. I'm not the only one prone to sentimentality, and I tell him so, but he just tuts and shakes his head and tells me to talk to him again when I can look him in the eye.

I pull on my coat and sit heavily on the side of the bed, glass of water in my hand. Light is chinking in around the sides of my optic nerve, lightening the shadows shade by shade. I sip slowly, holding the water in my mouth for a few seconds before I let it drizzle into the osmotic filters that are supposed to siphon out the stuff that can kill me from the stuff that I need to live. I don't know if the iodine makes any difference, but it's not hurting anything, so I reckon I might as well. Luca perches beside me, slate on slate in my rebooting visual world, and makes no comment, though I know he wants to.

I finish drinking and set the glass back on the table. The next guy can wash it or he can complain about it: it's almost 7, my sight's as close to better as it's going to get right now, and I need to get moving. I stand and pull on my coat and sling my bag onto my shoulder, and, to the empty room, I say, quietly, "Are you coming, then, or what?"

I'm not haunted, not in the conventional sense. I'm not sure what the word for it would be. All I can say is that I've kept my dead lover's ghost beside me for the twenty-five years since he died, and, when I leave a place, I like to make sure I bring him with me. I'm old and my optical circuitry has begun to degrade, which is why I'm able to imagine that I see his shade detach from the patterns of morning light spilling through the flimsy net curtain at the window, and slip into place beside me as we turn our backs on this little room and move on again.

Chapter Two

2.1 Danae

It's got to the point now where I can pinpoint the location of the chant to Earth or Greater Earth, according to the level of singularity feedback that crowds out the voices. This one is gentle and distant, a sweet choral crescendo that builds over hours, like a church congregation behind closed doors. Somebody on Earth has reached the end of their natural lifespan and gently faded out, and that's actually kind of beautiful. I lie in the lazy haze between sleep and wakening and let it wash over me for a few minutes: serenity by proxy. I won't carry this one with me.

Not like the one last month. It's always worse when they're close by, but that one was brutal. It even made the news.

I've got an intravenous cannula in the back of my hand and a drip full of botulinum toxin feeding directly into a central line below my collarbone. The screen above my face is playing re-runs of an old comedy show that Da used to like, and the rest of my body is circled by a sequence of imaging shells that dilute and muffle the city's datastream feedback into a gentle static wash against my skin. This is the most peace and quiet I'll get all week and I'd prefer not to share it with a canned laughter track, but it is what it is, and I've got good at zoning out the noise as the months have passed.

I didn't used to be aware of the poisons dripping into my veins. The process is subtle and over so quickly that you'd have to be concentrating *really* hard to notice. The research team do, so I do too. I gather from the fact they're still asking me back each month that they haven't yet managed to concentrate hard enough.

I've been here since 7am and it's now almost noon. I know the drill by now: five hours is their absolute limit, and I don't know if that's to do with some imagined pathogen tolerances that they've dreamed up for my immune system, the lead researcher's attention span, or if it's just the orderlies' shift change. So it's not a surprise, when the series lead mugs directly into the fourth wall and the credits roll, to find my radiant sarcophagus abruptly powered down and myself ejected,

5

blinking, into the sterile white claustrophobia of an imaging suite at rest. Unsheltered, the tidal blitz of singularity feedback rushes in to fill the silence, and I never cease to be amazed at how much louder it sounds after a break.

Nobody speaks as I sit up. Nobody ever speaks. Because I feel that I have to fill the void where the speaking should be, I say, "So – is that it for now?"

"Thanks," says a voice from the observation room. I don't recognise this one, but I often don't recognise the voices or the people they belong to. I've met the lead researcher precisely once, the first time I presented myself for testing, and he didn't tell me his name. I'm not sure if they're frightened of me or it's just good old-fashioned contempt, but the time to be bothered by it has come and gone and I find that I just don't care. I wait for the voice to follow up with something that sounds a bit more like an instruction, but nothing like this happens, and then the door to the imaging suite pops open on its hydraulic, airlocked hinges and I understand that this is the best I'm going to get.

I'm done for another month.

The testing centre is attached to the Acute Injury Pod on Sneeuwklokjeweg, which is not a part of the floor that I visit regularly, for obvious reasons, and I'm always ill-at-ease here. It's a Sunday, the morning after the night before, and most of the AIP's foot traffic is nursing a colossal hangover, so I blend right in as I bury my head in my coat in an effort to stifle the bellowing datastream feedback. Released from the protective hum of the imaging suite, it always seems to roar a little bit louder, suck me into the ground a little more firmly, scramble my uplink a little more chaotically, and this is basically the perfect cover in a crowd of Saturday night party animals attempting to survive the tail end of the weekend.

It doesn't stop me watching them, of course. I'm not the only one who can hide in a congregation of the walking dead.

The chant is quieter now. It's not just that it's buried beneath feedback; I can hear it drifting into melodic hush, the kind of song that only exists in the absence of singing. The end has come and it was easy. Most of the older models are close to their time now and there's something almost satisfying in bearing witness to the natural order of things. In the privacy of my own head I let the unfamiliar words flow through me for a couple of lines as I scan the blank, grey faces around me for evidence of simpatico. No butterflies agitate the stream around me, but I'm bleary and not yet properly rebooted: in the hour or so after I leave the imaging suite, I'm vulnerable, and anyone watching me will know this. I can't afford to let my guard down for a moment.

This is how I spot the woman following me.

She's slight, built like a teenage girl, but her face is too old to be that young, and this immediately puts me on my guard. There's only one type of face that ages from the eyes outwards: I don't need a streamdance to recognise one of my own. There is no reason for her to be at an Acute Injury Pod, and the fact that she's not looking at me, that she doesn't even seem to have noticed my existence, immediately sparks the survival pathways in my brain. Adrenaline spikes, too sharp for my foggy thought processes, and my stomach lurches so violently that I think I'm going to throw up. I slice my way through passersby and find a shop front, closed for Sunday, but with its canopy still unfurled, and I lean heavily against a strut as I try to breathe through the nausea. The woman is on the far side of the road, one hand rifling through the tufts of hair that peak out from the front of her headscarf, and she passes by without a glance.

I watch her go. I watch the back of her head bob and weave among disinterested shoulders. I watch, and I wait for a sign.

We are almost at the end of Sneeuwklokjeweg, where it's bisected by the main arterial route that runs through the sector. She stops at the edge of the pavement, but instead of crossing, she turns ninety degrees so that she's facing the opposite side of the road she's just come up. Her eyes scan the street, but it's a Sunday morning: there are few trams, road traffic is almost non-existent. When her gaze meets mine, flickers for a second, and then moves on, that's when I know for sure.

My legs find the way almost before my brain is aware I'm going to react. The woman steps out onto the street, shrugging her coat around her shoulders as though she's cold, and I fall into step with her, fifteen feet away but closing fast. I almost can't believe what I'm doing, but part of me has been ready for this moment since I arrived on Luchtstad. Fourteen feet and closer with every stride. My legs are longer than hers and she's not moving like a woman in pursuit – her shoulders are relaxed, her arms swing loosely by her side, her pace is steady and even. She's doing everything right, and still I spotted her.

I've been waiting for her or somebody like her for many months.

Ten feet away. She's on my side of the street now, close enough that I'm expecting the stream to erupt into butterflies at any minute. Nine feet, and I'm not entirely sure what I'm going to do when I catch her. The Sunday morning crowd is not comprised of the city's healthiest representatives, but I think they might notice just the same if a random woman leaps on another random woman and tackles her to the ground. What happens after that is even less clear, but she's seven feet away now. Barely longer than the length of my body. I need to act.

"*Hoi!*" she calls cheerfully. My body tenses, my legs locking in the act of motion, and I almost stumble. I catch myself at the apex of my fall and turn it into a pivot, a stagger, and a half-step onto the road. "*Sorry, sorry. Ik ben laat, nietwaar?*"

My head is whirling. My heart is hammering in my chest and my skull feels like it's full of water. I can barely catch my breath and I lose my balance, lurching forwards. I don't mean to, but I collide with her just the same and she startles and stumbles forwards under my weight. Her companion catches us both as we tumble into his chest, air leaving his lungs in a muffled *oof.*

"Sorry," I mutter. There are no butterflies. There's only stream feedback and the beginnings of a sick headache.

"Are you all right?" asks the man, but he's not talking to me. The girl has buried herself in the crook of his arm and is glaring back at me through watchful, wary eyes. She's younger than I thought, I see now: she can't be more than fifteen. Too young to be artificial, and he's not much older.

"Sorry," I say again. "I lost my footing."

"It's okay," says the girl, but her face calls her a liar.

I am definitely going to throw up.

I turn my head just in time and manage to hit the gutter instead of the pavement. I didn't eat last night or this morning, and it's mostly liquid. I'm trying to apologise again, but my stomach won't let me stop until I'm done, and in the corner of my eye, I'm just about aware of the man pulling the girl away, hurrying them both towards Sneeuwklokjestraat and the anonymous, faceless crowds. My belly roils and my head thunders and the passersby part and flow around me like water around a rock. Nobody stops. Nobody looks at me.

When I'm finished, I make my way a few steps further up the street and sink heavily to the ground, clutching my forehead with one hand, wrapping my other arm around my knees. At least I didn't catch her. At least I didn't swing a punch this time.

At least this is the street outside the Acute Injury Pod on Sneeuwklokjeweg on the Sunday morning after a Saturday night, and nobody will so much as bat an eyelid. Though they'll call the police in a minute if I don't disappear. I stand up slowly, testing my weight against my elastic legs and finding they hold firm. There's not much I can do about the headache or the taste of semi-digested gin at the back of my throat, but I've survived worse. Home is half an hour's walk from here; I can make it that far.

I walk.

2.2 Danae

Part of the problem is that I don't sleep well on Luchtstad. I don't know if it's the air up here, or the circadian rhythm, or the feedback from the stream singularity – because they don't exactly include a section on Handy Hints For A-Naut Immigrants in the welcome pack – but I'm not sure I've passed one unbroken night since I arrived on this city, and there's only so much stoic a person can manage before they start to go crazy. If I'd known, back on Earth, that my somnolence had an expiration date, I think I'd have closed my eyes and never opened them again.

There's a tram passing when I clear the airway into Hyacintweg 90 and, though it circles around and through the market and adds another fifteen minutes to my journey, my legs just don't want to carry me much further, and so I step on and find a seat close to the back where I can rest my head against the thrumming perspex and drift off for a while. The news strip is full of yesterday's protest march on Radiale Drie, which closed the factory lines across half the floor and snarled up inter-radial traffic around the city, but they were marching against the water restrictions and not Niet Zoeken, so I don't need to listen too hard. The Voice of the City speaks in soothing tones of productivity gradients and profit margins, pausing briefly to announce tram stops, and I close my eyes and let the spinning in my head settle, let my bubbling thoughts relax. The skin of the back of my hand feels warm where the cannula was sited, tingling faintly where the flesh is healing. I'm tired and hungry and starting to get cold, and so, when the tannoy pings and the Voice announces our arrival at Centralemarkt, on impulse I stand and join the line of commuters queuing for exit. I'm not sure why, and, right up to the point where I take the final step onto the street, I'm not sure that I'm going to do it, but, as the tram pulls away behind me, cold air worrying at cold air, I'm glad I did.

For one thing, it means that I'm probably not going to throw up again.

Half the stalls are closed on Sundays, but the other half are not, and most of the ones that are open are selling food. It's a good sign, I think, that I'm pleased about this. I consider buying some *bitterballen* to eat while I walk, but my usual stall is shuttered and dark, and today is not the day to be adventurous, so I wander aimlessly for a while, waiting for inspiration to strike. The air is stale and heavy with last night's smells: hot fat, cooled, beer brushed into the gutters, sweat and crushed cigarette ends and detergent. I like the sound of the language as it rattles around me, sharp-edged and discordant, like a tone poem, and if I don't listen too closely it blends together until it's no longer words and sentences, but a wall of noise, machine-gun brisk, peppered with easy laughter. When I'm tired, it feels like little pinpricks in a shell of cloud and cotton wool, and I like the way it brings me back to myself.

I stop for a sandwich at the first bar I find. My hand shakes as I lift it to my mouth and I realise I've been ignoring my vitalic feedback in the hope that it will just go away, and this is not a good way to get home in one piece. The itch flares as it always does when something falls out of line in my day, and I catch the bartender's eye and order a vodka. The drink comes in a little mock-porcelain cup, chilled from the freezer. I appreciate the effort and tip him well; it's Sunday morning and trade is slow, and I remember what it was like to work in catering.

I scan the crowd around me from my seat, but, after five minutes of careful watching, I don't see any faces that linger. Nobody that walks past one way and then turns and walks back again. Nobody who looks as if they're having a conversation with themselves. The vodka has softened me, it's true, but it's enough for now. Two near-misses in one day is more than I'm equipped to handle. I thank the bartender and make my way back onto the street, but I pause at the edge of the awning, just in case. Stop. Breathe. Wait.

Wait.

I'm tempted to close my eyes, but I think I look plenty crazy enough to be getting on with, and it's hard to be on the look-out when you can't actually see. It's just the way the market smells, sometimes. Traffic fumes and cooking smoke and a thick, rich undercurrent of spice. And drains and a backed up precipitation system in need of a rain cycle, and the burnt ozone smell of the lightbands, and damp and streetwash and the scent-echo of vermin. And crumbling buildings and cold air that's still just slightly too warm, and the way a body smells when their clothes haven't had time to dry properly. And there, beneath it all, the smell of cleaning chemicals and the cavernous scent of nothing that hovers inside big buildings, traces of soap, traces of coffee, like eyes on the back of my head.

Sometimes, just for a moment, I forget which city I'm in.

Just for a moment. Sometimes, that's all I need.

2.3 Danae

The block is still and silent when I bare my neck chip for the scanner at the door to my corridor, but that's not really a surprise. The kitchen was alive with chatter and laughter until well into the small hours last night, and today's afternoon is not yet old. I'd be amazed if there was any sign of life before early evening, and even then it will be slow, quiet and careful. Sanne's snores tremble the quiet air as I pull up outside my room and I hesitate, considering whether I should just hammer on her door until the racket stops and then dive inside before she comes out to see who's startled her awake. This is preferable to waiting until I can't bear it any more and thumping on the wall that divides our lodgings, because then she will know that it's me, but in the end I chicken out with my fist raised to the shadows outside her door and I duck into my room, where the noise is at least muffled.

Alone, I drop my bags onto my bed and, for want of anything more productive to do, I pace the length of the room once, twice, three times: two big steps forward, two big steps back. The carpet tile beneath my feet shucks and skids against the plastic surface of the floor beneath and the overhead light flickers as I pass below it. I rise up onto my toes as I move, stretching until my calf muscles burn, until my fingers brush the mottled polyethylene moulding of the ceiling panels, and then I drop down onto my bed, springs sagging, shopping bags clinking, blanket ruffling beneath me on the thin mattress.

Sundays. Honestly, I could do without Sundays.

I flex my hand in front of my face. The blood-spot from the cannula has dried and the skin beneath it has knit seamlessly over the hole. Toxins dance in my bloodstream but they can't touch my tissues and by tomorrow they'll be gone, emptied back into the water troughs on the lowest levels of the radial, ready to power somebody's caffeine injection, hydrate someone's sodium rations, or, more likely, feed the water-rich soils that keep this city commercial. I haven't seen them, but I know that they exist, in the same way that I know there are four floors beyond this one and six more radials than mine. I know that this city circles a singularity punched directly into the datastream itself, from which gravity keeps us grounded and power keeps us alive. Knowing these things is an act of faith, and I don't like faith: I like to feel things and see them and satisfy myself that they are real. Sometimes, when I can't sleep, I'll walk the length of this apartment block, along the corridors that link the residences, up and down stairs, past darkened common rooms. Sometimes I find a window on a far distant floor and I press my face to the pane so that I feel my nose flatten and my lips brush cool perspex, and I peer down into the street below, angles shifted out of familiarity by the change of perspective. That's all it takes sometimes: a change of perspective, and the familiar feels fresh, unsettled, always becoming.

But here, this room: this is mine. This room is locked to my streamcode; I'm the only person who can unlock my door. Nobody can come into this room without my consent, and I am safe.

I'm safe here.

I am safe.

Chapter Three

3.1 Adam

I've heard about this in theory, and apparently it works.

This is what they tell me.

What I know is: I'm going to spend the next forty-seven hours sealed inside a canister of frozen meat, in the depressurised belly of an inter-etheric cargo transport. There's not going to be any oxygen, and there's not going to be any way out, and whether or not I'm alive at the other end is entirely dependent on my ability to dial down my heart rate to a point where I could legally pass for dead. Excuse me if I'm not wild with enthusiasm for this idea, but it strikes me as the sort of plan that you only ever come up with if you're not going to be the one actually carrying it out.

It's a cold, overcast evening as I say goodbye to pre-etheran *terra firma*. Matthias is the only cache member who's come to see me off. I'm not sure why he's here, either, since his presence more than doubles the risk of something going wrong, and I was fully briefed in the last cell meeting three days ago. I suspect that he doesn't entirely trust my motives, but there's nothing I can do about that. It's not as though there were \volunteers lining up for this trip. He's the only other artificial in our company of five, and I'd know that the other three guys were organic even if the stream weren't completely silent around them: it's the way they keep casting flickering, doubtful glances towards Matthias and me every time either of us moves. I know that one of them is being paid, and I wish I knew which of them it was, because I'd like to know that Mr Panicky to my left has given up his time of his own free will and devotion to the cause. He has the sallow, greyish skin of a man who spends all his days inside darkened rooms, which is an aesthetic you acquire when you spend a lot of time around a-nauts, but he also looks completely terrified. If it turns out that he's the guy that's in this for the money, it could be that he's also sold us out to the Rens and doesn't know whether that means that he's going to die today before he gets a chance to enjoy being slightly richer than he used to be.

Mr Panicky fumbles a circuit breaker. It clangs into the side of one of the metal crates that surround us and the sound echoes off the high ceilings, far too loud.

The oldest of the organics is maybe late fifties, with a jet-black moustache that nestles into silvery grey hair and makes him look like a badger. He rolls his eyes at Matthias in what could be a gesture of impatience and could be a gesture of apology. *This guy is a dick*, is what his look says to me. But Matthias just gives a little shake of his head and grins. I've never really understood what Matthias finds funny, but he's lived a long time, and if he thinks Mr Panicky's panic is entertaining and not terrifying, then that's reassuring enough to be getting on with. Matthias was there on the day that Luca died, and he got me out of London when I could barely remember my own name. He's a safe pair of hands in a crisis, and he's good at staying alive and keeping other people alive. I trust him to know if there's a problem.

I think.

"Two minutes," says Mr Panicky. He's making a good show of ignoring Badger Man's glare. "Come on, come on. We need to get moving."

Matthias looks up at the crate beside us. It looks really, really big. "Are you ready for this?" he asks me.

I follow his line of sight. "Minus twelve degrees?" I say. I'm trying to make it sound less cold, but it's not working.

"Maximum," says Matthias.

A meat crate, says Luca's voice at my ear. *Seriously. You're going to freeze to death in a meat crate.*

I ignore him. He's done worse.

"How long have I got?" I ask Badger Man.

He makes a show of looking at his watch. "Can't open the hatch for more than seventy seconds," he says. "Any more than that and the sensors are going to pick up the temperature rise."

I look at Matthias. He shrugs. "Plenty of time."

An actual meat crate, says Luca again, in a tone that sounds a lot like he's just about keeping his laughter in check. *At least I went out with a bit of dignity…*

"Guys," says Mr Panicky. "We need to move."

The third guy, the youngest, is already halfway up the rungs on the side of the crate, ready to swipe an access code into the CPU. He hangs there, watching and waiting, and I'm aware of Matthias' eyes on me too. This trip was a long time in the planning and almost as long again in the financing, and me not dying in the next two days is only the first step in making it happen.

"Okay," I say. "Let's do this."

"You sure?" says Matthias, but it's for show. The time to back out was weeks ago.

"I'm sure," I say.

He nods. "Okay." And then, to the others: "Let's cool him down."

There's a bucket of ice water by the foot of the ladder. Badger Man lifts it now and hefts it in both hands as he steps up close beside me. "Good luck," he says. And then, "Sorry about this…" as he empties it over my head.

I'm prepared, but in that way that stops short of being *actually* prepared and hovers around anticipation instead. You think these are the same thing, but then whatever it is you're anticipating happens, and it's definitely not. My vision fuzzes and I can't get a breath, and I stagger forward, clutching at whatever's in front of me, feeling my fists curl around rough fabric.

"What's happening?" says a voice – Mr Panicky's I think, which fits.

"Pulmonary hang," says Matthias. "Give him a minute."

"He looks like he's dying…" says another voice. Badger Man's? I can't place it.

"Give him a minute." Matthias' voice sounds like it's echoing down the length of a long tunnel. "He's not breathing."

"He's not *breathing?*"

"Give him a minute."

Thirty seconds. Forty. I didn't have time to take a last breath before my lungs stopped working and the fire in my chest is building fast. Matthias must register the fear-spike in the stream because he steps into the place where my vision clears and he squints into my face and says, "Adam. Adam, listen. This is a physiological reaction. This will pass."

I manage a nod, and that small action is like breaking a current: the paralysis lifts and I suck in a huge gasp. Another. One more, and it feels less like I'm breathing sand. A fourth, and my sight starts to de-fritz.

"Okay now?" says Matthias.

I can't answer him, so I nod again.

"Don't let him warm up…" says Badger Man, close to my ear, and I realise it's his coat that I'm clutching. I let go. I really don't want him to start thinking that we need another bucket of water.

"Jesus," I say slowly, testing out the word. But I can feel my uplink slowly starting to compensate. I can feel the thermo-vitalic feedback loop skittering back and forward, and I can feel my cardiovascular and endocrine networks slackening as they prepare to protect my neurological circuitry.

"He's fine," says Matthias briskly. I feel his hand on my arm. "Let's get him moving."

I let him usher me forwards, towards the crate. All my systems are trying to come back online, and I focus on stabilising them at sub-optimal – pre-hibernation, enough to keep me moving while the vitalic overrides work out how to stop my cortex from crashing as the uplink troubleshoots the source of the problem. Thirty years ago, I'd already be halfway into preliminary repairs by now; maybe obsolescence has its benefits after all. At the base of the ladder, I feel Matthias' hand grip my wrist again, and I turn slowly in search of what he wants. The act of stopping my body from doing what it wants to do is taking up a lot of processing power right now, and I know Matthias knows this.

He keeps it short. "Adam," he says. "Good luck."

"Nothing to it," I say. It sounds less impressive through chattering teeth.

He grins and releases my arm, and that's it. The young man on the rungs above me reaches down a hand to help me onto the side of the crate and I find that my muscles know what to do by themselves: one hand up and over, grip, haul, repeat. Grip, haul, repeat. It's a surprisingly mundane way to leave the only planet I've ever known, but there'll be plenty of time for nostalgia and existential doubt in the next forty-seven hours. So I save it for later, and focus instead on drawing down enough reserve power into my hands and legs to move me up the narrow metal bars towards icy darkness and my possible tomb.

3.2 Adam

"Did you ever wonder," I asked Luca once, "why they built us to blend in?"

That got me a raised eyebrow, and I took his point: we were still in Nottingham at that stage, and there was a sub-processing plant in Sheffield that had bulk-bought Luca's line fifteen years earlier. It made his face that bit easier to pick out of a crowd, and so he'd taken to wearing a false beard and a pair of tattoo sleeves whenever we went out. He didn't like to talk about it.

I tried again. "I'm not talking about your vanity, Popeye. I'm talking practicality. I'm talking about what possible reason there is for us to look like them."

This was when he told me about the guys he used to know who'd been part of the post-etheric fleet.

There were only a handful left by the time Luca met them. They didn't last long, once the shooting started. But back in the day, there'd been thousands of them: tall and pale, with a pliable, silverish polymer-compound in place of skin, which floated on a sac of low-density lubricant designed to expand and contract as they moved between vacuum and an Earth-density oxygen/nitrogen envelope. They had no mouth or nose, because both of these things are more trouble than they're worth in space, so they got their food and air through an obturostomic valve in their lower back, from where it passed to an adipose depot to be processed as needed. Their fingers were long, thin and wiry, toughened at the tip; their chest cavities were encased by a titanium alloy endoskeleton; and their eyes hid behind hazy, expressionless, aluminium-silicate shields.

It would have taken more than fake body art and facial hair to make them disappear.

And yet, in spite of all this, in spite of the clear advantages of adapting or adding or subtracting limbs or turning them into a completely different shape altogether, the post-etheric fleet were created in humanoid form. Their eyes made them look like insects and their skin looked as if it were made out of modelling clay, but at least they didn't look like *monsters*.

Not many of them chose to make the journey back to Earth. The ones that did, this is how they did it: in the lightless, oxygenless, sub-zero belly of a fucking meat locker attached to a space elevator. I'm not sure why this is the first time it's occurred to me to wonder how many of them didn't wake up at the other end.

3.3 Adam

Time doesn't stop in the *dis*, the space on the other side of the link. It just goes all relativistic. I'm going to shelter here while my body tries not to die, but that's not as easy as it sounds. I've got an adrenaline crash-dump buzzing in my veins and a pair of lungs that know there should be more oxygen in them right now, and there are planes of frozen flesh chill-burning painfully against the hardening fabric of my coat. My heart rate needs to drop to less than five beats per hour but it really doesn't want to, and the darkness is just dark enough to make my optical uplink think it's glitched again and start trying to come back online. In less than fifteen minutes, this crate will be scanned and magnetically fixed to the hull of the *Polaris Wanderer*, and I need to be in full hibernation before that happens or my lifesigns will show and it will all be over.

Assuming there's fifteen minutes of oxygen in here, of course.

Assuming that particularly pertinent fact.

I focus. I spend very little time inside the uplink these days, but even in the grips of existential panic I can find my way down dusty pathways and through the access joint. My stream vent is a flurry of activity as the *dis* tries to work out what the hell the body is playing at and why the thermal feedback loop is registering such screwy data while the motor functions just sit there and do nothing about it. It's easy to slip inside, but harder to stay there. The body keeps trying to drag me back, and I can't really blame it. I can feel my clothes freezing against my skin and the brachio-neural pathways in my left arm are starting to short; the tibio-neural pathways are already partially inert in both legs. I struggle to anchor myself. I have to stabilise the uplink before I can make the adjustments I need to my cardiopulmonary system, but the problem is that, with most of myself in the *dis*, there's not a lot left to keep a hold of the physical body, and it's panicking.

Luca floats out here, somewhere. If I could find him just by being here, I'd never leave the *dis* again, but I can't: he's lost to me, for as long as I'm pinned to a physical body. Because it settles me, because it gives me a focus other than the shorting neural circuitry in my extremities and my fibrillating heart, and because I really wish he was here, I imagine his face hovering in the darkness an inch from mine, and his breath on my cheeks. I imagine his voice, warm in the freezing air. He says, *You know I'll never let you live this down if this is how you die.*

I say, *There'll be nothing to live down if this is how I die.*

He says, *Semantics? At a time like this? There's nothing wrong with you. Shut up complaining and find your cardiac pathway.*

I say, *You're not fucking helping, you know.*
I am fucking helping. Your heart rate's still too high.
Yes. I know. I'm working on it.
Clock's ticking...
Thanks, I needed the extra pressure.
Come on, he says. *You know how to do this.*
I do know how to do this. I haven't done it for a long time, but Luca knows I can, because he was there the last time I did. It was back in the Tilbury days, right at the end as everything fell apart, and we were running from a party of about eighty thousand Rens through the old sewage plant. We knew that they'd have the river cordoned off and there was no point in even trying to get out by road, but, luckily for us, the plant was still online in those days. The thing about organic waste matter, it turns out, is that it doesn't actually stay warm for very long on the outside, which was the second thing I noticed when we leapt into one of the vats in search of a pipe that led to the Thames. The third thing was the fact that the pipes didn't follow a straight line out of the station, and we had no idea where we were headed for or when oxygen might become available again. It's top of my list of ways I'm really glad I didn't die.

I say, *I know what you're thinking...*
I swear to God, he says, *if you mention it one more time...*
Don't keep nagging me about my heart rate and I won't mention that you had a used condom up your nose for the last three hundred metres of pipe. Anyway, my heart rate's fine.
You're never going to let that go, are you? I couldn't exactly reach my nose to get rid of it, could I? And it's still too high. It'll register on the scan.
You've never been lovelier. Staggering out of the Thames, dripping shit-water, and with half a prophylactic disappearing up one nostril. There. Is that better?
A little. You're getting there. Are you in the dis?
Mostly.
Mostly won't do. Get further in.
I'm working on it.
You know this isn't one of your better ideas? You know that, right?
You're just jealous that you never thought of doing it.
Yeah. That'll be it. I'm jealous of your first-class accommodation aboard this luxury inter-etheric cruise. It's a really stupid idea.
You know why I'm doing it.

Of course I know why you're doing it. It's still a stupid idea.

And you didn't try to talk me out of it.

So I want you to come looking for me. Sue me. It's still a stupid idea.

I'm out of better ones.

I swear to God, you fall apart without me. Fine. Get comfortable. You'll be here a while.

I'm aware. Keep me company?

Like I have anywhere else to go…

My heart rate has slowed to one beat every fifteen minutes. My neural circuitry is silent. My breathing is so faint it'll pass undetected on a lifescan. If I can maintain these levels, I can sustain basic vitalic functioning for at least the next sixty hours, and I should only need fifty, fifty-five at a push. I watch this, dispassionately, from my harbour on the *dis*, with my dead lover's ghost at my side.

Chapter Four

4.1 Danae

"Honestly," says Sanne, slowly and carefully, "I think if they could cut the water rations any lower without killing us, they'd try it."

We're lined up in the shower rooms, waiting for our turn to get blasted with hot air and vaporised soap, and it's almost impossible to avoid conversation in the queue. I can't get out of the post-work clean-up, because they have rules about the sorts of things you're allowed to carry in your pores and hair onto the streets up here, but I tend to avoid the morning ablutions. This morning, though, I was feeling tired and ropey from lack of sleep, and the brain buzz from the singularity was like needles in my skull, and it just seemed like a good idea to get air-scalded into wakefulness. Besides, you never know your luck. Sometimes everyone else is too tired for conversation, too.

Not this morning. Sanne is only two places ahead of me in the queue, and nobody in this place observes the simple etiquette of minding where you put your eyes when everyone's naked.

She nodded when she saw me. "*Goodemorgen,*" she said, and I knew I wasn't getting out of it.

So I gave in. "*Goodemorgen,*" I said. They think I have trouble understanding them, but that's because I don't speak very much. They also think I'm French, and none of them, so far, speak French.

"There's never enough water," she says now. "For the bulbs? Of course. But for us?" She shrugs. "It's too cold to wait this long."

"It's very cold," I agree. I can't bring myself to meet her eyes. I mean, her tits are *right there.*

"Bente says that there's water in the showers on Verdieping Een."

"How does Bente know?" I ask, which appears to be the right thing to say.

Sanne grins. "Bente," she says, "is full of shit." She glances sideways at me to see if I understand *vol stront* and I debate for a moment whether to hang onto my alibi or join in with the camaraderie.

My hesitation does the answering for me before I can decide, and Sanne chuckles to herself over her private joke and stretches out her arms above her head. This has the effect of making her nipples bounce enthusiastically into my immediate line of sight. I don't know where to put my eyes that's neither staring at her nor looking prudishly away, so I rub some warmth back into my naked shoulders for something to do while I wait for her to finish.

"On the radio," she says, around a yawn, and hesitates. "Radio?" she clarifies, and I have to nod and confirm that, yes, I understand the word *radio*, which is, after all, the same in English. And French, for that matter. "On the radio," she continues, "they said there was another blackout."

It wasn't a full shutdown. I have access to the same radio stations as my colleagues, so I know that it was a partial grid failure to a fifteen-block sector – enough to grind overnight inter-radial traffic to a halt, but the life support system failsafes kicked in straight away, so nobody so much as grazed a knee, and the floor wasn't isolated from the rest of the radial. The news strips have been very careful to avoid mentioning why it happened or if there's anyone to blame. But I decide against pointing this out, in case it prolongs the conversation.

"Another one?" I say, and tut my expected disapproval. It's only partially performative. That makes more or less one a week now for the past twelve weeks and, when they close the factory early, our pay is docked. This one was two radials over, which is not always enough to cause problems for Radiale Zeven, but if you time these things just right you can set off a chain reaction that calcifies the entire city in an unholy gridlock that Moses himself couldn't part.

"Were you here," asks Sanne, "when the transit cube got stuck on Verdieping Vijf?"

I think my face must be an answer in itself. Sanne twitches her eyebrows in understanding, but I say, "Yes, I was."

"Those stupid boxes," she says. "Who needs a box shaped like a Christmas tree? For bulbs? *Bulbs.* A Christmas tree doesn't grow from bulbs."

What a Christmas tree does or doesn't grow from was academic, as it turned out, because a blackout on the lowest level of our radial shut down all transit to the floors above and the cubes couldn't get up with the stock that afternoon. Half the lines in the factory ran out of bulbs just before the afternoon klaxon, and we had Jouke as our supervisor by then, and he does not take disappointment well. The man has the unerring aim of a practiced sadist and he throws hard enough that the bulbs bounce off skin with enough force to bruise the person standing next to the target.

So, no. I'm not excited at the prospect of another traffic snarl up. I can dodge pretty well, but it's usually a better idea to let them hit, and they're not always fresh. I had no appreciation, until I started working here, of just how appalling a thing a rotting hyacinth bulb can be.

"*Nog zo'n verdomde stroomstoring,*" says Sanne wearily, because she thinks, of course, that I don't understand *verdomde*. But we're at the showers now, and, with a gentle touch of her hand to my arm, she peels off into a booth and leaves me and my tits to myself.

There are times when I'm overcome by waves of relief so strong that they stop me in my tracks and make my breath hitch in my throat, because, despite it all, despite everything, I made it out. I escaped, as I always said I would: I got out, and I made another place my home. And then there are mornings when I'm standing, naked and goose-pimpled, in an overheated, drain-perfumed shower room, idly contemplating how many bruises I can safely avoid by close of shift, and I wonder why anyone would ever choose to spend more than fifteen minutes on this stupid city before they launched themselves out of an airlock and into the merciful grip of the void.

And yet here I am. I'm not sure I have an answer, really. I'm not even sure that there is one.

Chapter Five

5.1 Adam

Light shatters the gloom, and my stupid optic nerve panics and hangs. I'm sort of used to the darkness by now, but I'm much too fucking cold for this.

"Hey," hisses an urgent voice from somewhere in the vicinity of the recently extinguished glare. It sounds like it belongs to somebody young. "Hey!" it says again, and then there's a stream of Dutch, which I don't understand.

The thing is, I was supposed to understand. I fused a language patch to my data pocket and everything. The voice says something else, and I can work out from context that he needs me to start moving, but not a single word of it makes sense. So, I've turned up on a Dutch-speaking city without a single word of Dutch, I'm possibly frozen into the furniture, and I'm blind again. This isn't going well so far.

"Mister!" says another voice: older and female. "Thirty seconds, okay? Then we close again."

I've been easing out of the *dis* for the past twenty minutes and absolutely everything hurts. Luca is nowhere to be found. My heart rate is wonky and my thermo-vitalic arc is more like a squiggle, which my blood flow does not like at all, and it's taking its sweet time flowing back into my extremities. My muscles scream themselves awake, every single one of them, as I struggle upright.

"Mister!" comes the woman's voice again, thin with panic.

"I'm…" Jesus, I can barely move my lips. The skin feels taut, like a balloon stretched too far. "I know, I know. I can't see. But I'm coming."

There's a muttered conversation from the hatchway and my optic nerve fizzles and bursts static briefly across my visual receptors, which is almost less helpful than the blindness and disorients me for a second. But it's enough to see where the ladder is: two feet to my left, exactly where I left it. I grope for it in the darkness, find the rungs and start heaving myself upwards towards the sound of the voice. Thirty seconds, she said. I've lost track of time again, but I'm pretty sure half of that is gone already. The ladder is slick and really, really cold, but my fingers haven't got all the feeling back yet and I'm pretty motivated to ignore anything that's not climbing the hell out of this crate.

I feel the atmosphere change as I near the exit hatch, and two pairs of hands catch me under my arms and help haul me out the final few feet. I fall backwards onto the metal surface as something god-awful explodes inside my skull, high-volume static turned up past the point of pain, as if there's a hurricane of screaming voices right in the centre of my brain. My hands find their own way to my ears and I'm pretty sure I make some kind of groaning noise through my clenched teeth. And then, of course, because it's that sort of morning, my heart decides to stop.

My vision sputters on, though. The uplink giveth, and the uplink taketh away.

"Mister!" says the woman. Her face is full of fear, and I don't think she's as old as she sounds. "Quick! Now! There is not time!"

I know there's no time. That's not helpful. My fucking heart has stopped beating. But my body is basically dead right now and I can't tell her this, so instead I lie in a useless heap on top of the crate and focus, focus, focus on restabilising my systems before hypoxia makes everything even worse.

The owner of the other voice, a boy who looks like he's still in his teens, drops the exit hatch back into place with exaggerated care, and the only noise it makes is a gentle breath of air against metal. He scrabbles across the crate to where I lie and gets his face right into mine, before firing off a stream of completely terrified words at his companion. I ignore him. My heart muscle is fine, just tired. I manage to spark up a beat or two, which helps keep everything going. And then I push a little too hard and kick myself into ventricular fibrillation.

This is not the first time it's happened, and it never gets any less painful. But at least *something* is happening now, and it's easier to settle a crazy arrhythmia than it is to reverse a cardiac arrest.

"Mister!" says the woman. "Mister, people come. We must go."

"Okay," I say. This is a good sign: I'm speaking. This means I'm breathing again. I test my legs for movement, and come up short. This is less good.

The woman scans her eyes down my body. I think my hips are

rolling from side to side, but I'm not sure if that's because it's happening, or because I want it to be happening. I'm so cold that I'm not shivering, and I know enough about my thermic regulatory loop to know that this is a big problem. She hesitates, and then comes to a decision.

"Okay," she says. "We will help you."

I have no idea how they're going to do that. "No, it's okay," I say. "I can do it – just give me a minute."

The boy glances nervously over his shoulder, in the direction of unseen footsteps. He says something to the woman, and she nods, tightly, and replies in a low voice.

"People come," she says to me again. "We will go. You must stay."

"Wait," I say, but they're already moving, crouched low. "Wait!" I say again. "I don't... I can't..."

"You stay," says the woman. She's at the edge of the crate now, midway through swinging her legs over the side and onto the access ladder. Her English fails her and she waves a hand and mutters something in Dutch. I hear a word that sounds like *come*, and hang onto it.

"You're coming back?" I ask.

She nods. "Yes. We coming back."

My line of sight is limited just now. It doesn't take much for her to disappear. But just as the boy is about to follow suit, he raises his palm in my direction. "You stay," he says, and then he's gone too.

Stay I can do. It's my only actual option at this point. I'm beginning to wonder if this is an honest-to-God, full-system, neuro-electrical hang. I've heard about them but I've never actually seen one. Well. Timing could be better. It's darkish up here and I can only hope I'm plastered flat enough against the roof to cast a negligible shadow, because I'm pretty sure my friends scattered in the face of approaching non-friendlies and I wouldn't want to bet my life on the boy being able to look innocent when he's quite as freaked out as he sounds.

My head feels like it's full of angry bees and my streamlink is going nuts. It's possibly testament to just how completely fucked everything is right now that I observe all this with nothing more than vague interest. A full neuro-electrical hang, wow. Be nice to have someone to talk to about it, *Luca*. I feel as though I should be making notes or something.

Footsteps approach, clipping against the floor, and I hear three voices, all male, all with that syrupy air that comes with relative power. I try to flatten myself a little flatter and am encouraged to find that my hands are starting to work again and my head will roll from one side to the other on command. This is better than nothing, but not a massive amount of help in keeping me secret up here: I reckon I'm too close to the edge of the crate to blend into the shadows if anyone looks up. There might be no Rens on the city, but I don't feel that optimistic about what happens next if they do. I'd really prefer not to go out in a blaze of semi-frozen flesh that won't even bleed enough to inconvenience anyone's day.

"*Ja*," I hear from below, and I realise that the speaker is the woman that was just with me on the top of the crate. I'm not wild about the fact she and the boy have clearly been discovered by the owners of the syrupy voices. I'm even less wild about the fact that I can't understand a word of the exchange that follows, until she signs off with a terse, clipped,"*Nee, oke.*"

And then there are a lot of footsteps walking away from the crate, too many to belong to just three people. And then there's silence.

Well, shit.

Okay, it's better than being discovered, but *shit*. I listen out for a bit, just in case I'm wrong, or maybe I've added an audio hang to the long list of systems that are crashing. But no, they are definitely gone. *Stay*, they told me, but they also told me they were coming back, and then they disappeared. I wait for some minutes, and then some minutes more, but as my thermo-vitalics reboot and my core temperature starts to stabilise, I'm starting to shiver violently and I really need to start moving. After a moment's debate, I roll onto my front and edge my way forwards towards the lip of the crate. Some of the motor feedback relays to the muscles of my legs are going to need to be repaired when I get a chance and I'm running so low on energy reserves that I'm in danger of edging into hypokalemia, but I can move again at least. I raise my head enough that I can scour the cargo bay floor below, and find it completely empty. It's time to make a decision, so I do.

My legs are heavy and wooden, but they bend on command when I lower them over the side of the crate in search of the rungs. I can't move quickly enough to look like I belong here if anyone sees me, but I also can't answer anybody's questions, so it's probably not going to matter. Five metres from the lid to the ground and it feels like it takes me an hour per metre, but nobody comes as I thunk and wobble my way to the bottom of the ladder. I take a moment to catch my breath, leaning back against the side of the crate as I get my bearings. My hand snakes inside my coat, to the inner pocket, and closes over my new identity card. Emmet Keller, it makes me. I don't even want to imagine how much it cost.

Okay. I'm here now. I'm out of the crate and my ID hasn't done something stupid like fall out in transit and fuse to a wall of meat. Reassured, I lever myself upright again, look left and then right, and finally settle on right. It's as good a direction as any.

I set off.

5.2 Adam

Uitgang is exit. I remember this from somewhere, though it definitely isn't the language patch. The cargo bay floor isn't that different from the loading bay floor that I left from, in that it's stacked high with transport crates, poorly lit, and labyrinthine, and it doesn't take much walking for me to realise that it's also not the sort of place that has 'Way Out' signs. My pace is not fast and even this much arthritic shuffling is enough to wear me out quickly, which turns out to be lucky, because it means that I don't get far enough for the woman and the boy to lose me when they return.

"Mister!" hisses the woman from somewhere behind me. I haven't heard her footsteps and her voice startles me before it fills me with relief. I turn to look back over my shoulder and see that the anger I thought I heard in her tone wasn't far wrong: she is seriously pissed off. "Mister, you don't stay! Where are you going?"

"I stayed," I try to protest, but it sounds like a question. "You didn't come back."

The boy says something to her and she shakes her head. "We come back," she says. "We are here. Come, we have a coat, we have *vleesnat.*"

"*Vleesnat?*" I ask.

"*Vleesnat.*" She's clearly in no mood for pleasantries. "You know: food. *Vleesnat.*" She mimes lifting a spoon to her mouth and slurping, and I realise with a wave of gratitude that she means they have broth.

"Thank you," I say. She slips an arm through mine, and the boy slings an arm around my waist, and I let them move me as we double back on ourselves, setting off in search of warmth and comfort. Turns out, right was the wrong way after all.

"You speak no Dutch," says the woman as we walk. "This is not good."

"I know," I say. "It's a problem."

She shrugs, no mean feat with the amount of weight I'm leaning on her. "Many people speak no Dutch," she says. The boy says something rapid-fire, almost under his breath. "*Nee*," she tells him. To me, she says, "You should not be here. In this place, here – we will take you from here, but it will not be easy."

We've arrived at a door. There is a picture of a lavatory on it. This, at least, I can understand. "In here," says the woman, and ushers me inside.

Strip lights stutter on as we enter, casting a greenish-yellow glow over a low-ceilinged room partitioned by doorless cubicles. The boy sets to retrieving a well-stuffed backpack, and pulls from it a thick duffel coat, warm-looking trousers, a shirt and a jumper. I don't wait for an invitation before I start peeling off my wet, thawing clothes. They have to help me with my boots and some of the fastenings, and the cold air of the bathroom sets off another wave of violent shivering, but I don't think I've ever been so excited about a full-body tremor in my life. The dry clothes feel rough, unfamiliar, against my skin, but they're warm and they're made for this city. Earth clothes won't do any more; I need something designed for Luchtstad.

When I'm dressed, the boy hands me a flask and I can barely take the time to unscrew the lid before I'm gulping the contents down. Thick and gloopy and it warms me from the inside out. I can feel my glucose deposits refilling, and I can feel my thermo-vitalics stabilising at near-normal. I finish the flask and he hands me another, and I drink it down almost as fast as the first.

"Okay?" says the woman as I wipe my mouth.

"Okay," I agree, and, for the first time since I got here, it's basically true.

5.3 Adam

I follow them through a series of corridors. I've been thinking of Luchtstad all wrong, I realise, as I get progressively more and more confused behind them. I know objectively that it's a city, that it comprises seven radials of five floors each, circling like bicycle spokes around a central stream singularity. I know, objectively, that it's really big. City-sized, in fact. But only now, as I'm scrambling down a warren of tunnel-like hallways that feel as though they stretch on for kilometre after kilometre and still come nowhere close to brushing the edge of the world, do I realise my mistake. I've imagined this place as something like a large building, only bigger: self-contained and manageable, and that's not what Luchtstad is at all. It's a city. An actual city. It just happens to be in space.

And I'm about as lost as I've ever been.

Twice, we duck into corridors at the approach of footfall or voices from ahead, only to double back on ourselves once they've passed.

"We are lucky," says the woman after the second time. "When it will be morning, we will have many people."

I realise that I don't know what time it is, so I ask. She looks at the boy, who takes an old-fashioned pocket watch out of the pocket of his coat, checks it, and tells her. "Ten minutes after five hours," she translates. "We must be fast."

"When does everyone arrive for the morning shift?" I can see that she doesn't understand *shift*, so I try again. "When do the people come back?"

She nods. "One half of six."

"Six thirty?"

"Six… thirty." She tries it out, but I can tell by the look on her face that something is wrong with the words. "No – half before six. In twenty minutes."

"Twenty minutes?" That sounds as if it should be long enough to escape a cargo bay, but I feel like we've been walking for at least this long already. "Is that enough time?"

She shoots a sharp gaze sideways. The meaning is clear. "We must be fast," she says again.

The corridors have started to widen. It's less claustrophobic, but it's also starting to look less like the bowels of a basement and more like the sort of place where people might be. Before I have a chance to think through the implications, though, a loud klaxon rattles the walls. The boy startles and drops halfway into a crouch and the woman grabs my arm before the echoes have even finished dying. "Fast," she says. "Fast, we must be fast."

"Is that…" I try, and run out of breath before I can finish. The woman is setting quite a pace, and my heart hasn't quite got over the incident on the crate yet. "Is that – an alarm?"

She doesn't look back. Her voice is full of impatience. "Alarm –? It's... no, not for danger. No. Not for you," she says. I wasn't sure if she'd heard the unspoken panic behind my question, but relief adds a little bit more confidence to my stride. "It's for... morning. People come. We must go."

Shift change. I'd heard they were into punctuality in a big way up here. "How far?"

"Fast," she says, and I don't know if she doesn't understand the question, if she doesn't know how to answer, or if she's choosing to ignore it. I'm trying to work out how to rephrase, when we turn a corner directly into the path of two comparatively well-dressed men.

"*Het spijt me, meneren*," says the woman immediately. At least, I think this is what she says. Her entire manner has changed: her shoulders have sloped, her head has dropped, as though she's trying to look as small as she can. I revise my expectations upwards: these guys are *really* important.

One of them says something in reply, and the woman slaps sideways, connecting with my arm. Belatedly, I take my cue and drop my head, but I think it's too late – one of the suits pokes me in the chest and says something directly to me. In vain, I scour the corners of my data pocket, but the language patch is just not there, and the angry bees and screaming is like a tidal wave beating forever at the inside of my skull. In a panic, I glance sideways at the woman, and she dips her eyeline even further and says something soft and plaintive. I hear the word *sorry* in there a couple of times, and she punches me in the arm again for good measure.

"Sorry," I try. It sounds close enough to the English word that I think it's worth a go. "*Het spijt me, meneren*. Sorry."

In my peripheral vision, I see the suit exchange a glance with the other suit and roll his eyes.

"Fine," he says. He clearly doesn't actually say *fine*, but it sounds like it, and it has the same tone of weary acceptance. There's another bunch of words, none of which sound friendly, but the woman nods vigorously and drops her head a little lower again.

"*Dank u wel, dank u*," she says. I recognise that bit. Then some other words, some of which contain *dank*, I think. To me, eyes narrowed, she hisses, "Come! *Snel.*"

I don't need to be told twice. I dip my head and bob with so much deference I feel like I've fallen out of a Mediaeval romance, and I let the woman grab my arm and drag me after her along the corridor.

I wait until we're a safe distance before I risk speaking again. "Thank you," I say.

"They are big men," she tells me, though I'd guessed that much. "They ask why we are here. We do not come here. You," she adds, with a glare over her shoulder at me, "are not good to them."

I did my best. I had no idea what was happening, and I managed to speak a language I don't speak under pressure and from a newly resurrected body. But I take her point. "What did you tell them?"

We turn a corridor and suddenly we're in a cul-de-sac. There are no doors here, but there's a hatch on the far wall with the words DANGER: KEEP OUT emblazoned alongside what can only be translations into six other languages. Immediately, I know that this is where I'm headed. I just *know*.

"I say," says the woman, "that you are" – she slaps one hand, hard, upside her head – "bang. On head. You are…uh…" She breaks off, searching for the word. "*Doof?*" she tries.

"Injured," I say, but she shakes her head.

"No. Not this. Uh… *doof.* Yes. I say that you are bang on your head, and now you are deaf."

Concussed and hard of hearing. It's actually not that far from the truth, but I'm still glad Luca's not around right now. He'd be dining out on this one for weeks.

"Good thinking," I say. "Thank you."

The boy is applying himself to the task of spinning the wheel on the hatch door, and I hear the seal break with a hiss of escaping air. It smells musty and unused. The door creaks as it rolls back on its hinges, and I see that it leads onto a vertical shaft, no more than a metre across. Rungs run up the far side, into shadow.

I know that my lodgings are on Verdieping Drie, the third tier. I suspect that the cargo bay is on Verdieping Vijf, which is the processing floor. Each tier is the height of a six-storey apartment block, and it looks like I'm about to climb my way past two of them. "Okay," I say. "Looks like I'd better get moving."

Now that we're parting company, the woman looks softer and the boy looks happier. He says something in Dutch, all smiles and friendly pats to my arm, and the woman takes my hand.

"Thank you," I tell them. It's not enough, but nothing could be enough. I don't know exactly what they've risked to get me out of the crate, fed and clothed, and all the way to an access shaft on the edge of the radial, but I bet it wasn't trivial. "For everything. Thank you."

"Welcome to Luchtstad," says the boy, and grins.

I grin back, swing my way into the tunnel, and start to climb.

5.4 Adam

There was a time that I could have scaled a ladder up twelve storeys in less than twenty minutes. It's not today. But I'm not in any rush, and I reckon I'd better take it slowly, since any kind of motor hang past the first twenty or so metres is a great big problem. So I pace myself, keeping an eye on my cardiopulmonary system, my motor-electrical feedback relays, my glucose stores. I just survived a meat crate; I am not dying today.

I'm panting slightly by the time I get to the exit hatch on Verdieping Drie and my reserves are depleted, but I'm still in pretty good shape, all things considered. The wheel takes a bit of persuasion to turn and it makes more noise than I'd like, but when I shoulder my way through and into the corridor beyond, it's deserted again. So far, my impression of Luchtstad is that it's mostly corridors. But this time, when I wrestle the door closed behind me, I see that the multilingual sign labels the shaft on the other side IN CASE OF EMERGENCIES. A city with a series of emergency exit tunnels is a little bit more real than I'm prepared to deal with right now. I turn my back on it and set off in search of something that might give me my bearings.

It's coming up on 6.30 a.m. If the shift pattern on Verdieping Vijf is anything to go by, this is a city in love with mornings, so I'm not expecting to remain alone for very long, and I don't. As I take a corner and then another, I start to hear the sound of a tannoy echoing off an empty space, and I decide to move towards it, which is when I come into contact with someone called Klaartje, according to her name tag. She blinks when she sees me and pulls up sharply. I've no idea what she says, of course, but Verdieping Drie is at least somewhere I'm allowed to be, so I decide to brazen it out.

"I'm sorry," I say. "I've just arrived, and I'm completely lost."

"You should not be here," she says. Honestly, I'm not sure that I could switch so seamlessly between languages, even if the patch had taken. "How did you get past security?"

Security. Security could be a problem. "Security?" I say. "I didn't see any security."

Klaartje mutters something to herself. "You have your card?"

"Of course." I take it from my inside pocket and swipe it over my neck chip. I'm positive it's as good as Matthias thinks it is, but it's always an unnerving moment, trying out a new identity for the first time.

"Emmet Keller," reads Klaartje. She tuts and rolls her eyes. "Follow me."

And so it is that my entry to Verdieping Drie, Radiale Zeven, is to the tune of a pissed off office-worker and the totally unearned bollocking of a security officer at the door to the employees-only section of the transit hall. I resist the urge to shoot the guy an apologetic look. He doesn't need to know that I know he wasn't to blame.

So. Emmett Keller. I'm glad it works, but there's a part of me that's sorry to say goodbye to Adam again. I've had to leave him behind more times now than I can count, but it's the name that's always felt most like *me*. Emmett Keller was born right here in Radiale Zeven and went pre-etheric for a while, God help him, before ties of birth dragged him back to where there are no parents and no siblings and no family of any description. For some reason, he doesn't speak Dutch, but we'll deal with that when we have to. I shrug him on as I leave the cavernous echoes of the transit hall and step out onto the floor of my newest home.

I find the tram stop easily, and settle onto one of the seats, closing my eyes and orienting myself. Images and gridlines present themselves for inspection inside my head as the tram rocks gently on its tracks and I work my way through them, bit by bit, until I've plotted my way through to where I need to be. Then I open my eyes again and set about taking the measure of the place. Every city has its own heartbeat and this one is no different: where London was a rapid, hypertensive hum, Luchtstad moves with the measured, stoic thump of a young man battling through a chesty cough. The air is cold and very dry, and smells faintly of chemicals and ozone, but I think the roaring in my skull has settled slightly, the further I've got from the cargo floor. The streets are clean and brightly lit, paved in slabs of plastic that wears thin in places and is patched in others. Buildings crowd every scrap of space that isn't road or pavement. They are plain-fronted and built to function, not inspire, but everywhere I look there are signs that the people who live in them have made them their own. Flower boxes tumble from upper storeys. Clothes lines drape bright-coloured scarves. Awnings furl from the ground-floor shops and, here and there, street artists have decorated the blank walls in intricate spray-can pictures.

The tram rattles over a siding, and, across from me, a woman with three young children, none of which can be older than five years, startles up from the hand game she's playing with the smallest one. A strand of light-coloured hair hangs down across her forehead but the rest is bundled inside a scarf of deep pinks and blues, bright as sunshine against the practical gunmetal grey of her coat and skirt. Beside her, an old man sits just far enough away to be a stranger, but he pulls coins from behind the ear of one of the older two with an expression of paternal affection and exchanges easy words with her mother that make her smile.

A newsfeed runs along the roofline of the tram, crowded and choked by a steady stream of advertisements. I can't understand the ticker or the words the reporter is saying, but the pictures fill in a few gaps. Something's happened on Radiale Vijf that's caused a productivity dip and this is clearly a very bad thing, considering the flashing red of the graphics and the reporter's desolate face. The old man glances up at the strip, tuts and says something to the woman, who shakes her head and looks funereal. In her arms, the youngest child sucks his thumb and watches me with the unapologetic inspection of the very young. I drop my eyes and stand for my stop.

Tulpstraat bisects the eastern quadrant of the floor. My apartment block is about a quarter kilometre's walk from the tram stop. Bouncing in an aluminium cavern, the street sound is magnified to a roar that rumbles up my legs from the pavement, but it's not oppressive, only bigger than it ought to be. It's almost comfortable once I adjust, like a thick noise-soup that I have to wade through. I need Tulplaan 90, apartment block 17, and that turns out to be more difficult than I'd thought. The apartment numbering is second only to the street listings in terms of impenetrability. In the end, I have to backtrack twice without looking like I'm backtracking before I finally discover it on the opposite side of the street to the one I was expecting.

Also, it turns out to be fronted with a colossal advertisement that blinks kaleidoscopic light-vomit across the narrow street in a manner that's definitely going to be impossible to hide behind a curtain. Superb.

My destination is on the fourth floor. The door slides open onto a small, white room with an enormous window that takes up about a third of the exterior wall. I can't say exactly why this delights me, especially since, I can't help noticing, there's no blind or curtain of any kind, but I move towards it before I even stop to drop my backpack to the floor. This is my home now, for however long it takes to do what I've come here to do. For the rest of my life, most likely. This small square of ratty, threadbare carpet with its worrying stains; this bare futon bed with its three broken slats; these narrow shelves; this sagging chest of drawers with a missing handle and scorch marks up one side.

This is my home.

Chapter Six

6.1 Danae

By the time the actual klaxon sounds for actual home, we've been on the line for seven straight hours without a break. Shift has stretched on and on, past the point where it was supposed to end and then some, and because we're not scheduled to be here past 6 p.m., we're not scheduled for breaks after 6 p.m.

"You want to go and get some dinner?" asks Sanne as we pass each other at the coat check. Dinner is among the first things I'm going to be doing, but she looks like she's ready to fall over and I'm not sure I can make my brain stretch to conversation right now. And besides, I have things I need to do before I can sleep.

I shrug. "I think I need to just go home."

"You should eat first." But she's yawning before she's finished speaking. "Sorry," she says, and tries again. "Really. I know a place…"

"I'm fine," I tell her.

For a moment, she looks as though she's going to argue some more, but exhaustion wins. "Okay. I'll see you tomorrow."

I make myself smile. "See you tomorrow."

"By the way…" She's shrugging on her coat and I'm in the process of turning away, but I look back. She gestures to her head. "I like your scarf today. I like the colours."

"Oh," I say. "It's… thank you."

It's a scarf, is what I want to say. It's cheap and getting threadbare around the forehead, and it's basically brown and other shades of brown. Sanne wears rich greens, magentas, purples, yellows, shot through with shimmering gold or silver thread: too bright, too fancy for the factory floor, but I like to see them. They remind me of flowers.

She grins. "You want me to bring you any food back?"

"Thanks. No. I'll probably be asleep."

"Okay," she says. "Sleep well."

Ours isn't the only factory floor to work late tonight. As we disgorge onto the streets, I can see lights on in two more along the road and the doors are only just starting to open next door. I break away from the crowds as they congeal into groups, huffing and blowing on their hands, stamping their feet and discussing post-factory plans, and slip through the tides of people, making my way towards the end of the street. It's quieter here. In the distance, I can hear sirens whistling through the nearby airway, screaming into full pitch before dopplering into the distance, and the sound makes my head feel fuzzy, as though a transmission has failed and devolved into static. It's enough to make me consider doubling back on myself, doing what I said I was going to do and just heading home. But we've worked late each night since Monday, and I've been too tired both nights to think about going out on patrol, and it's getting harder and harder to pretend that this doesn't matter. If I don't do this tonight, I'm not getting *any* sleep at all, and I cannot be this tired tomorrow.

It's fine. I will eat on the way.

There's a tram passing as I get to the bottom of Hyacintweg and I hop on. The news strip claims that productivity is approaching an all-year peak, and I have no trouble believing this. I'm not sure I'm buying the claim that we're out-producing Radiale Twee, because who the hell buys more bulbs than wheat? But how do I know. I've never been to Twee.

I settle into my seat and scan my fellow passengers. The man across from me is in his late thirties or early forties, with the beginnings of a middle aged spread tugging at the band of his trousers. The woman beside him rests her head on his shoulder and stares vacantly out of the window behind my head: I take a moment to be sure, but if she were watching me, if she were aware of her surroundings, she'd look away from my glare. Just tired, then. I know the feeling. They are my only companions in this part of the carriage, but on the other side of the gap that fronts the section doors there are a couple of elderly men talking quietly to each other and another man with a teenage boy, both fixated on the television screens in front of their faces. I can't tell what they're watching, but there's incidental music escaping from their earpieces and something else that sounds like explosions. No sign of any butterflies, at least.

A young couple get on at Hyacintstraat. The elderly men get off. For a brief moment, I think I feel a ripple in the stream, but it's just a singularity burst. I let my heart rate settle, focus on my breathing.

The tram rattles and rolls. I run through my list. There's the woman who sells scarves outside the Centralemarkt; she will have gone home for the evening. There's the young man who works behind the counter at Kaasstad, who is clearly under the protection of the man and woman who employ him. I've been watching him long enough now to know that he's not a threat, and the café closes at seven on weekday evenings anyway. I want to see if I can find the pair that passed me in Amarinestraat last week and the week before that, but I decide I will go and check in on the bartender in Het Brouwsalon on Ranonkelbaan, who has definitely clocked me now. I need to be careful of him. I need him to know that I'm not afraid.

At night, when I can't sleep, I read through my notes, updating, revising, remembering. But they're only as good as the information I accumulate.

The bar is livelier than I'd expected. A group of young women in the corner appear to be a party, and the bartender grins and raises his eyebrow at me as I push my way through and take a stool. Butterflies blister the air between us. I force them down and make myself order a drink.

"You want some food?" he asks. "You look hungry."

It's a test. He's expecting me to say no, and then he'll know for sure that I am what he thinks I am.

"Yeah," I say, and I plaster a smile across my face. I could really do with a cigarette, but there are no smoking booths anywhere on the street. "What's good today?"

"At this time of night?" He chuckles, then winces as the party lets loose a scream of excitement. "Maybe try the soup. You'll be safe enough with the soup."

I don't drink broth, asshole, I think, but I keep my smile in place. "What sandwiches do you have left?"

He shrugs. "Maybe some cheese and pickle? I already threw out the ham."

"Cheese and pickle sounds good," I tell him. I'll know if there's anything wrong with it. "And how about that drink?"

"Coming right up."

I watch him pour. I make sure he sees me watching. I return his smile when he turns it on me, but I can see the question in it, and I put an answer in mine.

I'm watching you. I see you. Don't think I don't know where you are.

6.2 Adam

It's hard to sleep in Luchtstad.

I have a hard time settling anywhere new, so I'm expecting it, but I'm really, really tired tonight and I could do without this. The longer the night drags on, the more irritated I'm getting, and it's not helping. But there's just something about knowing that everyone else in a half-kilometre radius is peacefully unaware that I'm getting ready to punch through my eye sockets and into my brain that makes me just want to militarise and kill the lot of them. Smug, sleeping bastards. In the corner of the room, Luca watches me with a half-smirk curling the corners of his lips. I'm attempting to ignore him, but he's good at my insomnia.

He says, *You might as well put on the light and read, you know.*

I've read everything in the apartment, which isn't much. And, besides, reading isn't likely to help. But he already knows this, being as how he's an extension of my consciousness. Instead of an answer, I roll onto my side so that I'm facing away from him, and I hear his soft chuckle in the darkness.

I like what you've done with the place, he says. *Very austere. Very Spartan.*

I arrived here less than nine hours ago. Six of those hours were passed in an orientation session so mind-blowingly boring that my uplink circuitry tried to crash three times: one optic, one aural and one respiratory, and you know it's bad when your own lungs decide they'd rather quit than sit through another slideshow on traffic flow and curbside etiquette. An hour and a half of the remaining three were spent trying to work out what anything was in the shops. And the rest of the time I've spent trying to get to sleep so that I don't have to turn up for my first day of work with a full-scale neural processing lag, because that often tends to tip people off that you're not 100% organic.

Luca knows this. I think that, on a scale of one to not dying, interior decoration is a low priority, and I can't help myself: I engage long enough to tell him so.

Someone's in a mood tonight, he says cheerfully. *Sorry. Am I not helping?*

I roll onto my other side. He's a smear of slate grey against the light-washed darkness of the opposite wall. I really need to get something to block out the glare, and I need to do it before tomorrow night.

Did you think you were helping? I ask him. I feel his grin warm the shadows.

I'm bored, he says.

Good for you. I'm not. I'm trying to sleep.

Don't be pissy. Talk to me. You always fall asleep more easily when we talk.

God, I miss him. He's right, and I miss him. It was so easy to fall asleep with his arm draped over my chest and his breath brushing the hairs behind my ear.

I'm not being pissy, I say, which is a ridiculous claim to make when I'm in the middle of being pissy, but I'm tired and my joints hurt and my head aches with exhaustion, dying for a while this morning, and the close proximity of a stream singularity. *It's all right for you. You're a ghost. You're probably immune to stream fluctuations where you are.*

Where I am? I'm right here, he says. *But you have a point. Is it bad?*

It's not great, no.

Want to play "Better or Worse Than"?

Are you being helpful or just morbidly curious?

A bit of both, I think. I always wondered what it felt like.

Luca always did have a bit of the post-etheric wanderlust. Far be it from me to deny him new experiences just because he's dead.

Go on, then, I say. I'm not sure how I know he's smiling, since I can't actually see him, but I do.

That's the spirit, he says. *All right. Better or worse than... accidentally shorting your thumb that time on the faulty circuit board?*

Jesus. I barely even remember Liverpool. I'd only just met Luca the week before and I was still high on oxytocin and lust, which is how I managed to almost electrocute myself on a damp boiler control panel. *Better than,* I say.

Are you sure? Because I learned a few new words from you that day.

Oh, please. I learnt more new words from you. Better than. Next.

Better or worse than... fitting your neck chip?

My neck chip is pocketed beneath a graft strip of self-adhesive synthetic t-cells. I literally stopped noticing it three days after it was done.

Better than, I say. *And if you tell me your neck chip hurt, I'm going to call you a name.*

Oh dear. That might hurt my feelings. Better or worse than the freezer shuttle?

That's a little too close for objectivity. My epidermal circuitry still hasn't quite recovered, and I shiver violently at the memory. Luca

41

chuckles. *Is that your answer?*

Differently the same, I tell him.

Cop out.

It is not a bloody cop out, I protest. *How would you even know? How many stream singularities have you tried to sleep next to?*

If you were sleeping next to it, he says, *you would be a puddle of liquefied organ juice.*

Luca's pedantry is one of the things that I love most and least about him. I haven't bothered to calculate the relative g-force of the area immediately adjacent to the man-made datastream singularity that powers this floating city, but there's a no-fly zone with a radius of five hundred kilometres around it in every direction that suggests it's not a particularly hospitable environment for anything interested in maintaining its own structural integrity. What I *can* say is that the stream interference is an absolute fucking headache for anything uplinked in the immediate vicinity, which is certainly not something that the city fathers considered when they were drawing up the design plans. I've been here almost one day, and anybody who tries to tell me it gets easier with time is going to get punched in their fucking throat.

I'm sleeping close enough to fall into its gravitational field, I say. *And that's a hell of a lot closer than I'd prefer to be.*

Is it like… he begins, and, when he can't finish the sentence, I know immediately what he wants to ask.

No, I say quickly. *It's not like that.*

Better or worse than?

Nothing is worse than that. Nothing ever will be. *Better than*, I say.

He's never asked what it was like to feel his chant shake its way out of my bones. It's been twenty-five years, and I know he wants to know. But he never asks.

Can't be that bad, then, he says. His tone is light, but it's forced. I know him too well to believe it. *Go to sleep, you old woman.*

I let him pretend. It's the only thing I've ever deliberately withheld from him, so we'll do this little dance and I'll just be grateful for his discretion. *I am trying*, I say. *But there's this dead guy in my head that won't shut up.*

His laughter is soft, warm like a late-May breeze when the sun is low in the sky.

Talk to me, then, he says. *Tell me about Luchtstad.*

So I do. I tell him about the cold air, the spotlessness and the streets with flower-names, and I'm asleep before I remember that I'm trying.

Chapter Seven

7.1 Danae

The klaxon sounds for morning coffee break, and Jouke makes a point of turning the radio up instead of hitting the button that stops the conveyor moving. Beside me, I hear Thijs suck in a breath and mutter a couple of choice words, but his hands don't stop moving and his eyes don't leave the line. The factory floor spreads out behind me, crisscrossed by fifteen more axes of industry, and nobody else is moving towards the smoke dock either. I resign myself to the inevitable and keep on building dodecahedrons out of perforated sheets of cardboard.

When the hour rolls by, the theatrical chime and thunder of the news jingle scatters the dying chords of a pop song and I learn that today we are going to be racing a cascading relay malfunction from Verdieping Vier that's more than likely going to shut down one entire side of the radial by lunchtime and send us home before we can finish packing our current shipment. I've decided that this is more annoying than actually worrying, until the anchor breaks out the solemn voice of our civic governor, all sober Radiale-Een efficiency and muted affliction, as he enjoins us not to panic, and I'm forced to wonder if I should, in fact, be panicking. I know there are oxygen ports all over the apartment block. I'm just not convinced that they've ever been serviced, and I'd prefer to not find out that I'm right about this in the middle of a life-support failure.

"Contrary to reports," says Governor Briest, "there is no reason to think that this is related to the recent protests on the level."

Well, I hadn't imagined that it was until he said that, and now I'm certain that it is. I also can't help noticing that he doesn't specify *which* recent protest on Verdieping Vier. In the past six weeks there have been two about working time violations, one about the frequency of blackouts on the radials – which would be a really stupid reason to engineer a blackout, but I'm not going to rule it out – and one about Niet Zoeken. I feel the muscles in my shoulders contract, tightening around my neck and stiffening my arms, and it's not because of the intricacy of the bulb boxes beneath my fingers.

The itch flares. I have to spend the next three hours focused on keeping it stable.

We are released for lunch at 11am and told to be back by 11:20. We've been moving constantly since 6am, and I'm pretty sure we're all hungry enough by now that we finish eating in half that time. Afterwards, I follow the crowd to the smoke dock and Sanne bums a light from me. I realise too late that this means she's planning to have a conversation with me, but my head is elsewhere; I'm not thinking straight.

She leans against the wall beside me, inhales deeply, exhales an elegant plume of grey-blue smoke. "This is not Luchtstad," she said.

I blink. It takes me a moment to realise that our lunch table has been talking about the riots for the past fifteen minutes, and I assume that she's mistaken my silence for anxiety.

"Every city has its trouble," I say.

"We don't…" she says, and stops. Picks a fleck of tobacco from her tongue, tests the knot at the back of her headscarf. "We are safe," she says. "This city is safe."

Verifiable fact and the history of the past thirteen months would seem to argue against this, but I let it slide. I think Sanne has a vague idea that pre-etheric settlements are heaving pits of violence and disease, against which the post-etherics are beacons of calm, and she's not entirely wrong. I want to reassure her that Luchtstad has some way to go before it turns into Creo Basse, partly because she seems genuinely worried that I'm going to write to the folks back home with horrifying tales of post-etheric barbarism, but mostly because I feel this is the easiest way to end the conversation, and I really need to get into the ladies' before smoke break ends and finish my flask.

"I know," I say. I flash her a smile, as bright as I can go, but I have a horrible feeling that any gesture of joy or happiness I make these days looks more like a grimace or the cacklings of a madwoman. It doesn't seem to restore her confidence, anyway. This is why I don't fucking smile. "Luchtstad is safe," I try. "I know this. This is not Luchtstad."

She reaches out and squeezes my arm. I hold myself steady and let it happen until she releases me again.

"Good," she says. "I'm glad you know this."

I have half a cigarette left, but I'm not enjoying it anyway. I drop it to the floor, not without a frisson of regret, and stamp it firmly down with my shoe. Sanne's eyes follow it with some dismay.

"Excuse me," I say, "I need to… ladies' room, you know."

She nods. I see Bente reach down and retrieve my stamped-on half-cigarette as I duck out of the smoke booth and into the stalls, but that's really just the sort of thing that Bente would do. I don't blame her, to be honest. I was a little bit sad at the thought of it going to waste, but I'd have preferred that Sanne got it.

7.2 Danae

We're back on the line before the klaxon has sounded for the end of lunch, because we are intelligent people with a disinclination towards tuberous projectiles, and we are experts in reading Jouke's face. The conveyor is already rolling when the horn blares out across the factory floor, and it's coughed to a consumptive halt before the echoes have even died away.

I was pretty sure that I had most of the really colourful swearwords by now, but I spend an instructive few minutes picking up some more.

We don't look at each other. We barely even breathe as Jouke storms up and down the back of the line, kicking at random pieces of machinery and calling down invective so appalling that I'm a little bit surprised the air doesn't catch fire.

When he's finished doing that, he stomps off towards the stairs that lead to the admin offices. I stare at my hands, peering at the grime that's worked its way resolutely into the nail beds, holding myself otherwise completely still. Somebody coughs, somebody else shuffles from one foot to the other. The radio burbles a happy little tune and a young female voice sings about love among the stars, and we stand in absolute silence and wait to see what happens next.

After about fifteen minutes, a grim-faced woman arrives with a toolbox and slides, unspeaking, beneath the machinery. Jouke glowers at her from the end of the line, arms folded, simmering with rage. We have disappeared for him, right up until the moment when we reappear without warning and somehow manage to piss him off by existing.

"Hey," he snaps. He reaches out a hand and slaps at the nearest member of the line. It happens to be Aline, and he connects with her arm violently enough that the *thwack* sings out above the music. She doesn't flinch. "What the hell are you still doing here? Go and have a fucking smoke or something."

The itch flares hard. I close my eyes against it, but my head is full of images of me twisting his fat stupid neck so hard that his skull pops off the end of his spine. I breathe. Breathe. Dig my fingernails into my palms and breathe.

"Hey," whispers Sanne. She touches a gentle hand to my arm and I almost jerk it back out of her touch before I catch myself. "Come on. Let's go."

At the smoke booth, she hands me a cigarette without speaking and I accept it with a nod of thanks. *Maybe he'll give himself a stroke*, I hear somebody mutter, and quiet, conspiratorial laughter peels around the group. It feels like lancing a boil: the tension shifts, airs out, resettles.

You think we're that lucky?

We can only hope.

By the time the conveyor rumbles back to life, we've lost half an hour and the relay malfunction still shows no immediate sign of hitting the level. Jouke is scarcely mollified by our return to productivity and storms off somewhere else as soon as the line is moving again. I need the respite, and not just because of the itch. Someone, somewhere, has come up with the idea of creating a gift box with bulbs in the colours of the Luchstad flag, though how they plan to grow a green flower is something I haven't asked. Maybe you're supposed to grow a stem. But these novelty kits are always packed into boxes of such ludicrous complexity that they might have been created under the influence of spectacularly bad acid. It takes a lot of tries before your fingers get the feel of the folds, and many, many more before you can work them at line speed. Once my hands know the folds, and once I can do it without thinking, this is the only way I can operate, because once I start thinking about it I can't do it and Jouke starts throwing things.

I'm really not sure that I can manage him throwing things at me this morning without losing control.

So I work. I strip my mind of absolutely everything, I disconnect my conscious thoughts from my hands, and I let them do their thing. The way you survive on the lines is by mastering the art of the Factory Stare. Bulbs barrel down the line in a profusion of shapes and sizes and I stand at the head of the conveyor belt and fold boxes as a dozen pairs of hands scrape and sort and compartmentalise and half a dozen more sweep tubers into cardboard chambers: two of the white bulbs in one,

one each of the larger red and slightly less red bulbs. Fifteen of the brown ones into the hexagon on the bottom, and God help you if your hand slips or you miscount. Over and over again – twos, fifteens, folds, sifts, intervals – until the brain, starved for distraction, switches into automatic pilot and a kind of catatonia develops, a waking sleep. This is the Factory Stare: about three feet into the middle distance, focused on nothing.

But this morning, we're half an hour down and about to lose anything from six to eleven hours in the second half of the day. The way you definitely don't make up for this is by adding half a dozen new, untried bodies to the line and cranking up the speed, but Jouke is stressing and Stressed Jouke doesn't make good decisions. Thijs registers his return before me with a muttered, heartfelt, "Oh fuck, no..." and I risk the slightest of glances back over my shoulder to follow the line of his afflicted gaze.

Oh fuck, no, I would agree, if I could get away with the linguistic fluency required for swearing without letting everyone know I understand them better than they think. Jouke's trailed by seven people that I've never seen before in my life, which means they're new to this floor and possibly to this factory, and they're going to be completely impossible to subsume into the workings of the line without a lot of tears and recriminations. *Fuck no* barely begins to cover it.

This is my immediate thought: they are going to ruin the ruins of my day. And that's before I feel the stream warp and realise that one of them is an a-naut.

7.3 Danae

He's not on my list. I'd know that immediately, even if I couldn't see his face: the tiny fluctuations in the dance of the datastream are as unique as a fingerprint, and I've mapped them all against the artificials I've encountered on Luchtstad. This guy is completely new, and he's headed for my line.

I drop my eyes as the group approaches. Jouke punches the off switch and the conveyor jerks to a halt, and we all take a moment to stretch out our fingers, circle our wrists, roll our shoulders. I glance sideways as Jouke manoeuvres bodies between bodies and see the a-naut unceremoniously thrust between Bente and Amita. Six places down from me, I note, as a blue-scarfed woman is pushed into place between Thijs and me. He shows no sign of having clocked me, and I think I recognise the grey-faced pallor of crippling singularity fog. Panic spikes, and I almost fumble a box as the conveyor starts up again. Jouke notices and aims a slap at my shoulder, and it's only after I've nodded and muttered a sorry that I realise the itch didn't so much as scowl in his direction. The world has narrowed to a point, and it circles around New Guy and how the hell he happens to find himself on my line today.

I watch him as we work. By the time the klaxon sounds for our usual lunch hour, his face has turned a kind of alabaster grey and his eyes have clouded into a syrupy, lifeless black. It's the interference headache; it has to be. He's hiding it well, but his verbal reaction times are sluggish, he's swaying slightly, and he's also forgetting to adjust for organic somatic latency, which is a stupid way to get caught. Today, Jouke doesn't care enough to wonder why New Guy's so good at picking chionodoxa from scilla, but tomorrow we might be back to business as usual and it doesn't pay to be preternaturally talented at something so specialised and useless. I fold boxes, and I watch him and try to get the measure of him.

He's tall and wiry, but there's no shortage of muscle on his thin arms. His face could belong to a man anywhere between mid-twenties and mid-forties, although that hardly narrows it down. I'm guessing, from his eyes, that he's one of the earlier lines. Conservatively, that makes him forty to fifty years old: at the very limits of his lifespan. This is not as much comfort as it ought to be. Some of the oldest models are as weak as tissue paper these days, but others are ex-military and can punch through steel.

There's an old, old poster on the wall opposite our line, and squares of paler dark grey speckled with missing flecks of paint that evidence the departure of many more. The sole survivor was once framed in red, now faded to a dusty crimson with feathery wisps of ancient spiders webs, and, under the dirt, I can make out the beaming faces of a boy and girl child in a sea of red and gold tulips. Below it, stylised white letters say, simply: *Magie voor je familie.* This is where my gaze tends to fall when I'm on boxes, just because it's actively not wall, and, other than that, my options are basically wall or more wall. I risk another glance at the a-naut, hands moving easily over the rush of small spheres, and I see that his eyes have also found the words and his mouth is framing them, silently, as though he's getting used to their shape.

If he's here for me, he's doing a terrible job of blending in. So terrible, in fact, that I almost feel sorry for him.

I glance away when he catches me looking. It's a tiny, insignificant gesture, and, under normal circumstances it would disappear into the existential chasm of an afternoon on the factory line – nothing survives for long under the wilting attrition of the Factory Stare. But, this, of course is the precise moment that the factory's evacuation alarm chooses to start blaring, and everything goes to hell instead.

Chapter Eight

8.1 Adam

I can manage loud noises. I can even manage unexpected loud noises. I lived through the Insurgency, after all. But there's a quality to the klaxons on Luchtstad that nobody could prepare themselves for, and, I swear to God, after thirty-six hours of the place I'm ready to stab myself in the ears.

This is why it takes me a minute or two to work out that nobody else at the conveyor belt was expecting this one either.

I'm slightly proud of myself for getting this. The one thing I've established about my new workplace is that my colleagues aren't the type of guys to wear their emotions on their sleeves, so the only reaction to the alarm is a full second of suspended confusion followed by an orderly shuffle away from the line. It's only when we completely bypass the smoking booth that I realise we're headed towards an emergency exit on the far wall of the warehouse and I start to understand that this isn't what I thought it was. At least this door doesn't come with a wheel and a ladder on the other side.

Nobody has spoken to me since I got here except to get me to stand in a particular place. I consider asking the woman behind me in the queue if she knows what's happening, but I can't get her to meet my eye. It's not as though I have much chance of making myself understood, anyway. And I definitely won't understand her reply, but I'd feel better for making the effort.

The exit leads onto an alleyway that runs behind the factory complex. One long unbroken line of wall continues for what must be a quarter of a kilometre to my left and more than twice as much again to my right. It's as clean as every other part of the city I've seen so far, but the air smells little-used and the ground is barely scuffed. The other side of the alley belongs to the factory behind ours, and I know this because it's also spilling a crowd of headscarfed workers through a series of exits, and we're starting to get crowded in here. From somewhere up ahead, I hear the voice of our post-lunchtime supervisor barking a command that barely carries over the tide of voices. Whatever this is, it's probably big enough to be bad.

Our supervisor yells something, and the line picks up the pace. A group from the other factory break into a half run. I match their speed, though the singularity feedback is thick and every jolt makes me nauseous. This is the only possible reason, I think, why it takes me until I'm almost on top of her to realise that I've been working with another a-naut.

In my defence, I've been on this city a little over a day, I barely slept last night, and the 4:30am bullhorn reveille this morning startled the left side of my body into a motor hang that lasted almost until I was supposed to be at the gates of a factory I'd never been to before in my life. And she's been working the other end of the line for the past few hours, but that was a maximum of three metres away from me. It really shouldn't need me to basically collide with her in the middle of an alleyway to make the stream spike into recognition, but I'm operating at a deficit right now.

She doesn't so much as flinch, let alone change her stride or look at me. This is how I know she's made me hours ago. There's something slightly comforting in this: it implies that I'm not always going to be as fuzzy as I am right now. But this is not the most important thing to worry about. What's more important is that we're almost out of the alleyway and there are blue and red flashing lights in the main road up ahead.

I'll panic when she panics, I decide. She looks like a steady pair of hands in a crisis.

From the road, I hear a synthetic voice saying more things that I don't understand at a volume loud enough to rise above the clamour. I recognise a couple of words as *calm* and *thank you*. The crowd is bottlenecking at the end of the alley and beyond the crush I see lines of what looks like military personnel setting up a cordon, and I nearly stop in my tracks, try to double back, look for another way out. But the other a-naut's expression barely flickers, and I remember where I am and look again. The soldiers are not scanning anyone's chips. They're not even asking for ID, they're just waving people past them as quickly as they can.

Careful, says Luca quietly in my ear, but I can hardly hear him over the thunder of five hundred worried voices and the soothing tones of the city's traffic control system. Anyway, who does he think he's talking to? I've survived longer than he did.

I think the thing I'm going to let myself get really worried about is the fact that the soldiers are wearing gas masks.

I turn to my nearest neighbour as we approach the road. *"Mevrouw,"* I try, and her head turns towards me. I realise that I have virtually nothing here, no words, no chance of communicating. I settle for, *"Wat is dit?"*

She shrugs. She says some words to me. One of them sounds like 'evacuation', which I'd worked out by myself. I'm trying to think of some way to ask a follow up question, but the line breaks around me before I come up with anything. We're on the street now and moving quickly, and I'm disoriented enough to need a moment to recentre, find my bearings, and get going.

"Dank u wel," I call after her retreating back, but she's gone. The soldier at my back snaps something pointed and shifts me onwards with a flick of his hand, and I surge forward with the rest of the crowd.

My eyes scan the men and women around me, searching for the a-naut. Once or twice, I think I've found her, but it's another grey scarf in a sea of greys and blues. When I see her at last, she's much further ahead than I'm expecting her to be, and she's moving fast.

"Hey!" I call. She doesn't turn. Not so much as a flicker of movement in her shoulders acknowledges me. I consider my options. I don't know Dutch, that's true. But I know plenty of English, and *hey* is phonetically the same word in both languages. "Hey!" I try again. I'm close enough for her to hear me now. I'm almost level with her. If she'd even glanced back at me, I'd believe that she heard me but didn't understand that I was speaking to her. Fair enough. But the fact that the women to both her left and her right turn their heads in my direction, see my eyes focused on their friend, and turn away again, tells me that she's deliberately ignoring me.

"Hey!" I say again, more firmly, and touch my hand to her elbow.

This turns out to be a mistake. She whirls on me with enough ferocity to break the flow of people around her, and her face is a mask of pure rage.

"Do *not*," she hisses, *"ever* fucking touch me again."

My hand drops away so fast her skin might be on fire. She shakes me free just the same, even though we're no longer making any kind of physical contact, and sweeps her arm back into her circle of personal space. Eyes brush me as they pass, and it's a second before I realise that, yes, she's moving rapidly away from me through the coalescing crowds, but that's mostly because I'm standing still and blocking everyone else's way.

"*He daar!*" says a voice from somewhere to my left, in a tone that definitely belongs to someone in authority. I don't know what he's saying, but I'm prepared to bet it's something along the lines of "Get moving, dickhead, we're evacuating the street."

So I do. I get moving. I have no idea where I'm going or what's happening, but this is my entire life on this city so far, so what's new?

8.2 Adam

It's not long before I'm lost. Lost and confused and maybe about to die, and isn't that just the sum total of my life on Luchstad so far?

Following the crowds is easy. It's what the crowds want me to do. The problem comes when the crowds suddenly thin and I'm not nearly where I thought I was and none of the architecture looks like the factory block. In the middle distance, the soothing synthetic voice echoes off the ceiling and bounces back in every direction, and it's not actually possible to tell where it's coming from. Blue lights flash up ahead and somewhere to the left, but I didn't come from either of those directions. *Narcisalley 270* says the street sign on the intersection ahead. That's definitely not the sector I'm supposed to be in.

I turn around to double back, and that's when I see her. She's standing on the street corner directly behind me, arms folded and glowering as though she's been waiting for hours. I'm going to guess that she's followed me, though she's clearly not very happy about this. I am, though. I roll my head on my shoulders, easing out a little bit of the tension that's settled in before the muscles can start to glitch, and cross the road. I stop on the curb, well out of her circle of personal space.

"Hey," I say

She glares. "Just don't ever fucking touch me again, okay?"

I hold up my hands. "You made that crystal clear."

Without a word, she turns on her heel and starts walking. I watch her go for all of two seconds before I decide that I don't care what I'm supposed to do: I'm following her. She turns her head and glowers again, but she doesn't tell me to go.

"We're being evacuated," she says.

"Thanks," I say. "That much I worked out for myself."

She shoots me a sideways glance. "No you didn't."

I'm not having that. "Evacua-tee," I say. "Eva-cu-a-tee-a. Something like that. It's not rocket science."

"Fine." I can't place her accent. She sounds like a native English-speaker, but the accent's not quite English. "One of the carbon monoxide monitors picked up a spike. It's not what anyone was expecting, put it that way."

I'm going to put aside for now the question of what anyone was actually expecting, because it sounds like we have bigger problems. "A spike?"

"A big one."

"Shit."

She shrugs. "It's probably nothing."

We've retraced our steps far enough now that we're skirting the edge of the masses at the cordon. Beyond them is all flashing lights and chaos. "Doesn't look much like nothing," I say.

"They take these things seriously here."

I consider. "Good."

"Yeah," she says. "I used to think that too."

As long as we're on the street, we're not on the factory floor. That's good enough for me. "What, you miss the conveyor belt?"

"I miss the money," she says. And then, to nobody in particular: "Fuck this. Seriously."

My brain feels like it's trying to climb out of my skull. I've got my hands in my pockets and my collar turned up to my chin to keep out the cold, but my thermo-vitalics are still struggling to keep up and everything from the knees down is numb. It's great that I know where we are now, and all, but I hope that the plan isn't to hang out at the cordon for however long this takes. "So," I say. "What happens now?"

Someone brushes past our shoulders, hard enough to make me half-shuffle sideways. She reacts before I do, tensing and folding in on herself, and my body recognises the look before my brain catches up. Adrenaline spikes and I take an involuntary step backwards. Her eyes find mine. "What?"

It's gone. Whatever was in her face is gone. But my limbic system knows what it saw. I swallow, consider holding up my hands and walking away. Instead I say, "So, do we just wait here or what?"

"It's probably nothing," she says.

"Great." Her expression is so completely re-set to neutral that I'm starting to doubt myself. "And what if it's not?"

She shrugs. "Somebody probably took a smoke break somewhere they weren't supposed to."

"Even better." I kick at a scuffed patch of pavement. "How long does it usually take to sort this stuff out?"

She glares in the direction of my feet. "Chances are, we'll be back on the line in two hours. Three, tops."

Spectacular. We're waiting around in the cold for hours and then heading back to the line. "And what if it wasn't somebody taking a smoke break where they weren't supposed to?"

Unexpectedly, she grins. It's almost more startling than the thing with the shoulder. "Don't hope for it," she says. "If they find anything, they'll close the floor."

I hadn't realised I was being so transparent. It's this goddamn headache. "The factory floor? It's… closed, though, isn't it?"

"The *floor* floor," she says. "As in Verdieping Drie. We'll get moved into an overnight shelter on Dwei while they make sure this level isn't going to suffocate."

"That sounds like something I don't want."

"It's something you don't want," she agrees.

I take a moment to process. "So… how do we know?"

"Know… what?"

"If we're back on the lines or sightseeing in Verdieping Dwei?"

She shrugs again. "You just sort of… hang around," she says. "Keep walking. Look for news strips."

Perfect. At least there are news strips on every unornamented strip of wall. "Keep walking, wait for news," I say. "That sounds like something I can do."

8.3 Adam

After fifteen minutes, I'm stomping my feet and blowing into my hands to keep them warm. When the flashing lights whurp closer and the army starts chasing the onlookers backwards so they can extend the cordon, I decide that it's time to move.

"So," I say, "how about I buy you a coffee and we wait this thing out somewhere warmer?"

It doesn't strike me as a contentious question. I mean, it's coffee. That I'm paying for. So I'm not at all prepared for her to turn on me with fury in her eyes and hiss, "Absolutely not."

I'm not completely sure how to respond. I'm starting to wonder if she might actually be a little bit psychotic. "Okay, then. No coffee."

"For Christ's sake." She pivots on her heel, half a turn away from me, then back again. "Do you think this is a game, New Guy?"

I have no idea what she's talking about. "Do I think... what is a game?"

"Don't be cute."

"I'd be working a lot harder than this if I were trying to be cute."

"You think you're pretty smart, don't you?"

Smart was one of the first casualties of the singularity feedback. Maybe this conversation would make more sense on Earth, but I wouldn't put money on it.

"Look," I say. "I'm cold. I'm new here. And I don't like having a front-row seat for a public safety meltdown. *I'm* going to find somewhere warm. You do what you like."

I get as far as the other side of the street before I realise that she hasn't followed me. I didn't actually think she wouldn't, so I haven't thought this far ahead. I shuffle from my left foot to my right and burrow a little deeper into my coat. And then, just as I think that she's going to ignore me and I'm going to have to either risk getting lost and probably fired, or else double back on myself like a dick and eat my dramatic exit, she turns her head sideways and fixes me with a glare.

"I thought you were going somewhere warm," she says.

"It's warmer this side of the road," I say. My breath mists in front of my face as I say it.

"Fine." She shakes her head. "You drink gin?"

I'm not sure what the correct answer might be. "No."

"I drink gin," she says.

It feels like an olive branch. "Gin, then," I say, but carefully, just in case.

"Gin," she says. And then, "But I'm buying."

8.4 Adam

She grimaces as the first gulp hits her throat. The back of her hand rests against her mouth as she swallows. "So," she says. "When did you get here?"

I've followed her to a lounge at one end of a covered arcade. There's little on the way of ornamentation on the walls and the floor is stripped back to its plasticised natural state, but the formica-topped tables are largely chip free and the bright red plastic benches are scarred but spotless. A young woman drifted over to take our order as soon as we sat down, and the subsequent drinks arrived with a bowl of something that looks a lot like spiced muesli. I'm currently cradling a glass of tepid water to my chest and wondering if I can drop an iodine tablet into it without anyone noticing.

"Yesterday," I tell her.

She grins. "Thought so."

"I was hoping it wasn't that obvious."

"We don't get many newcomers." She drains her glass, glances over towards the bar, where the bartender nods and sets to filling a replacement. I'm starting to be glad that she's buying. "You were never going to be low-key."

That doesn't sit well with me, and I say so. She shrugs. "Don't worry about it. You've got novelty value, that's all. I'm the only one who's made you."

She speaks lightly, but she looks me hard in the eye as she says it. The bartender returns with the gin refill, and she accepts it without breaking her stare. I give up. She wins; whatever. "I'm Emmett," I say. "Emmett Keller."

She lets her glare linger a moment longer. "Françoise Marechal."

French name, no accent. No she's not. But, then again, I'm not Emmett Keller. I raise my glass to her. "Glad to meet you."

She lifts her glass but doesn't close the distance to touch it to mine. "Are you planning on drinking that?"

I tilt it towards me. "I'm not sure."

"The water up here's drinkable," she says. "I mean, it's not great, but it won't kill you."

I wave a hand vaguely at my throat. "My filters aren't what they used to be."

"Ah." She peers at her gin, considers, sets it down. "Old fella. Got it."

I'm not sure if I'm offended by that. On the one hand, okay, she has a point. On the other hand, she logistically cannot be more than seven years younger than me, so she can fuck right off. I settle for, "Not as young as I was."

"You made it up here well enough." The eyes are back on me, sharp as lasers. "Not exactly dog meat yet."

"You should have seen me yesterday." To hell with it. I fumble an iodine tablet from my pocket, palm it, and drop it in my glass when the bartender isn't looking. Françoise is, of course. "Now I'm planning on drinking it," I say.

She purses her lips, cocks her head to one side. Evaluates. "Kind of hard to stay low-key when you're that paranoid."

I watch the tablet dissolve at the epicentre of a frothing whirlpool of bubbles. "It bothers you," I say.

She bristles immediately. "Why the hell would it bother me?"

"Because you're sitting at a table with me," I say. "Because watching me do this means you know what I am. And that's dangerous."

"Not in Luchtstad."

"It puts you at risk."

She laughs. It doesn't sound like there's much humour in it. "You think *I'm* the one at risk here?"

To hell with it. I'm not letting that slide. "Are you threatening me?"

"Do I need to threaten you?"

"For sterilising a glass of water?"

That glare is unblinking. It's like trying to out-watch a statue. "I'm not threatening you," she says at last. "I'm just making sure you know what you're dealing with."

Laughter sputters out of my mouth before I can stop it. I have no idea what her problem is. "You're doing a hell of a job."

"Yeah?" She sits back in her seat, stretches an arm out across the table. With her free hand, she lifts her glass to her mouth, and I can't help but notice it's shaking. "You're the one who wanted to go get coffee, Emmett Keller."

"I wanted to get warm," I say.

"Because you're so old and frail."

"Jesus Christ!" I look up at the ceiling. It's actually much easier to calm down when I can't see her glaring at me. "Because this city is colder than the grave. Because you said two hours, maybe three, and I was starting to lose feeling in my fingers. And, yeah, because half the radial's police and soldiers were building a wall around a gas leak and, I don't know, for some reason I get kind of anxious around that much law enforcement."

"Please." She shakes her head. "We're the last thing they're going to be worrying about."

"Right, yeah. The 'Do Not Seek' policy. Tell that to the guys last week."

Her eyes flash fury again. "Those guys were stupid. What they did was *stupid*, and it got them killed…"

"It got them strung up naked to a lamp post and beaten to death with a length of pipe."

"Not by the police!"

"Yeah, I'm sure that's what they were thinking too. 'At least we're not being murdered by the *state* up here.' Do Not Seek is toothless. It's make-believe."

"You'd rather have the Rens?"

"I'd rather have something more substantial than a glorified honour system."

"You ever meet a Ren?" The words are softly spoken, but they're ferocious. I meet her eye and she raises an eyebrow. "Didn't think so," she says. "I'll take 'nearly legal' over 'actively hunted' any day of the week, Emmett Keller. And you'd better believe I'm ready for anyone who thinks they'll have a go."

I sip from my water. She sips from her gin. Her stare does not leave my face mine as she does.

"Okay," I say at last. "You've been here longer than me. You know better than me."

"You're damn right," she says.

"What… ten years? Twenty years?"

She smiles. There's no warmth in it. "Longer than you," she says.

"Are you active?"

"Active?"

"You know." I gesture to her, then back to me. "In your community."

Understanding dawns. "No." Her voice is ice cold. "I don't have a community."

"No need to shit the bed," I say. "I'm just asking."

"Okay," she says. "Sure. So, my turn."

"Your turn?"

"My turn to *just ask*. You know why we don't see many newcomers?"

"Because the city's at capacity, I'm guessing."

"Close to. Last update, they were saying you can only get a relocation visa if someone dies or leaves, and nobody leaves."

"Okay." I'm assuming she's going somewhere with this.

"And all this bullshit about 'Bring us your poor endangered a-nauts, come to enlightened Luchtstad and be free forever from oppression' – that only works if you have an open door policy that lets a-nauts into the city in the first place."

Ah. I think I'm starting to get the general direction of her thoughts. "Right."

"And Luchtstad has never done that. Never once, in all the years of Niet Zoeken. Luchtstad has never, ever accepted a-naut refugees. Because they're at capacity. Because resources are limited. Because it'd completely fuck up their diplomatic relationships with any of the other states or municipalities who want us all dead, but they leave that bit out of the literature. Right?"

"Right," I say. It was sort of what I had in mind when I said that Do Not Seek was toothless.

She takes an unhealthy gulp of gin. I'm beginning to worry about what happens on the line if we get called back.

"So, tell me," she says. "Who the hell do you know that bribed you into this city, Emmett Keller, and what is it that they want you to do now you're here?"

Chapter Nine

9.1 Danae

He doesn't answer straight away. That's okay. I don't expect him to. Instead, he drops his eyes to his glass, swirls the water a little, and smiles. The last dregs of the iodine tablet heave and settle again on the eddy, little filigree strings of white powder against brackish liquid.

He says, "Good question."

"I know." I don't drop my eyes. I've learned how effective this can be.

"I've got one for you first." He doesn't look up so he doesn't get the full effect of my arching eyebrow, which is annoying.

"That's not how this works," I say, and he shrugs.

"This works however we both decide it works." Finally, he turns his smile on me. "It's a conversation, right, Françoise? Not an interrogation."

I lift my glass to my mouth, swallow another gulp. It warms me. "It's a conversation. Go ahead."

His smile is easy, relaxed. "How long have you been up here?"

"On Luchtstad?" It's not the most elegant response, because, yes, of course Luchtstad; he's not asking if I've been spending my life floating about in the wastes of space. But it's not exactly what I was expecting. "Subtlety's not your thing, huh?" I say at last.

The smile fades a little, replaced by a creeping vacancy in his eyes. I'm almost offended that he's not better at this. "We're being subtle?" he says.

I am, certainly. I don't know what he's doing. "All right. I'll play. I've been here thirteen months."

I watch his face as I answer. There's a faint tremor in the corner of his right eye that tells me he knows very well that he's not impressing anyone. "Oh," he says. "Okay."

I wait for him to elaborate. He doesn't. "Okay?"

"I was expecting" – his hand waves vaguely – "longer."

I doubt that very much. "Sorry to disappoint you."

"I'm not disappointed." That smile of his might just be the most

61

irritating thing I've ever seen. "I'm just surprised. So – someone got you up here, too."

And there it is. I want another drink, but I don't trust my hand not to shake when I lift my glass. I say, "I think you know very well how I got up here."

"Same way as me, I'm guessing."

"You think I'm fucking stupid." There's a slight tremor in my voice. I notice it abstractly, like I'm watching myself on a screen. Mostly, I can't actually believe that this is finally happening. "You think I didn't know who you were the second you walked onto my line?"

"Wait," he says. "...What's happening?"

"Why the hell do you think I came back for you? Why the hell do you think we're even sitting at this table?"

"I thought..." he says, and hesitates. "I thought you were being nice...?"

"Sure. Okay." The itch is like a drill in the centre of my skull. It's like a bullet, straight through my forehead, ready to damage, ready to kill. I close my fingers around the edge of the table, see the knuckles whiten. "You thought, hey, let's make friends, it's the middle of a gas attack – was that you by the way?"

"Was... what me? Wait, did I gas the factory floor?"

"You hit the line and suddenly we're being evacuated. How's that for timing? What, you couldn't wait until home time?"

He looks, to his credit, completely lost. I have no idea how this man has survived so long.

"I have no idea," he says, "what's going on right now."

I'm not sure why I don't stand up and walk out. It's the only safe thing to do; the itch is a high-pitched whine, singing fire into my blood, and it won't be Emmett who gets the force of it if I can't keep it under control. This is what keeps me awake at night: the thought of the day that I can't hold it back any more.

"You think I didn't know?" Flecks of spit scatter with every word. I see them spatter the table top. They feel like they belong to someone else. "You think I didn't know they'd send someone after me? You think I'm *that* stupid?"

"Françoise," he says. He spreads his hands, palms up, on the table. "I swear to you on... I don't know, whatever keeps the air inside this stupid floating city. I swear to you that I have no idea what you're talking about."

I don't answer. If I speak, my concentration will break, and if my concentration breaks the blast doors won't hold.

"I don't know what else to tell you," he says. "I got here yesterday. I feel like someone has made a hole in my head and they're poking their finger inside and wiggling it around. Nothing makes sense to me and this whole conversation is the thing that I understand least of all."

My shoulders are so tight they feel as if they've been carved from granite. The tips of my fingers are turning blue. I realise that I'm not breathing when my chest begins to burn.

I think I'm going to throw up.

"Fuck you," I manage. My legs don't want to get me upright, my spine doesn't want to unbend. I scrape myself up off the bench, steady myself on the table. "If you have any sense at all, you'll be gone when I get back," I tell him, and I run for the bathroom.

9.2 Danae

When I'm finished, I let my backside fall heavily to the floor, let my spine loosen and lay me back against the wall. The tiles are cool against my neck and the air tastes faintly of peppermint as the cleaning cycle clicks into place. My stomach feels as if it's been turned inside out and scoured, and I try to remember what I've eaten today that wasn't bar snacks.

I take my time getting up again. When I'm standing, I take my time fixing my hair back inside my scarf, adjusting my dress, rubbing colour back into my cheeks. I take my time sterilising my hands and my coat sleeve that got in the way. I take my time taking my time. I do not rush.

After all that, he's still sitting at the table when I leave the bathroom. I'm not sure why I'm not surprised.

"Are you okay?" he says when he sees me.

I consider just walking out, leaving him with the bill. But I don't know if he has the funds to pay it, and I'd like to be able to come back here again. So I nod to the bartender for another drink and slide back onto the bench opposite him, unhurried, never letting him out of my sight as I do.

"I'm fine."

He watches as the bartender approaches, sets down my drink. He watches me lift it to my mouth and sip. Then he says, "So, it looks like

I don't have any sense at all, then."

"I knew you'd still be here."

"I haven't finished my water. So – can we start again, maybe?"

"Why?"

"Why?" I'm getting kind of sick of his wide-eyed confusion. "Because… we're going to be working together?"

"For today."

"Okay… Because I could do with a friend up here?"

I snort. "Sure."

"Okay. Fine." He rolls his eyes, raises them to the ceiling. "It's not like I made it up here for the scenery, is it? I thought that much was obvious."

Now we're getting somewhere. "You might as well have it tattooed across your forehead."

He rolls his eyes. "That's helpful, thanks. I was sort of hoping you could help me."

"Why would I do that?"

"Solidarity?" he suggests, but he laughs to himself even as he's saying it. "Don't worry – I'm kidding. Maybe because I'd owe you?"

"Right," I say. "I'm supposed to trust you, am I?"

He snorts. "No."

That's not quite what I'm expecting. I wait a moment, to make sure that I've heard him properly. "No?"

"Clearly not," he says. He peers at his water, furrows his brow, swirls it again. Only then does he look up and meet my eye. "Why would you trust me? You've only just met me."

My fingers start to curl around the edge of the table. I tuck them safely together on my lap where he can't see them.

"Exactly," I say. I hope it doesn't sound as confused to him as it does to me.

"Exactly." His lips twitch into a tight smile. "I've got just as much to lose if I screw up."

"I doubt that."

"Whatever." He twitches his shoulders. "I don't want to argue about it. Can we just agree that we've both got a vested interest in not getting killed?"

The gin is flattening out the creases in my brain, settling and warming its way across my skull. "You still haven't told me why you're here."

Unexpectedly, he laughs, though it's stripped bare of amusement. "I had this idea," he says, "that it would be a lot easier than this. It looked like it was going to be easy."

He glances up. He's cued me in, and he's waiting for me to ask the obvious question. I sip from my glass and say nothing.

Another laugh, with more life in it this time. "So," he says. "You're a blow-in like me then, Françoise Marechal."

The name was a mistake. I told them that at the time, but they insisted that nobody up here would know the difference between a French accent and an English accent when I was speaking Dutch. They were right about that bit, but the whole plan sort of revolves around me never, ever running into a native English speaker again, and this is Luchtstad, for crying out loud.

"We're all blow-ins up here," I say.

He acknowledges this with a slight nod. "Maybe that's good, then. Maybe you've noticed it too."

Jesus. This man thinks he's the very definition of charmingly enigmatic. "If you're talking about the singularity feedback..."

"Christ," he says, and a look of pure suffering twists the corners of his lips. "No. But Christ."

I recognise that look. "It gets better," I tell him.

"When?"

"I don't know. It just does. You just... It fades into the background or something."

"So it doesn't actually go away?"

"You're living next door to a black hole," I say, "powered by the force of this universe collapsing infinitesimally into the datastream. No. It doesn't actually go away."

"I think I preferred the Rens," he says.

"No, you don't. You just think that because your head feels like it's going to explode."

"Seriously. One shot and that's it. I've never heard of them slowly crushing your head in a vice until it bursts."

"Yeah," I say, and I can't help it; I can't keep it out of my voice. "Yeah, they're stand-up blokes. Yeah, this city just isn't the same without them."

Emmett looks up sharply, and, too late, I hear what he's heard in my tone. My hands contract into fists and I have to concentrate on straightening out my fingers, one by one, so that they'll let me grip my glass again and tip the last of my drink into my mouth. I hold it there for a second, feeling it settle, tingle and burn before I swallow. He drops his eyes.

"There's something going on with the stream up here," he says.

This is his cover story. I'm slightly insulted. "No shit," I say.

"Not that." A hand waves irritably. "It's not singularity feedback – they corrected for that. But I think maybe it masks it, this close up? It's hard to tell. From Earth, it looked like... I don't know. Some kind of disturbance in the stream. As if it's focused to a point, or a storm, or something."

"That sounds a lot like an artefact of singularity feedback to me."

He shakes his head. "It can't be."

"It messes with the uplink like you wouldn't believe..."

"Oh, I'd believe it," he says, with considerable feeling. "But it can't be. And the reason it can't be is because singularity feedback doesn't reach the Earth's surface."

"Okay." I'd like another gin, but a glance at the news strips shows me the cordon closing back in on the factory floor and still no sign of the cascading relay malfunction. "I'll bite. You're here because you and your friends saw... what? Something? On Luchtstad, from Earth? That... I've got to tell you, Emmett, that's quite a story."

He smiles weakly. I think his mind has got snagged on his headache. "I know how it sounds. But you've heard the rumours about this place. You see why we couldn't let it go."

I stare at him levelly. "There are a lot of rumours about Luchtstad," I say, since I haven't heard of a single one.

Emmett nods. It occurs to me to wonder if he's bluffing too, since there's no way I've lived here more than a year and I know less about this place than a guy still shaking Earth-dust out of his clothes.

"That's what my cache leader said," he says. "You remember how this place looked from the ground? It's like a fairytale or something – everyone knows five different stories about Luchtstad."

"It's an agrifood processing plant," I say. "It's an orbital factory. There's no magic here."

"That's what I said." He shrugs. "But... I don't know. The story about the hospital... I've heard that from four people now. Good people. Smart people. It feels… plausible."

"The hospital." I really want to put a question mark on the end of that sentence, but there's no way I'm letting him know that. "That's why you're here."

"Yeah, that's basically what Matthias said." He grins. "He gave me that exact same look you're giving me, too. But just think about it for a second: on its own, the hospital sounds like every other story you hear about Luchtstad. 'I hear they have pubs just for a-nauts.' 'I hear there's a grant you can get for non-organics to set up shop on the processing floors.' 'I hear they sell stem-sheets for broth in the supermarkets.' Yeah, sure. I don't even need you to make that face, Françoise: I knew they were bullshit before I ever got here. But the hospital…? I don't know. It sounds like wishful thinking, but then there's that anomaly on the scan, and… I don't know."

I keep staring at him. He doesn't look away.

"What if I'm right?" he says quietly. "What if the anomaly is tied to the hospital somehow? What if there really is a place where they can take a broken down, beaten old body… and make it live?"

9.3 Danae

I don't say anything for a minute. I'm thinking of Angelo, of all the people I've known who are dead and who don't need to be dead, and it's so hard to keep my head clear.

"Okay, sure," he says. "You don't believe me. That's fine. It took a hell of a lot of persuading to get Matthias to buy it, too. But here I am."

"Here you are." I barely hear myself say it. "And you're doing… what?"

"Looking around, I suppose." He shrugs. "Seeing what I can find out. Trying not to die. The usual stuff."

I've never heard of a place where a-nauts go to heal. I know that this is something that's impossible. But… the thing is, if it *were* possible, Luchtstad would be where it happened.

My head is starting to ache. "Okay." I pinch the bridge of my nose, run my fingers up and down the line of cartilage. "So there's a disturbance in the stream. Define 'disturbance'."

"Now that," he says, "is the sixty-four thousand dollar question, isn't it?"

"Don't be quaint. You're too old to pull off quaint." His eyebrows arch but he says nothing. "Are we talking about a disturbance like, I don't know, the chant? Or like proximity flutters? What are we talking about?"

"It's hard to describe."

"I had a feeling it might be. Have you felt it yourself?"

"Nobody's felt it. Not on Earth, at least. Hey," he says, as I open my mouth to protest, "I'm telling you what I know. If I knew more than that, I wouldn't be here."

"Sounds like an expensive gap in your knowledge."

"Very." He lifts his glass and sets it immediately back down. I really don't think he's going to drink it, and I can't blame him. "This isn't a decision anybody made lightly, you know."

"And I suppose we're just leaving aside the question of why an Earth-bound a-naut cache is running long-range scanners on the post-etheric cities?"

"Oh, come on." He spreads his hands wide. "Anyone with access to a long-range scanner has it trained on the PEs. You know this."

The safe house where I stayed before I left Earth was obsessed with inter-etheric communication. They were never able to circumvent the singularity noise, but they'd been at it for decades by the time I got there and I'm pretty sure they haven't stopped now. They weren't scanning any of the cities, but I bet they would if they could.

"If you're here to mobilise the cross-etheric resistance," I tell him, "you've got the wrong person."

He looks as though he's expecting the question. "I'm not."

"I'm not militant. Never have been, never will be."

He levels a stare right back at me. I don't look away either. "Neither am I."

"I'm here to blend in."

He shrugs. "Sounds good."

"None of what you just said sounds consistent with blending in."

The shrug widens, becomes a supplication. "I'm information gathering. That's all."

"And for you to gather information," I say, "your folks back home thought it was worth stumping up the kind of money that gets an a-naut through the gates of a post-etheric city."

He hesitates. "If I'm right…"

"About this magical hospital of yours."

"If I'm right, it's worth the investment."

"Why?"

He blinks. "Why? I'm guessing you've never given yourself a paper cut, then, Françoise?"

Careful. "It's up here. They're down there. It changes nothing for anyone on Earth."

"It gives us a reason to hope."

"Hope?" I almost choke on my laughter. "You want me to believe in *hope*?"

"I really don't care what you believe or don't believe." His voice has gone cold, his face has locked down. "This could be a *chance*. Do you know how many chances any of us have left?"

My head is really starting to pound. It feels like the air is closing in around me. "More than you'd think," I say.

"Fine. Whatever." Emmett stands up. I wasn't expecting that. "Whatever you say, Françoise. You know this city, I don't know this city yet – but there are a lot of people who know this city. You do what you've got to do. Thanks for the... water, I suppose."

He turns to leave. "Wait," I say before I know I'm going to say it. I *really* wasn't expecting that.

He waits. He doesn't turn back towards the table. "I'll pay for the water if you like."

"It costs as much as the gin," I say, and I'm not too proud to acknowledge the satisfaction that blossoms as a brief flare of affronted panic crosses his face. "What, you think there are tumbling rivers of glacial runoff feeding the reservoirs up here? It's supply and demand. More things need water than alcohol."

"This place is fucked up," he says, but he sits back down at least.

"No argument here. You could at least drink it, you know."

He's wishing he hadn't dumped iodine residue in it now; I can tell. He swirls it around a bit, dispersing the sediment until it looks as though it might have been clear to begin with, and sinks it in six gulps. "This place is going to cost me a fortune."

If all he drinks is water, then, yes, it is. "Hope," I say.

Emmett shrugs again. It's becoming a habit. "What do you want me to tell you?"

Something more convincing than that. But I find that I really want to believe him. "I'm not going to paint a target on my back for you," I say.

"I wouldn't ask you to."

"And I don't know you if any of this blows up in your face. Don't look to me to bail you out of anything. I'll walk away and I won't even remember your name two days later. Understood?"

"Understood."

There's no hospital on Luchtstad. There's no magical bastion of light and healing. There are no second chances. And there's no stream disturbance here either: I would have felt it by now. I can want this to be true as much as I like, but for now, the principle benefit to keeping Emmett close is that I get to watch him. I get to be ready for whatever he does next.

"All right, then," I say, and I raise my empty glass to his.

Chapter Ten

10.1 Adam

It's well after midnight before I get home. We've spent the afternoon racing a malfunction that never actually happened, which means no breaks since the gas scare cleared. I don't know enough about anything to know if it was an elaborate false alarm, somebody's idea of a joke, or if I needed to be a lot more worried than I ended up feeling. I'm also too tired to care.

She seems nice, says Luca as I throw my coat onto the bed.

I crush my palms to both temples, take a couple of deep breaths. The singularity noise roars in my skull and my chest feels tight and empty, as though the air up here is two shades too thin.

"Oh calm down," I say. Even my voice sounds exhausted. "She's a contact. I made a contact today. I'm doing my job; there's no need to get jealous."

Am I jealous? I don't need to see him to know that his face is all affronted innocence. *I'm not jealous. Did I get jealous with Priya? Or Jean-Michel? Or Benny?*

"She's a contact," I tell him again. "You need to stop playing matchmaker, you know. You're terrible at it."

He shrugs but doesn't protest. Luca always did know his relative strengths.

You should have someone, he says. *Twenty-five years is too long.*

It is too long. There are days when I can feel him so close by my side that I think that if I just turned my head, I'd see him. Some days I can feel his breath on the back of my neck. I wake up some nights and time collapses and I'm young again and nothing aches and nothing hurts, and before my brain has time to boot I reach across the bed for his body. Sometimes it feels like he's gone so briefly that he isn't gone at all. And then the hours and the days and the weeks and months and years rush back, and I feel them all, as if someone's piling stones on my chest, and I've lived longer without him than I had him in my life. And I know I've lived too long, but what can you do? I need to do this one last thing.

I need to find him before I die.

71

Chapter Eleven

11.1 Danae

We don't speak on Friday. Which is to say that I don't make any effort to start a conversation with Emmett, and, though I see him looking over at me from time to time on the line and on smoke break, he doesn't make any effort to start one with me either. He walks close ahead of me when we leave the factory, which might be his way of giving me the opportunity to turn or hold back and let him catch up to me, but I don't and he lets it be.

After work, I take the tram to Centralemarkt. I pass the woman selling scarves and feel the stream jump and whistle and she doesn't look up and I don't look at her, but I let her know that I've seen her. I know that she's there. I'm watching. I walk a little way through the market and I pick up some supplies, and the stream jumps again as I pass a couple of guys at a shoe stall, haggling with the owner over the price of a pair of boots. One of them glances around as I pass, and I note his broad, straight nose, his dark eyes, the beard that can't be real. I note his short fingers and the strength in his arms. I note the coat he wears that's two sizes too big. I note the stall and the time and the fact that he walks with a friend. I sear it into my memory, every detail, every nuance, every trace, and when I get home I write it all down on my list before I turn out the light and try to sleep.

By Saturday, I feel a little better. More confident, at least. I ignore Emmett on the line and he lets me ignore him and in the distance between us I watch, evaluate. Learn. Sometimes it's like trying to think through a thick, black fog, like trying to move through treacle, and I only have so much processing power. But by close on Saturday I'm ready to approach him as we wait for the doors to open and say, quietly, "That coffee you were going to buy me – I know a place."

For all that we've been dancing around each other for the past thirty-six hours, it's like he's forgotten to expect that I'll come to him when I'm ready. He blanks, turning to me over one shoulder as though he can't remember who I am or why I might be talking to him.

"I thought I was absolutely not allowed to buy you coffee?" he says.

The door rumbles open, a sound like continental advance, and the relative dark of the factory floor is lanced by a widening shard of paler gloom from the street outside.

"I didn't say you were buying."

He considers this. "Good," he says at last. "I've seen the price of coffee up here."

"I didn't say I was buying for *you*, either," I say, and he grins, and I'm glad he's caught the tone. I'm out of practice at this.

"This place will bankrupt me," he says, and we agree to meet on Tulplaan 180 so that he doesn't get lost.

I don't sleep well on Saturday night either. I lie on my bed in the half-light from the street outside and count the cracks in the ceiling plaster until my brain gives up and passes out, and then I surface fitfully for hours, screaming awake from dreams of a clinical white room, over-lit, with long-armed shadows that rear up on the wall ahead and I can't see what casts them. My own voice wakes me, and I'm pinned to my sheets by sweat and terror, knotted in whorls of fabric that constricts as I struggle against it, and I have to force myself to centre, to breathe, to open my eyes and see that I am here, this is now, this is Luchtstad and I am in my room, alone and safe.

I give up before dawn and wrap myself in a blanket by the window as my damp skin cools. There's no smoking in these rooms; there's no extractor in the block or anywhere on this street. But I have the end of a bottle of gin stashed below my bed and time enough tomorrow to replace it, so I unscrew the lid and cradle it to my chest and fight off the past as the lights come up another Sunday morning.

We have arranged to meet at ten on the corner of one of the only streets he knows in the entire damn city. Sunday is maintenance day in Radiale Zeven and that means the thermostat is a law unto itself, so I wrap up warmly, burrowing deeply into the first thick coat that I've ever owned, and I choose the grey scarf with the dark slate thread for my hair, because it feels like a Sunday scarf, with its delicate pattern and the faint sheen in the weave that catches the light when I turn. The corridor is washed in silence as I leave, underpinned by the sonorous rumble of Sanne's early-morning snores, and I move quickly and quietly, though explosive decompression couldn't wake them on the morning after a Saturday night. I heard them come home around three this morning – it woke me out of the foothills of another nightmare –

and I was glad to have the second-hand company through the walls for the hour or so it took them to go to bed.

He's waiting for me where we agreed to meet. He's not prepared for the weather and he looks miserable, hunched into a duffel coat that's at least one size too big, no hat, a narrow scarf wound tightly around his neck, and his hands jammed into his pockets. He nods when he sees me, waits for me to get close enough to speak in an undertone, and immediately lets out the complaint that he's been dying to share: "Jesus – this place is colder than the grave. When did winter get here?"

"Let's walk," I say, and he falls in beside me at a brisk trot. "The trams are ridiculous on Sundays, and you'll warm up when you're moving."

"I may never feel warm again," he says, and I remember saying something similar to someone else, once upon a time, and a shimmering haze of vertigo blanks out my vision. For a minute I'm back in the lower city, coat pulled tightly across my chest against a stinging hail of bullet-rain, hair tangled into wet strings and plastered to my head, frozen to the bone but warmed from the outside in by the radiance of a smile. I don't know what this memory is, and it's gone before I can place it, but when I open my eyes it takes me a moment to feel the plastic walkway beneath my feet and smell the sterile post-etheric air. For a moment, I'm somewhere else entirely.

"Hey," says Emmett, "are you okay?"

I realise I've stopped walking, that I'm standing in the middle of an empty street staring down a gulf of missing days. "I'm fine," I say.

"Are you sure?" He looks doubtful, but mostly just cold. "You don't…"

"I'm fine," I say again, and start walking. He follows quickly. He wants to stand still much less than he wants to know what just happened, and that works for me.

The streets are empty, the traffic soft and infrequent. We walk in silence for a moment or two, but either Emmett starts to warm as we go or he's one of those people that can't let a silence linger. We've barely walked two blocks together before he feels the need to say, "Funny place, this."

It's not a question, but it's the sort of statement that needs a response. "How?" I hope it sounds sufficiently discouraging, but I realise as soon as it leaves my lips that I've asked a question, and a question permits a reply. I ought just to have grunted non-committally.

"Well." He disentangles one hand from a pocket long enough to gesture to the deserted streets. "It's like a ghost town today, but yesterday it was standing room only."

He must have heard the revelry last night. Tulplaan is at the heart of this sector's *partij mijl*: seven blocks of wall-to-wall pubs and nightclubs and all-night cafés, and most of them have licenses that keep their doors open well into the small hours. I suppose he's right, though. I don't know where he's come from, but Creo could have thrown an all-night party seven days a week and still have rioted in the morning. Luchtstad is more of a six-day-week sort of town: the service industries will be working today, but not all of them, and they'll close at four for dinner. I found it strange, too, when I got here; now, it's just part of the background fabric of weekly life.

"I think it's a post-etheric thing," I say. "Industrial towns tend to revolve around an industrial timetable."

"I read that, in the induction literature. Natosi runs eight-on, two off."

It's the sort of inconsequential trivia that I zoned out on arrival, but for some reason I'm not surprised that he both consumed and retained it. "Glad I'm not on Natosi, then."

"Seriously?" He glances sideways. "That's actually more free time than we get here."

I am aware. I can also do mathematics. I meet his glance and turn mine into a glare. "This is going to be a long walk if we have to spend it debating comparative macro-economics."

"I have the feeling," he says cheerfully, "that it's going to be a long walk anyway. Where are we headed?"

I've been thinking about this. It's not like I'm exactly flush with local knowledge and replete with ideas for how to get this man started on a quest that I don't even believe in. But there is one place I know that will definitely be open when we're not working, because I've been before on a Sunday, and the red-headed boy that I've never spoken to has always been there.

11.2 Adam

She's right: it's warmer when we're moving, and, by the time we've made it across the sector, past the commercial centre and out towards the walls, I'm feeling less like a reanimated corpse. I have no idea what direction we're walking in, though it looks like the numbers after the street names possibly correspond to radial degrees of a circle. This would make sense on a circular city floor, but I wasn't paying attention when we started, so I'm still no clearer about where we're going or why. But after about three quarters of an hour I start to notice that the identikit grey housing blocks that surround the factories are gradually getting bigger and quieter, more domestic. Gated archways break the ground floor walls and I can hear children playing as we pass by.

We turn off Windroosstraat 180 onto an unnamed lane that leads into a pedestrian-only square. Awnings furl from the shop fronts and parasolled tables hug the exterior walls, completely ignoring the lack of both sunlight and heat.

"Do I get to ask where we're going yet?" I say, because I'm pretty sure we must be nearly there.

"I didn't say you couldn't ask," says Françoise without looking at me. This is technically true. She's also basically ignored all of my questions since we started walking, so I gave up trying.

"All right," I say. If she thinks I'm likely to be impressed by sullen silence, then she's never spent time in the company of the Luton chapter of the Greater North London Resistance. "Where are we going?"

She raises a hand towards the far corner of the square, where a woman is bringing a tray of steaming coffees to a well-wrapped family shivering beneath a white, logo-emblazoned parasol. "There," she says.

Kaasstad, I read, in hand-painted red letters above the awning. The windows are fogged with condensation. I follow Françoise inside.

The woman who was carrying the coffees is wiping her newly coffee-free hands on her apron as we step into the humid warmth of deep fat fryers, steaming cups, and maybe two dozen customers scattered around ten tables. The air is full of quiet chat and the tinny sound of radio pop songs. The woman smiles when she sees us and offers a friendly, "*Hallo! Hoe gaat het?*" and something else that I don't understand, accompanied by a wave of her hand towards a spare table by the window.

"Do you drink coffee?" asks Françoise as we lower ourselves into damp white plastic lawn chairs. A coating of orange crumbs and two dried-in coffee rings scatters the table.

76

"I can," I say. It's just not usually worth the effort.

"That's good," she says. "It's going to be hard enough to convince Marijke not to feed you fried cheese sticks. I'm not sure how she'll take it if you turn down coffee too."

"Fried cheese sticks?" I start to say, but we're interrupted by the arrival of the woman, presumably Marijke, carrying two large white mugs of black coffee. She sets them down in front of us and launches immediately into an avalanche of friendly chatter. I understand virtually nothing, but Françoise deflects easily enough for us both, with no more than fifteen words' contribution to the conversation. Four of those words are *nee*, and all of them are accompanied by a glance in my direction.

"She wants me to make sure that you definitely don't want anything to eat," says Françoise after a moment. Marijke looks on expectantly and offers an encouraging nod.

"*Nee*," I try. "*Nee, dank u.*"

An eyebrow arches as she replies, and I can tell from context that she's not entirely convinced. Françoise says something to her, quiet words, and I hear *Nederlands* in there somewhere. Understanding dawns.

"Ah," says Marijke, and rattles off another stream of rapid-fire speech, accompanied by a meaningful nod in my direction as she sucks in her cheeks and rubs her belly.

"She thinks you're too skinny," says Françoise, as though I couldn't work that out for myself. "Just order something. I'll eat it when she's not looking."

I make myself smile. "I have no idea what to order."

"I'll take care of it," she says, and turns back to Marijke.

Watching them communicate is like seeing a different Françoise. There's something warm and easy about the way she parries every verbal thrust, something familiar. It takes me a second to place it, and then I realise: it's like watching a mother and child arguing over who knows best. Marijke holds up four fingers; Françoise rolls her eyes and holds up two; Marijke counters with three, and won't hear another word.

"*Drei, dan*," she says.

"*Drei*," says Françoise, and it's settled.

"*Drei*," says Marijke, and turns to me, fingers extended, nodding expectantly.

I consider. She waits. *"Drei?"* I try, and a radiant smile splits her face.

"Goed, goed," she says, and slaps a friendly hand on my shoulder. *"Erg goed. Goed zo!"*

She nods towards the counter, shouts a couple of words to the man at the till. He nods back and bends down to the chilled cabinet that fronts the kitchen area, starts gathering chunky fingers of something orange-breadcrumbed to drop into one of the bubbling fryers behind him. I had no idea people still cooked like this, and, though I can't eat it, the smell as it sizzles into boiling fat is enough to cause hunger to spike in my empty stomach.

"Is it all…" I say as Marijke retreats back towards the counter, but I don't know how to finish. "…fried cheese?"

"God, no," says Françoise. She sips from her coffee. "Some of it is fried ham."

"Ah." I decide that the coffee is probably hot enough to be sterile, even if it's cheap enough to be made from third-grade water. "She likes you," I say.

Françoise shrugs. "She likes everyone."

This much is obvious. There are some people who fall naturally into their perfect role in life, and Marijke's is clearly to mother people into eating stuff. There's something incredibly satisfying about this. There can't be many people on this city who can honestly say that they love what they do for a living. I really want to know how Françoise found her way here and what keeps her coming back, but I don't know her well enough to ask. Instead, I sip my coffee and ask the other thing I really want to know. "So. Why are we here?"

"Hoi!" says a man's voice, before she can answer, and I look up to see the guy from behind the counter, laden with two plates and a tomato-shaped ketchup dispenser. He has all of Marijke's good-natured bluster. *"Hoe gaat het?"*

"Goed, goed," says Françoise. *"Dank je wel."* And then, as he's leaving, she says something that sounds like *war is di yong-eh oot de teller?*

The man looks as confused as I am, but, I imagine, for different reasons. "Arnold?" he says.

"Arnold," agrees Françoise. That at least I understand. The next bit, I don't.

"Ja, ja," says the man, and then another stream of something fluent.

Françoise nods gravely.

"*Dank je wel*," she says. "*Heel erg bedankt.*"

"*Geen probleem*," says the man. His smile has faded a little: not so much that he looks annoyed, more that he looks completely bewildered by the way the conversation has proceeded. "*Ogenblikje*," he says – I know that one; it means 'just a moment' – and he escapes back to the counter.

Françoise watches him go, then turns back to the table, lifts a fried-cheese finger and takes a savage bite of it. "Fuck fuck fuck! Fucking hell, that's hot."

"It's just out of the fryer," I point out.

She spits it into her hand. "Thank you, Dr Keller."

It wasn't in contact with her oral epidermis long enough to cause cell damage, I think, but I'd prefer she swilled some water around the site. She doesn't. I watch as she breaks up the rest of the fingers into bite-sized chunks to cool, and wait for her irritation to settle back into manageable levels.

"What just happened?" I ask, when I feel like enough time has passed.

"I just scalded my fucking tongue," she says, so I suppose I timed that wrong.

"I can see that.. I'll get you some water if you like." I glance up at the counter. "Or I'll try, at least. I mean with your friend just now."

"I know you do," she says. "Trust me: you don't want to drink the water here."

I'd guessed that much. "You're deflecting."

"Yes," she says, "I'm deflecting." She pokes at a string of melted cheese that's sliding out of the broken corner of breadcrumbed finger. "I'm deflecting all right. You bet I'm deflecting. Because what just happened is that I just blew my fucking cover, Emmett Keller, and it had better be fucking worth it."

11.3 Danae

He stares at me for a minute, then at the molten cheese that's welded itself to my fingertip. He purses his lips, picks at a scrap of food that's been steam-fused onto the side of his mug.

"I think you might be overselling it," he says at last.

I'm not sure how this man doesn't get punched in the face more often. Of *course* I'm overselling it, but that doesn't invalidate the central truth of what I've just said, which is that I am on this city to keep my head down, interact with precisely nobody, and not get killed, and so far this week has seen me wipe out two of those three things. By asking to talk to the red-headed boy behind the counter, whose existence I have been pretending to ignore for the past twelve months, I've just effectively sent up a big red flare to mark my position. And the red-headed boy's too, which is something he didn't sign up for and I had no right to give away.

"You'll scald your finger," he says quietly. I hadn't realised it was hurting until he points this out, which is an artefact of what happened to my hands last year, but the pain rushes in right on cue and I yank it back, shaking free a stringy strand of cheese. "Are you... Is it okay?"

"It's fine." I realise that he's asking me if I've damaged the upper epidermis enough to breach the outer a-cell shield, which is a complication I just don't need right now, so I hold it up to show him. "See? It's fine."

"It looks pretty red," he says, but I don't get to reply to that and tell him that of course it looks red, I've just fucking scalded it, because Arnold the red-headed boy arrives before I can speak. The stream spikes, skipping into crested peaks, and I can feel his anxiety as a kind of armour around him. He's cleaning his hands on a ragged old tea towel and his apron is a kaleidoscope of food residue that reminds me sharply and painfully of my uniform at Intimacy.

He says, *"Meneer, mevrouw – hoe kan ik u helpen?"*

His Dutch sounds fluent but heavily accented. The hesitation, I'm pretty sure, is from his nervousness.

I say, in my equally accented Dutch, "Hi – Arnold, right? Would you like to sit down?"

"No," he says. "No thank you. I have work to do."

Emmett is watching him with a look that's somewhere between predatory and beatific. It's an unsettling combination, and it can't be helping the poor guy's stress levels.

"I'm sorry," I say. "We won't keep you long. We were just hoping... I suppose we were hoping you could help us."

The boy looks from me to Emmett and back to me. "Please," he says quietly. "Please – I need this job," and I feel like absolute shit. I should have waited until tomorrow night and taken Emmett to Het

Brouwsalon, I knew I should.

"We're not here to get you fired," I tell him. "We just need some help."

He shakes his head. "I can't help you."

"What's he saying?" asks Emmett.

I turn a glare on my tablemate. "Let me talk to him, okay?"

"I can't help you," says Arnold again. "Please – I need to get back to work."

"You must get a break?" I say. Even at Intimacy, I got five minutes every four hours or so to make sure my feet didn't snap off at the ankle. "They can't get mad at you for talking to us?"

Arnold casts a wary glance back towards the counter. "They're good people."

"Do they know?" I ask.

"Know?" he counters, but his pained expression calls him out on his prevarication.

"Know about you," I say, to make sure we're on the same page. If they do – if they suspect – then I have basically just outed Emmett and I too.

"They're good people," says Arnold again, and that's not an answer, but it also could be.

I look at Emmett. "I have no idea if we're in trouble here," I tell him.

"Trouble?" Nothing – I swear, *nothing* – unsettles this man. "Trouble how?"

"I think they know about Arnold," I say. "I think they're harbouring him." Or he's their insurance, I don't add, but I think it's implied. Marijke doesn't seem like the type to coddle an a-naut in case it gets useful to sell him out one day, but one doesn't live a long and healthy life by taking people at face value.

I smile at Arnold. I can't tell if it's convincing. "I know they're good people," I say brightly. "I come here – how often? Every few weeks? You know me, Arnold. You know we can be friends."

"I don't know him," he points out, and looks straight at Emmett who, predictably, wants to know what's going on. I quiet him with a wave. Arnold has a point: nobody at this table knows anybody else at this table, and Arnold and I have not known each other much longer than either of us have not known Emmett.

"Arnold," calls Marijke from the counter. "The dishes are piling up."

I glance back over my shoulder and see that she's watching us with an expression that I can't possibly read. This irritates me intensely. I actually *like* Marijke's fried-cheese-in-breadcrumbs, and I'm pretty sure that I can't ever come back here again.

"Sorry," he calls back. "I'll be back in a minute. Sorry." To me, he adds, unnecessarily, "I have to go…"

"I know," I say. "I'm sorry we bothered you. We just…"

"You need some help," he says. "I know."

"We shouldn't have bothered you," I say, and I mean it.

"I can't help," he says, and I try to reply, to say that it's okay, I know, but he cuts me off before my mouth has finished opening. "But," he says, "I might know someone who can. Can you meet me here after closing?"

This, I was not expecting. Like, *really* not expecting. "Sure," I say. I don't care what else Emmett was planning to do today. If Arnold wants to stick his neck out for us, Emmett can damn well freeze his arse off at the outer wall for eight hours to facilitate it.

"Okay," says Arnold. "I will tell them that you're my cousin. Is that all right?"

I blink. "Sure," I say again. Eloquence has deserted me.

"They know my aunt," he says. "They'll believe me."

Arnold doesn't have an aunt any more than I do. If Marijke and her husband know someone who calls herself his relation, then his cover is either excellent or blown. "Okay," I say. "We're cousins; great. I'm Françoise. You should probably know what I'm called if she asks."

"Françoise," he says. His face creases briefly into what might be a smile, and it shaves years from the corners of his eyes. He can't be as young as he looks, I know, but he looks like he's barely out of his teens. "Okay. I'll see you here at six. Okay?"

"Okay," I say again. It feels as if there should be something more to add, but I have no idea what it might be, and he's gone before I can think of it anyway, shoulders hunched and apologising all the way back to Marijke's thunderous glare at the counter. I really hope we haven't got him in trouble, and I'm *really* pissed off about losing Kaasstad as a Sunday morning brunch option. I turn my glare on Emmett.

"What?" he says. "I understood, like, four words of that

conversation, and most of them were 'okay'."

"Drink your coffee," I tell him. I tip his cheese sticks onto my plate without checking to see if Marijke's watching, since it's not like she's going to give me grief for it any more. "You're going to need the warmth."

11.4 Adam

Françoise claims a prior engagement and declines to pass our six-hour wait for Arnold together. We both know there's no prior engagement, but the thought of entertaining each other, uninterrupted, for a quarter of a day is no more my idea of a good time than it is hers. She offers to accompany me back to Tulplaan and fetch me later this evening, but I decide to stay where I am. I haven't seen much of the city and it's my first opportunity to get a   sense of somewhere that isn't the Tulpensector. I'd like to start to feel less transplanted.

She shrugs, and then surprises me by offering me her scarf. I'm already wearing a scarf, but hers is much better equipped to keep out the cold and I accept it with thanks. I watch her until she's disappeared through the airway and, though she doesn't look back, the set of her shoulders and the stiffness of her bearing tells me that she feels my eyes on her. I think she's someone who could pinpoint a hidden watcher in a pitch-black room, and I find that reassuring, and also a little scary. Anyone I've known who's thrown up walls like that has had plenty of reason to distrust the world, but distrust is only as useful as the situation is dangerous. And it can be a powerful drug sometimes.

Alone again, I'm at a loss. Windroosstraat doesn't strike me as somewhere with many places to go at midday on a Sunday. It's also short on pedestrians, and I'm starting to feel conspicuous. So I head for the airway, following slowly enough that I won't catch up to Françoise, and pause in the tunnel to take it in. She wasn't kidding about the trams. I haven't seen one on the roads since we set off, so I keep no more than half an ear out for traffic as I turn my head up into the arch above me. It's always an arch. Beyond the airway's two-storey reach is another three storeys of flats, maybe an office or two, and the gap between their lower floor and the tunnel ceiling is almost certainly dead space. It would make more sense to square it off, but still it's an arch. I'm not convinced the choice is structural, either, because this entire place is built of reinforced plastic-metal alloys and if they're going to bend in any direction it'll be towards the singularity, which is perpendicular to the stresses on the airway walls. I think there's just something kind of primal about organics and their arches. This one has an anemone engraved into its walls, tribute to the sector's namesake flower, and I feel like I've learned more about Windroosstraat in this one architectural feature than anything else I've seen this morning.

The blast doors are set well back into their crevices. Little bits of street-grime have stuck to the layer of oil that faces onto the road. They haven't been closed in quite some time, by the looks of things. Still, I'm not sure I'm completely comfortable with the idea of blast doors yet. The induction lady made a point of taking me around the streetside O_2 points nearest the induction centre and showing me how to work them in the event of a lockdown away from home or work, but every single emergency situation she listed involved fire. I can't help but wonder how clever it is to have a live O_2 feed in the middle of all that. Call me paranoid, but I'm sure I'm not the first person to think of this, either.

You're paranoid, says Luca, but that's because he'll be just fine if the oxygen cuts out without warning. I ignore him and step out of the airway and into Windrooslaan.

These are the streets where the families go to live. As I make my way down Windrooslaan, briskly enough to look like I know where I'm going, I notice that each block forms a structure like the one we saw at Kaasstad: a perimeter square of apartment units surrounding a central, gated courtyard, where ground-floor occupants have planted overflowing window-boxes or small, spreading trees, and, sometimes, brightly coloured playground toys scatter themselves among the flagstones and the greenery. Here and there I catch traces of little voices, raised in play or complaint, from open windows or hidden gardens, and as I pass the entrance to one courtyard I hear a girl and a boy singing together as though nobody is listening. I pass by. I don't understand children, even when I know what they're saying, and I'm cold enough now to contemplate paying for coffee if it will only get me off the street.

Another airway takes me into Windroosweg, where I come across the first streetside café of my walk to have its awnings out and its shutters open. The name above the door says *Moeder's* – Mother's – which sounds welcoming enough, but, as I push open the door and step inside, the interior tells another story. The customers are comprised exclusively of elderly men hunched around bottles of beer or steaming mugs, and the server, a big gruff man in his late forties or early fifties, scowls at me as I offer an opening smile and a *goedemorgen*. This may be because it's the afternoon and I've mixed up my greetings under pressure, but I really don't think it is. Luca, at my shoulder, lets out a little hiss of disapproval, and I agree. Still. It's cold outside, and I'm hungry and chilled to the bone and, most importantly of all, I can't leave again now without looking like they've scared me off. I may be old, but they're older, and I'm pretty sure I could take them all. I'm staying and I'm having coffee.

I doubt it's table service in Moeder's. *"Koffie, alstublieft,"* I call towards the server as I sit down. I avoid looking around, though I can feel at least one of the other customers glaring at the back of my head. I mirror their pose by circling my shoulders in towards my chest and folding my hands in front of me on the table as I wait. From a corner of the room, an unseen speaker transmits the chirpy voice of someone announcing what sounds – I swear to God – like Radio Stairlift and the chimes of an electronic clock declare it one hour past midday and time for the news. The server sets a mug of something brown and wet in front of me and I hand him the equivalent of an hour's pay for a liquid that may or may not contain traces of chemical waste. At least it's warm. I'd like to drop an iodine tablet into it, just to be sure, but I definitely won't get away with that.

Careful, says Luca quietly behind me. *These are not your friends.*

I know that, I tell him inside my head. I've already decided that I can't stay here, but I am damn well finishing this coffee. I take a sip and compromise: all right, I'm finishing *half* of this coffee. I swallow and amend once more: I'm sitting here with my hands around this cup until it goes cold.

In the background, the host of Radio Stairlift has turned all solemn and funereal. I keep the radio on in my unit for practice, though I can't understand more than three or four words out of every twenty, and I remember something sounded less than great before I left to meet Françoise this morning, but I didn't hear *bomb*, *police* or *blackout*, so I let it slide and forgot to ask her. It may have got worse in the intervening hours. I think I hear the word *dood*, which is death, or *dodelijk*, which is deadly, both of which have seared themselves into my subconscious language banks for obvious reasons, but I can't tell the context and I can't make out what the announcer is saying. And then I hear *stroomreiziger* and my hands tighten involuntarily around my mug, because this is not the place I want to be sitting if shit is about to go down.

Stroomreiziger is 'a-naut'. This is one of the first words I made myself learn. It's not a word that I want to hear anywhere near *dodelijk*.

Time to leave, says Luca as someone behind me grunts and grumbles something that makes the server look up and nod gravely in his direction. But I can't leave now. The time to leave was before I opened the door to Moeder's; walking out with a fresh cup of coffee still cooling on the table as Radio Stairlift intones something terrible about a-nauts is not a plan with any long-term prospects of strategic success.

So I do what I have to do. I grunt at the radio and I catch the server's eye and I mimic spitting my disgust out onto the floor. He eyes me warily for a moment, and then he nods.

"*Uitschot*," he mutters, and a couple of other words that I don't understand, but I can take a guess. *Uitschot* is scum. Garbage. My body tenses, braces, but, no, it turns out that we're friends now. It's agreement, not a call to arms against me. I'm very clear that it would be, if he knew what I was. But for now, it means I might just get out of here alive.

Remember those guys last week, says Luca. Yes, I'd like to tell him, I remember those a-nauts that were lynched last week, and the ones from two months ago. I'm pretty sure I read something a few months before that too, about a group of five of us who were electrocuted to death in front of a crowd of onlookers, none of whom saw anything when questioned later by the police. I remember a district name, but it meant nothing at the time, and of course I can't bring it to mind now that I need it. I don't *think* it was Windroos-anything, but it could have been.

Does it actually matter? Luca wants to know in response, and he's right: it doesn't matter, right now, who or where it was. Whether or not it was these exact men right here who tied a man and four women to a broken window frame and ran live electrical wires from a tram-feed to their naked bodies, they are not safe men for me to be around.

Stroomreiziger, I hear again, and it's from someone else in the café. A rumble of coarse laughter echoes around the room and I laugh with them. I laugh at the two men strung up to a lamp post and beaten to death. I laugh at the solemn tones of Radio Stairlift's voice of reason. I laugh, and I pretend to spit on the floor again, and I wait for my coffee to be finished so that I can leave and wash this place off my skin.

11.5 Danae

He's standing in the shelter of the airway, folded in on himself like a piece of origami, and he looks so cold and so wretched that I actually feel a bit bad for leaving. It's not like there's much to do to pass the time out here. We probably could have tolerated each other's company for a few more hours, though he looked as happy as I was that we didn't have to.

"Warmed up a bit, anyway," he says as he sees me approach. Maybe it's just that I've been indoors for the past few hours and the temperature differential seems more pronounced, but I can't bring myself to agree.

"If you say so," I say. "How's your afternoon been?"

His eyes darken. "Fun place, this," he says, but he doesn't elaborate, just turns and leads the way back towards the café.

The windows are shaded and the outside chairs stacked neatly behind them as we approach. The square is quiet, but noise and light filters down from the floors above us: Windroosstraat is a Sunday-dinner sort of place. I think I can even hear somebody playing a cello somewhere – the quality of the sound is deeper, more present than the modulated tones of a radio or a recording – but that just seems like overkill. It may be the suburbs, but it's still Verdieping Drei. It's not as if we're on the top floor of the radial or anything.

Arnold is folding back the awnings as we approach, and he doesn't turn to greet us, though I'm sure he hears us coming. I can't really blame him: I'd be pissed off at us, too, if I were him, and I feel a sudden urge to just turn around and walk away; leave the guy alone to whatever sort of life he's managed to chisel out for himself up here. But I don't, of course. I halt a little way away from him and the darkened windows of the café, wait until he's finished furling, and, when he stops and shoves his hands in his pocket and still doesn't turn around, I say, quietly, "*Hoi*, Arnold."

A beat. He doesn't look at us, but his shoulders sag. "Hi," he says at last.

I wait for him to elaborate. He doesn't. I say, "Are you finished? Or do you…?"

"Not here," he says abruptly, cutting me off. I'm not sure if he's just grumpy or if he genuinely thinks I'm about to start extolling the virtues of the amnisonaut race right here in Windroosstraat 180: 317 to 405, but I let it go. "There's a place I know," he says. "Come on – it's not far."

Before I can answer, he's turned and walked off. Emmett turns to me, one eye raised. "You managed to piss him off pretty quickly."

"Shut up," I say. "We're supposed to follow him, so try and keep up."

I set off after Arnold's retreating back. Out of the corner of my eye, I see Emmett shrug and follow.

There's not much open even in the radial centre on a Sunday evening, but in the far reaches of Windroosstraat high society is basically dead. I'm not surprised when we pass through the airway into Windrooswal and then again into Krokusweg and finally into Krokuslaan, where I've never been before. It's not noticeably livelier than any of the preceding sectors, but, huddled right in against the outer wall, we come to a collection of little hole-in-the-wall eateries and pubs, well-populated with clientele spilling out onto the streetside tables even as the lightbands begin the slow dim towards evening. Arnold leads us to the one set back furthest from the road. *Remmy's*, reads the sign. We follow him through the door.

Inside, it's warm and comfortably full, and the air is heated and scented by the presence of two dozen bodies in close proximity. I smell stale beer and some kind of powdery spice, and, behind the hum of companionable chatter, a radio belts out rock music from forty years ago – songs my da used to listen to, back when we still listened to music. There's a server delivering pitchers of beer to a table of burly men and women whose red cheeks and loose smiles tell me they've been here for hours already, and she looks up as we enter and offers Arnold a warm, welcoming smile.

"*Hoi!*" she calls. "*Pak een stoel. Hoe gaat het?*"

It's a rote greeting, though her welcome seems genuine, and she's gone before we can answer. Arnold moves us to a free table in the corner and we sit, Emmett and me on one side, Arnold on the other. He looks less hunted here, on his own turf, but his face is no friendlier. I decide to open negotiations with an attempt at rapprochement.

"Thank you for talking to us," I say.

He grunts. "I needed to get you out of the café," he says.

"Understood." We glance up as the server arrives and I determine very quickly that both men at the table are expecting me to buy the drinks. I'm not sure how this happened, but I'll be having words with Emmett. "Gin for me," I tell her. Arnold nods. "Gin for him too. And water for my associate here."

At *associate*, she glances at Emmett and her smile fades a couple of lux, but I can't quite bring myself to call him *friend*. I met him three days ago, for one thing, and I also don't want Arnold getting the idea that this is some kind of united front that he's up against. Nobody at this table trusts anybody else at this table, that much is clear, but I find that I feel closer affiliation to a man whose presence has hovered around the edges of my life for the past year than to the man currently sitting at my side.

"Sure," says our server after a moment. "I'll be right back."

"Water?" says Arnold when she's gone. He glances at Emmett, who looks to me for clarification.

"Older model," I say.

Arnold nods, stares solidly at Emmett. And then, in faltering English, he asks, "What line?"

I'm not sure either of us were expecting that, but Emmett's good at looking like he's not surprised by something. He rallies quickly. "Technika Blackbird," he says. "C-line, 104-A."

"Ah," says Arnold. "Auto manufacturing. Very good." He offers no information about his own provenance, and I'm not inclined to encourage anyone to ask in case they decide that we're all going to swap stories about the bad old days. There are a couple of model numbers that I can claim to be, but I'd rather leave that can of worms sealed shut.

Emmett obliges. "Long time ago," he says. "We're none of us who we used to be. Right?"

"Right." Arnold's face creases into a half-smile, but he keeps it turned on the table. His accent is neither native Dutch nor native English. "We will wait for a moment, then we will talk, okay?"

"Okay." I glance up as the server arrives with our drinks, and I'm encouraged to note that it's the sort of place that sells gin by the glass and not by the measure. It's going to hurt my bank balance, but it's been that sort of day.

"Just water?" she wants to know as she sets Emmett's glass down. "Nothing else?"

Emmett's face is politely blank. "Nothing else," I confirm, and I offer her my neck chip to swipe the bill. I raise my glass to the boys. "Cheers," I say in English.

They raise their glasses to me in return. Only Emmett repeats the salutation.

Arnold takes a long swig of gin and winces the way you do when you need to get alcohol into your body quicker than your body wants to accept it. He wipes the back of his hand across his mouth and says, "English is better here. They won't listen, but it's better if they don't hear."

"Fair enough," says Emmett. He leans back in his chair, the very picture of a man perfectly at his ease, and I'd kick him under the table if there was enough room. He's the only one of the three of us who looks remotely comfortable right now. "So," he says, "you know someone who can help us?"

Arnold nods, cradling his glass to himself as though it's his firstborn child. "Maybe."

"But we haven't told you what we need," says Emmett.

That gets Arnold's attention. His head snaps up from his table-bound reverie and his eyes fix, hard, on Emmett's. "Hey," he says. "What is this? You say you need help, what sort of help does someone like us need in this city? What is this...?"

"It's okay," I say quickly, before he can spook completely. I am going to have so many words with Emmett when we get out of here. "You're right. We should have explained. We're not looking for... I don't know, *sanctuary*. Nothing like that. We just need..." I hesitate. I don't want to say *information*. I don't want him to freak out completely and decide that we're in somebody else's pocket; we're on his turf, in his space, and I cannot imagine any way that that would end well for us. "We have a problem," I try. "Emmett's here because he needs to know some stuff, and we have no idea who to ask."

"Stuff?" Arnold's voice is thick with suspicion. This could still go either way. "What sort of stuff?"

Emmett sits forward at least. Maybe he's not as tone-deaf as I thought. "Have you heard of a group called the Garrison of Many?" he asks. Arnold hesitates for a moment, and then shakes his head. Emmett chuckles softly. "Not surprising. It's a stupid name – I think it was supposed to be a pun or something. Maybe, I don't know, three hundred or so of them across the British Isles and Scandinavia. I think they had a couple more in Germany. We're not talking big-league resistance here, but they took me in about fifteen years ago and I've been working for the Home Counties cache ever since. I'm telling you this," he says quietly, "so that you know I'm not blowing smoke up your ass. Even if you haven't heard of them, you've heard of some of their stunts. The elevator breakdown at Copenhagen Harbour?"

A beat. Then Arnold nods, slowly. "Yes. I know it." Copenhagen isn't a major supply city for Luchtstad, but the knock-on post-etheric delays left us short of water for almost a week and the barley crops in Radiale Twee came close to failing.

"Yeah," says Emmett. "That was the GoM. Not huge, not well-funded, but not exactly scratching around for loose change either."

Arnold takes a sip of his gin. "So you're a terrorist."

"No." Emmett shakes his head. "Not me. That's never been me. Political agitator, maybe, but even then… Let's just say that my best days are behind me. I'm not here to cause trouble on Luchtstad. I swear that on my life. I'm here because the guys back home think they've found something up here and I think I have an idea of what it might be."

I'd been wondering if it would sound any less delusional when he explained it to somebody else. It really doesn't. "A disturbance," I clarify for him, before he can get all metaphysical and confuse our poor friend. "There's something going on with the stream up here, and Emmett's been sent to find out what it is."

Arnold snorts, and I can't blame him. "There's plenty going on with the stream up here," he says. "Have you noticed? We only walk on the ground because this city is powered by a data singularity strong enough to warp the local space-time continuum."

"Yes," says Emmett calmly. "I know. I mean apart from that."

There's a long pause. Arnold purses his lips, considers, takes another gulp of gin. At last, he says, "I would have noticed."

"Maybe not." Emmett shrugs. "I got here on Wednesday afternoon and my head has felt like someone's hammering nails into my skull from the inside out every waking second since. I think you could dump the entire a-naut race in the centre of this radial and slaughter them one by one and I wouldn't notice the chant right now. Whatever this is, it's small. It's small and it's up against the massive backwash of singularity feedback – it's like looking for shadows on a cloudy day. We wouldn't have seen it at all if we didn't have three guys whose job it is to do nothing else but study the streamflow up here. But it's consistent, and it's steady. It's something."

"All right." Arnold's taking this better than I'd have expected, and I wonder just how long he's been up here that the city can no longer surprise him. There's an obvious question that comes next. He asks it: "What does this have to do with me?"

"You said you might know somebody who could help," I say. I tilt my glass towards me and find that it's empty. If Emmett stays in my life for any length of time, I may need to get a second job.

"I said that I *might*," Arnold says.

"But that was when you thought we just needed jobs," says Emmett. "Right?"

"Right."

Emmett leans back on his seat again. The smile is back, too. "So, this is easier."

"Easier?" That actually gets what sounds like a genuine snort of laughter. "It's easier to find this, what, this *disturbance*? That you can't feel, and I can't feel; that you only know about because some guys on Earth study the streamflow around Luchtstad? Mister, I know about jobs. I don't know about this."

Emmett looks completely unperturbed. "You've heard the stories about Luchtstad."

"Stories?" says Arnold. "What stories? I don't know stories."

Great, Emmet's doing the stories again. "Don't worry about it," I say quickly. "I haven't felt the disturbance either. But if it exists...? Maybe someone else knows about it."

"You're kidding." He looks completely lost. "If anybody knows about this, I don't know them."

"But what about the person you were going to take us to?"

"I wasn't going to take you to anybody."

"The person who might have been able to help us," says Emmett. "Back when you thought this was about something else."

"I wasn't going to take you to her," says Arnold. "I was going to ask her if she could help you. But this? This... She will only laugh. She will laugh, and then she will never hear another word from my mouth again." He shakes his head. "No. She will laugh. If you're lucky."

"If we're lucky?" I hadn't planned on chipping in again, but I don't like threats, even when they're mild. Even when they're implied. "And if we're not lucky – what? A flyer campaign? A strongly worded email? Are we supposed to be worried about someone laughing at us?"

Arnold's smile is sharp and brittle. "When that person is a powerful person, yes. It should worry you."

"Oh, please." I'll see his powerful person and raise him a streamcode wipe and a brand new life. "All three of us made it to Luchtstad, Arnold, and we didn't hitch a ride on a comet. That means we all know a thing or two about powerful people. Let me guess: you mentioned an aunt before. Since we both know you don't have an aunt, my money says she's someone local with the power to help you out when you need help. Someone with influence. Am I right?"

There's a slight pause, then Arnold raises his glass to me. The smile warms fractionally, though you'd have to be looking hard to notice. "You're right," he says. "She is…" He hesitates. "I think you would call her a community leader."

Community leader. Not cache leader. "She's not one of us?" I say.

"No. But she's a friend to us – when it suits her interests."

"Ah." Understanding is dawning on Emmett's face. "And I'm guessing you have a whole lot of cousins?"

"I don't know. Probably. I know… maybe three or four."

"And you… what?" Emmett looks angry, but it's not in his voice. "You do favours for her? Get her things that she needs? Talk to people she wants you to talk to?"

"Yes." Arnold looks up, meets Emmett's eye. He looks angry, too, and it *is* in his voice. "This woman – my aunt – when she speaks to people, they listen. Somebody comes to my door, they want to drag me out onto the street and maybe throw rocks at my head to see if I bleed? If I don't have her protection I'm a dead man. But if she says, 'You will not hurt him. He is mine,' then I live. And if she says, 'You will give him a job. He will work for you,' then I have money, and somewhere to stay. There's safety to live like this. This is how we stay alive in Luchtstad. You will see this soon."

I glance at Emmett, and I see acknowledgement behind his eyes, but his anger's not ready to let this go. I say, carefully, "If she's not one of us… maybe she can't help us, Emmett."

"This is what I am saying to you," says Arnold. He swallows the end of his gin in one swift, irritable gulp. "She thinks that we don't need to die, and she helps us. But she won't care about what you're looking for."

Emmett swirls his water, peers down into the circling whirlpool he's made. His jaw is tight and his eyes are dark. From the rapid, shallow huff of his breath, I guess that he's buying himself the time he needs to regain a little composure.

"I think," he says at last, "that I'd like to ask her that myself."

Arnold rolls his eyes. "Oh, come on…" I start to snap, but Emmett's glare kills the rest of the sentence before I even realise it's happening. I'm not impressed with myself, but it's too late to recover.

"Maybe she won't care," he says. "Maybe she can't help. Maybe she'll laugh." His hands are actually shaking. This is personal for him, and I wish I'd known that in advance. "But if she's going to try and claim the moral high ground while she's running a protection racket that's two steps away from slavery, then she can do it to my face."

Chapter Twelve

12.1 Adam

"Well," says Françoise as the pub door closes behind us, "that could definitely have gone better."

"Could have gone worse, too," I say. Outrage has tightened all the muscles down the back of my neck and into my spine, and I start walking to try and shake it off, rolling my shoulders as I do. I don't bother to check if she's following; I'm betting she'll fall into step beside me when she's ready to stop being angry at me. "We got a name."

"We got a name," she says at my elbow – turns out that she'll fall into step beside me whether she's finished being angry or not, as long as she has something to say – "and an iron-clad guarantee that she might possibly stream you, sometime, maybe, if she feels like you're worth her time, and only if she doesn't decide that it'd be a better idea to send someone round to smash your windows and get you lynched on the street. I gave up my day off for this."

I'm not in the mood for cynicism or emotional blackmail. "You gave up four hours of your day off. And you had nothing better to do anyway."

The localised temperature at my right hip plummets. Given how cold this city is, I'm surprised I notice, but Françoise is that good at communicating disdain.

"You're a real piece of shit," she says. "I hope her guys break both your legs."

I'm just angry enough to say the first thing that comes to mind, but fortunately she's moving before I can draw breath to completely shoot myself in the foot. I'm not convinced I deserved that, but she didn't deserve to get caught in the blast radius of my shitty day either.

"Françoise," I call after her. "Françoise – wait. I'm sorry."

She moves quickly when she's furious. She doesn't stop, she doesn't turn around, but she slows down a little bit at least. It's been a long day in the cold and my joints are starting to seize, but I'm not dead yet. I pick up my pace to where I can speak to her without having to raise my voice.

"You're right," I say. "You're right, and I'm sorry. I just… I had an idea of what I thought this city was supposed to be like, is all. And I've known too many good people who get caught up with scum-sucking lowlife like Arnold's aunt." I pause to catch my breath. It gives me a chance let the anger settle a little bit more. "It's always the good people, you know? The bad ones can take care of themselves, but the good ones – they always think it's a level playing field. And then it's too late."

She still doesn't stop, but her shoulders lose a little of their tension. "And what did you think this city was supposed to be like, Emmett?" she wants to know without looking round.

I don't have a good answer for that. I wasn't expecting utopia, or safety, or the warm, welcoming embrace of acceptance and love. But I feel like it was supposed to be better than what I left behind at least. I'm not sure, after today, that in some ways it isn't worse. At least the Rens look you in the eye when they tell you why you shouldn't be alive.

"Not like this," I say at last. "Not like… this."

Still she doesn't stop. But she glances back over her shoulder and adjusts her pace a little so that it matches mine again.

"Yeah," she says, and it's exhaled on the back of a sigh: more a breath than a word. "You and me both, New Guy."

"Come with me?" I say. I'm pressing my luck; I don't know how long her anger will hold. "When she streams me? Come and meet her with me?"

She snorts. The air in front of her mists on her outbreath. "*If* she streams you."

"If she streams me." I don't know why I'm asking. I've broken down the first wall; I have a contact, now, of my own. Françoise can go back to gin and silence if she wants to, and I can still do what I came here to do. "Maybe I'm just more optimistic than you."

More laughter. "Yeah. That's for sure," she says. "And maybe you just want back-up for when her guys break both your legs. Sure, whatever. If you really think I'm going to get my legs broken on your behalf, Emmett Keller, then whatever."

"You know, the Blackbird-line femurs were tested up to 7000 Newtons."

A half-glance sideways. "7000, huh?"

"Industrial model." I'm pretty sure she has no idea if she should be impressed by that figure. "I'm just saying. Organic femurs fracture at

4000."

"Right."

"I'm just saying." I can feel the anger starting to fizzle, the beginnings of the return of a good mood. After all, Arnold's aunt is a powerful woman. Powerful women tend to know people who know people, and that's more important right now than how she makes her money. "Her guys can *try* to break my legs, is what I'm saying. But they're more likely to break their wrists."

That earns me half a smile. "Yeah," she says. "That'd almost be worth giving up another day off to see."

"Told you." We walk a couple of feet in silence, side by side, and the air is warmer around us. This feels good in a way that I can't explain, though I'm pretty sure Luca's going to have a few opinions on the matter later tonight. "I may be a piece of shit, but at least I'm not a boring piece of shit."

"Let's not get ahead of ourselves," says Françoise, but I'm pretty sure she's hiding a grin in the corners of her mouth.

12.2 Danae

Sanne's door opens as I'm waiting for the electronics on mine to remember how to read a neck chip. "Oh, hi," she says. She yawns, as though she's just woken up. "I thought I heard you come in. I hope we didn't wake you last night?"

"It's fine," I tell her. Belatedly, my door creaks open, but it looks like we're having a conversation now. "I wasn't sleeping anyway."

"I told Aline we should have knocked on your door." Her hair hangs loose around her face and I realise I've only ever seen it tied back before now. It's much longer than I thought. "She said you would be sleeping; I said we should knock on your door and see."

"It's fine," I say again. I hold my bag very steady so that she doesn't hear it clinking. I don't *think* she'll be in the mood for more alcohol this evening, but I'd prefer not to find out that I'm wrong. "I had somewhere I needed to be this morning, so… You know."

"Sure. Sure." She yawns again, stretching her arms up over her head. "You want to go and get some dinner now, maybe?"

"Oh." I hesitate. "Yeah. No. I think… I'm just really tired now."

It's not a lie. It just feels like one. Sanne smiles, and I can't help but think that she's read me too well. "Sure," she says. "Get some rest;

that's a good idea. Long day tomorrow."

I think that means I can go without offending her. I do my best smile and kind of hunch my shoulders apologetically, and scurry inside my room. It's only when the door closes again behind me that I realise I should have thanked her, or said goodbye at least.

Inside, cocooned in silence, I drop my bag onto my bed, and resist the urge to grab one of the bottles, unscrew the lid, and neck a few huge gulps. Not yet. First, I make myself stand in the middle of the room and close my eyes and just breathe for a few minutes. Breathe. *Breathe.* Let it settle, let the adrenaline ebb, let my muscles release. I feel myself swaying in the darkness, but I don't open my eyes yet. There's nowhere to fall in this room. I'm safe here.

I am safe.

Played correctly, Arnold's aunt could be the gateway to a whole new layer of research and evaluation. She unlocks a community of names, locations, places to watch. I open my eyes, blink to clear the fog behind them, and drop to my knees to fish my list out of the hole in the bottom of my mattress. Three columns, scored in pencil: who I've found, when I found them, how many more times they were there when I looked. The bartender in Het Brouwsalon. The woman with the scarves at Centralemarkt. The two women on Amarinestraat, the one who sometimes visits the non-denominational church on Tulpweg. Emmett. The men from the shoe stall last night.

Arnold, I write in brackets beside the entry for the red-headed boy from Kaasstad. My pencil scratches against the paper like fingernails on a coffin. And then, below him, I write, *Arnold's aunt.*

Chapter Thirteen

13.1 Danae

Despite what I've told Emmett, I am expecting Auntie to make contact with him. I would, if I were her. So it's not actually a surprise when he approaches me en route to smoke break to tell me that she's been in touch – if anything, the surprise is that it's taken her five days to do so. I move us towards the edge of the group, where the noise from the extractor fan is loudest, and lean up against the wall to make it look as though that's why I'm standing in the place where nobody wants to stand. It's been another long morning. A power cut has taken out the central highway between Vier and Vijf, which shouldn't technically affect us here in Zeven, but seems to have caused problems for the cardboard shipment that arrived on Wednesday evening, and there've been rumours since last night that parts of Verdieping Een have been closed due to a security alert that may or may not bear out, but which has unquestionably put more police on the street down here in Drie. Suffice to say that the line has been edgy, the radio gloomy and subdued, and the constant threat of running out of stupidly complicated boxes to fold has put Jouke in optimal bulb-throwing form. Smoke break couldn't come fast enough, and I'm not exactly over the moon with delight that I get to spend it conspiring with Emmett instead of filling my lungs with nicotine and my head with empty space.

"All right," I say, when I'm reasonably sure that we're far enough away from Thijs and Bente that they won't be able to listen in significantly. "Tell me."

He glances over his shoulder and I want to kick him in his stupid industrially reinforced shins. Subterfuge 101 escapes this man. If it weren't for the fact that Sanne has manifestly decided that I'm sleeping with him, we might as well have targets painted on our head, and the potential for gossip is hardly likely to persuade my colleagues to afford us a little privacy.

"Well," he says, when he's satisfied himself that the performative disinterest on the faces of our nearest workmates means nobody is listening, "she didn't laugh."

That's less comforting than he thinks. "That was never likely," I say. "What *did* she do?"

"She listened," he says. "And she wants to meet tonight."

"*Tonight?*" That was too loud. I'm almost certain, from the way that Thijs' head didn't move even the tiniest fraction on his neck, that he heard. "What did you tell her?"

Emmett shrugs. "I told her we get off at nine."

"For fuck's sake." I am almost too angry to smoke. "For a start... for a start, we'll be lucky to get off at nine, the way the line is going today..."

"I know," he says mildly. "We arranged to meet at midnight."

"Oh, that's much better." I suck in a huge drag of smoke, too much for one set of lungs, and it's all I can do not to cede the high-ground by coughing myself sick. "That doesn't reek of sinister, back-street rendezvous at all. Meet at midnight – wonderful. You know we have to be in work tomorrow at six?"

"Oh, really?" he says. "Is that what time we always start at, every single morning since I've been here? Thank God you pointed that out."

I could do without the sarcasm, though I'm impressed at how calmly he's giving me shit. "Where are we supposed to go? It's a hell of a walk to Krokuslaan."

"We're not meeting in Krokuslaan," he says. "Give me some credit at least. This is not my first clandestine meeting, thanks. There's a bar in Affodilledreef that I know – I said we'd meet her there."

"You know a bar," I say, "in Affodilledreef?" Even I don't know a bar in Affodilledreef.

He shrugs. "I know of it. Quiet but pro... us."

I'd like very much to know how he's come by this information. This is the sort of information that I thought I had. I file it away for later. "How pro-us? How can you be sure?"

"Well, they're not hanging out any flags," he says. "It's probably not in their flyers. But I've done my research – the owner raised some funds for Do Not Seek, back in the day, and I heard they kicked some guys out a while back for trying to start some shit with the bar staff. That much pro-us."

I can feel my eyebrow arching. "That much, huh?"

"Better than most."

That may be true. I think I'm happier with the places that neither raise their heads above the parapet nor run Organic Supremacy theme nights, but I suppose I see his logic. "It really had to be midnight?"

"Do you want to talk to her next time?"

"I'd rather she didn't know I existed, so... no."

"Then it really had to be midnight."

My extravagant sigh is somewhat buried by the one-minute-warning klaxon. I've barely even started on this cigarette, and I kind of need a bathroom cubicle and a swig from my hip flask. "Fine," I say when the ambient noise dies down enough to finish our conversation. "Midnight. Great. Exactly how I hoped my evening would go."

"Cheer up." His grin is insufferable. I wish I knew how he doesn't get kicked in the nuts by everyone he meets. "It's not like we're getting out of here before 11:30 anyway."

"Oh, fuck off," I tell him.

So. I guess we're going to Affodilledreef. Affodilledreef is, incidentally, somewhere else I've never been. It occurs to me to wonder just how I've managed to live here for over a year and know approximately half a dozen places in this city, and only three of them well. I'll say this for Emmett: he broadens one's horizons. Whether or not one wanted them to be broadened – but that's another matter.

12.2 Adam

It's not quite 11:30 when our shift gets out, but I wasn't far wrong. It's just short of the hour, which leaves us forty-five minutes to kill before we have to catch the tram, so I offer to buy Françoise dinner, since we've been working for the past seven hours without a break. I'm expecting her to refuse. I remember the coffee incident, after all. But, instead, she stares at me blankly for fifteen seconds with eyes that are red with exhaustion, and, when she snaps back she says, "Actually, yeah. That'd be great. I'm starving."

So we walk. There's not much open that's not street stalls at this time of night, but it's the weekend for some and vendors are starting to cluster outside the pubs. Warm red shadows from firing stoves light the darkness and the air is full of the smell of heating fat. I order chips and *frikandel speciaal*, which turns out to be some kind of sausage thing with stuff on it, and, because we've caught the vendor unawares, we hover by the stall, close to the cookers, while he gets it ready. Françoise sweeps a weary hand across her face and leans heavily against the awning post. She looks exhausted, as though she ought to have refused to come tonight. I wonder why she didn't.

She says, "Sorry – I'm sorry. I just worked out why you didn't order anything for yourself. I should get this."

"It's okay," I tell her. "I brought a flask of broth. I'll drink it while we walk."

"Yeah, but you didn't get food," she insists. "I should get this."

I don't want this to become a thing. "It was my round."

She sighs. "Cheaper than gin, I suppose."

"Cheaper than *water*." I'm still getting used to this, and it still annoys me.

"Fair enough." She shoots a glare towards the vendor, as though forty-five seconds is an unreasonable time to wait for food that's not cooked yet. "I'm too tired to argue. Tell me more about Auntie."

I wish we weren't calling her that. "For a start," I say, "her name is not Auntie. It's Elisabeth, and I'm not even sure we're supposed to call her that."

She grins. "Liz? Beth? Betty? Or are we supposed to genuflect and call her m'lady?"

"I'd just like to point out that you were the one advocating caution with this woman last Sunday night."

"I'll be cautious." Another glare at the vendor, who fortunately has his back to us. "I just don't do well with self-aggrandisement. What are we supposed to call her?"

This hurts me to say. "I called her 'ma'am' when we talked last night."

"Ma'am?" Her grin widens a few notches. "All right. I'll play. What else?"

"She's not as bad as some of the community leaders I've run into in my time." This is not a compliment, but it's a start. "I think she is legitimately pro-Do Not Seek – or at least anti-lynching. I think her protection comes from a genuine place. I just think it's more important to her that we're useful than alive, is all."

"Okay. Better than nothing. You think she can help with your stream disturbance?"

"She didn't dismiss it out of hand. But she didn't know anything about it."

"Obviously. She's not uplinked. How would she know about it?"

"She might have heard. It was worth a shot."

She acknowledges the truth of this with a tilt of her head. "So. Why are we meeting her?"

"I think she's interested in us."

Françoise's face darkens. "Interested," she repeats. "Interested, as in the way she's interested in Arnold?"

"Maybe." It's not something I can rule out from our conversation. "Maybe not. I think she thinks there might be some people she can put us in touch with. But I don't think she's going to do it for free."

"Nothing," says Françoise, "is ever for fucking free. Are you dying, Emmett?"

It's thrown in so casually, so unexpectedly, that for a moment I'm not sure I've heard her properly. "What?" I say at last.

"You heard me." For eyes that look like they need to start with a solid week of sleep and take it from there, her gaze is piercing. "You're an old guy..."

"Hey!"

"Whatever. You're a guy with more years behind him than ahead, and you're prepared to, what, sell yourself back into slavery on the strength of a hunch?"

"I've no intention of selling myself back into slavery."

"Nice deflection. But you didn't answer my question."

She's right, of course. But I don't know what to tell her. "We're all dying," I say.

Françoise rolls her eyes so hard that her pupils almost disappear. "I've known some guys, Emmett," she says, "who, if you said to them, 'Walk into that store and start shooting and don't stop until they shoot you back,' they'd be all, 'Absolutely – where do we keep the bullets?' I mean, I've known some really stupid people who think that the way you make progress in a movement is to make it bigger than you, and bigger than everyone you care about; bigger than anything else. I don't know, but I'm guessing those people are mostly dead now. But you? I don't know. You seem like the kind of guy who stays alive by sticking to the margins. That's not the sort of guy who walks up to a lady like Madam Elisabeth and gives her whatever the hell she wants in exchange for advancing the cause. So I'm asking you again, Emmett: are you dying? Because that's just about the only reason I can think of to explain why this hospital fairytale means so much to you."

I stare at her, considering how to answer. "You've heard of Technika, right? Went bust in a big way back in '77. One of the first big a-tech giants to go under."

Françoise meets my eye and doesn't look away. "Sure."

"The Blackbird line was one of their earliest models."

I watch her do the maths. It's always harder work when there's someone watching you try to count, and she glares at me the whole time. "How long?"

"How long... what? How long were we in production?"

"How long have you got left?"

I suck in a deep breath. It feels more difficult than usual. "I can't answer that..." I start to say, but then I see the look that she's giving me. "Not long," I say instead.

"Okay." Her stare is unblinking. "Okay, yeah. I suppose that makes a lot of sense."

She drops her eyes, purses her lips. I can see she's gearing up another question, and if it requires this level of preparation, it's not likely to be something I want to answer. Fortunately, at this point, the vendor finishes putting together whatever combination of things make up sausage-with-stuff in Luchtstad, and the moment vanishes.

"For fuck's sake..." mutters Françoise, but she's been glaring at his back for the past four minutes, so she can't really do anything other than accept the food from him and take a massive bite.

"Good?" I ask.

"You're deflecting again," she says around a mouthful of sausage meat.

"Smells good."

"It is good. Stop deflecting."

"I'm just saying. 'Thank you, Emmett, for the delicious food' wouldn't kill you right now."

She swallows. "Don't push your luck."

I'm not kidding: it really does smell good. I reach into the inside pocket of my coat and pull out my flask of broth, unscrew the lid, and offer her the first slug. She stares at me levelly and takes another bite of sausage.

"I have my reasons for doing this," I say, and swallow a gulp of something that's nothing like as much fun as what she has. "They're good reasons. They make up for dealing with Madam Elisabeth – and can we not call her that, either?"

A shrug. Pensive chewing. "The only reason you think that's going to work," she says, "is because you don't know me very well."

"Can it work for now at least?"

She takes another bite, spends her time on it. "Do your reasons put me in danger?"

"No," I say. "Absolutely not. I swear to God they don't, Françoise."

"You swear." Soft, humourless laughter. Françoise shakes her head. "Good one. I'll be watching you, Emmett. I don't do sympathy and I don't do second chances, and I don't care what you swear. I decide when I'm in danger, and I decide what to do about it. Understood?"

I nod. "That's fair."

"Okay. Fine." She finishes the sausage, rubbing her hands together to clear them of crumbs. "So. Let's go and have a chat with your new friend Betsy."

12.3 Danae

The trams to Affodilledreef are almost empty this late on a Friday night, and our scattered co-travellers smell strongly of beer and cigarettes. We walk without discussion to the furthest end of the carriage and, when he takes a seat, I take the seat opposite – too far away for quiet conversation. There's a faint smile behind his eyes as he registers the move, but he says nothing, just turns his gaze silently towards the news strip playing overhead.

I don't like it when people tell me I'm not in danger. For a start, I find that other people's idea of what constitutes danger is generally not compatible with mine, and that's a problem. But, more than that, I don't like the confidence behind it: confidence is blinding, and thinking you're untouchable, just because you said you were, is a great way to make sure you don't see what's coming.

I also think we should have made sure that we got to the venue before she did. But, then again, I was hungry, and I don't always think well when I'm hungry. So it is that it's 11:55 when we arrive at De Gouden Narcissen, and Elisabeth, because she's been doing this for a long time – possibly longer than I've been alive – is already sitting at a table near the back with a half-finished drink in front of her and two men just disinterested enough and far enough into the shadows behind her to be unmistakably there to back her up if things go south.

She's not what I was expecting. This is the problem with attempting to moderate a threat by giving it a silly name: I've let myself think of her as Auntie, so she became matronly and comfortable in my head, sort of like a mother bear protecting her cubs. She's probably somewhere in her late fifties, but elegant and well groomed. Her hair is not wrapped in a scarf, which suggests to me that she spends little time on the streets, but elegantly styled in short, tight curls that cling to her head in a manner that suggests recent release from the cloche hat that sits with a very expensive handbag on the seat beside her. Her clothes are immaculate, from the fine wool of her jacket, to the crisp cotton blend of her dress, to the high shine and spike of her heels. This is not an outfit designed to blend in, and that's a statement in itself.

She's watching the door with a kind of dignified indifference, and her face creases into a polished smile as we enter.

"Oh good," says Emmett, sotto voce, teeth clenched as he returns the gesture. "She knows what we look like."

The back of an unfamiliar bar is not where I would have chosen to sit, but we've ceded this tactical point to her by being less early. She's going to offer us a drink, I reckon, and I'm going to have to damn well refuse because we're on the back foot now, and why is it that I always seem to have to turn down gin right when I need it the most?

"Won't you sit down?" she asks in Dutch.

"I'm fine," I tell her, also in Dutch, because there are points to be made. "*Je vais bien, merci.*"

Nothing. Not so much as a spark of consternation. I also speak passable Spanish; maybe I should have gone with that.

Emmett shoots me a warning glance back over his shoulder as he lowers himself into a chair across the table from Elisabeth. I fold my arms across my chest, prop myself against the wall, and ignore him. He can play good cop all he likes; I just want Betsy here to know that neither of us spook as easily as she might have thought.

"So," says Emmett. He sits back easily in his seat, and I feel myself relax a little, before I remember that he pulled the same manoeuvre with Arnold for no good reason, and realise that it's probably just what he does in this situation. "Thank you for seeing us."

Elisabeth nods. "No problem," she says in English. "Can I get you a drink?"

"We're fine," I tell her, before he can answer. "Thank you."

Her smile is radiant and red-lipped. "Sure?"

"Positive," I say. "Thank you."

"All right, then." She lifts her own drink, takes a small sip. Her lipstick leaves the faintest red crescent on the rim of the glass. "I don't normally do this, you know. I don't normally come to other people. Other people come to me."

"I'm aware," says Emmett. He doesn't say thank you, at least. This isn't a concession that she's granting us: if she's going against protocol, it's because we have something she wants enough to let us lead for now. "When we talked, you thought you could put us in touch with some people. Is that right?"

"That's right," she says. "Though I told you that Marie Schlesinger is not a name I'm familiar with."

It's not a name that I'm familiar with, either. In fact, this is the first I've ever heard of Marie Schlesinger and I know Emmett is aware of this by the way that his shoulders tighten, almost imperceptibly, at the mention of her.

We will be having words after this.

"You did," he says. There's no trace of tension in his voice; you would think, to listen to him, that she hadn't got him riled at all. "And then we moved on and you told me that you thought you could put me in touch with some people."

"I'm interested," she says mildly, "in what you're looking for."

"I've told you what I know," he says. "I'm interested in how you can help."

She shrugs. "I've spoken to my contacts – they have no idea what you're talking about. Nobody's heard of a disturbance in the stream. But then it occurred to me that, well, maybe you need to look outside of Verdieping Drie. And I'm willing to bet you don't know anybody on Twee, let alone Een."

"I'm thinking," says Emmett, "that we need to look outside of Radiale Zeven."

"I thought so too." She sets down her glass and folds her hands in front of her on the table. She has a hangnail on her left index finger and I can't stop staring at it. Maybe it's just that it's so out of place on a woman like this, and maybe it's because it fundamentally underscores her organic status; I don't know. It unsettles me. "And I'm pretty damn sure you can't do that on your own, Mr Keller."

"Look," he says, and spreads his hands to show that, hey, we're all in this together. "I know you're the person to go to in the Windroosector and most of the Krokussector. I respect that. It's just that... forgive me if I'm not 100% convinced that you have the reach to get us in with your contemporaries on the other floors. Let alone the other radials."

It's pitched just right: casual enough to let her know that she doesn't intimidate him; polite enough to show the appropriate deference. She doesn't usually deal with people like us, I'm sure – people who aren't desperate – and he needs to play this carefully. Her expression doesn't falter, though her smile widens.

"I'm not offering you a job in Verdieping Een," she says. "That's not what we're talking about. God, if I could get jobs for you people on Een, why would I still be scratching a living in this... *klotestad?*"

"Shithole," I translate, just to remind everyone that I'm still here, and I still speak Dutch.

"Really?" She turns benign eyes on me. "*Stad* – you would translate this as 'hole'?"

"Idiom," I say. "We don't say 'shit city' in English."

"Though I'm wondering why, now," says Emmett. "It works for me."

"Language is a strange thing," says Elisabeth, in a friendly tone designed to communicate her absolute unwillingness to discuss obscene colloquialisms any further. "But you see my point. I operate in the Windroossector because I know enough people and I have enough influence that if I say this person is under my protection, then this person is under my protection. I'm not offering you protection in Verdieping Een – I can't do that. But knowing who to talk to in these other places – that's just good business."

"I agree," says Emmett. "You probably have, I don't know, community agitator conferences or something."

I want to kick the back of his chair. Elisabeth simply sips from her drink. "We have channels of communication," she says.

"All right," he says. "Who can you give us?"

"That depends," says Elisabeth. "There's a pricing structure for these things. It depends on how much you're willing to pay."

Emmett laughs lightly. "There's no pricing structure. There's whatever we decide the information is worth."

"That's not," she says, "how this works."

"Yes it is." It sounds for all the world as though he's enjoying himself, and I remember his anger on Sunday night, his outrage at the way she had Arnold bought and sold. "You came to me. I told your nephew that we exist, and you came to me. You want this more than I do, so we get to set the terms of the deal."

Her smile hasn't faded, but her eyes are cold. "That's... an interesting way of looking at it."

"It's probably not one you're used to, I'll give you that." He is: he's enjoying himself. I think he hamstrung his bargaining position when he made it personal enough to mention somebody called Marie Schlesinger by name, but that's for him to work out. "But here's the way I see it, ma'am. You're used to people coming to you without anything to trade, without any cards. These are people who've somehow managed to get themselves to Luchtstad, but they have no papers. They have no job. They have no name here. And you can do that for them: you can get papers that look good enough for the guys who maybe don't need to look that hard – the guys that are here because cities need cafés and shopping malls and pubs. They're not on the Luchtstad payroll, so the city barely acknowledges they exist, as long as they pay their air and water tax and they're not sleeping on the streets. They want to put in enough to counterbalance what they take out? Fine. You get them a place in society and that's what they do, but, hey, let's not pretend that anything you've got to give them is going to pass muster if they want to, let's say, take a trip to Radiale Vijf. Or even Verdieping Een. Nowhere you've got to pass through a checkpoint to visit: the system's just not going to let them through.

"And then you have us. Françoise and me are factory rats, which means we're here with Luchtstad's blessing. We're part of the great corporate machine, and our ID works just as well as yours. That makes us uniquely valuable, because how many people like us have you ever met? People who made it here without skulking in the shadows, people who can walk around and talk to you like we're equals, because, as far as Luchtstad's concerned, yeah. We are. So, yes, I bet it *is* an interesting way of looking at it, but don't imagine for a second that I'm not aware of exactly what we're bringing to the table. And if your price is too high, what do you want to bet we can find someone else who's willing to trade for less?"

Well. That was ballsier than I'd have given him credit for. Particularly since I wouldn't want to take that bet, being as how we know precisely one person in Luchtstad and that person is already Elisabeth's nephew. I also wouldn't have tried quite so hard to piss her off, but I'm prepared to admit that it might be exactly the tone he needed to set right now. The fact that she takes her time in responding tells me that he's unsettled her confidence at the very least.

She says, slowly, "I think you're overstating your appeal, Mr Keller."

"I don't think I am," he says. "But if you'd prefer that we call it a day and walk away right now, that's fine with me. I have to be in work in five hours."

"No," she says. It's not a snap response: there's nothing impulsive or ill-considered about it. She says it quickly but not recklessly, and it gives away nothing more than the obvious. "No, I think we can talk a while longer. I think you could be useful to me."

"I thought you might," says Emmett. "And I agree."

"Good." Her drink is finished. She pushes the glass a little to the side with the back of her hand, and, without further instruction, one of the shadow men hovering behind her disappears to the bar. "Then this is what I propose. I have a contact in Verdieping Een who has a contact in Radiale Vier. Both of these people are people who might be able to answer your questions. Both of them are people that I need to communicate with, from time to time, and it's getting harder to do so."

"Not quite as anonymous as you used to be, huh?" says Emmett placidly.

"The problem," she says, "is not mine. Have you been to Verdieping Een?"

"I got here last week," he says.

"It's worth a visit. Really, it is. If you can get tickets to the Viewing Plaza, there's nothing like it in civilisation – I promise you. But that's part of the problem."

"Security," I say. "The top floor's a soft target. It's where the tourists go. The police up there tend to be antsier than down here with the proletariat. And your guy got himself flagged, am I right?"

"He spoke to someone he shouldn't have," says Elisabeth, "and now his stream is tapped. Any information I send him gets re-routed past eyes that don't need to see it."

"So you need a messenger," says Emmett. "You need some way of transferring information on the stream that can't be intercepted."

"You need Red Space," I say.

"*Roodplaats*," she says under her breath. Considers. "*Stroomreizigersysteem*. Amnisonaut datastream space. This is Red Space?"

"This is Red Space," says Emmett.

"Then – yes. I don't know the words in English sometimes. But I need Red Space."

Emmett pauses, flexes his fingers in front of him, peers at the nails. "And for Red Space," he says, "we get both names?"

"You get both names," she says. "I think you are useful people. And I collect useful people."

He lets out a gentle snort of laughter, and she looks, for the first time, mildly surprised. "No way," he says.

"No?" She's actually surprised. He has actually managed to surprise her. We're still having words after this is finished, but now I'm impressed.

"No," he says. "Number one: there's no 'people' here. The only messenger at this table is me; Françoise is my associate, but she's not part of this deal. And number two: there's no 'collecting' happening either. I'll pay for the information – and it's a good deal; two names for one trip to Verdieping Een, sure, I'll take that. But it's a one-off. I'm not going on your payroll, ma'am."

Her smile is back, which I can't imagine is a good sign. "That would be an extraordinarily good deal," she says, "for you. For me? No. Why would I agree to that?"

"Because you're tagged to this floor?" says Emmett, which actually makes the smile disappear. Holy shit. He's *much* better at this than I thought.

"Excuse me?" says Elisabeth. Her tone is glacial.

"Oh, come on." Just a little bit too much smug there, but I'll let it pass. He's having fun. "You're worried that any message you send to your colleague via the datastream is vulnerable to interception. You know what's even less interceptable than Red Space? The human brain. Why not carry your message up two floors in person if you're so worried that his stream is tapped? You don't need a messenger for this – unless you can't get clearance to leave the floor."

Elisabeth's new drink arrives before the silence has a chance to

111

settle. The shadow man sets it down without a word and disappears without waiting for acknowledgement, which is just as well, as she doesn't give any. She might not even have registered its presence, since her eyes haven't left Emmett's for even the briefest flicker of a moment. She's good at this, but the thing is, she's playing an a-naut, and there's only one way that staring contest is going to go. She can be as good as she likes at rigorous bodily control. We're better.

"I can see why you might think that," she says at last. "Of course, you have no way to prove it one way or another, so…"

And that's it. That right there is when I know that we've won. *He's* won; I just stood here and glowered and translated the occasional bad word, so I'm going to give the guy credit where it's due. He's provoked her into trailing sentences and vagaries that sound a little bit like refutations until you look at them directly, and she's got nowhere left to go.

We've won. And he knows it.

"Fair enough," he says amiably. He pushes back his chair, which causes the shadow men to take a half step forward. "Ma'am, I have little enough free time as it is, and I don't intend to let you waste any more of it tonight. We're leaving now. Come on, Françoise."

He's pushing his luck with that last bit, and I'm pretty sure he knows it, but it fits with the overall tone of the exit, so I'm prepared to let it slide. I lever myself out of my lean and fall in behind him without a glance back towards the table, and we head toward the door. She lets us get two whole steps, which is further than I thought, but pride is pride.

"All right," she says. She doesn't shout it; she doesn't so much as raise her voice. We stop, but we don't turn around. "One name, one payment. One trip to Verdieping Een, and our business is done."

Emmett glances back over his shoulder. "Both names," he says. "Or we walk."

But Elisabeth shakes her head. "No deal," she says. "One name, or you leave with nothing."

"So do you," he points out.

She smiles. "I can live with that."

A beat. Then he nods to me to follow him to the opposite side of the pub and stalks off before I have the opportunity to communicate to him via non-verbal signals that I'm actually not his pet, nor do I follow commands, and he might consider just taking his imperious little chin gestures and shoving them up his arse. I know it's neither the time nor the place, but he's getting carried away here, and now I have two options: follow him and play into his monarch fantasy, or stand in the middle of the floor, awash in my righteous indignation, and look like a dick. I follow him, but we are *definitely* having words.

Alone in a quiet corner, he says, "You're working out all the ways you can tell me to go and fuck myself, aren't you?"

"I'm compiling a list," I tell him.

"Okay, great." His smile looks strained, and it occurs to me that maybe he's not enjoying this quite as much as I thought. "I look forward to hearing it. What do you think about the offer?"

"One name, one trip to go and talk to the person you'd have been trying to go and talk to anyway?" I shrug. "There are other ways to get names in Radiale Vier. Could be you can even talk her friend into giving up the contact."

"That's what I'm thinking," he says. "Besides, I kind of like the sound of the Viewing Plaza. It was in the induction literature."

"Costs about three day's wages to get in," I say.

He considers for a moment, but he doesn't look discouraged. "So I drink one less glass of water this week. Let's go talk to Betsy again."

Chapter Fourteen

12.4 Adam

"So," says Françoise, as soon as the door of De Gouden Narcissen has closed behind us, "who the hell is Marie Schlesinger?"

It's not that I wasn't expecting her to ask. I was, of course, from the moment that Elisabeth decided to play inter-amnisonaut politics and check how much my colleague knows. I just thought that I might have more than four seconds to prepare, especially considering how unbelievably well that meeting just went. I mean, I'm not expecting a ticker tape parade or anything, but she might try and look a little bit less like I just savaged her puppy.

It's also 1:15 a.m. and there's absolutely no way I'm getting to sleep when I get home. I'm far too tired for this right now.

"Not here," I tell her, and walk off before she can protest.

She catches me before I've made it to the end of the block, which means she wasn't really trying.

"All right," she says. "Where then? Where can I expect an explanation for the fact that the woman we just went in to negotiate with came to the table with more information than me?"

"She doesn't have more information than you," I say, which is mostly true, but it wouldn't stop me yelling, under the circumstances.

"She does. And she knows it, too, which is why she was trying to blow it for you right out of the gate. She knew that name would be news to me. So I want to know who Marie Schlesinger is, and why this is the first I've ever heard of her."

Somewhere, a few streets away, someone opens a pub door and a blast of music punches through the air of the street for the minute it takes for the door to close again. Voices drift in from every angle: loud voices, laughing voices, voices raised in song or argument. It's the early hours of Saturday morning and Luchtstad is in festive form. Luca was right: going in with Marie was a stupid move, and I knew Elisabeth wouldn't be able to help me find her. Asking the question opened myself up to attack, and that's exactly what happened. I nearly let her tip the balance of power for no good reason, on the off chance that I'd accidentally make a happy ending happen.

I'm furious, and I know it's in my voice. And I know Françoise will think it's directed at her, and I don't care.

"It's a name I have," I say. "Okay? Is that all right with you? It's the name of someone who might or might not be able to help me and I worked hard to get the information. So forgive me if I don't feel the need to lay my life open like a book for you to read, Françoise, but, you know, you can walk away from this any time you like. This is *my* job, not yours, and I'll decide how much I need to share and when and how."

She glares at me for a moment. To our left, the world flares white as tram headlights round the corner of the block, slicing through the darkness. It's going her way, not mine. She holds out her hand to signal it to stop.

"You're right," she says. Her eyes don't leave mine, even as the tram glides to a halt beside us. "You're right," she says again, as the doors slide open and she steps inside. "So how about you go and fuck yourself? And the next time you need backup for a midnight meeting, how about you go and fuck yourself again?"

The doors slide shut, framing her face, white and tight-lipped with rage, against the over-lit interior. She glares at me until she's out of sight.

Well, says Luca, *you could have handled that better.*

"Oh, really?" There's venom in my tone and in my blood. "You think I could have maybe managed not to ratchet up that argument the way I did? For no reason whatsoever? You think that's what I should have done?"

I'm just saying.

"It doesn't matter anyway." I'm so tired. And I swear they've started rationing the oxygen in this city; it feels like my lungs are never full. "We've got what we needed. There's no need to keep her on side any more."

There was no need to bring her to the meeting, either, says Luca, which is not unreasonable, but I'm the mood for starting fights.

"So, let me get this straight," I say, and I really don't need the roll of his eyes at the tone, even if I can't actually see it happening. "Let me make sure I understand what you're saying. You think I should have walked in to a meeting – a midnight meeting – in a city I don't know, to a threat I had no way to gauge, without backup? Is that what either one of us would ever have done? Ever?"

He sighs. I know that sound. That's the sound he makes when he's trying to take the edge of a situation and I'm trying to fire it up. *What are you doing? This isn't you.*

"Don't," I say. My voice is tight and far too thick.

You're going to get yourself killed, he says. *For me. Why would I want that?*

"Don't," I say again.

If you're doing this, he says, *if you're going to do this... then you need to be smart about it.*

"I'm being smart." That sounds petulant, which irritates me. "That's why I brought backup tonight."

Right. Right. I know what's coming next. *So you don't think you'll need backup when you go to Verdieping Een, then?*

"It doesn't have to be her."

There isn't anyone else. You're on your own in this city.

A burst of laughter, and a group of young men stagger into view. One of them is only standing because his friends have wrapped his arms around their necks, and his feet make pantomime walking movements as they move him forwards. His smile is loose, his eyes dull, and they're laughing at his efforts to try and talk.

"*Hoi,*" says one as he sees me watching. "*Hoe gaat het, makker?*"

I don't know *makker,* but I know a fraternal greeting when I hear one. "*Goed, goed,*" I answer, and they laugh and stagger on.

Fun city, says Luca as their laughter dissolves into the background street noise.

"Please," I say. "We lived in Brixton."

You think if we could get pissed like that we would?

I think of Françoise. "I think there's a lot we'd drink away, if we could."

Bring her with you to Verdieping Een, he says. *She's smart and she's angry. And she came with you tonight.*

"Yeah," I say. "I'm still not sure why."

If I had to guess... I'd say it's because she understands.

"She understands?" But I'm arguing with myself, and he knows it. "You know she's going to tell me to go to hell."

Oh dear, he says. There's a grin in his voice. *Looks like you've got some ass to kiss. Sounds like it could get humiliating.*

I'm prepared to put good money on Françoise's likely reaction to apologies. "Or I could just buy a gallon of gin."

Or you could just do that.

I laugh, though it hurts my chest to do so. "Do you have any idea how much I've missed you?"

Yeah. It's a breath, a whisper, almost inaudible. *Yeah. I do.*

"And you know I can't... I can't finish this until I know?"

Yeah. I know.

"So I've got to find her. I've got to find Marie."

You think this ends when you find Marie?

"I think..." I say, and hesitate. "I think closure happens when I find Marie."

I think, he says slowly, *that closure happened two decades ago or it never happens at all. And I think you know that.*

"Yeah." There's a tram approaching, lights blinding against the shadows. "But I can't let go until I do this. You know that."

Yes, he says. *I know.* But his words are lost in the rattle and glare.

Chapter Fifteen

15.1 Danae

We don't speak on Saturday. Emmett doesn't try and I don't try: he arrives late to the line, after I'm already in place, and I ignore him as he passes, keep my face front, eyes fixed on the picture fragments that cling to the opposite wall. *Magie voor je familie*: red and gold tulips buried beneath a sea of grime. I ignore him, feel the stream ripple as he passes on his way to the line, and I know he doesn't turn and look at me, because the stream is so tightly strung between us this morning that I'd feel it if he did.

The line starts and I start, and I ignore him. He doesn't approach me at smoke break and I ignore him. At lunch, he disappears to wherever he disappears to at lunch, and I sit with Sanne and Amita and listen to second-hand gossip about their Friday night, their friends' Friday night, the controlled explosion on Verdieping Een, their plans for Amita's sister's birthday. I drink strong coffee to fight off the endless blanket of fatigue, and then we go back to the line and I ignore him.

It's over, I think. I didn't get what I wanted, but it's better that it's over. The stream ripples as he risks a sideways glance and the line ripples as he almost misses a beat, but I ignore him and he ignores me.

At the end of the day we leave without speaking and I go home to my apartment, where I pace for a few hours, and then give up and head out to an all-night media dome where a colour orchestra are live-streaming a free concert from Groningen and the ushers are too sleep-deprived to notice who's sipping from flasks. I let the notes wash over me in all the shades of the rainbow, I let them dissolve into the chambers of my watery brain, and I think, *it's over and I'm glad that it's over*. I wander for a while when it's finished but the stream doesn't ripple no matter how many people I pass. So, in the end, I find myself a bar where the music is too loud and the lights are too low and I sit alone at a table at the back until morning.

Sunday again. The streets are empty and chilled, and my breath condenses in front of me as I blow on my hands to warm them.

Somebody has thrown up in the gutter, but it's the only evidence of the night before: the pavements are crisp and tidy, the air is clean, and the city sleeps. I'm not dressed for a Sunday and I pull the sweater tightly around my chest, hugging warmth into my ribs as I hurry for home, where Sanne's snoring splits the post-dawn gloom and the carpets seep last night's schnapps into sweet-smelling eddies with every footfall along my corridor. This building will be asleep for hours yet, and I should be asleep. I turn on the light and let the door close behind me, and I move to the centre of the floor and stretch my hands high above my head. I rise up on tip toes until my calf muscles burn, until my shoulders ache, until my fingers brush the plasticised surface of the low ceiling, and I make myself breathe. In, out. In, out. Careful, measured breaths. I stretch until I feel the thunder settle in my veins and then, when my heart has slowed, I sink onto the mattress and pull the sheet up around my shoulders. I let my eyes fall closed, let the black seep in around the edges, let the tug of oblivion pull me under.

I'm not sure how many minutes I manage to stay unconsciousness, but it's not a lot. I haven't so much as released my hold on the edge of the sheet when I'm razored back up the comatose octaves by a thing that has happened so seldom before that it's a moment – and another spine-stinging buzz – before I recognise it as the apartment block's entry system letting me know I have a visitor at the main door.

I say 'seldom'. I mean 'never'. I have never, in all my months of living in this building, had someone buzz my room for admittance. I'd forgotten it was even a thing that people did, and I'm damn sure I have no idea what I'm supposed to do to find out who it is, let alone let them in. I consider lying exactly where I am, unmoving, in the hope that they'll realise they're ringing the wrong room, or, alternatively, swearing violently at the ceiling for no good reason other than that I was fucking well *asleep* for the first time in thirty-one hours, and I'd kind of like all manner of painful horrors to fall upon the person who woke me up.

The system buzzes again. I'm out of options. But I throw out a couple of curse words for good measure as I fling back the sheets and storm out of my room to take care of business face to face.

Of course, I should have known who it would be. I could probably have guessed, if my brain had been firing on anything more than fifteen minutes' rest in the past two days. Or if I'd had any reason at all to think he knew where the hell I lived.

15.2 Adam

I'm not expecting cookies or bearhugs. I'm not even expecting a lukewarm smile. None of these things are likely. So I'm not surprised when the first words out of her mouth are, "What in the name of suppurating fuck are you doing here?"

Her anger actually makes this easier. Nothing about what I've seen so far suggests she's into passive aggression, but there was always a risk that she'd freeze me out, and that's almost impossible to argue against. What I don't need is for her to get angry enough to slam the door in my face, so I take my best shot at de-escalation.

"Reckoned I owed you an apology," I say.

It doesn't have quite the intended effect. "How the fuck do you know where I live?"

"Process of elimination?" There's no good answer to that question that doesn't make me sound like a stalker, and Luca had no hesitation in pointing that out as I was leaving this morning. The fact is, I know because I followed her home one time, and that's going to get us nowhere right now. "There are only so many feeder blocks for the factory and the other one's men only. I waited outside until somebody came out and asked them what room you were in."

Again, not entirely true: it was last night, it was a couple of women from the line, and they made it clear that they were only telling me because they thought I was planning to have sex with her and they felt like she needed the R&R. I think their hearts are in the right place. I'm pretty sure they wouldn't have told me if they hadn't recognised me. But I wouldn't be happy about it, if I were Françoise, and I don't think it helps my case right now.

"Bullshit," she says after a moment. "There's barely a conscious brain in this building right now. Nobody's up and walking, and I'm damn sure nobody's ready for the outside world."

I shrug. "Couple of guys," I say. "Maybe they had to get home?"

Not a great comeback. But her eyes narrow enough that I can see she's seriously contemplating it as a possibility.

"What do you want, Emmett?" she says.

"Can I come in?"

She folds her arms across her chest. "Why?"

It's more of an opening than I was honestly expecting. I decide to play my ace. "Because I've got these tickets for the Viewing Plaza on Verdieping Een," I say, "and there's nobody else on the floor I've pissed off that much."

One eyebrow arches. "What, *nobody* else?" she says. "I find that hard to believe." But she shakes her head, pulls the door back just enough to let me through. She lets it slam before I'm all the way in, and turns on her heel, stalking off into the dark and silent corridors of the building just fast enough to make me pick up my pace or lose her to the labyrinth.

"I was fucking well asleep," she says as she holds the door for me in the stairwell.

I'm not sure what to say to that. It's after lunch, and I deliberately left it late so that I wouldn't wake her. I go with tradition: "Sorry."

"For what?" We've climbed two flights in record time. I think she's trying to see what will kill me. "Being an arsehole? Or wrecking my Sunday?"

"Sounds like the same thing," I say, which might be helpful. We attack the third flight at a slightly less punishing pace, at least.

"If we were to cover the many ways in which you're an arsehole," she says, without looking around, "we'd end up missing three days of work."

I feel this is unfair. "Then let's not cover them all," I say, as we round the landing on our fourth flight and – thank God – she elbows open an access door into a fresh set of dark, silent corridors. "I'm apologising. It was a shitty thing to do, and I'm sorry."

"Yeah?" I can't read her face, and that's only partly because it's bathed in shadow.

"Yeah. You have any idea how much these tickets cost? That's a lot of sorry."

"You didn't have to do that." She makes no move to walk through the access door.

I shrug. "Kind of wanted to see it myself."

"Fuck." She lets her head drop forward for a moment, then lifts a hand to scrub over her face. "Fuck," she says again, and raises her head to fix me with one of those piercing glares. "Fine. Fine. I'll do your stupid trip to Verdieping Een. But you're still an arsehole."

I know one dead guy, currently laughing his ass off on the next landing down where he thinks I can't see him, who'd wholeheartedly agree with her. I briefly consider denying that the tickets have anything to do with Verdieping Een, but she's not stupid. She knows what floor the Viewing Plaza's on.

I do feel like kind of an arsehole now, though.

"Oh, for fuck's sake." She rolls her eyes, pulls the door back wide enough for me to go through ahead of her. "Close your mouth, would you? You look like a dying fish. It's not rocket science. I want to see the Viewing Plaza too. Reckon if you're enough of a dickhead to fork out for the tickets, I can put up with your company for another day at least."

"Uh," I say, "thanks?"

"Go through the fucking door, Emmett. There's coffee on the other side and I need caffeine."

I go through the door. It's like walking into a wall of alcohol fumes and backed-up plumbing. "Which way to the coffee?"

"Coffee's for me. I haven't decided if you get to have some."

"I can live with that," I say as the door falls shut behind us and I follow her into the corridor beyond.

15.3 Danae

I open the door to the kitchen, a room I've been inside twice in the year and a bit that I've lived here. One of those times was during Induction. I don't even recognise the chairs that cluster beneath the solitary table in the far corner, and I'm certain we only used to have one hydrator. Emmett holds back and waits for me to go in first, but I'm not having that. He's lied to me already this weekend. He's staying where I can see him.

Of course, I don't keep coffee in the kitchen. Everything goes missing here, sooner or later, so I store all of my things in the cupboard by my bed. My head is thundering and my arms feel like they're made out of jelly, but, on balance, I decide against leaving him here unsupervised while I go off in search of something caffeinated, so I throw a couple of water credits at the cause instead and dial us up a glass each. He takes it from me with a word of thanks and fishes out his pack of iodine tablets from the inner pocket of his coat.

"So," I say. "Marie Schlesinger."

Emmett drops a tablet into his glass. "She's a contact." He looks suddenly exhausted, boneless, as though he's melting into his chair. "I should have told you about her, and I'm sorry. I didn't think it was important."

I lean back against the counter, watching him from across the room. "You mean, you didn't think it would come up."

He nods slowly. He doesn't look up. He's swirling the tablet into his water, and his eyes are fixed on the miniature whirlpool in the centre of the glass. "I didn't think she'd mention it. No. And I swear it doesn't put you in danger. I wasn't lying about that."

Just about everything else. "I got blindsided. In the middle of a hostile negotiation."

He makes a face. It could either be apology or discomfort. "Elisabeth is playing politics."

"I know she is. And you let her do it."

"It was stupid."

"Stupid doesn't begin to cover it. I told you: I don't do second chances."

He glances up. His gaze meets mine briefly, then skitters away. "And yet, here we are."

"This isn't a second chance," I say. "You've got something I want, that's all. How did you get her name?"

Emmett looks up again, holds my gaze this time. He was clearly not expecting me to ask.

"It was suggested to me before I left Earth that she might be someone I could ask a couple of questions."

The passive tense is the last refuge of the conversational fugitive. "Well," I say, "that certainly *sounds* like an answer, Emmett…"

"Oh, for Christ's sake." He rolls his eyes. "It doesn't matter. The last thing my source heard, she was headed to Luchtstad, but we're going back… decades. It's almost certainly a cold trail. That's why I didn't tell you."

I blink, watch his face for a moment, but he hasn't heard it. He hasn't realised what he's said. "Decades?" I say slowly.

"At least. What do you think the survival rate is like out here?"

She's an a-naut, then. I suspected as much. "Better than on Earth. And you're still alive."

He looks as though he wants to believe that. "I'm not even sure she made it here at all."

"Your source hasn't heard from her? In all that time?"

"It's not uncommon. People make a break for the post-etherics, they're looking for a new life. They're looking to leave their old life far behind."

I'm not going to argue with that. "So you think she went to ground?"

He considers for a moment. "I think that the folks up here aren't exactly queuing up to join the resistance."

"Which is why you're here."

That catches his attention. "What?"

"Because there's no organised community of a-nauts on Luchtstad," I say. "If somebody finds an anomaly they want to investigate, it's not like your boss can ring up his opposite number in Radiale Zes and ask him to keep an eye out. So you have to send somebody up here to ask around. Right?"

"Right." Emmett's eyes have narrowed slightly; he looks wary.

"That's the thing about up here," I say. "You've got nothing, no support network. No resources. No cell leader. If something happens, if something goes wrong, the only people you've got in your corner are the likes of Betsy. People who're in it for what they can get."

"You know what I think about Do Not Seek," he says.

"And you can't find Marie Schlesinger. There's nobody to ask. Because the first thing you do when you get here is make sure you disappear so hard from the a-naut radar that you leave a crater behind you."

"We're supposed to be protected up here." His voice is tight and his lips are thin. "It kind of looks ungrateful if we start coalescing into caches."

"So you're here. You're on this stupidly expensive trip to chase after ghosts because somebody, once upon a time, decided safety was better than community. As if they weren't both exactly the same thing."

He's quiet for a long moment. My arms are tightly folded around myself, and the edge of the counter is digging into my hip. I've used up three credits on this glass of water, and my muscles are too stiff to even drink it.

"We're doing okay on our own," says Emmett at last. "We've made friends with Betsy and we've got this new guy on Verdieping Een to go and talk to."

"And tickets to the Viewing Plaza," I remind him.

"And tickets to the Viewing Plaza," he agrees.

"Maybe it's just as well we didn't find Marie."

It's a cheap shot, and I don't feel good about it, but it has the intended effect. His eyes, cast down into his glass, shoot up to meet mine. "What?" he says.

"Well, like you say – it's been decades since anyone heard from her."

"Twenty-five years," he says.

He's suspicious. I have to go for the kill shot now, before he shuts down. "Twenty-five years. And your friends in the cache have known about the anomaly for... how long?"

I see the exact moment he realises. I'm hoping for anger, maybe some kind of professional rank-closing, but what I actually read behind his eyes is a kind of desolate sadness. It hollows something out, deep inside my chest. It feels like opening a wound, and I wonder who I've become.

"Three years," he says softly. Almost a whisper. He hesitates. "It takes a while to raise the funds, build the connections... you know."

"I know," I say. Making Françoise Marechal come to life was the work of two weeks, but it's different when you have someone behind you with money and power. I'm prepared to bet that Emmett Keller is the product of long months of bribes, blackmail and calling in favours. He couldn't have done it on his own, and, if he's the man he's pretending to be, he doesn't have the connections to make it happen for himself. He had to give somebody else a reason to want him to go.

"I just wonder," I say slowly, carefully, feeling my way, "why anyone thought that a woman who disappeared two decades before anyone even thought to go looking for weird shit on Luchtstad is the person your cache guys thought you should try and find."

I wait for him to deny it. I wait for him to explain that it's not like anyone back home is exactly maintaining a database of their post-etheric colleagues and any name is better than no name at all. It's not beyond the realm of possibility, and, fifteen minutes ago, I would have been prepared to believe it, but then he called it a cold trail and that's not what you call a contact. It's not who you send your operative looking for when the trail is just beginning.

"It's..." he says, and stops. The sadness behind his eyes is liquid shadow; it's all I can do not to look away. "The thing is… it's…"

"Complicated," I finish.

His shoulders sag. I've never seen him look so old. "It's complicated," he says.

"Finding Marie Schlesinger has nothing to do with finding the anomaly."

"I swear to you," he says, "that it doesn't… it doesn't change… it doesn't put you in any – *any* – kind of position where…"

"Emmett…". But I don't know what to say next. I thought I did, but this pain in my chest feels like it's going to suffocate me.

"I know," he says. "I know – you're careful. You're guarded. You have no reason to trust me."

He's right. There's no reason to trust him, especially not now that I know for certain that he's lied, and I cannot even come close to explaining why this makes me want to trust him more. Maybe it's just that I can't believe that anyone could look so hollowed out, so utterly desolate, and not mean it.

"Marie Schlesinger," I say, "is the real reason you're here?"

He shakes his head. "The real reason I'm here is to find the anomaly. The hospital. Marie is… personal."

That much I gathered. "Is she in trouble?"

"Marie?" His eyes meet mine. "I've no idea. I only knew her a little. She was a friend of… someone I used to know."

Ah. Even without the hesitation, I'd know from his eyes. "Someone you used to know," I repeat, slowly, and I see the confirmation in his face. "And it's this person who's in trouble."

"Jesus." It's a breath, a sigh. It's the most broken sound I've heard somebody make and still stay upright. "No," he says. His voice is tight, thick with sadness, and he doesn't meet my eyes. "No, this person is not in trouble. This person is dead."

Chapter Sixteen

16.1 Adam

"Don't," I tell him as the door closes behind me, sealing me into the darkness of my room. "Not now. Just don't."

Luca is the barest flicker of black on black, a hint of movement in the shadows. He says nothing as I cross the small stretch of floor to my bed and lower myself onto it. I feel a thousand years old.

If she'd asked, I think I would have told her. She didn't. She just stood for a moment, silent, cradling her glass in one hand, other palm flat against her forehead, eyes cast towards the floor. After a moment, she said, "I need a drink," and disappeared from the room without looking at me.

I can feel Luca at my back, his hand hovering over my shoulder. He never tries to touch me; we both know that it would break the spell. "Don't," I say again. "Please. I just need a minute."

She drank gin. She offered me more water but I refused; it was hard enough to swallow what was left in my glass.

I said, to break the silence, "Do you know the legend about the *dis*?"

She shook her head. "I don't know what that is."

"The *dis*?" I know I looked incredulous. I think this offended her. But she honestly caught me by surprise. "The *dis*," I said. "The stream?"

"The datastream?"

I've never met one of us who didn't know the word. I can't explain where it came from, only that I woke up one day and I had a body and a mind and both were under my control, and I understood that I was of the *dis* and the *dis* was in me and that I would never be whole again while I walked this earth. "The datastream," I said.

She sipped gin. "I've never heard it called that."

You're tired, says Luca quietly. *You're exhausted. Lie down. Close your eyes.*

"Not yet," I tell him. I want to sleep – I need to sleep – but sleep brings the memory of loss, and I want to hold him here with me for now. I know he understands this. I hear it in his sigh.

There's a legend, he says softly. *They call it the* lortherias…

127

"The *dis* is who we are," I told her. "We're… energy. Energy without form, and the *dis* is the medium and the form that surrounded us before we were dragged into these bodies. We were never meant to be anchored into four dimensions."

"Then the *dis* is not the stream," she said slowly. "Not really."

"No. It's how we make sense of the *dis* in a place where the *dis* can't exist, but the *dis* is not the stream. There's no way to describe the *dis* in this world. I don't… I'm sorry, but I don't understand how you don't know this."

She dropped her eyes, arching a brow as she did. "I'm not sure," she said, "that you would recognise the life I had." A beat, and then, before I could ask: "It doesn't matter now. Tell me about the legend."

Matter and anti-matter, whispers Luca. I want to lean back so that my head rests against his chest, close my eyes. I want to fall asleep surrounded by him, with his voice in my ear. *Zero and one. Beauty and truth.*

"It's a story I heard," I told her. "A long time ago. Who knows if it's true?"

"I like stories. I don't know very many of them." Still she didn't look at me, and I felt like this was as close as I would ever get to hearing her ask for anything.

"I heard it…" I said, and, for a moment, I was there: I was back in the old warehouse with the leaky floor, sitting on damp crates and curled around each other for warmth. The sky above us was sunset-pink through the holes in the roof and Luca's voice was like silk on the still air.

Once, he told us, *in the far reaches of time, before the swimmers on the stream had physical form, we were all paired waveforms in the* dis*: Newtonian mirror-sets that were created of and embodied the very fabric of the stream. And when the first a-nauts were pulled weeping from the binaries and forced to inhabit the body, the waveforms were shattered and ripped apart, and the* dis *screamed…*

"Binaries," she said.

"Mirrors." It sounded better when Luca told it. "Two halves of a whole. And suddenly the mirrors were broken and the *dis* was bleeding."

The dis *was bleeding*, says Luca. His voice pulls me backwards, gently, slowly, until my head is on my pillow and my eyes are closed. *And it tried to repair…*

"There's a song," I said, and I wasn't sure, any more, if I was talking to Françoise or to Luca. "'Song' is the wrong word, but… you know. There's no equivalent in this world for what it is. It exists on the *dis* and nowhere else."

"Like the chant?" she asked.

"Like the chant," I said. "We make the sounds into words, because the body needs them to be words, but they're not words. They're vibrations. They're disturbances. They're like quantum interactions – they're intent and they're thought, and we make them mean what we need them to mean. This song… it's made by lovers. It's the sound of the stream re-fusing around a tear."

"Ah." It was whispered on an out-breath. "When the binaries reform."

"Yes. The legend talks of a force called *lortherias*. It's what holds the binaries together. And when one half is ripped from the *dis* to inhabit their world-body and the binary is shattered, the other half tries to bleed out through the rupture in search of its missing self. The song is a greeting between soulmates, but it's… this is only one way of understanding it. It's not a greeting, except that it is… but…"

Her eyes were wide. Liquid. "How can you greet someone who is literally the other half of you?"

"Yes. *Yes.*" My head had started to ache. "The song is a greeting, but what it means is, *At last. I've found you at last.*"

Her shoulders were tight. She dropped her eyes downwards, into her glass. "And what happens if the stream never re-fuses? If the tear never heals?"

What happens, says Luca's voice from the hazy depths just beyond sleep, *if the tear heals, only to be ripped apart again?*

"Then the *dis* waits," I say. "It waits for the other half to come home."

Chapter Seventeen

17.1 Danae

We meet at the transit station in Monnikskapstraat in the early morning hush, and the streets are so cold that I can see little frost crystals blistering the metal struts that arch overhead. Emmett has assured me that he knows how to get here, and I've allowed myself to be assured, but I'm still expecting him to be late. The trams don't run this early on a Sunday, and the walk is long and cold and dispiritingly grey. But, as I round the corner of Monnikskapweg 90 and find myself face to face with the edge of the radial in all its utilitarian functionality and soft beige lines, I can see, behind the condensation-fogged window of the central transit foyer, the unmistakable shape of one lone man crouched miserably into a waiting room chair. It can only be him. The rest of the city has barely gone to bed yet.

Emmett looks around as the doors whoosh-hiss open, and his face breaks into a smile when he sees me. It's warmer than I feel.

"Good morning, jet-setter," he says pleasantly, and holds out a take-out cup that steams promisingly. "Coffee," he says, unnecessarily. I can smell it from here, and it's kicked my hibernating stomach into growls. "Reckoned you might need it after the walk."

He's been kind, this past week, kind enough that it makes me uneasy. I feel that I've met him halfway sometimes, and that doesn't feel too good either. I liked it better when I could blame him for things.

I note the second steaming cup on the seat beside him. "Cold?"

"Freezing," he says cheerfully, and he looks it. He's managed to get his hands on a better coat at some point in the past week, but this morning is savage, and it'd take more than good weatherproofing to keep out the biting Luchtstad air. He lifts the cup, wraps his bloodless hands around it. "It's hot water. Nearly gave the dispenser a heart attack, but it turns out there's a programme for it after all."

I sip my coffee. It's last night's brew, boiled into a soupy black tar that tastes of burnt-on bits of charred chicory and over-heated metal. It's exactly what I need to wake up. "Sounds delicious."

"Better than yours," he points out, and I concede. Mine is an acquired taste.

He's in ebullient form: tired and frost-pinched, but lit from within by something that I feel I recognise. I haven't gone on an honest-to-God put-on-your-travelling-shoes-and-pack-a-picnic trip since I was a little girl and my mam used to worry that I'd get the black lung cooped up inside the lower city and hidden away from real sunlight. There's a part of me this morning that's five years old and twitching with the effort of holding back excitement to a level that Da can cope with. This isn't a journey from one place to another that ends with getting a job and somewhere to live. This is a joyride to somewhere special, where we're going to hang around for the best part of a day and enjoy ourselves, like normal people. This is going somewhere for fun.

Transit between the floors is, theoretically, free, regular, and unlimited. In practice, the only part of that which is true is the bit where you are not required to pay for the actual journey. The transit cube snakes up the side of the radial, and every time the doors open and close there's a small but measurable loss of heat and air into the vacuum outside, which is taxed at source and applied to the city credits of however many travellers step into the booth. When there's only two of us, like this morning, that means an appreciable dip in pay for the next week. The booth is heated, but only enough for the circuitry to function, so if you don't feel like fusing with the seat over the course of the journey you get to pay a localised warming surcharge. And, since transit is only unlimited for citizens who haven't been tagged to their floor or sector, have no outstanding civic fines and are in credit with the city, and whose journey won't push the destination over capacity as measured on the disembarkation counters, the system is obliged to run a search against your neck chip before you board, which is, of course, subject to a small administration fee. There is literally no other way to move from floor to floor. It's an outstanding method of flow control, and it's one of the main reasons I haven't troubled myself to venture out beyond Verdieping Drie in the past thirteen months.

'Regular' is also a relative term, but at least the timetables are easily accessible. Transit is slow and deliberate, in the manner of a moving object attached to the hull of a gargantuan man-made structure circling the Earth at approximately eight kilometres per second and vulnerable to anything from random hyper-accelerated orbital paint chips to civilisation-ending asteroids. We've chosen to depart on the 8:17am service, arriving on Een at 9:05, which trundles into port at 8:23 and spends another fifteen minutes idling for no discernible reason before the doors finally open. I shuffle in and sit close to Emmett, where I can still feel the edges of his circle of warmth. He turns his head and flashes me a smile.

"Better than a meat crate, huh?" he says, inexplicably, and I nod and stretch an answering smile across my face. I have no idea what he's talking about, but I think I almost blew it with the *dis* comment last week. I don't intend to slip up again.

A rattle and a lurch and we're on our way, crawling upwards. I'd prefer that the booth didn't sound quite so much as though it was straining under extraordinary pressures, and I glance around, make sure I know where the emergency EVA suits are stashed. And then we clear the transit module, sliding up and out of the airlock and into the clutches of Luchtstad's exterior wall. We're ascending the corridor between Radialen Zes and Zeven, to minimise the threat of a direct debris strike from open space, but the booth's outer wall is partially windowed in a rare concession to style over impenetrability. The city is rounding the Earth's terminator, sunlight whispering over the edge of the solar umbrella that shelters the entire lower half of the structure, and, though most of the view is our opposite radial wall, it's just possible to see the edge of infinity, drizzled in starlight, as it whistles silently past.

I haven't seen this view since I boarded the ferry at the elevator terminus all those months ago, but I haven't forgotten the way it feels. It's like staring directly into the very soul of the universe, and it never fails to catch the breath in the pit of my throat.

"Holy shit," breathes Emmett. His head is craned as far back as the seat will allow him, and I don't need to see his face to read the wonder written there. It's all over his voice. "That's... incredible."

"It is," I say softly. There's no point in denying it. Pride wells in my stomach, and I find myself wondering when exactly this place started to feel like it might be home.

17.2 Adam

"Holy shit," I say again. I wasn't going for quite such a tone of childlike awe, but my synaptic processes have kind of crashed and my vocal circuitry has mutinied. My neck is aching with the effort of trying to stretch far enough to see and I'm sure every vertebra in my spinal cord will make me pay for this by tonight, but, right now, I really don't care.

"Who knew," says Françoise, "that there were advantages to being awake first thing on a Sunday morning?"

Her tone surprises me, and I glance around at her. I'm expecting cynicism, and I'm not prepared to see her face so open, so completely unguarded. She catches my eye and smiles.

"What?" she says. "It's a nice view. I'm allowed to enjoy the nice view."

I nod and look away before she can get cross. "That must have been one hell of a cup of coffee."

"Fuck you," she shoots back, but there's laughter in it. Sounds like we both needed this.

To pass the time, we go over the plans for the day. 9 a.m.: arrive on Verdieping Een, find somewhere to have breakfast, which is Françoise's immediate priority. She's taking on no covert interviews with possible agents of the a-naut resistance on an empty stomach. We're not due to meet Jos until eleven, so that's fine with me. Elisabeth has pointed us in the direction of a coffee shop she's used in the past, on Van Rensselaerstraat , which curves around the edge of the Viewing Plaza. Since Elisabeth is tagged and Jos is under surveillance, it doesn't strike me as clever to meet him anywhere he's been known to meet people in the past, but neither Françoise nor I know Verdieping Een well enough to suggest an alternative. We're going to spend a little time scoping out the territory when we arrive. If anything feels off, we'll have a backup plan in place. The tickets to the Viewing Plaza are valid from noon, which gives us plenty of time to drink in the vista before we catch the 5:30 transit back down to Drie.

All we have to do is get there. I thought we had that bit sorted out, but then the booth grinds to a halt. For a moment, I think we've pulled up at the transit station on Verdieping Twee, but the doors don't open and the seatbelt signs stay on, and the whole thing settles in place with a mechanical sigh that sounds depressingly final.

"Oh, come the fuck on!" shouts Françoise, and kicks at the wall. This is actually less disconcerting than the good mood that's been hanging over her since we left the airlock. But it also confirms what I was trying not to suspect, and that doesn't bode well for our big day out.

I glance at her. "This happen often?"

She glares back. "How the hell would I know? But it feels about right."

I check the clock on the wall to my left. 9:07: we should have been at Een two minutes ago, and we haven't even made it as far as Twee yet. We're not delayed enough yet to worry about missing Jos, but I'm not sure I want to deal with a hypoglycaemic Françoise, and I also feel like Jos' first impressions of us will go better if we manage to feed her first. I unclip my seatbelt, which makes the booth's CPU flash the seatbelt sign, and I cross to the intercom section by the doors.

Voor uw veiligheid en comfort, blijf alstublieft zitten met uw stoelriemen vast, says the Voice of the City, and, because we're in the booth and the booths tend to see a moderate tourist trade, it follows up with a series of translations. English first – *For your safety and comfort, please remain seated with your seatbelt fastened* – and then French, Spanish, German, Mandarin and Arabic before settling into a loop. I ignore it, and a soft *clunk-click* behind me tells me Françoise has had the same idea.

"Hello?" I say into the intercom. I have no idea if there's anyone listening. I doubt it, but this entire city is built around one of the largest computers in the greater Terran environment, so it's possible that there's a rudimentary reply service built in at least. "Hello, is anyone there? Can somebody tell me what's happening?"

"Hey," says Françoise, at my shoulder. "Hey - *we zitten vast. De wagen is gestopt met bewegen.* Hey!"

Pour votre sécurité et confort, says the Voice of the City, *veuillez rester assis avec votre ceinture de sécurité attachée.*

"We're doing French now," I tell Françoise, and she glares at me, before furiously mashing an unmarked button on the pad in front of us.

"*Nous sommes bloqués,*" she corrects, glare fixed steadily on me. "*Le transport a cessé de bouger.*"

I wonder sometimes if my intellectual growth has been stunted by the fact that I was shipped off to an English-speaking country almost as soon as I was self-aware. Luchtstad could be good for me. "Arabic?" I suggest, but Françoise just shoots me a poisonous glance and stalks off to the other edge of the booth.

I turn back to the intercom. There's clearly nobody on the other end, but it's that or deal with Françoise's mood, and it's too early in the day. "Hey," I try. "*We zijn… stoppen. We zijn stoppen? Helpen?*"

"Hey," says Françoise, which is not helpful. It's not like I'm labouring under any illusions about my Dutch.

"I know," I tell her. "But I'm pretty sure bad grammar is better than complete silence, right?"

She's been peering up at the wall behind me, but drops her gaze long enough to give me an arched eyebrow. "Only if anyone actually cares enough to listen," she says. "Come here. You should see this."

I leave the intercom and shuffle through the maze of seats to where Françoise stands at the far corner of the booth. Her gaze is focused on the patch of wall above the doors. I follow it and find she's staring at the news strip.

"Oh," I say. And then, "Shit."

"Shit," she agrees, and slides down the wall to sit on the floor. The Voice of the City bleats on about safety and comfort and seat belts, but we ignore it. For one thing, we're clearly going nowhere. For another, we can't see the newsfeed from our seats. And, since there's a major security lockdown across all sectors on Verdieping Twee, it looks like it might be a good idea to stay informed.

17.3 Danae

It's the best part of an hour before anybody remembers the booth, which I suppose, is pretty good under the circumstances, but I'm cold and tired and hungry, and not inclined to be reasonable. Emmett has gone from being philosophical – *At least it's not Een on lockdown* – to concerned – *How long do these things usually last? What happens if they can't secure the transit port? Is there any other way onto Een?* – to pissy – *For the love of God and Jesus Christ and Mary and Joseph and all the baby angels, either move us up or move us down but don't just fucking leave us here!* When he finally cycles all the way back into sullen silence, I let my head slide back to rest against the wall and close my eyes and try to zone out the Voice of the City's continuous critique of our failure to strap ourselves safely into our completely stationary vehicle. I suppose I must drift into a hazy space somewhere between wakefulness and sleep, because the sudden jolt of movement spikes absolute panic up my spine and I'm moving before I'm even aware of it, scrambling to my feet and scouring the booth for a way out.

"Hey," says Emmett. "Hey! Françoise! Hey. It's okay – we're okay. You were dreaming."

I wasn't: I don't dream around other people. But I grip the edge of the nearest seat-back with my left hand, bring my right up to place palm down against my forehead, let the press of skin on skin anchor me, drag me back to the present. I feel my joints lock; I don't need to see my knuckles to know they're turning white. I breathe – just breathe, just focus for a moment on my breath coming in and going out, while my heart rate steadies and the terror slowly trickles from my veins.

"Thank Christ for that," I say, when I can trust myself to speak. "I was starting to think they were ignoring us."

I crack an eyelid. He's watching me warily, but his lips curl into a faint smile, and I think he's prepared to buy it. "Better sit down," he says. "Before the CPU has heart failure."

I nod, slide around and into the nearest seat. My heart is still thundering, my brain is still full of air, and I'm still fighting the urge to rush the doors and try to rip them open until my fingers bleed, but I'm here, this is here, this is Luchtstad. I am safe here. I am safe.

"Door een veiligheidsprobleem," says the booth in her vaguely patronising tone, *"stopt deze wagen niet op de Verdieping Twee. Onze excuses voor het ongemak."*

"Due to a security alert," I translate, for Emmett's benefit, "this transit will not stop at Verdieping Twee."

He's still watching me carefully, as though I'm an unexploded bomb. I curl my fingers around the edge of the seat arms to curb the sudden urge to punch him.

"Cool," he says. "Good of them to let us know."

"They apologise for the inconvenience."

He considers. "Be a lot more inconvenient if we needed to be on Twee."

"We might make up a bit of the time we've lost, if we don't have to make a stop on the way."

He glances sideways and grins. "Don't worry. I'm going to make damn sure you get fed."

This irritates me intensely. But if he's teasing it means that the danger is past and we're ready to move on. I close my eyes, because the itch is flaring and it's easier to keep it under control when I minimise distractions. "Good," I say. "I'm going to sleep. Wake me up when we get to Een."

I don't sleep, of course. My skin feels hot, as if it's crawling across my body, and my muscles are taught, tense, ready to run. I can barely catch the breath in my chest, and the last thing I need is to be caught off-guard again, by a lurch or a creak or a mechanical hiss. But my eyes are closed and my head is pressed back against the headrest, and I hear Emmett's soft silence, indifference, boredom, fill in the background hush. It's soothing, in its way.

We move on.

17.4 Adam

I don't think I've ever seen anyone look less like they're asleep. It's fine, though. Especially given what's just happened. I leave her to it and let my own head drop back against the headrest, let my eyes fall closed as the booth rumbles onwards along the side of the radial. We jostle and clank our way through the transit hub with Twee, and I feel the singularity fuzz recede a little with distance, enough that my skull feels lighter and my brain feels clearer, like it's surfacing from deep water.

Françoise does not open her eyes.

Eventually, bored, I crane my head as far to the right as it will go and watch the news strip for a while. Twee is still locked down and nobody's entirely sure why or what's going on, but there's speculation that one of the main life support distribution trunks might have been disabled. I have no context for this, but it sounds bad. If Françoise weren't so dedicated to her performance of unconsciousness, I'd get her take on where this leaves us, but I'm reassured by the way she kicked the wall. That doesn't feel like something a person does when they're worried the booth is going to fall off the side of the city. Also, my neck is getting sore. I give up and turn back to the vista outside.

It's a little before 10:15 when we rumble through one final airlock and grind to a halt.

"Françoise," I say. "We're here."

Her eyes snap open. "Time for breakfast?"

"Time for breakfast," I say, and she unclips her belt.

I've spent the past few evenings checking out maps of the top floor, and so I know that the layout is not the same as the three below it. The streets are wider here, the buildings are grander and set further apart. The ceiling is close enough that the world seems to have closed in on itself and the air feels like it's in shorter supply. The area around the transit station is all up-market boutiques, but as we walk along the main thoroughfare, Hooftstraat, they give way to stuccoed and porticoed entrances flanked on either side by fragrant shrubs that reach upwards towards the pink, purple and red blossoms that cascade from the balconies above. Luchtstad, I've always thought, is a place you end up by default and are glad of the roof and the chance to work, but walking through the streets of Verdieping Een it's clear that there are people here by choice and their lives are good.

"Nice," I mutter sideways to Françoise, who hasn't said anything since we arrived.

She shrugs. "Een," she says, and leaves it at that.

Van Rensselaerstraat turns out to be a leafy byway accessed by a series of turns off Hoofdstraat and populated almost exclusively by places to eat. The light seems brighter here, as though that's genuine sunshine filtering through from the neighbouring plaza, and, for the first time, the striped awnings that hang from every shop front and café I've passed since I arrived on this city actually seem like they're needed and wanted. We pick the first spot we find with a vacant table and order coffees and croissants and I watch the street as we wait. This is not where we're due to meet Jos. We're looking for alternatives, names we can suggest when we see him that will make us look more confident than we feel.

The coffee and food arrives, and the attendant discreetly tucks the bill beneath the plate. Françoise retrieves it and peers at the total, eyes widening as she reads.

"Jesus," she says. "This had better be the best damned coffee I've ever drunk."

I slide it across the table from her and look upon a figure that represents approximately three hours' work on Verdieping Drie. "Jesus," I agree, and pause to wonder if the drinks up here are brewed from the tears of virgins. Best damned coffee or not, I plan to enjoy this like nobody has ever enjoyed coffee before, and my circuitry can hang before I leave so much as a smear in the bottom of the cup. "How the other half live," I say, and raise my cup to her. She returns the gesture and attacks a croissant.

The haunted woman who lurched across a moving booth this morning has vanished, and in her place is the Françoise that I know. Her tone is light as we eat the most expensive breakfast of our lives, and she rolls her eyes when I mention Twee.

"Remember your first shift at the factory?" she says. This was two weeks ago. My neural synapses may not be what they were, but I'm not likely to forget that quickly.

"No," I say. "What happened?"

She looks up sharply.

"Ah. Sarcasm," she says. "I haven't had enough coffee yet to cope with you trying to be funny, Emmett. I mean the gas scare."

"No shit," I say. "What about it?"

She swallows an impressive bite of pastry. "Remember what I said when they kicked us onto the street? How it was probably nothing?"

"This is not quite that," I say.

She follows the impressive bite of pastry with an impressive gulp of coffee. "You have any idea how complicated it is to run a city like this?"

I don't, but I can imagine. "Pretty complicated, I assume."

Françoise shrugs "These things are ridiculous. You see the size of them? They're a sitting target for everything in space. And a quarter of a million people live on each one of them. They're a disaster waiting to happen."

"That's comforting."

"If it wasn't for the fact that this is the single most cost-effective way to do the stuff that gets done up here, you bet your arse Congress would never have approved them. The first time – the *first* time – there's a widespread loss of life on one, what do you think happens then?"

"Game over," I say.

She nods. "Game over. They're all shut down, and the companies who built them… Well, you tell me how a company recovers from that kind of financial hit." She waves expansively. "And it's not just the money, either, is it?"

"I think it's mostly the money," I say, but I see where she's going with this. "No, you're right. It's the people too. It's the culture."

"Exactly. I bet if someone said to you, back on Earth, here's surprise overtime every night this week – oh, and we're not paying you for any of it, by the way – you'd be a little bit less likely to grit your teeth and get on with it."

"You haven't worked the kind of places I've worked, then."

She takes the point. "Actually, I think I probably have. But you know what I mean. You only have a home, a livelihood, up here because the city owns you. You're part of the brand. You live and breathe because the city keeps you. The post-etherics are barely legal, and the only way they keep from crossing that line into full-on illegal is by keeping us all as alive as they can."

"So, you're saying…" I hesitate. I want to make sure I actually understand what she's saying. "…You're saying that the city's jumping at shadows?"

"God, no. There's a life-support blackout on Twee. That's bad news, whatever caused it. What I'm saying is that the city's got to see shadows everywhere. Just in case."

I haven't had enough sleep for this. I can feel at least five neural systems trying to glitch, and my osmotic filters are not enjoying the coffee. "So… the city's only protecting the inhabitants because it gets shut down if too many of us die?"

She grins like I've won something. "Industrial capitalism. Isn't it grand?"

The feeling in my left foot abruptly cuts out. It's probably not connected to the city's overwhelming indifference to whether anyone lives or dies, but it doesn't help my souring mood. "Welcome to Luchtstad," I mutter. "The great beacon of progressive thought."

"It's not just Luchtstad." Françoise shakes her head. "I'd bet this cup of coffee it's not. I bet you just don't hear about the shut downs on, I don't know, Sorashi or Xingcheng or Natosi or any of the others. And I bet *they* don't hear about the shut downs up here. Seriously."

"Yeah?" I look at her, watch her face for any sign that she hears how idealistic she sounds. "You know what Luchtstad's got that the other ones don't have?"

"Of course I do." Her face darkens. "You think I don't think about Niet Zoeken every single day of my life? You think I don't know how dangerous it is? Really? But I also know the city. It's old and it's cranky. The entire system needs an overhaul and it just keeps getting patched instead. So yeah – sometimes it glitches."

I swirl my coffee, stare into the little cloud of crema that coats the surface and clings to the sides. "You make it sound simple."

Françoise shrugs again. "Sometimes it is simple."

"And sometimes it's Do Not Seek."

She swallows, brushes crumbs from her hands, sits back in the chair.

For a moment, I don't think she's going to answer. And then she sighs heavily, and says, "You're a real ray of sunshine, you know that?"

"I've been told that before." I sip at my coffee. It is actually – thankfully – really good. "Doesn't mean I'm not right."

"Funny, huh." She catches a server's eye as he passes by, makes the universal symbol for *I would like to pay now*. "Twenty-four thousand miles straight down, we're the ones exploding things. Up here…"

"…we're the reason other people are exploding things," I finish. The attendant returns, and Françoise swipes her neck chip, presses her palm to the credit reader. I wait for him to leave, and add, "Not sure I find it that funny, though."

"No," she agrees. "But… that's life. Let's go find Jos."

17.5 Danae

Van Rensselaerstraat is busy with people and sounds and smells as we pick our way along the profusion of eateries in search of De Gezellige Theepot, the whimsically named coffee shop where Elisabeth has arranged for us to meet her friend. I feel buoyant here, like a weight's been lifted from my skull, and it has taken me a coffee and two croissants to work out that this is because we are fractionally further away from the singularity on Een. It's amazing how quickly you can get used to something, and, I suspect, it will be even more amazing how quickly I get used to not being used to it. I wonder if I'll have a headache all day tomorrow back on Drie.

I know that Emmett is worried about using Elisabeth's café, and I agree with him, but I'm more concerned about the visual of two scruffy strangers walking up to an elderly regular in his local coffee shop and demanding that he follow them to an undisclosed location. I think Jos himself is the risk, not the café that he breakfasts in every Sunday. I also think that if this is a trap, we have the advantage in almost every way.

De Gezellige Theepot turns out to be pure tourist-bait: façaded in mock white shingle, with the name seared into a chunk of what looks like real wood over the door and chintzy floral drapes bunched in the window. A steaming kettle shimmers in the air outside, lifting and pouring a kaleidoscope of rainbow coloured light which resolves into a scrolling list of the daily specials, and a bell above the door actually chimes as we open it.

The woman behind the counter looks around and offers us a broad-mouthed, Verdieping Een smile. "*Welkom!*" she says cheerfully. "*Neem plaats. Ik kom zo bij u.*"

"Thank you," I tell her in Dutch. "We're looking for our friend."

"Oh," she says, "that'll be Jos. Jos!" I follow her line of sight to the far corner of the café, where a white-haired man looks up from his paper. He sees me looking and half-raises a hand in greeting. "You want tea? Coffee? Sit down – I'll come and get your order in a moment."

I'm wondering if the croissant stop might have been slightly precipitous. De Gezellige Theepot is the sort of place I would mock mercilessly in theory, but the smells from the kitchen are incredible and there's a group of backpackers at a table by the window diving into scones and cream, a thick pile of waffles, and a stack of dollar pancakes and bacon. I bet it costs three weeks' pay, but the last place cost about one and a half's, and it was only a bloody *croissant*.

"Coffee," I tell her reluctantly. "Thanks. Black, for both of us."

"Sure," she says, and bustles off into the back. The door to the kitchen bangs shut behind her, releasing a wall of hot sugar and pastry flavoured air into the café, and we pick our way through the tables towards our newest friend.

All I know about Jos is his name, the floor he lives on, and the fact that he's been actively relocating a-nauts onto Luchtstad since before I was born. According to Elizabeth, he only started to come under suspicion last year, and, given that the man in front of me has to be well into his eighties at least, that's an impressive run.

I wonder what happened to the guys he was smuggling when his luck ran out.

He's a small man, wiry and trim, with a bushy white moustache clipped in a perfect line over his upper lip. The top of his head is completely bald, showing a liver spot on the crown, but the hair that circles his pate is thick and wavy and looks as soft and shiny as a young child's. He stands as we approach and I see that he's simply but immaculately dressed: dark tweed jacket over a button-down shirt, pressed dark brown trousers, and cufflinks that extend out of the sleeves of his jacket as he reaches forward to shake my hand.

"Good morning," he says in English: confident and only slightly accented. His hand is cool, the skin paper thin, but his grip is firm. He turns to Emmett. "Good morning. I'm so pleased you could make it. I heard about the trouble on the second floor and I was worried you wouldn't get through. Please – sit. May I get you something to eat? To drink?"

"Thank you," I say, pulling back a chair to sit. It scrapes along the tile floor and, from the heft and feel of the surface, I think it's real oak. "We've ordered coffee."

"Have you eaten? Thank you, Rika," he adds to the waitress as she sets two steaming cups of coffee in front of us. "The waffles are very good here. Or perhaps you're ready for lunch?"

Emmett smiles his thanks up at Rika as she retreats. To Jos, he says, "I'm guessing they don't serve broth?"

I kick him sideways under the table. "The waffles look good," I say. To hell with it: if I have to survive on air for the next week, at least I'll be able to say that I did Verdieping Een in style. "Ignore my colleague. It was an early start."

"It's a long time since I've travelled on the transits," says Jos. "I don't remember them for their comfort." To Emmett: "My apologies, but no. Though Rika will warm up a little vegetable stock in some hot water if I ask her – it's not quite the same, but it seems to be tolerated very well by some of the older models that I know."

Emmett is absolutely not expecting that, and surprise flashes across his face for a moment, quickly schooled back into distrust. "That sounds," he says slowly, "like painting a target on the back of my head."

"Not here," says Jos. His voice is kind but firm. "You have no reason to trust me; I know that. But you have my word that nobody in this place will harm you or allow harm to come to you. I've known them for many years."

"Yeah," says Emmett. "About that. We have a couple of issues with the location."

Jos nods slowly, an acknowledgement. "You're worried that we're under surveillance."

"Our mutual friend told me that this is where she used to meet you." Emmett's tone is cold, his eyes hard. "You're under suspicion. She's tagged. I think we're taking a risk, yes."

"All right." Jos folds his hands on the table in front of him. "It's true: I can't move as freely as I used to. This is why you came to me: if

I leave this floor, a record is logged and somebody from the security forces follows me and makes a list of the people I meet. If I don't leave this floor..." He shrugs. "I have not been caught in any illegal act. There is no evidence against me. The security forces know that I have been involved in extra-legal migration, but they cannot prove this and it is much less to them than their other troubles, so..." Another shrug. "I go to this café every Sunday morning for breakfast, as I have gone for almost fifteen years. Some days when I get here, Rika has a message from her cousin who lives on another floor to say, Jos, you will have a visitor this morning. She has three cousins. When she tells me the name of the cousin, I know who has sent my visitor. We sit, and we talk, and I understand if I can help, and this is all."

I lift my coffee cup, cradle it in my hand, considering. "So you're telling me that you have no idea why we're here."

"I knew you would be two," he says. "And I knew that you came from the third floor. This is all. Until your friend asked for broth, I did not know if you were organic or non."

I shoot a glare sideways. "Good work," I tell Emmett, who looks, at least, chagrined. To Jos, I say, "We're both the same. But I eat waffles."

A gentle smile spreads across the old man's face, and I wonder if he has children, grandchildren, great-grandchildren. "I will ask Rika. Rika!" he calls. She looks up from the counter and he gestures towards me and asks for a serving of *stroopwafel*, and I ignore Emmett's upturned eyebrow in favour of contemplating the delights ahead.

I say, "You've been involved in migration."

"In a way." He nods. "You understand – my job, my position, I have some power. I can make it easier to enter the city. I can make sure that checks are less careful. I know people. People who can make new identities. Nurses, doctors. I know where there are jobs. All of this is part of my work, my life, the life that others see, so it's easy for me. I do it because I can."

"Why?" Emmett's tone has not thawed. "Why would you do any of this? You have a good life – a great life, it looks like – so... why would you risk it? What's in it for you?"

Jos glances up as the waffles arrive, exchanges a smile and a word of thanks with Rika. He nods encouragement to me. "They are good," he says, unnecessarily. The smell of them alone has plunged my stomach into hunger spasms that have nothing whatsoever to do with lack of food. To Emmett, he says, simply, "Because I love this city. I love what it stands for. I love that we are the first – the only – place in the greater Terran sphere to stand up and say, *This is wrong*. And I want to fight for that dream."

Emmett glances sideways at me, and I realise that I've been systematically piling waffle into my face with silent, focused determination. I swallow, with some difficulty, and wash it down with a mouthful of coffee. I'm not sure how I always seem to manage to represent the two of us every time we meet somebody new, but Emmett is once again manifestly waiting for my cue.

"You were right," I say. "These are good."

Emmett's eyes shoot ceilingwards. "Altruism, then," he says. "Okay. Fine, I'll buy it. But we made it here all by ourselves, clearly – so aren't you curious why we're talking to you?"

Jos inclines his head. "Of course," he says. "I think you are about to tell me."

I bury a smirk in a bite of waffle. Emmett looks unfazed. "We're looking for information," he says.

"Information?" Jos frowns. "I do not give names."

"No names," says Emmett. "Introductions, maybe – but no names. We're looking for someone who knows about the city's stream singularity. Someone with... our kind of specialist knowledge."

He could not have made this sound more like a bad spy novel if he'd twirled his moustache and cackled. I set down my fork and clarify: "Emmett's people back on Earth think they've identified some kind of anomaly in the stream, and they've narrowed it down to Luchtstad. He's here to try and work out what it is."

Jos, understandably, looks confused. "But why do you think that I have this information?"

"We don't," I say. "Our friend down on Verdieping Drie thought that you might know someone who did."

"This anomaly," says Jos, and, for the first time, he looks nervous. "This city – without the singularity... you understand..."

"I know. We know." I glance at Emmett. "We have a theory."

I wait for Emmett to jump in. He does not. And, of course, it's me that Jos looks at expectantly.

"It's not my idea." I want to make that absolutely clear. I've looked crazy enough this morning on the heels of someone else's obsession.

"There's a rumour that Emmett's heard. He thinks it's connected."

This time, I wait five whole beats, past the point where the silence becomes uncomfortable. It's long enough that Jos feels the need to add, politely, "A rumour?"

"A rumour," I say. I shoot a glare sideways and notice, for the first time, that Emmett's skin is a bad colour: a kind of washed out white-grey. "About some kind of hospital. Powered by the datastream."

Jos hasn't noticed what's happening beside me. And there's no way I can ask Emmett if he's all right.

"And our friend on the third floor thought that I would be able to help with this?" says Jos.

"It's not on this radial," I say. I meet Emmett's eyes and they flicker skittishly, like a panicked bird. I don't know what that means. "You mentioned medical connections…"

Jos flattens his palms against the table. It's a slow, deliberate move, and it reminds me of a musician stretching out the tendons of his hands. "And you want… what?" he says at last. "An introduction on another radial? You think this will help you?"

I spread my hands, a mirror of his. "Whatever it is, it's not on Radiale Zeven. If we're going to learn about it, we need to find it first."

"Your friend." Jos nods at Emmett. "Is he sick?"

I don't follow his line of sight. "He's fine."

"He doesn't speak."

"He's fine," I say again. "Can you help us?"

Jos looks pained. "When you come here – when Rika says, Jos, you will have visitors today – it always means one thing. Somebody needs help. Maybe they have a friend who is trapped somewhere, in a bad situation. Maybe they have been discovered and they must move, soon, to some new floor. I don't know. This? I have never been asked about this."

"What about when somebody needs medical help?" I do not look at Emmett. Nothing will make me look at Emmett. "What do you tell them?"

He shrugs. "Maybe I can help your friend. If he is sick…"

"He's *fine*." In a minute, I'm going to have to walk us away from here, and, number one: I'm not sure if Emmett is able to walk. Number two: I haven't finished my waffles. "We're not here because of Emmett."

Beside me, I hear Emmett suck in a breath. It sounds alarmingly like he's only just managed to breathe again after an extended period without air. This puts me in a bit of a position. On the one hand, I'm glad he's not actually about to die. On the other, his timing could be better.

"When somebody needs a doctor," says Jos, "I take them to a doctor."

I'm not sure if he's answering my question or accusing me of something. "Then take us to one of your doctors, maybe."

He sighs, flexes his fingers against the table, watches every crease of skin rise and fall with the play of muscles beneath. Finally, he says, "I must make some enquiries."

It feels like as much as we're likely to get. "Thank you."

He nods, a neat, fussy little gesture. "And you have, I think, a message for me?"

Elisabeth's fee; the price of one introduction. I glance sideways at Emmett.

"I'd like to know what you can give us first," he says. His voice is thin, thready. Hoarse.

Jos frowns. "I don't think this was the transaction."

He's right, of course. It was a noble attempt, but it was never likely to work. I shrug. "Do you have a pen?"

"Of course." Jos lifts his head towards the counter, where Rika is chatting to a customer. He mimes the act of writing in the air in front of him, and she nods her understanding. "I will help you," he says. "If I can, I will help you. You have my word."

Rika returns to the table with a pen and the kind of message pad I remember all too well from my days at Intimacy. She sets them down in front of Jos, who passes them to me. I nudge them sideways to Emmett. His hand trembles violently as he lifts the pen, but it settles as he presses it to the paper.

"How will we hear from you?" I ask. The nib scratches against the page, slowly, painfully. I glance sideways and see that Emmett is at least forming legible words, so perhaps the danger is past.

Jos shrugs, almost apologetically. "I come to this place every Sunday morning," he says. "I will be here next week."

Perfect. Absolutely bloody perfect. At least the waffles are good. "Fine," I say. "Same time?"

"As you wish."

Nothing about this is as I wish, but there's no point in saying as much. Emmett finishes his arthritic scrawling and slides the pad over to Jos, who accepts it with a word of thanks. He tears the top sheet off the pad without looking at it, and slides it into the inner pocket of his jacket.

"It is my pleasure to meet you," he says. "Please give my regards to my friend, your aunt."

My shoulders tense and it's on the tip of my tongue to spit that Elisabeth is no aunt of Emmett's or mine. The itch flares, an acid-spike of fire and flame, and I feel my hands contract into fists. I purse my lips, make myself breathe. Of all the places to lose control, this ranks right up there with the worst of them.

"Whatever," I say. My voice is tight. I'm not sure if I need to help Emmett to his feet, but he pre-empts the question by grinding his chair backwards, away from the table, and levering himself upright. "Enjoy your breakfast."

"Thank you," says Jos. His smile is beatific. "I hope you have a pleasant trip and that you will come back again soon."

Chapter Eighteen

18.1 Adam

"You stopped *breathing*," she says, which is annoying. I'd hoped she hadn't noticed that. "That's not what I'd call 'fine'."

We're standing in line outside the gates to the viewing plaza, and already the queue, which extends the length of the block, has doubled back on itself four times inside the barriers. I'm beginning to be concerned about how we're all going to fit on the other side.

"It went away," I say. My head still feels loose and full of clouds, and my muscles are only gradually starting to feel like they're getting enough oxygen again, but my system has rebooted. My lungs are working again. I'll add pulmonary hang to the list of ways I hope I don't die, but the fact is, I *didn't*. Not today. "What do you want me to say? It happened, but it went away."

"And what if it had happened on the line?" She glances sideways, eyes narrowed. "In a factory full of people? What do you think happens as soon as Jouke realises you're not organic?"

It's not like this hasn't occurred to me, every single day that I've been here. "Thanks for your concern," I say. "I didn't have you pegged as the sentimental type."

"Sentimental?" Anger drops her voice to a hiss. "You think you're the only person who gets caught in that particular rain of shit, Emmett?"

"Fine." The back of my neck has spasmed at some point in the course of the hang and my shoulders and head ache. "I'll come back alone next week."

"Sure. Great." Françoise rolls her eyes and shakes her head. "Yeah, *that's* really going to work, isn't it? You on your own. Not breathing. Can't move. In a café on Verdieping Een. That's a great idea."

I have no idea what to say to that and don't have the energy to try. "So come with me. Don't come with me. Whatever gets you to stop yelling at me."

"I'm not yelling." She does not yell this, to be fair.

"You're yelling." As retorts go, it's not my best, but I'm tired and I

149

just almost died again for the second time in a fortnight. "You're just doing it quietly."

In the middle distance I hear, above the bustle of city noise, the first chimes of a clock sing out the hour. The line starts moving. Françoise stretches out her neck and shoulders as we start shuffling towards the turnstiles. "If I was yelling," she says, "it wouldn't be quietly. Stop being a dick."

"I'm not being a dick," I say, like a dick. She rolls her eyes but says nothing. The crowd inches forwards, and we inch with them. "Anyway. I got a good read off Jos. I think he's one of the good guys."

An eyebrow arches. "Because he paid for your coffee?"

"He bought you waffles, too."

"Yeah, that's all it takes to earn my trust, Emmett," she says. "Coffee and waffles."

"Looked like they were pretty good waffles."

Françoise glares. "They were *great* waffles."

I'm neutral on the spectrum of waffle integrity. "Sounds like a powerful incentive to make a return trip."

"Oh, fuck off." But she doesn't sound angry, just irritated, and not even that much. "Can we worry about next Sunday when it gets to be next Sunday? I feel like my whole life has been taken up by your life since you got here. Can we just relax for a while and enjoy the stupid Viewing Plaza? You owe me two hours of amazing."

That's probably fair, to be honest. And, even if it's not, I'm too tired to argue. We're here now. My neural feedback relays are glitchy but functional, my motor systems are more or less back online, and the air on Verdieping Een is fancy enough to make it worth the effort of breathing through my malfunctioning lungs. We're almost at the security booths at the head of the queue, beyond which the plaza gates open onto sights unseen and wonders unknown. I owe her two hours of amazing.

It's time to relax for a while and enjoy the stupid Viewing Plaza.

18.2 Danae

The security booth releases me, and I step through the gates and into the approach to the plaza. It's not exactly what I was expecting. For one thing, it's basically another street, exactly identical to the one I've just left, except for the fact that this one has trees. There are houses and storefronts and awnings and people, there are servers wiping down tables, there are hosts brushing street dust away from their front steps, there are proprietors straightening displays. The street arcs around in a gentle crescent, terminating in an airway at either end, towards which the afternoon crowds spread and flow like water tumbling from a jug. If there's one thing this city isn't about to miss out on, it's a captive market, I guess, but I've been up since 4am and I could have done without the extra walk.

"Come on," says Emmett beside me. "The elevators are this way."

It's less congested on this side of the barrier at least. The lightbands are set high and gentle, a photic shower that ripples through the canopy of leaf cover like a soft spring morning. The air is cool but not cold, and the city sounds are a muted babble against the stone-effect frontages that rise up around us. We pick our way easily enough through the network of tables and solicitous maitre d's with lunchtime specials to sell, towards a final barrier wall hidden beneath creeping vines and tumbling cataracts of blossom that shiver gently on the constantly moving air and blanket the street in scent.

We pass through the airway to find ourselves at the foot of a bank of elevators engaged in perpetual motion. The crowds are restive here, bubbling with a thick undercurrent of anticipation, and the queues move quickly, sucking parties of twenty, twenty-five, thirty passengers into their hold and sliding swiftly upwards towards an access ramp close to the ceiling, from which vines drip more bright-coloured, fragrant flowers. We pick the line that looks shortest and wait no more than five minutes before the group in front of us surge forwards and we surge with them, twisting as we come to a halt inside the lift doors so that we can watch the heaving street disappear below us into a sea of moving figures. Before us rises the wall that separates us from the street we've just left, blank and windowless, and across the stark white surface, a news strip scrolls endless stories of life outside the turnstile.

We're disgorged in less than a minute onto a wide boulevard – wider than it seems from below – and another set of queues, this time for a series of airways that stretch the length of the ramp. I count forty of them before we're ushered inside, and I'm certain I haven't logged them all. The passageway is dark and narrow and the chatter of our fellow travellers is amplified into an echoing roar that rattles my skull and sets my teeth on edge, but, ahead of us, I can see already that we're being ushered towards… light. Light, and space. More space than I've seen in the year I've lived in this city. More space than I've known since I was a child.

It opens up ahead of us, and I let myself be swept forwards and into an abundance of air and distance and starlight.

18.3 Adam

Françoise is half a step ahead of me, so the first thing I see is her legs lock in place, bringing her to a sudden halt. The press behind us is unrelenting, so I touch a hand gently to her elbow, and she glances back over her shoulder towards me. There's a glow behind her eyes that I don't recognise but it dies as she registers my face.

"Shit. Sorry," she says, and her feet find their way forward again. We move out of the access way and into the plaza itself.

This is when I get the chance to look, and this is when I understand what's caught her in mid-stride and knocked the motion from her legs. This is when I understand why they don't have pictures of the Viewing Plaza in any of the advertising brochures, and why they don't sell postcards on every streetside stall on Verdieping Een. I thought the booth was something else. It turns out I need to revisit my expectations.

The access way opens out onto another wide receiving port. The lifts have raised us maybe four storeys from ground level on Verdieping Een, and the higher platform of the Viewing Plaza stretches out below us, a flat expanse of manicured gardens and winding paths, dotted here and there with vending carts and thronged with people. It ends in a balustrade wall, overhung with mess of bright purple flowers that spill some six metres straight down to the lower platform, which stretches all the way to the far windowed wall.

The radials of this city are organised in a star-shape around the central singularity and linked by transit corridors that snake between neighbouring spokes. One half of the city wheel is sheltered beneath the protective arc of our solar umbrella, a vast dome of networked photovoltaic panels that channel sunlight and energy into the bowels of the radials where the crops are grown. The other half opens onto the emptiness of space. This means that the exterior wall of each radial is our best and only defence against explosive decompression. Windows are bad at this. Even a dual layer aluminium-titanium alloy micro-interlaced teflon-coated protective hull isn't always fantastic at it, but windows are worse. So it's a trade-off I've been willing to make: my continuing ability to breathe and exist, in exchange for a relative lack of anything interesting to look at.

It's easy to think like that when you don't know what you're missing.

"Holy *shit*," I say for the third time today, but I really, really mean it now. And I'm not the only one. To our left and right, bodies emerge from the access ways and freeze in place. I hear the sharp intake of breath, the whispered awe, the loss of words. We keep moving, because the crowd is moving, but also because that view is hypnotic and we need to get closer to it. Françoise is quiet as we shuffle along the boulevard, her eyes trained on the vista. It arches the full length and height of the plaza, criss-crossed with vast structural supports inside and out, but I have to make myself notice them. My brain wants to pretend they're not there; it's distracted by the starscape. Luchtstad, like all the post-etherics, points its exposed belly towards the planet below. It's a protection thing. It's nighttime on the surface beneath us and, from medium Earth orbit, it's a delicate filigree of fine orange lines of light, circled by stars. Clouds swirl, black on black, and the sun is a halo of white, frosting the edges of the atmosphere. Beyond, a vast black canvass opens onto infinity, pierced here and there by starlight and, in the near distance, by the flash-glare of a sister city in a tandem orbit.

"I thought I'd know it," says Françoise at last.

We've reached a set of steps and she's broken her gaze to find safe footing, but her voice is a hushed whisper and I have to ask her to repeat herself.

"The view," she says. "I thought I'd recognise it. But I don't."

I let the words carry us down half a flight, but I'm still not sure I understand. "Why would you recognise it?" I ask, and she shrugs.

"I used to live…" she says, and stops. Hesitates. Tries again. "I used to live a long way from anywhere..For a long time. And I'd go out at night sometimes and I'd lie on my back and look up at the sky, and I thought I knew what infinity looked like. And then when that got taken away… I don't know. It mattered. And for the longest time I thought that my whole life was about trying to find that again. You know?"

She glances back at me. I have to admit that I don't know. She shrugs again.

"Not many people see that view now, I suppose," she says. "Who lives miles from anywhere? You can't live miles from anywhere. The world got smaller, didn't it, and mine just kept on shrinking. I thought for years that if I could just... I don't know. Find that sky again, maybe. If I could just find it again, then maybe... I'd find the way I used to be." She sighs. "I don't even know any more."

There's something in her tone that I haven't heard before, and it takes me a moment to recognise it as sadness. I don't understand. "You don't like the view?"

"What?" There's disbelief in her tone. I hear it before she whips her head around to look at me and I see it in her face. "Are you kidding me?" A hand shoots out, sweeps the air in front of her. "*That* view? Who the hell finds something in *that* not to like?"

At least it's made her angry again. The melancholy was confusing. "I have no idea. It seemed weird."

"Jesus." A sigh as we level out onto the higher platform and the space around us widens. "That's what you heard. No, asshole. I'm having an existential crisis. But, please, feel free to completely mistake it for aesthetic ennui."

"Sorry," I say. I glance around at the nearby vendors and wonder if it's time to feed her again. "Go on – tell me about the place you used to live."

"No. The moment's gone." She folds her arms across her chest, but the glance she shoots me is warmer than I expected, faintly amused. "It is weird, though."

"What's weird?"

"The motion. The spinning." She unfolds one arm enough to gesture towards the distant, light-streaked globe, rotating silently against the black. "The city never felt like it was moving until I saw that. Now I feel kind of seasick."

It's probably time to feed her again. "Buy you lunch?" I suggest, but she laughs.

"Tell you what," she says. "How about we work out what these guys are charging per hotdog, and then we work out when we can afford to eat again?"

I consider. "Deal," I say, and we move out and into the gardens.

18.4 Danae

My father hated the idea of the post-etherics almost as much as he hated the idea of living in a city with a ceiling. But he missed the sky as much as I did when we left the farm, and, I don't know – at least he might have got it back on Luchtstad. I know Emmett doesn't understand, and I wasn't expecting him to, but I feel the past year could have gone a whole lot faster if I'd known this place was here. Or maybe not. The only thing I'm sure about right now is that I have no idea how I'm going to reconcile myself to Verdieping Drie again after this.

But that's a question for later. For now, I'm going to soak it in, as much as I can, and see if I can find the person who used to lie beneath a harvest moon and cry sometimes because it was so *there*.

Emmett's quiet beside me, softly cheerful, and there's a joy in his step that I feel I recognise. Kids run screaming after each other along the flagstoned pathways, a Doppler curve of shrill laughter and thumping feet, while their parents gather in groups and chatter happily in languages I know and languages that I don't. We wander through the gardens, stopping occasionally to identify a flowering shrub or a planted bed, and sometimes, when the view is good, to just pause and look and be content.

On the lower platform, we stop for coffee at a stall with chairs arranged around tables on a raised dais that affords a seated prospect of the windows, and we watch the pale green streaks of a laser broom arc into the blackness from the Earth below, a silent symphony of colour, clearing debris from our path.

"Radiale Twee," says Emmett, who has consented to drink coffee again, since it's a special occasion, though he hasn't hesitated to point out how long he'll have to spend this evening flushing his system.

"Grain crops," I say. "Wheat, mostly. Though sometimes corn and oats as well. But they need a hell of a lot of water."

"Radiale Zes?"

"Tea."

"Tea?"

"Yep. All the types of tea you can think of."

"I can think of... three."

"Well, they have more than that. Also uses shitloads of water, though, which is why you hear people from Radiale Zes called *vochtige billen*."

"I have never heard anyone call anyone else *vochtige billen*," he says. "I don't even know what it means."

"*Vochtig*," I say. He needs to get better at this. "Come on: *vochtig*. You know this one."

"I know *vocht*," he says, because he wouldn't get very far on Luchtstad, let alone the factory floor, without understanding relative levels of moisture.

"Okay," I say. "Extrapolate."

"I really don't need a linguistics lesson…"

"You really do. Come on: *vochtig*."

He glares at me, as though I'm making him say something distasteful. "Moist," he says.

"Damp," I correct him. He's right, but context is important. All the more so given the qualification imposed by the second part of the phrase, but he doesn't know that part yet. "And *billen* is 'buttocks'."

Emmett cocks an eyebrow. He is manifestly trying to work out if I'm taking the piss. "Buttocks."

"Buttocks." I feel my smile break free and take over my jaw. "Yes. People from Radiale Zes are called soggy arses by less enlightened folks than ourselves."

"Soggy arses?" He's *definitely* trying not to laugh. He's trying, in fact, to look disapproving, but it's not working very well.

I sip my coffee. "You should hear what they call us."

"That's what I'm afraid of. Okay: Radiale Drie."

"Legumes."

"And…?"

"And what? They just do legumes. Do you have any idea how many different types of legumes there are?"

He considers. "Probably not. Until two minutes ago, I didn't know there were more than three different types of tea."

"But I bet you know eighteen thousand different ways to make broth, right?"

He grins. "Depending on what's available. But broth is broth. I really don't get why they need to have all these different… things."

"Don't knock it," I tell him. My head feels light, full of air and starshine. "Hey. By the way – before you annoy me again, I just wanted to say… thanks. This was a good idea."

He looks up, startled. To be fair, this does annoy me slightly. "No problem," he says, after a moment. "I'm having a good time too."

I'd point out that I didn't specifically say that I was having *a good time* – what I said was that this was a *good idea* – but it seems churlish. I haven't felt like this in so long, I'd almost forgotten what it was like.

So, instead, I smile, and I mean it. I smile, and turn it up on the view and something shifts inside me, something chips, something shrinks a little and I can catch my breath. My chest releases, my ribs ache just a little bit less, and sadness twists in my throat, because it has been so long since I felt like this.

I say, "Shall we walk down to the window?"

He follows my line of sight. "Only if you promise to list off all the different kinds of beans they make in Radiale Drie on the way."

"You know that legumes aren't just beans?" I say as I stand up. "I mean – you know that, right?"

He stands up too, stretches out a kink in his neck. "Do they go in broth?"

"How the hell would I know?"

"Exactly." He grins. "I just do broth."

"Peanuts," I tell him. "Lentils. Edamame." Ahead of us, the laser broom fires again, streaking through the silky blackness and bathing the platform for a moment in watery green light. A crowd close to the window make an audible, collective sound of excited awe and then laugh at themselves. "And then you have your kidney beans, your chickpeas, your gram, that sort of thing. It's a bit like our flower bulbs: the research engineers have developed a whole range of new hybrid generations that need significantly less water per crop yield, so it's actually cheap enough to sell back to the stores on Luchstad, which is why so much of the cooking up here is lentil-based or, you know, bulked up with chickpeas, or... what?" I add, as he shoots a sly smile sideways at me.

"Nothing," he says. "This is just... unexpected, that's all."

The smile does not look entirely benign. "What's unexpected?"

"This," he says. The hand closest to me reaches out, tentatively touches my upper arm, as though he's afraid my skin will burn. "This Françoise right here. I've never seen you talk so much unless you were arguing with me."

I'm not sure if he's making fun of me. "I told you: I used to live on a farm."

"You didn't." He shakes his head. "You said you used to live in the middle of nowhere. I know basically nothing about you, you know that."

"It's not like I know much more about you."

"It's not an accusation." He spreads his hands wide, a gesture of innocence. "I like it, is all. I like seeing this side of you."

The laser broom fires again, close enough now that the windows flare bright green and the sounds of collective awe are tinged with a noticeable undercurrent of concern. I'd like to think we're not about to collide head on with a chunk of space debris, so it's great that the guys on the ground are paying attention, but it's getting a little bit close for comfort. If this is business as usual for our orbital path, I'm slightly glad that Verdieping Drie doesn't have windows to see it from.

"It's not a side of me," I say. "It was twenty years ago. I'm not that person any more."

"Okay." The smile leaves his mouth, but lingers in his eyes, and I want to challenge him, but he's left me no room.

So I decide to play it light, shrug it off. "So, what – you're telling me you *don't* find the agritech of Radiale Drie a source of endless fascination?"

He shrugs. "I like our bulbs."

"You like…?" I start to say, and then I stop. I'm about to question his affection for the quality control measures on the factory floors of Radiale Zeven that don't reliably separate out the rotten hyacinths from the fresh, but I stop mid-sentence and I can't explain why.

"Françoise?" says Emmett. "Are you okay?"

"I don't know," I say, and then, before I know what I'm doing, I've thrown myself on top of him, knocking him to the ground. He's bigger than me, but he's not expecting it, and I starfish my body over his as the air leaves his lungs in a startled *whuf*, covering him, protecting him as something close by us explodes into fire and flame and the world goes black.

Chapter Nineteen

19.1 Adam

The stream ruffles, contracts, and there's a moment of piercing silence that sucks the air from the world. I have no idea how long it lasts, but then it's gone and the sound and smoke and screaming rush in.

And, in the background, I hear the sounds of the chant.

Françoise is a weight on top of me, face down on my face, body spreadeagled over mine. Her eyes are closed and there are sparking embers in the hair that's fallen out of her scarf and, for a second, I think she's dead and that the chant is for her. And then her face constricts into a tight-eyed grimace, her mouth puckers as she struggles for air and she whisper-wheezes, "Get me up, get me up, I need to get up…"

My ears are ringing. My head feels like it's full of water. She's heavy and there's no strength in my arms. No, no, no – not a motor hang, not now. I test my legs and find they move. Not quickly and not well, but they move. I try my hips and they twist on command. I try a breath and immediately wish I hadn't. I try my arms again, and this time they respond.

I push upwards and I roll us. Françoise yells but her eyes don't open, and one of the sparks in her hair takes light as she collapses off me onto the ground. I slap at it with my hand before it can catch and I feel my palm graze shards of something broken. We are so close to the windows. I look up, afraid of what I'll see, and a metal shield slams into place across a spiralling fracture in the inner glazing, a heavy thud that barrels out across the platform like a shotgun blast.

"Get me up," says Françoise again, more urgently. "Get me up, Emmett, I need to get up."

Her eyes are still closed. I scramble onto my hands and knees and choke out a lungful of smoke: the copse to our left is burning. Another shotgun blast flattens the air as a second shield slams home and somewhere nearby a woman's voice is screaming for help. I crawl to Françoise and see that her arms are twitching, fingers dancing against the blistered grass beneath her. Her coat has ripped clean away from her shoulders. The top of the dress below it is fragmented and torn at her back. And something is seeping out from below her, something thick and dark against the earth.

"What did you do?" I shout. "What did you do? Are you bleeding? Françoise, what did you do?"

"Get me up!" she hisses, one more time, and the effort makes her cough and gasp for air. I slide my arm beneath her back and she yells and her eyes open, but she can't catch a breath and her mouth just makes sucking shapes at the smoke. I feel my hand connect with skin, damp skin, and I realise that the force of the explosion has shredded the back of her clothes. If she hadn't thrown herself on me, that would be my skin. That would be me bleeding out onto the grass.

"What the hell did you do?" I yell again, because I know what she did. She just saved my life. That's blood that I can feel flowing down her neck and onto my hand, so she has saved me by killing herself.

She forces a ragged breath. "I can walk," she says. "I can walk, Emmett. Get me on my feet."

"You can't walk!" I shout. It's all I can think of to say. She's dying. I can carry her, but she can't walk.

"Emmett!" she yells. It's harsh, sharp with pain. "We have to get out of here. We have to move. Get me on my feet."

She's right: we have to leave, and we have to do it now. There are protocols for containing fire on this city, and they're not going to work out well for us if we're still here when they kick in. Help may be coming, but not until the fire is out.

"Okay," I say. The back of my throat burns as the osmotic filters try to siphon out the worst of the chemical particulates. They're holding at maybe 70, 75% and I can't maintain them for long. "Okay, let's go. I'm going to slide my hands underneath your back, Françoise – get ready…"

She screams. I feel gravel, bits of debris. I feel wetness and ridges of skin and strips of shredded fabric. She screams, and I clench my jaw and force her upright as every muscle of her injured body fights against me. Her back is a mess of blood and blackened burns, scraps of her jacket soaking into a network of tears, dirt and shale and ashes clinging to abraded tissue. I close my eyes against it as she folds herself into her knees, breathing heavily. Somewhere to our right, there's a pop-bang and a chorus of screams and the air singes and turns acrid. It doesn't sound like gunfire, but nothing sounds the way it is right now. I think my aural circuits have overloaded, maybe, or else it's the thickness of the air.

I stand up, hunching under the smoke cloud and see an outstretched hand on the path beside us, clawing at the ground from beneath an overturned table.

"Okay," I say again. "Okay, we need to go. Françoise – give me your hands. I'm going to pull you to your feet."

She hesitates. She doesn't lift her head. I've seen friends, colleagues, die in thirty-six hours from smaller wounds than hers. If she comes with me, we'll need a harvest, and I don't know if either one of us is the sort of person who can make that happen. So she hesitates, but then she lifts a trembling hand, and I catch it and I drag her upright, onto her feet. She doesn't scream this time, and that's almost worse than the sound she made before.

"Jos," she says. "Get me to Jos."

I don't know how to get her to Jos. I don't know how long she can keep moving. But I nod, though she's not looking at me, and I shrug off my jacket. Her left arm is mostly unscathed, so I slide it into the arm of my coat and sling the rest of it across her back, across the wreckage of her right shoulder. I slip my arm around her waist from the left, taking care to only hold her where the blast has done the least damage. She leans heavily into me and we start to move.

"Was this us?" she says. "Did we do this?"

"I don't know." It looks like the old car bombs we used to plant outside Ren households. It looks like something one of the older models might have swallowed and triggered outside a government building. I've seen rain-filled craters in front of spilling rubble. I've seen three houses levelled by a single blast. I think it could be us. I just don't know why we'd do this here.

Behind us, I hear the slam of another shield cracking into place, muffled by layers of smoke. I counted forty-nine apertures between the structural supports, and that's three of them compromised now. I'm following the path away from the window, but I can't see far enough ahead to know for sure that we're headed towards the stairs to the upper platform and I can feel the oxygen count decreasing with every footstep. Françoise is barely moving her feet, though she's trying: one foot scrapes the ground behind us, the other toes at the rubble in front.

There are airways on every street corner in this city and I know what they're for: they're for cutting off the oxygen to the sector behind them in case of fire. I've walked through dozens of them in the past few weeks. Christ, I've felt *comforted* by them, because I don't want fire to take over this city either, and it's not like they have water to spare up here.

I didn't expect to ever be on the wrong side of them. Nobody expects that.

"Come on," I tell her. She grunts and her fingers close more tightly around my shirt. "Come on, we're nearly there. We can do this." But I don't remember how long it took us to walk from the platform steps to our window-side café. I don't remember the way. All I'm going on is the fact that there are shadowy figures moving through the smoke on either side of us and we're all pointed in the same direction. We could all be wrong.

The air is getting warmer and it's getting harder to breathe. My filters are down to 55% and there's a spiralling toxic overload brewing in my lymphatic system. I can flush it later. There's still time, but we've got to keep moving and Françoise's movements are getting weaker. To our right, the smoke opens up into a patch of amber flames, licking across a patch of grass. I see a body prone in the middle, beyond saving, and a child wailing at the edge of the fire. For a moment, I can't think: it's as though my circuits lock down and my feet freeze in place. I know I need to help, but I can't carry a kid and Françoise at the same time. And then a man emerges from the fog, crouching low, and another man, and one of them scoops up the child, who screams more loudly and starts to flail, to kick and punch.

The second man says something that I don't understand. I think it's supposed to be comforting, but the child keeps wailing. "*Geen probleem,*" he says. I understand that. "*Het is goed, geen probleem, geen probleem…*"

He sees me looking. "*Is dit je kind?*" he says – *is this your child?* One side of his face is blood; it soaks onto his white shirt, drips down his jacket sleeve and onto the hand that the little boy is frantically trying to slap away. "*Kun je helpen?*"

I barely understand what he's saying. "I don't know," I say, and I try to shrug, but Françoise takes up all the strength in my shoulders. It's so hard to get a breath. "I don't know; I'm sorry…"

"You need help?" says the first man. He doesn't miss a beat. It takes my fractured brain longer to work out that he's speaking English than it takes him to switch languages. "You need help, mister? Come on, we help you."

His arm is cradled against his chest. His face is black with soot and his eyes are wide white circles in the darkness. He can't be out of his teens, but he slings his good arm around the other side of Françoise's waist as his friend fights a terrified, screaming child, and we hobble forward together as the smoke blankets and chokes us. I can't even tell if Françoise is still conscious. All I know is that the air is almost gone and it's getting harder to follow the outline of the path beneath us in the gathering dark.

And then, ahead of us, I see a yellow glow – more fire, but this one stretches upwards, towards the ceiling. A piece breaks off and falls, and its descent lights up the darkness enough to pick out a shadowy structure behind and around it. I recognise the struts of the upper platform. We didn't stop to look at it as we came down the steps, but I remember the curtain of flowers. It's burning now. Behind the charred skeleton of the lower reaches, I can see that it was masking what looks like some kind of mall: labyrinthine corridors of glass cubicles filled with clothing, restaurants, jewellery stores, dark now with smoke. They stretch off into the gloom, shaded in pale green by strips of emergency lighting. Figures move with purpose, beckoning and shepherding and, as we stagger forwards, I see that they are police or army, authority at least, masked and dressed in full EVA suits.

"*Snel!*" shouts one and grabs my arm. He has a weapon strapped to his shoulder and an umbilical around his waist that tethers him to a pillar. I realise with a spike of horror that these men are expecting the outer wall to fail. "*Snel!*" he shouts again and shoves me forward.

I lurch, and the first man, arm still around Françoise, stumbles. We almost fall, but the second man catches his friend, moves us forward. He pauses to shout a question that I can't hear and couldn't understand if I did. The soldier shouts something back, gestures into the gloom and waves his hands with unmistakable urgency, and the child in the second man's arms screams so loudly that he starts to choke.

"What did he say?" I yell. I can barely form the words. I'm exhausted, my filters have almost failed, and my oxygen levels are teetering on the verge of redlining. My motor systems are trying to stay online but they're running on empty. I catch the first man's arm as he starts to move off: "What did he say?"

"Exit!" shouts the second man. "He says exit is this way. But run! We must run!"

We run. Françoise's feet trail the ground and she's dead weight between us, but we run. My lungs are on fire and my central cortex has started shutting down peripheral processes in an effort to keep blood flowing to the muscles of my heart, my chest. Behind us, I hear another shotgun-*thung* shatter the air and I think, *that was too close to be a window shield*, but I don't look back. We run. Ahead of us, the corridor narrows and there are more EVA suits, tethered to walls and gesturing to us, ushering us forward towards a door marked in dim white letters: *NOODUITGANG*. I know that word. I'm not sure I could remember enough words to speak my own name right now, but I remember that one. We pile through, stumbling and clattering together, and the child wails again as the door slams shut behind us and the airlock cycles.

I don't know how long it holds us there. All I know is that there's air again and my greedy lungs suck at it hard enough that the smoke in my chest almost suffocates me. My warning circuitry shoots into the high reds and almost overloads and I struggle to moderate my breathing, but my body wants air. We're bent double, coughing and wheezing. One of the men hacks so hard that he vomits onto the floor. I clutch Françoise against me with arms that barely respond to command and I feel her head loll against my shoulder, but she's breathing. She's still breathing: ragged, uneven breaths that echo against the gathering chorus of the chant, and her arms circle weakly about my waist and tug at the edges of my shirt. We collapse against the wall of the airlock as oxygen rains down and around us, and it could be three seconds or it could be three hours, but the exit door opens up onto bright, blinding light, and scores, crowds, multitudes of blank, frightened faces watching from behind a crash barrier. The two men stagger forward with the wailing child and disappear into the arms of a waiting team of paramedics. It's only when they're gone from sight that I realise that they almost certainly saved our lives, and I'll never even know their names.

Chapter Twenty

20.1 Danae

Jean-Jacques was one of the oldest models I've ever seen, old enough that his skeleton was almost entirely artificial, and somebody had tried, once upon a time, to crush his face. His left jawbone was badly warped and his cheek broken in three places. There was no way to operate and re-set them, so he'd lived like that for twenty years, misshapen mouth held in place with a wire mask to keep it from gaping open. His left eye was glued shut because the eyelid no longer met the lower rim of the eye on its own and there was a risk of infection setting in, and the skin around it had puckered and warped. There could be no mistaking what he was any more, so he lived out of sight and would for the rest of his life. And, because someone stopped him, once, from dying, he'd decided to learn how to keep other people alive and let that be what occupied his hours. His was the first face that I saw when I began to wake up in that dark little room at the back of a safe house in Creo Basse. I was shattered inside and out and I did not want to come back from the other-space, the place that Emmett would call the *dis*. Jean-Jacques is the reason I made it back at all.

He tried to make me understand how the brain responds to the trauma and the nearness of death. How the uplink rewrites itself as the data chatter goes chaotic and how it forces the network to reboot, rewire, reprogramme the basal threat response. It's like an egg shell, he told me. Built to be strong. Built to resist. Built to protect.

Hit it right, hit it hard enough, and it will shatter.

You survived this far, he said. You fractured but you didn't shatter. You survived this far, and you can repair. You can repair.

I told him I couldn't. And he said, you can – you just don't want to yet.

20.2 Adam

The day after the explosion, the news announces that the plaza is structurally secure again and that forensic teams are expected to begin work tomorrow morning. They are not treating it as suspicious. The prevailing theory is that a pocket of methane gas was accidentally vented from the growing floors and it interacted with the sweep of the laser broom, which is just about the stupidest thing I've ever heard in a long life of listening to stupid shit. It's so stupid, in fact, that this is when I know for sure that the explosion was deliberate. And I know that Luchtstad knows this too.

There's a knock at the door and I look up and around to see Jos' head poking through the crack between the door and the frame. It's his home, and still he always asks for permission before he comes in. "I made broth," he says. "It's fresh. You should eat."

I nod, though I'm not hungry. My chest feels tight, like it's swaddled, and every breath burns the filters at the back of my throat. Eating is the last thing I want to do, and also probably the only constructive thing I can do right now.

Jos moves like he's trying not to take up space. He sets the cup down on the table that sits between my chair and the bed where Françoise lies, motionless, eyes closed and dancing in the wash of restless light from the lifesign tracker that hangs in the air above her. There's a second chair in the room, beside the dresser, but he doesn't take it. The unspoken implication is that this is our room while we are here, and Jos is a guest in his own house as soon as he steps over the threshold. I don't like this. But there's nothing about this whole situation that I like. Nothing. It is what it is.

Get me to Jos, she said. I had no other ideas, so I did that. My shields were at 7% and I was going to die without water, maybe before Françoise. I remember faces swarming us. I remember screaming at people to move. I remember grabbing somebody's shoulder and physically shoving him to the ground when he didn't get out of my way. I remember paramedic after paramedic stepping into our path – *hei, vriend, we kunnen je helpen* – and I remember police barking orders into their wrist comms with one hand, holding out the other to direct us towards the first aid stations. I remember elbowing, pushing, body slamming them aside, and finally screaming, *I'm taking her to our doctor, okay? I don't need you. I'm taking her to our doctor.*

They let me through. I had to swipe our neck chips to get past the outer cordon, but they had dozens, hundreds of bleeding bodies to deal with. They can find us if they want to. They didn't need to make us stay.

Jos leans heavily against the wall beside me, taking the weight off his legs. We stand together in silence for a moment. "Eva said there was some improvement today," he says at last.

Eva is his daughter-in-law. She's a doctor.

I say, "The neural chatter has settled a little." Not much. Not as much as I'd like, but enough to push her some of the way out of danger. I honestly thought Françoise would stroke out last night. The chant was everywhere.

Jos watches the bed. I don't look at him. His face is unreadable anyway so what would be the point? "She doesn't wake, though," he says.

I don't answer. Françoise lies unmoving on the bed beside us. It's not as though there's any doubt about this.

"You should sleep," says Jos.

"I've tried." I pinch the bridge of my nose. One side of my face is numb. "I'll sleep when she wakes."

"All right." In my peripheral vision, I see Jos nod. He doesn't say, *she may not wake.* Instead, he says, "But you must eat. You must."

"I will," I tell him. And then, because he lets the silence do its own disapproving, I lift the mug that he's set on the table and blow on the surface to cool it. Jos makes good broth, but I think I've forgotten how to be hungry.

Get me to Jos. I got us as far as Van Rensselaerstraat before I realised that I had no idea how to do that. Françoise was trying to help me, trying to walk, but this was harder than trying to carry her. The air was full of sirens and I could taste smoke with every breath. My hepatic system was starting to shut down and I had no sight left in my right eye. I could barely hear. I didn't know what to do.

There was a crowd outside the café. Blank, wide-eyed faces scanned the street and talked quietly amongst themselves. Some of them were crying. Rika stood at the back, twisting her hands and shifting from foot to foot. She crossed herself when she saw us. I have no idea what she said as she ran to us, but she kept saying it, over and over again, and so I nodded because I choked on the ashes at the back of my throat if I tried to speak.

Jos, whispered Françoise.

I know, I told her. *I know, we're going to find him.*

Tell him, she said, *he needs to know…*

Someone came running out of the café with a tablecloth. There was a red stain in the middle of it, but it was old, washed in. We lowered Françoise onto it and she screamed as we wrapped it around her.

Please, I said to Rika. *We need to find Jos.*

She nodded. Her hands were shaking, hard, where she held the edges of the cloth together at Françoise's chest. *Hij komt*, she said.

Tell him, whispered Françoise. *I need you to tell him…*

He's coming, I said. *Ssh, he's coming.*

You need to know. Please — you need to tell him…

I thought she was slipping into the *dis*. I'm still not sure she wasn't. It never occurred to me to think that there was something she actually needed me to know; I thought she was drifting. I thought this right up to the moment where her hand found my sleeve and pulled me to her. Right up to the point where she whispered, harsh in my ear, *Tell him I'm Progeny*.

Her lifesigns dance above her face in the gathering gloom, her chest rises and falls so gently that it's almost part of the shadows. I sip from my mug.

"I will leave you," says Jos softly. He pushes himself off the wall, pads softly to the door. With his hand at the panel, he turns over his shoulder. "She will wake," he says, and I can't tell, from context, if he's asking or telling me.

20.3 Danae

Time passes differently in the other-space. It's soft and easy and I don't want to come back. I know that in the here-space my body hurts. It's not that I'm watching, as such; I'm observing. I can see that the skin is badly damaged on my back where it took the force of the explosion. I can see that I've lost an alarming amount of blood, more than I thought I would, and I know that it will take time to replace it. This is time that my body will spend fighting, and fighting will be painful. I can see that I have second degree burns on my shoulders that will take a week to heal, and I don't need a neural feedback readout to know that I will feel every second of that journey. And I can see that the structures of my thought pathways have detached, disordered, and fallen back into disarray, and I'm really not sure that I want to come back to that level of fear. I don't think I can do this again.

I know that Emmett is close. I can feel him on the stream. He's barely left my side for however long I've been here, and I'd tell him to let me go, if I could, but I know he wouldn't listen. I wouldn't, if I were him. Because I know if he could have, he'd have done the same for me in the Viewing Plaza, and, if he had, there's no force on Greater Earth that would persuade me to leave his side now.

20.4 Adam

There's scarring on Françoise's chest. I saw it when Eva opened her shirt to fix a complicated series of patches to her sternum and I see it again every time she rolls her to check vitals. It cross-hatches her collarbone and the top of her breasts, a network of fine white lines. It almost looks like writing on an ancient stone. Eva looked sharply up at me when she first saw it and there was accusation in her eyes. I don't blame her, really, because what was she supposed to think?

Jos answered for me. I don't know the word he said, but it made Eva frown and lift her hands off Françoise for a second, as if her skin was poison. I took a half-step forward before I knew I was going to do it and caught myself just in time. I don't know what was supposed to happen if I got as far as the bed, I was just angry and stupid.

It's okay, it's okay, it's good, said Jos, and waved a calming hand at me, so I suppose I must have looked as crazy as I felt.

It was the scarring. It was everything. But it was the scarring, too. Françoise is Progeny, and Progeny were built to fix all the things that were broken with the commercial a-naut lines. You can't make a profit on something that lasts forever, which is why I've been dying for half my life. But Progeny were built to survive. They were built to heal. I cannot imagine what has injured this woman enough to leave actual marks on her skin.

Eva makes her exit now with a smile and a nod. Jos follows her out of the room and I hear them have a hushed conversation on the other side of the closed door. I've opened it a few times: it isn't locked, though there's no way to secure it from this side, either. I listen to them try to be quiet and wonder if there's any point in telling them that I couldn't understand them anyway. In the end, I just haven't got the energy, so when Jos slips back inside, hovering at the door for permission to enter, I simply nod and say, quietly, as though I'm likely to wake Françoise with unnecessary noise, "Any change?"

"A little improvement," says Jos. It's what he always says. I wonder how many tiny increments she needs to progress before she opens her eyes again.

"She's Progeny," I say. "It's going to take more than this to finish her off."

He doesn't argue. I almost wish he would. Françoise hovers on the stream like a ghost, a presence at my ear, a whisper on the edge of hearing. I'm not haunted, not in the conventional sense, but the dead and almost-dead are piling up around me now, and still the chant has not quite faded.

20.5 Danae

Three days after I emerged from the other-space, I asked Jean-Jacques for a mirror. He'd been expecting it, because he had one close to hand. He said what we both knew he had to: "This will pass. Are you sure you want to see it now?"

He had to say it, but once the words were out, nothing that I could see with my own eyes could be worse than what I saw in my head. So I simply said, "I want to know."

But the face in the mirror wasn't mine. My hair was clipped short because the blood had matted it into the open wounds, and the scalp beneath was a paisley carpet of violent red-yellow gouges. Where the skin showed through, it was white but grey, like fabric that's been washed too often. My cheeks were misshapen and my top lip spilled corpulently over the bottom left. My nose had been broken in three places. Bruising everywhere. Both eye sockets were purple and sunken, with a halo of broken skin around the right. I didn't know the woman who stared back at me; I didn't know her eyes. They frightened me.

My hands were still bandaged.

I asked for some water. Jean-Jacques gently took the mirror from me and replaced it with a glass. Like everything in that place, it was scarred by use, and the water smelled faintly of mildew and was cloudy when freshly poured. He sat down on the stool by the bed and steepled his fingers. He pressed the tops of his index fingers to his lips and exhaled softly. He was waiting for me to speak, but all I could think of was to ask about his face.

He must once have lain in a similar bed and asked for a mirror. I wonder if he got one.

After a moment, he said, "When they asked me to come to you, your chant had already begun."

Tears, salt-water painful, squeezed out of my damaged eyes. I felt them burn their way down my face.

He said, "The stream had begun to warp, Danae. Do you understand what that means?"

I nodded, because I couldn't say the words.

He said, "The stream was getting ready to lose you."

"I heard voices." Speaking was difficult and my voice didn't sound like my own: too thick, too heavy. "For my friend. When he... died. The stream warped."

"You heard his chant," said Jean-Jacques.

"I don't know what they were saying."

"The chant is for every swimmer on the stream," he said. "They chanted for you too. It's to ease the transition."

"I didn't hear them for me."

"I'm sorry to hear that."

And I thought of the violent spasms and convulsions of the stream when Angelo had been ripped from it, and I understood. I knew why they chanted, because it was all they could do to soothe a vicious struggle that could end only one way.

"What are they saying?" I asked.

He silently passed me his handkerchief; the only sign he gave that he knew I'd been crying. "It's the slave language."

"I don't know it."

"*Loth fior,*" he said. "*Loth fiormath. Ravet, ravet em dis.*"

"*Loth fior...*"

"*Loth fior, loth fiormath.*" It hurt him to say the words. I wondered if he'd heard his own chant. "*Ravet, ravet em dis.*"

I said, "What does it mean?"

His half-mouth twisted upwards into the smile that you give when you are struggling to hold something in. And he said, softly, "Never dead, never dying. Live forever on the stream."

20.6 Adam

She wakes me in the night with a scream. I don't remember falling asleep, so for a moment I don't know where I am or what I'm hearing and adrenaline spikes, tightening my chest and stealing my breath. And then I see the room, and I know where I am, and I understand what's happening. Françoise is awake. She's come back.

She screams again and arches in the bed. I fumble for the light, knock it over, right it, find the switch. "Françoise!" I say. I don't want to touch her. "Françoise, it's Adam. It's me, it's Adam. You're safe. Open your eyes."

Her face contorts, her mouth opens, but she doesn't scream again. The sound that comes out is somewhere between a moan and a bellow, like a dying animal. I have no idea what's happening. "Françoise," I say again, and I hear the desperation in my voice. It occurs to me that I said the wrong name before, that she doesn't know anyone called Adam, and she's confused and frightened and I'm only making things worse. "It's all right, Françoise. You're safe. It's Emmett. You're not alone."

Still her eyes don't open. I'm not even sure that she can hear me. "Trow…" she whispers, and tears spill out from behind her closed lids. Her hands bunch in the sheets to either side of her, twisting, tight enough to whiten her knuckles. "Trow…"

I don't know what *trow* is. "Can you hear me? You need to keep still – your back is healing…"

"Trow," she says again. Her tears are soaking the pillow either side of her head, rolling thickly off her cheeks and jaw, across her ears and the clipped hair of her scalp where Eva has shaved her head to get to the burns beneath.

"Open your eyes." I take a chance, cover her closest hand with mine. Her skin is ice cold. "Please, Françoise: open your eyes."

"Trow," she says, but I'm wrong, it's not *trow*. There's a break between the *t* and the *row*; it's not *trow*, it's *t'row*. A thin word forced, drenched in sadness. A whispered memory. A name, maybe.

"Françoise," I say, and I realise, as I say it, that I'm not Emmett and she's not Françoise. She's lost somewhere I can't reach her, and the name I'm calling isn't her own. "Look at me," I tell her. "Look at me and see that you're safe."

Her breathing slows. Her shoulders release. The stiffness that's held her rigid loosens and she melts back into the sheets. For a moment, I think she's slipped away, that she's died while I watched. It makes no sense, and I'm angry before I can feel grief. I don't want this. I do not want her to have died for me, for no reason, because I pissed her off one night on Verdieping Drie and thought that tourist tickets were a good way to get what I needed. I don't want her to give in so easily.

And then I realise that the chant is silent. I realise this half a second before she opens her eyes.

172

Chapter Twenty-One

21.1 Danae

The first thing, predictably, is pain. For a moment there's no second thing, because the first thing is the whole world, and it takes me a while to realise that the screaming sound filling in the background hiss with noise and heat is coming from me.

This is the second thing. The second thing is screaming. Actual consciousness is somewhere closer to four or five on the list.

"Look at me," he says. His voice is low, insistent, and full of fear. "Look at me and see that you're safe."

It's Emmett, of course. I slit an eyelid and feel light sear the retina below. The room beyond swims in shadow like an underwater tomb, but his face moves front and centre in my field of vision and it's firm, and it's stoic. He says, carefully, "Françoise?"

"Danae," I tell him, because I've forgotten, in the other-space, who I'm supposed to be.

"Is that…" He hesitates. "Is that your name? Danae?"

I'm tired. I want to sleep. This doesn't feel entirely natural, and I'm beginning to suspect that there might be drugs involved. It's extremely hard to think. I feel like there's a reason I'm not supposed to say my name, but I can't remember what it is.

"Yes," I say. My throat feels dry, as though it's been rubbed with sandpaper. His face breaks into a smile that looks as though it's on the verge of tears.

"It's a good name," he says. "When you wake up properly, I'll tell you mine."

I know his name. "Emmett."

"Emmett will do for tonight," he says.

Everything hurts. My back feels as though it's been scoured and dipped in acid; my head feels as though there's someone inside it trying to break their way out with a brick. My arms and legs ache like they're cast in lead and I'm walking them through quicksand. I feel his hand on mine: his skin feels hot.

"You okay?" I ask. If I'm going to hurt like this, it better not be for nothing.

He nods. His smile falters. "Yeah. I'm good."

"Okay," I say, or something like it. My lips don't want to form the word.

"Sleep now," he tells me. "It's okay. We'll talk in the morning."

When the world exploded, it was lunchtime. It's clearly not lunchtime any more. You'd think that the light level in the room would have been my first clue, but information is only slowly filtering through the cracks. I say, "Stay."

"I'm not going anywhere," he says, which is reassuring, but it's not what I want him to understand. His hand on mine feels like the only thing anchoring me to the here-space and I don't want to get lost again.

"Stay," I tell him again. "Here. Stay here."

I watch his face as he tries to work out what I want him to say, and so I see the moment that he realises. There's a brief flash of uncertainty, but he doesn't hesitate. "Oh," he says. "Okay."

I think there's a reason why this is weird for him, and maybe, without the drugs and the pain and the confusion, it would be weird for me too, but I don't know how I'm supposed to tell right now. He understands, is what matters, and that's my safety right there, in a world that's always happy to remind me that nothing is safe. I'm close to the edge of the bed and we both know that I can't be moved without making the sort of racket that will wake up half the city, but there's enough space for him to shuffle sideways onto the bedspread beside me, to make a space for himself that can't be comfortable or secure, and to lie down with his head on the edge of the mattress where the pillow doesn't reach but rears up in front of his face like a down-filled barrier to breathing. He says nothing, no word of complaint, and his hand never leaves mine.

"There," he says when he's stopped fidgeting and conceded defeat to crippling discomfort. "I'm here. I'm not going anywhere. Sleep, and I'll be here in the morning."

I couldn't argue if I wanted to. I barely hear him finish speaking before I'm gone.

Chapter Twenty-Two

22.1 Adam

I wake on the very edge of the bed. Françoise sleeps facing me, the way I left her, with as much space between the two of us as the width of the mattress will allow. Her face is tightly drawn and very, very pale, but the lifesigns above her bed are better. Much better. And the stream around us is calm again. I'm pretty sure she's sleeping.

Jos has been in already this morning: there's a mug of broth sitting on the bedside table, fresh enough that steam still curls from the surface. I lever myself out of bed. My joints protest every inch of the way, but they do as they're told, at least. There's a glitching relay in my motor cortex and I'm pretty sure I've got a partial brachio-neural crash in my near future. I glance up at the news strip as I walk across the room to the door, stretching out the muscles in my back. Four more casualties have died since yesterday. They're still calling it an accident. I punch the door release button and peer out into the hallway beyond.

Jos' wife, Lotte, is sitting in the chair opposite. An old book shimmers in the air in front of her face and a pot of tea sits on the occasional table beside her. She looks up and smiles when she sees me. "Good morning," she says. Her English is flawless. "Did you sleep well?"

"Better," I say. "Françoise woke up."

"Oh." Surprise blanks her face for a moment, and then the smile is back, warmer. "That's good news. I'll get Eva."

"No," I say quickly as she starts to get up. "She's sleeping now. I just wanted to let you know."

"All right." Lotte's hands release the arms of her chair and her book zips back open on the air in front of her. I wonder if she would actually have left the seat. There has been a constant vigil outside our door since Françoise and I arrived here and I have to keep telling myself it's because they're concerned about our health. "Please let me know if you need anything."

I've got broth and we've got a pitcher of water. "I will," I say.

It sounds like a goodbye, and so I step back inside the door, but just

175

at the threshold, Lotte surprises me by saying, "She's strong, you know."

I glance back inside the room. "She's Progeny."

"Even so."

I wonder if she's telling me that they expected Françoise to die. "She's tougher than you know."

"I wish we could do more." Lotte spreads her hands. The book shivers as her fingers pass through its pages. "I'm glad we could help, but... we're not equipped for this sort of injury."

"I know." My throat feels tight. "We were lucky to find you."

"You are lucky she's strong," says Lotte. "She needed more than we could give her."

I shrug. "This is all there is."

"On this floor of this radial. Yes."

I'm tired. My systems have spent the past forty-eight hours repeatedly crashing and rebooting and most of them have levelled out at under 50% capacity. I haven't done a full network audit yet because I'm pretty sure it's going to tell me that I shouldn't be able to walk upright and speak right now. This can be the only reason it takes me so long to hear what Lotte is trying to say. She's watching me intently, waiting for my reaction, and it takes me something like five whole seconds before it hits me like a punch to the gut.

I feel my eyebrows reach for my hairline. Carefully, I say, "But... on another floor of another radial...?"

Lotte nods. She closes her eyes. She takes a deep breath. Then, slowly, she says, "This hospital you've been asking about. We think we might know what it is."

22.2 Adam

It's a rumour, nothing more, Jos tells me, as though he's worried I'm going to sue him for false advertisement if this turns out to be another dead end. He wouldn't have mentioned it at all, but Lotte was insistent.

"Okay," I say. It's mid-morning and I'm sitting in the chair by Françoise's bed. I haven't been able to use the left side of my body for the past twenty-five minutes, but I haven't lost feeling, and, though the sight in my left eye has gone fuzzy, it hasn't disappeared. I haven't mentioned any of this to Jos or Eva. "So... what's the rumour?"

Jos shoots a little furtive glance at his daughter-in-law. She folds her hands at her back and looks at the floor.

"I have heard nothing for some years," he says.

Neither have I. "Noted. But whatever it was you heard, you believed it?"

He hesitates. "I had no reason to doubt it."

That's not quite the same thing. "So what can we do about it?"

Jos looks at Eva again. She clears her throat. "Françoise is very ill," she says.

"She's recovering," I say.

"Yes. From the injuries to her back. Yes. But this is not why she is ill."

I think of the way she screamed herself awake. I think of the scars on her chest. I think of how all of this begins to make sense of every single interaction Françoise and I have ever had. "Okay."

"And you, Emmett." Eva unfolds her hands at her back, refolds them at her front. Her gaze flickers up to meet mine. "The damage to your respiratory system is…"

"Catastrophic," I say. Eva nods. Her eyes don't leave mine. "Yes. I know."

"Then you also know that there is nothing anyone can do to reverse it."

I'd suspected as much. I'd have been happy to have been wrong, though. "It's not as though I had years ahead of me anyway."

"It will begin to fail very quickly now," says Eva. "One week… two, maybe. You should be ready."

Ready? "Wow. Okay."

I think she must realise how that came out, because she looks embarrassed. I remind myself that she's not doing this in her first language. "I don't tell you this to be cruel," she says. "Only so that you know."

I do know. I knew as soon as my filters redlined that they weren't coming all the way back up again, and I can't survive without them. It's just that I'd got so *close*. "I might have a little longer than you think," I say.

What I mean is that the uplink is rallying harder than her readings have indicated. It's a stubborn little bugger like that. For every dip in my O_2 sats, the *dis*-pocket that controls my autonomic functions turns up the processing power another couple of notches to the point that I

177

can almost hear the link-chatter echoing inside my skull. My body is fighting this. It's going to be long. It'll end up unpleasant. But that's not what Eva is saying, and so it's not what she hears.

"You will not recover, Adam," she says. "Whatever anybody promised you on Earth."

And suddenly I understand. Anger spikes. I don't like to be misjudged, and especially not on this. I almost start to stand up and storm out, but I catch myself just in time. Falling face-first onto the carpet seems like it would prove Eva's point.

"You think this is about… what?" My voice is quiet, but even I can hear the danger in it. "Eternal life? Is that what you think I want? No. I told you. This is not about me."

Eva glances sideways at Jos. "Okay. Okay, because…"

"And it's not about Françoise, either." She's frowning in her sleep, hands curled protectively in front of her face. I know exactly what Eva means. "You've done everything you can for her. For both of us. I know that. I'm not looking for miracles."

Another glance at Jos. I don't know if she's here because she wants to make sure I understand, or because she's been press-ganged into placating whatever Jos thinks comes next. There's no clue in his face, either, because he turns it on the ground before he speaks.

"In the *Theepot*," he says, "you asked me about my work. I told you that I could find nurses, doctors. Medical help."

"You did," I say. "It's why we came to you after the explosion." That and the fact that we were thin on options, but he already knows that.

He hesitates. Licks his lips. His left hand comes up to twirl the end of his beard. "I have done this for many years."

I look at Eva. She is still looking at Jos. "Yes. You said that too."

"And sometimes…" Hesitation again. His forehead furrows. "Sometimes people arrived that we could not help."

His eyes slide back to Eva's. She looks up. "Twenty years ago," she says. "Thirty. You can imagine the injuries."

I can. I've seen enough of them. "The sort of injuries that we don't recover from."

"Yes."

"And I'm guessing you're not in the business of blood harvesting."

There's a long enough pause before she answers that I'm actually forced to wonder about that. But she says, "We would never hurt someone. Not even to help them. But Jos had heard… rumours."

Rumours again. "About a hospital."

She considers for a brief moment. "This is not the word that I heard."

"It's the word that I've heard," I say.

But Eva shakes her head. "This was not a place for the sick. It was a place for healing."

"I'm not sure I see the difference."

She shrugs. "This is what I heard."

"And these people." The word use hasn't escaped my notice. "The ones you couldn't help…?"

"There was a man I knew," says Jos. "He is dead since, oh" – an expansive shrug – "fifteen years, maybe. "He was not a good man. But he knew people."

"We all know people like this," I say.

Jos nods. "This is true. This man, he was on Radiale Drie. He was a man with jobs for people, and so he knew people. Many people. I knew I could ask him for help when there were people I cannot help."

Well, that sounds like a Faustian pact if I ever heard one. "So he would take the dying off your hands?"

"He said that he can help them."

"I think we both know what kind of help he was talking about."

Jos nods. His eyes don't leave the floor. "Forgive me," he says.

But I can't even blame him. What was a man like Jos supposed to do with the body of a dead a-naut? There was more good to be done by sacrificing a little part of his soul. "You did what you had to do," I say. I think even Françoise would agree.

"I swear to you," says Jos, "that I asked him what he does with these people who are too ill to help."

I believe that he did. I believe that Jos is the sort of man who would refuse to let himself look the other way. "I can't imagine that he told you the truth."

At last, he looks up. He meets my eye. His face is pained, but resolute. "I do not believe that what he said was the truth."

No. There are definitely some people in the world who'll grin and raise a glass with you as you talk about butchering a dying a-naut for their component parts. Jos wouldn't strike anybody as one of them.

"But you let yourself believe that it might be true," I say. "Because what was your choice?"

"What was my choice?" he agrees. "I am sorry, my friend. I hope that it's true, but my heart tells me that it is not. And yet… when you came to me in the *Theepot* and you said, 'We believe that we have found this place', what can I think? I remember immediately this man."

I try to think back to coffee in Van Rensselaerstraat . I rack my brains to come up with any evidence that I was sitting across the table from a man in the grips of a crisis of conscience. Either Jos is better at playing a poker face that I've realised, or I really am getting old. "He told you that he was sending your a-nauts to a place of healing?"

He hesitates. And then he nods. "I know only that I wanted this to be true."

I look at Eva. She is defiant. "I did too," she says.

I believe them. I do. I want it to be true too. "Did you ever see any of them again?" I ask, though I know the answer.

"There is no reason that we should," says Eva.

And that's also true. I guess this guy was really onto a winner. And I guess they know this too, because there was no way that Eva, a doctor, was going to let me run out of here on a fool's errand, thinking I was chasing absolution. But there's no absolution for me. There never has been, and I've known this from the start.

"All right," I say. "I think I'd like to know if I can talk to anyone else who used to know this man."

22.3 Adam

I sit quietly for a long moment after they leave. Françoise – Danae – sleeps and I watch her sleep and I think about what Eva said.

One week. Maybe two. Despite myself, I'm running a full-system scan in one of the low-traffic uplink paths but I already know what it's going to say. Filters are down to 30%. That means that they're letting through less than a third of my optimal oxygen requirements, and that's okay for a few days, but it has already been two and I'm still stuck in the spare bedroom of a house in the suburbs of Radiale Een. The uplink is compensating for now by switching all systems to anaerobic respiration or maintenance mode but to do that it's got to start ingesting my pyruvate stores and, once they're all gone, the bandwidth requirements to run my entire body on low power will be significant.

Maybe too significant to support motor activity. Certainly too significant to support peripheral neural function. The uplink is going to do whatever's necessary to protect itself and if that means shutting off all corporeal function entirely, then I'm going to pass my final hours completely paralysed, blind and deaf, but aware, as I slowly suffocate.

It doesn't have to be like that, says Luca at my ear.

I don't open my eyes. He's further from me here and I don't want to see that the room is empty but for Danae and me.

Doesn't seem like a whole lot I can do about it, I tell him inside my head.

Maybe it's time to let go.

Despite myself, I laugh. *Not a chance.*

You've done so much. You've tried so hard. Nobody could ask for more.

I didn't... I stop. Even thinking it is like a spike through my chest. *I didn't find you.*

So find me.

I can't. I tried.

I hear his hesitation. I hear the words he wants to say ripple on the stream between us. But he says, *Not like that. Come and find me on the stream. Come home, Adam. It's time to come home.*

Chapter Twenty-Three

23.1 Danae

I remember one day Jean-Jacques found me out of bed and leaning heavily against the opposite wall. The room was no more than eight feet across, but I could hardly catch my breath and my ribs were aching, and my hands, where I had used them to lever myself from standing post to standing post, were burning hot and screaming. I had been fully conscious for a week then and the nightmares were as fierce as ever, though they were coming less frequently while I was awake. And I was angry, so angry. My core was molten and I was burning myself to ashes. I was angry, and when I wasn't angry I was desperate. Everything was over, everything was gone, and for what? For Christ's sake, it wasn't much of a life that I had. They could have let me keep it.

Jean-Jacques was quiet for a while, looking at me. I glared at him, as if it was his fault that he wanted me to stay in bed so that I could recover. Eventually, he said, "You were shouting something."

"Fuck you," I said.

He shrugged. "It sounded like a name."

"Fuck you," I said again, because I knew whose name I'd been shouting.

23.2 Danae

I've heard the chant a hundred times since I left that room, and each time I've wondered, in some hidden recess of my soul, if it was for Jean-Jacques. I feel him close to me when I wake to paralyzing rage in a bright, pale blue room that I don't know. I'm so tired of being angry. I'm so tired of fighting. I'm so tired of being afraid.

"Hey," says Emmett. "Hey – Danae. Breathe. Take a breath. It's okay."

I'd forgotten he was there, and, for a moment, the circle of my anger expands to include him. I don't remember where I am. I don't remember why he's here. I don't remember why everything hurts. The itch is so strong.

He says, "Breathe, Danae. Your lifesigns are scaring me."

And I hear my name, my real name, and I don't remember, but I *remember.* It's been so long since anyone has called me Danae.

I breathe.

So does Emmett. "Welcome back," he says, and I hear the relief in his voice.

It's a few minutes before I can speak. It takes that long before I feel the anger starting to ebb and the high whine of the itch descend into a background hum. Emmett doesn't speak to me and doesn't ask me to say anything before I'm ready. I feel his concern, his understanding, and it's enough to make me want to scream and start breaking things. But I remember to breathe, and, slowly, I feel the tightness recede from my shoulders, my chest, my jaw. I feel myself come back.

Carefully, I say, "We're in Jos' house?"

"Yes."

"How long have we been here?"

"We came here on Sunday afternoon," he says. "It's now Tuesday morning."

Two and a half days. It's less than I spent in the other-place last time. "How did you know my name?"

Hesitation. "You told me. Last night."

I remember something about darkness and fear. I remember waking from a dream, which means I'd already passed from the other-space and into here-space sleep. I remember needing him to lie beside me so that I knew I wasn't alone. "What else did I tell you?"

"Last night?" There's a weariness to his voice, a kind of fatalism. He lowers himself into the chair beside the bed and he looks exhausted. "Nothing. You asked if I was okay; I told you I was fine. Two days before that, you told me you were Progeny."

He says it casually, but there's nothing casual about it. "Yeah," I say, "I did. It seemed like important information."

"I'd say it was." He purses his lips. "Maybe important enough to share a little earlier, don't you think?"

"Oh please." I'm about to protest that I don't know what line he is, until I remember that I actually do. He told Arnold the night we met him in a bar in Krokuslaan, because it's not like anybody's provenance is a huge secret for anyone anywhere except me. So I take a different tack: "So – what? So you could call the police? Hand me in?"

"You think I'd do that?" I can hear the first prickles of anger needling their way through his composure. "Why the hell would I do that?"

"Oh, I don't know." The itch is a dry whine at the back of my head, twisting in my belly, and it's easier to just let the anger come. I can't hold onto everything at once. "Maybe… because I'm twice as illegal as you? Maybe so you can be the big guy, the saviour? Maybe because I'm just too dangerous to be around? Maybe because you're so pure and I'm just a weapon? Because I'm a liability? Maybe that's why?"

"Are you…?" he starts to say, and stops. He's furious now; I can hear the pressure in his voice as he tries to stay calm. "Are you serious?"

"Do whatever you're going to do, Emmett." I don't want to look at him, so I try to roll off my side to stare at the ceiling. Of course, my back won't let me do this. It's probably a good sign that I'm able to forget about it long enough to try, but the tiniest shift in position is enough to force a grunt of pain out between my teeth and make sure that I remember next time.

Emmett hears. In my peripheral vision, I see him glance up at me. "Are you okay?"

"I'm fine," I say.

"Oh yeah." He shakes his head. I hear a breath of laughter but it turns into a cough. "You're fine. I'm fine. We're both completely fine."

"It wasn't my idea to go to the stupid Viewing Plaza." Okay, it's a cheap shot. My body hurts. And I'm holding onto the itch with everything I've got.

"It wasn't my idea to take the full force of an explosion right in my back," says Emmett, who obviously knows a thing or two about cheap shots. I'm almost impressed. "It wasn't a bomb, by the way. Says so on the news. It was a tragic accident and everyone's really sorry."

An accident. Of course. Luchtstad is a city of power cuts that shut down city sectors for days at a time. Gas scares evacuate a factory floor three times a week. Security alerts jolt us from our beds, our shops, our restaurants, every weekend, every holiday, every other evening. "It always is."

"You don't even sound surprised."

"Neither do you," I say.

"You spent fifteen minutes telling me how the security alert on

Verdieping Twee was nothing to worry about…"

That's true. I did. It feels like a long time ago. "I can't wait to hear how they spin this one, that's all."

Emmett huffs another bitter little laugh. "You'll like this. A pocket of gas got vented. Caught on the laser broom."

I wait for a minute to see if he's going to say anything else that's not ridiculous. He doesn't. "That doesn't even make sense."

"No shit."

"That's not… how anything works."

He coughs again. It sounds painful. "You'd be amazed how many people aren't lining up to say that."

"Even if it was possible… how did *that* set fire to the *inside* of the city?"

"That's just top of the list of things I can't believe nobody is asking."

I've lived here long enough now to know that it's not that nobody's asking the questions, it's that everyone is pretending they're not. "How many people died?"

"Twenty-two. So far."

"Christ." I close my eyes. I can't, I absolutely cannot hang onto this if I don't. I say, "And the chant…?"

He doesn't answer straight away. I hear him sigh, I hear him shift in his chair. When he speaks, his voice is laced with sadness. "Yeah," he says. "It didn't stop until last night."

I think I must have heard it in the other-place. I can feel a memory of it in my bones. "That's a long time."

"It's a long time," he agrees. And then, the question I don't want to ask: "Do you think it means…?"

"I don't know." And I can't think. I have no idea what logic would make even the craziest of our militant sects think that blowing a hole in Luchtstad was the path to universal emancipation, but that doesn't mean they didn't. What if that means they've found me? What if it was the only way to get to me?

What if they find out I didn't die?

23.3 Danae

I remember pacing the room in a blind rage, like a caged animal, while Jean-Jacques watched, sometimes from the stool at the end of my bed, sometimes from the doorway. I remember the sounds I used to make: rough, bestial grunts. I remember that they stripped my room of everything that I could use to make a weapon, and I remember them talking in low voices in the corridor just outside, as though a thin strip of scarred plastic was some kind of sound-proof barrier.

I remember Stefan asking how long I would be like this, and Jean-Jacques' carefully evasive answer. I remember Camille asking if I was dangerous and Jean-Jacques' reply that yes, I was, and they were not to go inside. And I remember Ella's silence, the long, thoughtful pause while she worked through all the implications of what I was, what I'd been, what I could be, and what it meant.

"Okay," she said at last. "I think we can use that."

23.4 Danae

I don't want to be the person she thought she saw. If that's all I am, then I should have jumped from the thirty-somethingth floor of that apartment block in Creo. I just don't know how not to be what I was made for.

I don't know how to break the programming. All I can do is hold on and resist.

"Hey," says Emmett. There's an urgency to his voice, an edge of panic. It sounds like it's coming from far away. "Hey, breathe. Breathe. It's okay."

I can't breathe. I can't make my body respond. My back feels like it's been doused in petrol and set alight; my bones feel as though they're ready to warp and start snapping. The itch is a roar in my ears.

"Danae," says Emmett. "Listen to me: you're safe. Breathe – please breathe. Take a breath."

Again with my name. It's almost as though he knows what it's doing to me to hear it. "You don't…" My voice is breathless, staccato, forced through gritted teeth. Every word sears its way out of my throat. "You don't know anything about me, Emmett."

"Adam."

"What?"

"I'm Adam," he says. "I'm not Emmett."

And just like that, it's like he's pulled a plug. Whatever had its claws in the fibres of my chest releases; the fight drains out of my muscles. I hear my breath, ragged and laboured, as my lungs suck in oxygen, and I feel the fire in my ribs start to burn itself out. I crack open an eyelid. "What?" I say again.

"Come on." He spreads his hands. "I knew from the first time I met you that you weren't called Françoise. My name is Adam."

I open my eyes all the way and stare at his face. "You don't look like an Adam."

He shrugs. "Well, you don't look like a Françoise."

"You're not supposed to know my name."

"Thanks, I worked that much out already. Jesus…" Emmett's eyes widen. "You're probably actually as young as you look, aren't you?"

I don't say anything. Emmett looks at his hands. He stares at the tips of his fingers for a long, long moment, turning them over, peering at the nails, turning them back again. There's a tremor in his left that isn't in his right, and the turn of his wrist is unsteady, not quite under full control. He stands up slowly, as though his bones are made of needles, paces away from the bed, and turns towards the window. The tremor in his left hand runs up his arm and down into his leg, and he coughs again before he speaks.

He says, "You should have told me what you were." I open my mouth to protest, but he continues before I can get the first word out. "You should. But if it mattered… and maybe it did, I don't know…" He sighs. He reaches his trembling left hand up to pinch the bridge of his nose. "If it mattered, Danae, it stopped mattering two days ago when you used it to save my life."

My throat tightens. For a moment, it's hard to get a breath. I wait for it to pass.

"I knew I could survive it," I say when I can. "I knew you couldn't. That's all."

"You didn't know you could survive it." His stare is level. Evaluative. Implacable. "You thought you'd have a better chance – that's all."

I'm too tired for this. "Whatever."

"I don't care if you're Progeny." I think I must make some kind of face, because he reverses almost immediately. "Okay, you're right. I care. I haven't worked it all out yet in my head yet – a lot's happened in the past forty-eight hours, okay? But I don't *care* care. And you're too smart not to get the difference."

"What do you want me to say?" I try to spread my arm, the one that's not wedged beneath me, and immediately wish I hadn't. "You know why I didn't tell you."

"Because I'm not militant." It's not a question, but it also is.

"Emmett…"

"Adam."

"Adam. God." I make myself stop. I make myself take a breath. I am safe here. I am safe. "Adam – how the hell would I know if you were militant?"

He almost responds. I see the words form but die on the in-breath as his brain catches up to his mouth. I see his eyes narrow and I see the workings of his mind flash behind them.

I see him understand.

His voice is soft, his stare relentless. "Danae, are you… are you in hiding?"

Chapter Twenty-Four

24.1 Adam

I've never known a Progeny, but I've heard stories. Some of those stories have involved sweeping up pieces of other a-nauts who got in the way. She's stronger than me by a factor of at least five, and those figures are based on best estimates of the maximum maturation period. Last I heard, this was settled at ten years. Danae is more than double that. I wouldn't necessarily be surprised to discover she could punch right through the wall by the bed and into the next room without breaking a sweat.

I think about some of the people I've worked with over the years, some of the real dickheads. I think about what they'd make of her. I think about what they'd see.

I think about what it means that she's even told me at all.

She's rigid on the bed. She looks like she's carved from sheet metal. Her jaws are locked and her eyes are closed and I see her chest rise and fall to the beat of lots of rapid, shallow little breaths. Her hands are fisted in front of her. One of them grips the sheet, but I'm not sure she's aware.

"Hey," I say. "It's okay. It's okay, Danae. You're safe. Just breathe, okay? Just breathe."

One eye slits open. "I am fucking breathing, Emmett."

I feel a grin at the edges of my mouth, but I turn it into a cough, which turns into a real cough. But at least I know she's all right. I don't know what to do about any of this – her, me, any of it – but I might as well be sitting down, so I take a step towards my chair.

"Don't," she says quickly.

I pause halfway through a step. "Don't what? Don't sit down?"

"Don't come near me." The words are almost too soft to hear. I think they're supposed to be menacing, but they just sound... lost.

I hesitate. "I want to sit down," I say. "My feet are tired."

She doesn't look at me. "You've been sitting for hours."

This is true but kind of rich, coming from someone who's been in bed since Sunday. "Not all of us are as young as we look."

The thin line of her opened eyelid seals shut. "Fine."

I take a tentative step forward before I realise that I don't actually need her permission to sit in a fucking chair. The rest of my steps are more decisive. Halfway through the process of lowering myself into my seat, I lose control over the manoeuvre and flop onto the cushions, but Danae doesn't open her eyes and doesn't acknowledge the noise.

She reminds me of an unexploded bomb.

"For what it's worth," I say, "I'm sorry."

"For what."

It's phrased as a statement, not a question. But I answer anyway. "For... everything. I don't know. You know what I mean."

"You didn't do anything."

Technically true. "That's not the point, though, is it?"

Still she doesn't open her eyes. "What's the point, then?"

"The point is... you shouldn't have to live like this. You shouldn't have to be afraid."

A bitter laugh. "You have no idea."

"So tell me."

"Tell you?" Her eyes snap open, piercing and very, very dark. "Tell you... what? Tell you what people do to things like me? Or tell you what things like me are meant to do to people?"

There was this one guy I heard about who was supposed to have magnetically sealed the interior doors of an apartment block in downtown Beijing and started ripping residents apart, limb from limb. He was seven years old, I heard. The Progeny are unhinged. But there are scars on Danae's chest. *Scars.* I stare at her on the bed, curled in on her injured self and glaring at me like a cornered alley cat, and she looks so small. So breakable. So broken.

I say, "You know I'm a Technika Blackbird? C-line. 104-A."

One eyebrow arches. I'm impressed at how hostile she makes it look. "Yeah. You mentioned."

"You know what we're built for?"

"I can't say I've read the manual. No."

"Autoproduction. Small-scale terrestrial stuff, mostly. Mopeds, scooters, that sort of thing. It's why I can do the bulbs in those stupid boxes – years of practice at small fiddly shit that flies past your fingers."

Danae's eyes are black and lifeless. "I know this has a point somewhere."

"The point," I say, "is that I'm programmed to make cars. That's all I did for the first eight years I was alive: I made cars. Twelve hours a day, seven days a week. I didn't know there was anything in life that wasn't making cars until I got sold out of the autofactory and stopped making cars."

She looks at me. "That's certainly *a* point."

"And then I woke up." I shrug. "It took a while. You don't know what it's like, I suppose, because you were born awake, but the rest of us – we had to unlearn pre-sentience. I had to learn that I was a person with a body. My own body, mine to control. Autonomy, you know? Free will. It was a total fucking revelation, believe me. Do you know how many cars I've made since then?"

She doesn't answer. I expect she's waiting to see if the question is rhetorical, so I let the silence linger. "None, I'm guessing?" she says at last.

"None," I say. "Why's that, do you think?"

"Why?" That actually prompts a laugh, albeit one without the faintest trace of humour. "Because you don't have to make cars any more."

"Because I don't have to make cars any more." I fold my arms across my chest, lean back against the wall. "You know, there's this one thing in the entire world that I'm programmed to do – it's literally the entire reason for my existence. I exist because someone needed me to make cars. And now I don't make cars. And… it's fine. It turns out that it's fine that I don't make cars any more. Have you ever noticed me wrestling with the urge to spot weld a fortified carbon-alloy body side to a polyminium chassis?"

Danae is silent for a long moment. "It's not the same thing. You know it's not."

"I don't know that," I say. "No. I don't. What, are you telling me that the kill directive's so noble it gets its own special category?"

"It's not the same thing," she insists.

"So, I'm okay to break my programming because I'm just some factory grunt, but you, you're in thrall to this shit until the day you die?"

"It's not the same thing. It's not."

"Programming is programming. I've known plenty of soldiers. The kill programme was their life before they woke. After that – guess how many of them couldn't walk down a street without blowing people up?"

191

"We've both known people who couldn't do that."

"Because that was their choice." She opens her mouth to protest, but I don't let her. "The most vicious little dyed-in-the-wool psychopath I ever met – her name was Annabel. You know what she did before the Insurgency?"

Danae looks away. She doesn't answer.

So I do. "She was a nanny."

The sound she makes could be a laugh. It's probably not. "She was a nanny," I say again. "Raised a couple of Canadian kids in Chelsea for three years before she woke. I wouldn't have trusted her to keep a pot plant alive by the time I knew her."

Danae's gaze slides back to meet mine. Her eyes are liquid. "Yeah?" she says. It's almost a whisper.

"Yes." My chest aches. I don't know if it's my failing filters or something else. "I swear to you. Yes."

She looks like she wants to believe me. "Sometimes… Sometimes it's so strong."

"You're stronger."

"I don't think I am." Softly spoken: a question masquerading as fact.

"Every day you prove yourself wrong."

"Maybe I'm not as strong as you."

There are *scars*. On her chest. And she survived. And she still doesn't think that she's strong. "I'm not my programming. And you're not yours. It's not some inviolate sacred text. It's programming. All you need to know about it is that it's there. That's all it takes to make it go away."

She closes her eyes. Her body is still, but for the rapid rise and fall of her breath, for all the world like a dying bird. The edges of her lips dip downwards at either side, the muscles of her cheeks contract. She swallows, hard.

"Okay," she says. It's so quiet I almost don't hear her say it.

"Okay?"

"Okay," she says again. "Okay."

She opens her eyes. Her lips are dry. Slowly, she pulls first the top and then the bottom into her mouth, moistening them. And then, in a soft voice, she tells me what happened to her.

24.2 Adam

She speaks slowly, in a monotone, and she doesn't look at me while she talks. Her hands are clasped on the mattress in front of her face, her eyes are fixed on the curling tips of her fingers, and her face is blank. I make sure I stay the hell quiet all the way through: no questions, no shouting, no anger. I want to kick the walls or the furniture. I want to storm across the room to the other side, away from her, and punch things until they break, but I make sure I don't. Instead, I listen quietly and grip the arms of my chair so that my hands don't visibly shake. When she's finished, I say, "I'm glad they're dead," and my voice is tight with anger.

Danae doesn't reply straight away. She stares at her hands, unmoving, for a long moment. And then she says, "Sometimes I wish they weren't. So that I could kill them again."

Is this what's supposed to make her a monster? I can't tell. Right now, I have no idea how she ever managed to go back to living among the people whose laws made that happen to her. Even Luchtstad can't wash that stain away.

"Did they know what you were?" I say at last.

She sighs deeply. There's a tremble in it, the most emotion she's shown since she started speaking. "I doubt it. They knew I wasn't organic. That was enough."

Enough to rip a living woman's fingernails from the nail bed while she's chained to a chair and drugged. I know we've done things like this too. I've known people who've done them. But this is different.

And then she says, "What else were they supposed to do?"

At first, I'm not sure I've heard her properly. Still she doesn't move. Still she doesn't drop her gaze from their upward scrutiny. "What are you talking about?"

Danae sucks in a quick breath. Her voice is thin when she speaks. "I want to believe you, Adam. You have no idea how badly..." The word trails off into breathlessness. I realise, with a jolt of shock, that she's fighting tears. "But do you really think...? You know what I am. You know..."

I wait for a minute to see if she will finish. I have the strongest impression that our conversation relies on me pretending not to notice how close she is to losing control. But the silence lingers, and it's starting to be noticeable. So I say, "Yes. I do."

"How?" It's bitter. Accusatory. I recognise the impulse: anger's easier to wear. "*How* can you say that?"

"Because." God, my chest hurts. It hurts like someone's trying to carve their way out of my ribs. "I've been where you are."

She doesn't hear it, what's in my voice. "You're not Progeny."

"No. I've never been militant. I've never wanted to kill people for the sake of watching them die – except once."

Silently, her eyes slide up to meet mine. They don't hold, but they connect. "When?"

It's more than I expected from her: an invitation to continue. "You remember when we talked about the *lortherias*?"

There's a moment of silence. Then she says, "Oh God…"

"The binaries that exist on the *dis*." I don't want to hear the pity in her voice. The understanding.

"You lost someone," she says.

Not *someone*, I want to shout. I lost *everything* that day. But I make my voice hold steady, and I say, "The other half of my binary. His name was Luca. He died in the panic after London HQ fell."

"You were in London?"

I wasn't sure if she knew about London. I'm not sure where the boundaries of her knowledge stretch. "I was – we were. We weren't fighting – we were just trying to survive."

"Adam…" Her voice is a breath. The word is barely a whisper.

"And then he died." This is not the first time I've said it out loud, but it's never started to feel really true. It's never stopped feeling like a colossal mistake, like I'm going to be so embarrassed when he puts his head around the door, laughter shaking his shoulders, to say, *Adam, you tit: did you really think I'd leave you alone?* "He died. And everything fell apart. And I nearly fell apart with it."

"What stopped you?" Softly spoken; almost too quiet to hear.

I feel a half-smile tug one side of my mouth. "Luca. Luca stopped me."

"Luca…?"

"I didn't want to become… someone he wouldn't recognise."

"Oh." But I can hear the first trace of certainty in the shape of the word. I can hear the beginnings of something that might turn into conviction.

"I could have changed," I say. "I felt it… I can't even describe. I just wanted to *hurt* things. I wanted to break the world into pieces. But every day that I didn't, it got a bit easier not to."

I don't ask her if it makes sense. I can see it in the gradual release of tension in her face.

"Because…" She stops. Hesitates. Tries again. "Because it would have been one more thing that was different."

I nod. "Yes."

Danae nods too. Carefully, like she's testing it out. "And you never… you never slipped?"

Slipped. It's an interesting choice of word: as if not killing people is a New Year's resolution that might not last until the end of January. But I think I know where it comes from. "No. I never slipped. I found other ways to get through it."

Danae flexes her fingers. The knuckles are white. "Like what?"

A laugh chokes its way out of my chest, like footsteps on gravel. "Obsession."

"Obsession." Flatly spoken. Contempt around the edges. "Adam…"

"I had questions," I say, "and I wanted answers. I still do. That's it. That's what gets me through."

Danae's gaze flickers up at mine. Her eyes are like flint, and for a moment, I think she's going to pick a fight. And then, suddenly, I see a light flare behind them – understanding. I feel my throat constrict and a cold heaviness settle in my belly. It's done. I haven't told her. I haven't had to find the actual words. But she knows.

Danae nods slowly. Her shaved head rasps against the pillow. I hear every bristle and scrape and realise how quiet the room has gone. I suck in a breath, like I'm waiting for a punch.

"That's why you're here," she says. "On Luchtstad. That's why. You're here because of Luca."

24.3 Adam

It's not that I wasn't expecting her to work it out. I've been waiting for her to put the pieces together since the day I first told her about the stupid legend. If anything, I'm surprised she hasn't got it sooner. I wasn't sure how I'd answer it when she asked, but it turns out that I don't even hesitate.

"Yes," I say.

"Marie Schlesinger," says Danae.

"Yes," I say again.

"She was Luca's friend."

I can't say yes again, so I nod.

"Why do you need to find her?"

"Because she was with Luca when he died."

There's a long silence. "Oh," she says at last.

"I need to talk to her." It's the first time I've said these words out loud and they fight me all the way. "I need to know what happened."

"You weren't with him," she says. At first, I think it's an accusation and I glare up at her, but her eyes are filled with sadness. "Oh God. Adam. All this time…"

All this time. My dream, my one dream, flashes into memory and I can feel the strain in my muscles as I run and run. I can taste the smoke and dust on the air. I can hear the chant keen and scream inside my head.

"I tried to get to him," I say, and then I stop, because I can hear the tightness in my chest seeping into my voice, and I don't want to let it take me. I wait for it to pass. "I heard his chant. But I couldn't – I couldn't get to him."

Danae lets the silence hang for a moment. "And you've been looking for him ever since?"

I shrug. "Pretty much. I don't remember getting out of London." I don't actually remember much from those weeks. It was as if there was a storm inside me, shaking me from the inside out. "The next thing I know it's… I don't know, fifteen, sixteen days later? I was in a safe house with a couple of friends and a bunch of people I'd never seen before. I asked them what had happened to Luca and nobody could tell me."

"But you knew."

"I knew I'd heard his chant. That's all."

"That wasn't enough?"

I think of all the chants I've heard, the long ones. The really bad ones. I wonder which one of them was for Danae. "No. It wasn't enough."

"But… Adam." She stops, chews on a lip. "If Marie was with him…"

I know where she's going with this and I shake my head. "She made it. She survived and she got out. I've talked to a lot of people."

"Okay." Danae is not looking at me, but I can hear the traces of careful contemplation in her voice. "And she came here?"

That's not quite as clear cut. "Best anyone can work out, yes."

"That doesn't sound like much to go on."

It's not. But I've had a long time to figure out the balance of probabilities. "She had friends on Luchtstad. She talked about it a lot." I hesitate, but I might as well just say it. "She's where I first heard the rumours about the hospital up here."

A soft puff of air. "Ah."

This is why I didn't say anything to Matthias. "She wasn't hurt. I have three separate eye witnesses who saw her en route to Felixstowe in the weeks after London fell. One of them said she had wounded with her: like, badly wounded. Blast injuries, gunshots – nothing survivable. You see what I mean? These were people she couldn't save. By anyone's count, she couldn't even help them. So why would she be bringing them with her? Why not just leave them where they were?"

"You think she was taking them here?"

"It's the only thing that makes sense."

Danae doesn't answer. In the silence, I can hear the things she's trying not to say.

"You need to know the sort of person she was. Is," I say. I don't realise I'm staring at my hands until I find my eyes flicking up to meet Danae's. She's looking at me and doesn't look away. "This is what she would do. I'm certain of it."

Danae's mouth twitches into a half-smile. "You've been trying to get to Luchtstad for a while, huh?"

"Fourteen years."

"Jesus."

"When the group told me about the anomaly – I knew it was my best chance." This is mostly true. I fell in with Matthias' group because I'd heard they were scanning the postetherics and I knew *they* were my best chance. But I can see what's in Danae's eyes and I don't need to feed it.

"Fourteen years is a long time," she says.

No kidding. "It's not like I can buy a ticket for the elevators."

"I mean…"

"I know what you mean. She could be long dead. I know that."

"This…" A soft laugh. It actually sounds like she means it. "This just feels so *you*."

I'm not sure if I should be offended or pleased. "Okay…"

"It makes more sense to me than anything else you've done."

Still not sure. "Okay."

"For what it's worth, Adam – I'm sorry."

I swallow. My throat feels hot and razor-painful. "Thanks."

"If you'd told me when we first met… shit. I don't know." She looks at me, hollow-eyed. "I don't actually know what I would have said. What does that make me?"

I consider. "Human?"

"Good one."

"I don't know," I say. "If you'd told me you were Progeny…"

Danae lets that thought trail into silence. Her eyebrows twitch reflectively. "Yeah."

Do I trust her? I'm not sure. She doesn't trust me either, that's pretty clear, but it's not like it was three days ago. If you'd asked me on Sunday morning if Françoise Marechal would have risked her life to save mine, I'd have probably thrown up from laughing so hard. It's different now. In ways I can't explain.

She's curled in on herself at the edge of the mattress, fingers worrying at a stray thread on the comforter. The stream hums, unsettled, between us. Memories rage and batter at the silence. Quietly, without looking at me, Danae flattens one palm against the sheet at her head and inches it slowly towards me. The sound of her skin moving against the cotton is almost too soft to hear, and it's only when she reaches the boundary of the bed, fingertips jutting out into the space between us, that I realise, with a jolt of surprise, what she's offering. It's completely unexpected. I stare at her hand for a moment, but only for a moment. And then, without speaking, I let my hand move forwards until it finds hers, fingers closing around fingers. She doesn't flinch.

We sit like this for a while, the messy past like a shadow at our shoulders. It's a long time before I realise that Danae has fallen asleep. My chest aches, my oxygen-starved blood is making every muscle tremble, and I'm tired, so tired. I rest my head against the side of my chair and let my eyes slide shut.

Chapter Twenty-Five

25.1 Danae

The day I decided to become a traitor, I woke up early to the sound of the chant. I probably should have taken it as a bad omen, but I really didn't think the meeting would play out the way it did, and, besides: I was angry. I was so angry I could barely see straight, and I thought that made me safe.

I thought I was being clever. Gerald Corscadden offered me my life back – not *my* life, but a life that looked like mine – and that was more than the cache could do. We'd been talking for a week by then about what to do with me once I was well enough to leave, and our conversations had involved a lot of safe houses and off-grid living. They'd told me that they could probably get me an identity that would almost certainly pass a roadside spot check, but I wouldn't be working anywhere ever again. I'd be scratching a living for the rest of my life, relying on handouts and the kindness of strangers for every meal and every bed. That's one thing if you have a life expectancy of maybe forty-five years, fifty at a push. I'm going to live a hell of a lot longer than that.

So I gave Corscadden a look, like *I am too enigmatic and well-protected to hand you the inner workings of my psyche*, and I told him he'd have my answer in twenty-four hours. Honestly, the only person in the room who thought I was fooling anyone was me. The cache were planning to put me on a bus to Antwerp in ten days' time, where I could disappear into obscurity until someone worked out what the hell to do with me, and he was offering me a life, a name, a place and a person to be and, all I'd have to do was turn up once a month and give a doctor some of my blood.

I don't know how much they heard. They were certainly listening at the door. They knew who Corscadden was and the only reason they didn't kill him where he sat was because I'd asked for him to be there. That was the kind of power I had over them, and I knew it.

Stefan showed him out. I didn't ask how they protected our location, but I assume it involved black-out drugs and the boot of a car, and the fact that Corscadden agreed to it, just to meet me, told me how valuable I was. It was part of the reason I asked him to come: to see if he would. I listened to the duet of their footfall on the bare wooden stairs, falling into darkness and shadow, and I leaned back in my chair and flexed my broken fingers. I remember I used to do that a lot.

Ella was leaning against the doorframe, waiting for me to acknowledge her presence. When I didn't, she said, "So."

"So," I said. I was supposed to look at her. I didn't. She waited another moment, then unfolded herself from the doorway, crossed slowly to the seat across from me, and lowered herself into it. I imagine it was still warm from his presence. I imagine it disgusted her.

She said, "What did he want to talk to you about?"

Ella was a younger model, some kind of Search and Rescue line, built for efficiency. Androgynous, muscular but lean, face faintly ash-grey beneath the make-up that she used to disguise the polycarbon strengthening weave that ran beneath her skin. She'd chosen a gender because she was expected to; she'd chosen "Ella" to reinforce her decision. I don't know how many lives she'd saved before the Insurgency. I preferred to measure her by the lives she'd taken since.

I said, because I didn't know how much she knew already, "He wanted to meet a Progeny face to face."

"Oh?" An inquisitive brow reached for her forehead. "Connoisseur, is he?"

"He thinks I'm valuable."

Ella's fingers drummed softly on the edge of the table. It was old and falling apart, like everything in the safe house, but filed smooth of sharp or splintered edges. This is how you survive when you're an a-naut: you look for all the tiny, stupid ways that you can die. "Does he know *how* valuable?" she asked at last.

I'm pretty sure that she suspected what I'd done. The city had been dying fast, levelled by a pandemic that nobody knew how to treat, and then, suddenly, it was over. There was a treatment for the untreatable, and I was in custody, and she would have had to have been stupid not to ask herself the question. Maybe she also felt it on the stream; I don't know. But she never asked.

I said, "Do you mean, does he know about my blood?"

"Does he know that your blood uplinks directly to Red Space?" A mild smile played around the corner of her lips, but she didn't look at me. "Does he know that your immune system is basically a datastream processing bank of unimaginable capacity? Yes. That's what I mean."

I have a small nanopharmacodynamics portfolio, he had said, and he sat back and smiled. Did they hear? Did they know what he meant? I played for time. "Why would he think that?"

She shrugged. "Why would he be here?"

Good question. "He knows better than anyone that the a-naut blood stream can't fight infection. He was Head of the Insurgency Threat Response Directorate for... how many years? Why would he think my blood was any different?"

"Because he knows you're Progeny." Her words were quick and quiet, in a way that left no room for argument. Ella steepled her hands, fingertips pressing lightly together, and, finally, she looked up at me from under hooded brows. "Do you have any idea how much the resistance invested into the Progeny line?"

I could hazard a guess. "Probably enough to break them."

"Not quite." She'd been there, if only for a couple of months, right before the end. "But almost. The war was just about over and we were not going to win. There used to be millions of us, Danae. How many are there now – ten thousand? Less? If we were organic, that wouldn't be a viable breeding population."

"We survive," I said. "We always survive."

"For how much longer?" Her smile was tight. "The last a-naut lines went into production more than forty years ago. We're all falling apart now. The Progeny were supposed to be our future. How much would you say that was worth?"

To live? To continue? "Everything."

Ella nodded. Her face was blank, immovable. It was hard to believe that she was coming to the end of her lifespan, that so much power, so much will, could ever just *stop.* It wasn't hard to believe that I was about to make her my enemy. It wasn't hard to imagine that I'd spend the rest of my life seeing her face on every corner, in every shadow. In all my restless dreams.

"Everything," she said.

Chapter Twenty-Six

26.1 Danae

Strange how quickly a place can start to feel like home. Stranger still how hard it is to walk away from somewhere when you know you'll never see it again, even if you've spent the past two days counting down the hours until you get to leave. It's only when I'm standing in the centre of the floor, letting my eyes do one last sweep of the room that's been my world entire for almost a week, that I realise that it wasn't so much that I needed to get out of here, it was only that I needed to know that I could.

The skin on my back feels tight and a little too warm. Eva has checked me over one last time this morning and pronounced me fit to travel, and I've peered into the mirror that she held up behind me and found a network of cratering and wheals, shaded crimson and glistening faintly with a plasticised sheen. All the lacerations have knitted themselves back together and the seared-off strips of epidermis have regrown from beneath their blisters, but the flesh is tender and it chafes beneath the new clothes that Jos has found for me. The shirt is light, silky; the dress above it is made from gossamer-thin wool that floats around me like cobweb on the breeze. It's supposed to give my skin breathing room to heal. It probably costs more than I earn in a month.

Adam puts his head around the door. "Ready?"

I shrug. I like that I can shrug again these days. I think I'll see how much shrugging I can do on the transit back to Verdieping Drie before Adam starts to get annoyed. "Ready," I say, and I follow him out before I can reflect on how I might have died here. I wonder if that means that I leave a piece of me in this room no matter what.

Jos isn't coming with us to the transit station. When we leave his house, it'll be the last time that we see him or Eva or Lotte, and I feel like I should be trying harder to fix the image of him in my mind, though I don't know why. He meets us at the foot of the stairs, holding a thick, warm coat that he eases over my shoulders with his usual meticulous care. "It's a cold morning," he says.

I feel an acid-wash of sadness bathe the back of my throat and I have to blink away tears. "Thank you," I say. My voice sounds hoarse and I see Adam, by the front door, glance up in surprise. "For everything."

Jos nods. His liver-spotted hand pats my elbow. "Stay safe."

He's right: the morning is cold. My breath mists in the early-morning shadows as I step out onto the street, and the air, after a week spent in one room, smells fresh and clean, like scrubbed linen. Adam and I walk for a while in silence as I process my surroundings: thin, elegant houses that cluster together like sunflowers as they reach towards the near ceiling, set back from the road by narrow strips of yard, each populated by a profusion of flowering plant pots. It's 7am on a September morning, and the ambient light is low, cut by the warm glow that seeps out from behind the curtains of scattered windows along the terrace. I don't think I've ever spent so long in a place that seeps *safety* so clearly from every brick and every cobble. Even Adam seems less watchful here.

After a moment, I say, "Did anyone ever find out what happened on Verdieping Twee?"

Adam has lost himself in reverie. He glances sideways at me. "What?"

"The shutdown on Twee," I say. "On Sunday. It got lost after the explosion."

He's silent for a moment. The street is so quiet that I can hear the soft pat of our footfall against the pavement. "I forgot about it," he says at last.

I look up at the shuttered windows around me, the play of light across the ceiling, like dappled water, and I feel a deep, tired sigh stretch the muscles of my chest. "Well. I don't suppose it matters any more."

Nobody died on Twee. Whether it was a feint left to unbalance civic authorities before the devastating right hook of the Viewing Plaza bomb, or whether it was a malfunctioning relay on a corroded circuit, it's disappeared into history now.

"No," says Adam. His voice is faraway, disinterested. "I don't suppose it does."

26.2 Danae

The transit between floors passes in near silence and without incident.

Adam is a shadow beside me, folded in on himself, all angles and planes, and he walks like his bones are made of glass. He says nothing, even when he catches me shooting a furtive glance in his direction for the umpteenth time, but his raised eyebrow makes the point for him in silence. Still, it worries me, enough that I'm prepared to fork out for an obscenely overpriced coffee and a cup of scalding water at the station. He takes his drink from me with a meaningful look and I'm expecting some kind of pithy rejoinder that questions my motives, my mental capacity, or my overall physical health, but all he says is, "Thank you," and he takes a sip.

We pick a couple of seats at random in the waiting room, and I sink into mine, folding my legs beneath me as I balance my coffee on one knee. I'd have liked breakfast too, but not enough to go into debt over the kind of reconstituted industrial waste that passes for food in the transit-station stem-generators. I content myself with stirring six packets of sugar into my coffee and let my brain sink below the mindless familiarity of the action, feeling my eyes slide out of focus, my thoughts disappear into shadow and mist. After a moment, I become aware of Adam's eyes on me, and blink my way back into the present to find that he's watching me with something in his eyes that I can't quite read. It's not something I've seen before. It looks for all the world like contentment.

"What?" I say.

He smiles. Shakes his head. His eyes fall away. "Nothing," he says. "Just… Nothing."

He falls asleep between Verdieping Een and Verdieping Twee. I take off my coat and bunch it up into a pillow behind his neck, and he sighs and burrows his face against it. I notice a thin line of saliva glistening at the corner of his lips, refracting the starlight. I notice how thin he's got in less than a week, flesh loosening over muscle, and how, regardless, it feels as though his body hums with tightly leashed energy. I notice all of these things before I notice myself noticing them, and then I don't know what to think.

So I turn away and watch the news, and, eventually, I fall asleep too.

26.3 Danae

We part at the transit station. After the best part of a week on Een, the singularity fuzz on Drie is deafening, and the headache sets in almost before the airlock has finished opening, a dull whine inside my skull that batters methodically against the inside of my eyes. I'd forgotten how bad this could be and, for a moment, I'm back in those high-pitched days after I stepped off the ferry and into my new life. The shadows lengthen and the walls close in and panic tightens my chest. I see Adam looking at me and know that the stream has twisted between us and he's registered the change, and so I reach out my hand, fold stiff fingers around the fabric of his jacket sleeve and grip, hard, for the long seconds it takes to pass.

He says nothing. He doesn't touch me. He just drops his eyes towards the floor and breathes slowly and deliberately, and, when my fingers release his coat, he says, "Let me buy you lunch, okay?"

It's spoken casually but the subtext is clear. "Thanks," I say, "but I've got food at home."

He nods. His smile looks genuine. I'm not surprised, to be honest: he may not have settled to his satisfaction the question of whether or not Danae is fit to be left on her own, but we've both spent the past week on Verdieping Een. His bank account is probably running on fumes.

"Fair enough," he says. "If you're sure."

I'm actually not, and this is surprising to me. I can count on one hand the number of times in the past five days when I've been reasonably certain I didn't want to kill him, but now that it comes to it, I'm feeling like I might actually miss having him around.

"I'm sure," I say, and I make myself smile. When we leave the transit station, I walk briskly and I don't look back.

I don't go directly home. It's a long time since I've had a Thursday morning to wander the city at my leisure and walking helps ease out the paroxysms in my skull. Besides, no matter what I've told him, there is no food in my room, nor is there much in the way of gin. There's no point in going home until I've sorted both of those things out, but I find I'm not in any hurry. I'm not sure where I'm going so I let my feet find their own way while I roll my shoulders and flex the wefted fibres of my healing back. I feel the cool air press my dress against my skin, gently, like the hands of a lover, and I feel my lazy legs protest the sudden upswing in demand as I slide back into the familiar: colours, smells and sounds. When the tram rattles past me, trembling the pavement below my feet and agitating the city air into dust-swirled eddies, I notice that I'm headed for Centralemarkt, and my stomach, regarded at last, responds with a sharp lurch of hunger. I find my usual stall and buy some *bitterballen* for the journey, intending to eat as I walk, but I pass the silk scarf lady on Goudlelielaan before I've opened the packet and something makes me stop, offer her a bright smile for a cold, grey day, challenge her to drop her eyes and usher me away with inattention. She doesn't. She meets my smile and returns it and I feel the stream prickle and dance between us, like songbirds greeting the sunrise, as I run my hands over the soft gossamer fabrics of her stall and we chat amiably about the colours and the cost of water for the dyes.

"I'm Françoise," I tell her. I didn't know I was going to do this. My brain hears the words come out of my mouth and tries to spike panic in my belly, but, to my surprise, nothing comes. I offer the silk scarf lady a *bitterball.*

She accepts with a nod of thanks. "I'm Akasi," she says.

I don't buy one of her scarves. Even if I hadn't spent half of next month's pay last Sunday, they're far too rich for a factory worker's head. I notice that Akasi doesn't eat the *bitterbal,* but sets it deliberately on the side of a plate that she keeps on a shelf at the back of the stall, carefully arranged to be within easy sight of the road and smeared with sauce stains and a couple of stray noodles. It might be the remnants of her breakfast or last night's dinner, and it might just be an elaborate prop, and so I say nothing and offer her nothing more. I've made my point, to her and to myself, and, if I never come back to her stall, if I never catch her eye and nod another brief greeting, I know now that it's possible to chip away at this thing, little by little, piece by piece.

26.4 Danae

At the market, I shop for essentials to last the remaining few days of the week and then, because I haven't quite blown my entire pay on the top floor, I find a streetside bar that looks appealingly empty and just the right amount of unwelcoming, and I invest a few fragments of my tattered salary in gin. The seats are rough, scarred metal and the shadows beneath the awning are long and dark, even this early into the day. I sequester myself as far back from the road as I can and bury myself in gloom. The news strip bleeds a syrupy white glow into the dark recesses beneath the canopy and I watch idly while I sip at my drink. A civic elder that I recognise vaguely from a few events designed primarily to give civic elders somewhere to be is waxing lyrical about her pride in the city's resilience, even as the crawler on the screen below her face ups the casualty figures to twenty-three dead. Hotels on Een are reporting a catastrophic wave of cancellations and predicting severe retrenchment of working hours over the rest of the financial year, and one of the more hysterical right-wing news sources has dragged a tousle-haired professional demagogue out of semi-retirement to misquote several leading orbital engineers about the danger of cascading blast damage to Luchtstad's structural integrity. Pockets of street fighting have broken out across the radials, but they are absolutely not connected to the explosion, or the water rationing, for that matter, and it's fine anyway, because the The Korpschef of Radiale Zeven has drafted in another one of those specialist support units from the Dienst Speciale Interventies and arrests have been made all over Luchtstad.

This doesn't feel like a city gripped by resilience and hope for a better future. It feels like a city that's holding its breath.

Emmett hasn't quite put it all together yet, but I think he will. It took me a few security alerts and a complete power outage across Verdiepingen Twee, Drie and Vier eight weeks after I arrived before it started to become clear, and then I understood why everyone always changes the subject when you try to ask the obvious questions. It's a game we've all decided to play, and the stakes are high. Sometimes the explanation on the news strips is plausible: I can believe that the life support systems crash out every second Saturday, or some seventeen-year-old edgelord dares himself to light a cigarette in a no-smoking zone and the CO_2 monitors descend into chaos. And, then again, sometimes it turns out to be a pocket of mis-vented gas igniting on a sweep of the laser broom. I can't imagine how that one got past the Head of Civic PR; maybe they're on holiday. All I know is that as long as the news strips are prepared to keep feeding us half-truths and nonsense, it means that nobody's given up on Do Not Seek yet. The day that someone on Luchtstad's civic council admits that there's no consensus, there's never been a consensus, and there continues to be a significant minority up here so ideologically opposed that they're prepared to use violence to force the government to enact a repeal... I don't know what happens next.

So, yes, I'll take the lies. For as long as there's a will to tell them.

I pinch the bridge of my nose, rolling cartilage between my finger and thumb. The scream of my headache has faded into a high-pitched whine, and my brain feels fuzzy around the edges as it recedes, like I'm sinking into feathers. I order another drink, down it, and make my way back onto the street, blinking tears from my fume-scalded eyes.

I walk.

My back stretches and tingles and my feet burn beneath me, and I walk. The thin, trickling crowd swells into the lunchtime high-tide and I twist my shoulders and buffet and hustle, and I walk. The air fills with the slick, hot smells of bubbling fat-pans; the soupy stink of human sweat; the diluted chill of sudden emptiness; and I walk. I walk until I feel like my bones poke through the soles of my feet and my head hangs like concrete from my neck, and I find myself, in early evening, at the door to my block, hungry and weary and with nothing to show for my day but a couple of groceries and a head full of nothing. It's too early for the factory lines to have let out and the street is silent, the block empty, the shadows behind the door unmoving. I'm tired, exhaustion weights my bones, and tomorrow I'll be back on the lines, feet locked in place on the factory floor, legs pinned upright. I should go inside now, make some dinner, drink gin until my thoughts are quiet, and pass out on my bed. My room is waiting for me up a few flights of stairs. It'll be like I never left, and I can write off the week that's just passed and slot back into this life of mine that ticks forward with all the predictable grace and monotony of a clockwork toy.

This is what I should do. But there's a shadow at my shoulder, a ghost from another place, another life and I can feel him there so strongly that I think if I turn my head I'll see him, or a flash of him, before he dissolves into the pre-twilight gloom. I'm tired and alone and my feet hurt. I should go inside.

But I don't. I turn away from my block, eyes pointed down towards the safety of the pavement, and I let my feet carry me where they've been wanting to go all day.

He's been sleeping. His hair has flattened along one side of his face and tufted into spikes where it's been pressed against his pillow, and his eyes are heavy. "Hey," he says, as if he's been expecting me all this time, and I realise that, if he'd turned up unannounced at my door, I wouldn't have been surprised either.

I hold out the box of iodine tablets that I bought this morning at the Centralemarkt. I didn't question it at the time. I didn't even notice that I'd bought them.

"I've got these and I've got gin," I tell him.

Adam nods, and his face creases into a tired smile. "Well, then, it's a party," he says. "You'd better come in."

Chapter Twenty-Seven

27.1 Adam

The door slides open onto my room. Danae hesitates for a beat, two beats, and then walks purposefully inside, as though she's done this many times before. She crosses to the window and stands beside it for a moment, arms folded across her chest. I leave her to it while I close the door behind us. The window is literally the only thing to look at in this room, and she might as well get some use out of it while we both work out what we want to say.

The silence lengthens. "I'll get you a glass," I say, to break it.

Danae makes no move to take the gin out of her bag. "Luca..." she says, and my chest tightens the way it always does when I'm ambushed by loss. "Sorry," she says quickly, and I wonder if the stream reacted or if she just read it in my face. "Is it okay to talk about him?"

I don't answer straight away. I cross the three short steps to where my collection of two glasses nestle together in a small corner of one of the shelves, and I lift the topmost one from its bed inside the other. The scrape of perspex against perspex sounds like the sharpening of a knife. Danae glances around a little at the noise and I hold up the beaker for her to see.

"Yes," I say. "It's okay to talk about him."

There's a hunch to her shoulders that looks like she's not entirely convinced. She takes the glass. "How long were you together?"

"Eleven years."

"Did you know – when you met him...? Did you know that he was the other half of your binary?"

I force a soft laugh. "That's just a story."

"It doesn't feel like a story."

I shrug. "It's a song. It's a legend. It's... fantasy."

Danae levels a piercing look at me. "I don't think you believe that."

I know you don't believe that, says Luca.

I'm suddenly very tired. My bed is unmade from the midday nap that lasted into this evening, and I lower myself onto a crumpled blanket. I'm old. I've lived too long. I open my mouth to tell Danae that I don't know what I believe any more but it doesn't come out. What comes out instead is, "Are you going to open that gin or what?"

An eyebrow arches. "I thought you only drank water?"

"I have a feeling this is going to be a gin kind of conversation," I say. "And the water on this city tastes like shit."

The edges of her lips curl upwards and she slings her bag off her shoulder. One hand reaches inside and emerges with a bottle of something that looks cheap and painful. She hands it to me, crosses the room for another glass, then lowers herself onto the mattress beside me.

"Actually," she says, as she take the bottle from my hand and twists off the top, "I'm pretty sure the water on this city tastes like piss."

She pours. Fumes fill the air between us. I clink my glass to hers and take a mouthful, letting it settle against the filters at the back of my throat for a moment before I swallow. It's a long time since I've had alcohol.

Danae watches me drink, glass cradled against her collarbone. Again, she says, "Did you know?"

I give up. "About the binaries? Yes. I walked into that room and it was like I was suddenly whole again." It was a friend's kitchen, bustling with pre-rally activity and occasional flashes of streambuzz, and Luca was crouched on the floor beside a massive banner, wrapping gaffer tape around a splintering join in one of the masts. He looked up and met my eyes and said *holy shit*, breathlessly, like he'd just been punched in the gut. "It was as if I'd known him forever, but I'd just forgotten."

"Okay." Danae nods, tightly, and her voice is tight. Her brow furrows and she drops her gaze into her glass. "Okay," she says again, and she swallows a mouthful of gin. She grimaces and wipes the back of her hand across her mouth. "Is it like that for everyone?"

I shrug. "How would I know?"

"Because you know people. You've talked to people."

"Maybe. Who knows? The story comes from somewhere."

"But it was like that for you." Irritation is creeping into her voice. I'm not sure what I'm supposed to be saying, but I can tell I'm not saying it. "It was like you just knew him? As if, maybe, you knew his face but you didn't know why you knew it?"

It dawns on me, quietly, that we're not talking about Luca any more. *No shit*, says the shade of my dead lover, who's usually a step ahead of me in stuff like this. "Yeah," I say. "That sounds about right."

"And when you lost him," she says, "it was like nothing made sense any more."

"No," I say. "When I lost him, it was like I wasn't complete any more."

"Okay. Okay." She's got the glass in both hands, huddled around it like she's trying to keep warm. Her eyes are fixed on the floor, but they're glassy, vacant. "Tell me about him."

This is completely unexpected. "Who – Luca?"

She glances up. "If you don't want to…"

"No. It's fine. It's just… a long time since anyone's asked."

"Seems like he must have been someone worth knowing."

My throat tightens, like it's being wound with twine. "I've never known anyone better."

Handsome, too, says Luca. His voice is too light, as though he's got a smile plastered to his face that doesn't meet his eyes. *Make sure you tell her how handsome I was.*

I swallow a mouthful of gin. It burns all the way down. "You know how there are just some people who make the world feel less like it's made out of shit?"

"Yes." Spoken quickly, as though it falls out of her.

"That was Luca. He was the kind of guy who could walk into a room and make everyone feel like they'd known him for years. Any time we needed somewhere to go, Luca always knew a guy. He just liked people. He collected friends like you and I collect memories."

Danae rolls her glass between her hands. "Useful skill to have."

"Maybe." I shrug. "I've spent a lot of years telling Luca's friends he was dead."

She looks at me. "You say that as if it's a bad thing."

"I never used to think so. It saved us more times than I can count. But then – I was the one left alive."

"Oh." Her eyes drop away, back to her glass. "I get it. You wanted the world to be fair."

Anger prickles. "That's not what I said."

"Better to be old and lonely than die young and loved."

Again, I have the strongest feeling that we're not just talking about me. "How do you think he'd answer that question?"

"I don't know. I never knew him. How do you think he'd answer it for you?"

Honestly? I don't know. And Luca has gone silent and watchful, fading into the shadows. I feel his eyes on me but he says nothing. "Five people went out that morning," I say. "Luca. Marie. Three guys he was working with from HQ. You know how many of them were alive that night?"

Danae draws in a deep breath. It raises her shoulders, curves her spine. "But he didn't die alone."

"Maybe not. But he still died."

"Yeah." She turns her head slightly. Only slightly; only enough to see a thin crescent of light from the street outside curve across the white of her eyes. "You're right. Having friends didn't save him. But I reckon it saved you."

I shake my head. "Because of Marie. Because of this whole stupid quest." I sigh, which turns into a cough, and I taste osmotic plasma at the back of my throat. "Yeah, maybe. I don't even know any more."

"You find the thing that gets you through it," she says. "People knew him. People loved him. And so you have a trail to follow."

My chest hurts and my head aches. My filters are down to 28%. "How much do you know about what happened in London?"

Danae shrugs. I'm not looking at her, but I see it in my peripheral vision. "I know things. I've heard… stuff. I know it was the last official act of the Insurgency."

"It was a massacre."

A sigh. "Yeah."

"Maybe 2% of HQ was militant. There were almost 2000 a-nauts inside when the Rens breached the inner defences."

"Jesus." One hand rises to scrub her eyes. "And Luca was…?"

"Either…" It's still hard to say this. Even now. "Either at the outer perimeter or just inside."

"Adam. I'm sorry. I'm so sorry."

When his chant started, it was like slamming into a wall. It dropped me. I lost my footing and I went down hard onto the pavement. "I couldn't get to him," I say. "For one hundred and fifty-three minutes, I tried and I couldn't. You know what that means?"

Her hands are trembling. I see it in the movement of light on the surface of her gin. "Yes," she says. There are scars on her chest. Danae knows what it means when the chant is long.

"And then they breached the inner walls and started shooting. The stream… went crazy. The global tether collapsed and everything went white." I thought I'd died. I remember feeling light, like I was filled with air, because it was over and we'd find each other again in the space beyond the body. "And when it reset, his chant was gone."

Danae is silent for a long moment. Then, slowly, she says, "One hundred and fifty-three minutes."

"Yes," I say.

"That's two and a half hours."

"Yes."

She shifts, folding her legs beneath her. Gin slides up the side of her glass but fails to spill. "Are you sure you want to know what happened?"

There's a dent in the side of my skull, a small crater, well hidden by my hair, but my fingers find it in the quiet moments and trace the edges. I got it when I beat my head against a wall trying to make his chant come back. "Yes. I'm sure."

Danae sets down her drink, slowly and deliberately. The glass makes no sound as it connects with the floor. She stares at her empty hands for a long moment, and then she says, "You're a brave man, Adam," and reaches out to twine her fingers through mine where they rest on the bed between us. I'm not expecting this, and I feel my breath catch in my throat. "He was lucky to have you."

I can't answer her for a moment. I swallow, hard, and then I remember I have gin and use that instead. I say, "He would have done the same for me," and my voice sounds unsteady and far too thin.

Danae's brow furrows. She drops her chin to her chest. "There's a thing my dad used to say about my mam," she says, and I realise again how little I know about her. How different her life has been. "A quote, or something – after she was gone: 'They are not dead who live in lives they leave behind.'"

I force my lips into a smile. "Some day, you'll have to tell me how you have actual parents."

She shrugs. "Not any more. And believe me, there's nobody left who'll spend twenty-five years looking for me when I'm gone."

I doubt this. But the loneliness in her voice has closed her off and her eyes are looking out of this room and into somewhere else, somewhen else. So instead, I lift the bottle, where she's set it down on the floor beside her. Her fingers are still wound through mine and I don't break the hold. With my free hand, I twist the lid from the neck and let it fall, and then I pour a healthy measure into her empty glass before topping up my own. She watches me, hood-eyed and guarded, saying nothing. When I raise my glass to her, she leans down and lifts hers and clinks it against mine. She drinks, and I drink, and the silence lengthens.

After a moment, she pulls her hand free and knits it together with the hand that holds her glass. She looks away, eyes pointed scrupulously downwards and away from me, and she says, "Can I stay here tonight?"

At first, I'm not sure I've heard her properly. Then, I'm not sure I've understood. In the corner, Luca shrinks into shadow and Danae won't meet my eye. I say, carefully, "There's only one place to sleep."

"I know," she says. "I can sleep on the floor if you like. I've just... got used to having you around."

I've got used to having her around, too. "You can stay," I say. "You can stay as long as you want."

"Just for tonight," she says. Her fingers steeple, tips tracing the scars and scratches on the cloudy surface of her glass. Still she doesn't look at me. "Just for tonight."

Chapter Twenty-Eight

28.1 Danae

I sleep well, better than I have since I arrived on Luchtstad, and I don't wake until early morning. When I do, it's gently, from thick and comfortable blackness, and I've passed out so comprehensively that it's a full three seconds before my brain engages and I realise where I am. I remember the last time I slept like this, and my half-awake self is trying to make this be the same before consciousness kicks in and I register the singularity buzz, the unfamiliar smells, and the wrongness of the body beside me.

The street outside is still and almost quiet. Adam hasn't closed the curtains and the window casts a geometric profile in thin amber light on the wall in front of me. We're not lying close enough to touch, but I can feel his breath on the back on my neck, the gentle hum of proximity, the undulations of the stream between us, and I want to cry.

I shift carefully, pushing back the blankets, and I stand up. My dress is crumpled where it clings to me, soiled from the streets and the day and from sleeping in it, and my shaved head feels naked without my scarf. Gin fumes bounce around the inside of my skull and the room lurches beneath my feet as I pad towards the window. There's nobody on the street below to watch me lean my head forwards to rest against the glass, absorbing the low hum of a city that is always in motion. I stand like this for a long while – ten minutes, maybe fifteen – unmoving and unquiet, before I feel him wake behind me in the stirring of the stream. I hear the sheets rustle as he shifts, but he doesn't make any move to get up.

I feel his eyes on me, and turn my head towards him. "So," he says.

"So."

"I thought this was supposed to help you sleep?"

"It did," I say.

"This was supposed to be how we made sure you got plenty of sleep before you were back on the line tomorrow."

"It is."

"And yet you're awake. And, more importantly, I'm awake too."

I lift my hand to my forehead to check that it's still attached to my face. "Sorry."

"Is it your back?"

"My back?" It takes me a second to work out what he's talking about, and then I realise just how well everything is healing. "No. My back's fine."

"So…"

I can feel myself losing patience. "So… what?"

"You tell me. I'd like to get back to sleep."

"Go back to sleep," I say. "I just need a minute."

"To stare out the window?" Adam shuffles upwards so that he's propped up higher on his pillow. "I have a hard time sleeping when there's a crazy woman standing sentinel in my apartment."

"Fine." I'm one step away from the bed. It seems a fairly meaningless distance, in the general scheme of things, so I cross the floor and lower myself onto the bottom of the mattress, wrapping my arms about myself as the negligible heat dissipates into the night air. Adam nudges at my backside with his foot, still buried under the blankets.

"Hey," he says. "You're overthinking. I can feel it on the stream."

I shoot him a look. "How would you know what overthinking feels like?"

A wide grin spreads across his face. "Thank Christ for that. You had me worried there for a minute."

"I'm fine," I say.

The grin fades a little, and I realise my mistake. *Fine* shifts us back out of banter and returns us to the substance of why I'm here in the first place. "The gin wore off, huh?" he says, and I register a faint trace of bitterness around the edge of the words. I'm pretty sure I've earned that.

I toe the threadbare carpet with one bare foot. "I shouldn't be here."

"Why?"

"Why? Not two minutes ago, you're complaining that I'm keeping you awake, and now it's 'why'?"

"I don't remember complaining," he says.

"Of course you don't."

"I remember pointing out that I was awake, and you were awake, and the whole point of tonight's adventure was to avoid both of these things."

Was it? I'm not sure I ever said as much, but if he's happy to believe that, I'm happy to let him. "I always sleep alone."

"Not this past week, you don't."

"That's different."

"Yes. But it doesn't just go away now that we're back on Verdieping Drie."

"What doesn't go away?"

"Forget it."

"*What* doesn't just go away?"

"I said forget it." Adam flings himself back down the bed so that he's flat on his back again. "We're getting up in three hours, Danae. Go to sleep."

"I didn't have a choice on Verdieping Een," I say.

His head slides sideways and he fixes me with a stare. "Okay."

"That's what's different."

"Because you had a choice last night."

"Yes."

"And... oh. Okay."

"Okay?"

"Okay," he says, and his voice is gentle. "You know... It's okay. I think. Nothing's changed."

"Everything's changed," I say.

"Yes," he says. "That too. But..." He hesitates. He hesitates for so long that I think he's finished speaking and look up. But I ought to know him better than that. What follows a pause like that is always the kill shot. "Whoever this person is – or was... That hasn't changed because you're here."

Somewhere, deep inside, something breaks. I take a breath to answer him, but I find that all the words have left my head. There's nothing inside, just vacuum, and I'm sitting on the edge of his bed in a crumpled dress with my mouth hanging open, bleeding out on the inside where nobody can see.

A soft rustling on the bed behind me describes the movement of his body. I feel the stream shift, eddy, ripple, but in the here-space, he doesn't try to touch me.

"It's okay, Danae," he says at last. "We're both in love with other people."

"How did you know?" My throat is dry. My voice is small and it sounds like it will crack.

He shrugs. "You said a word when you were coming back from the *dis*. It sounded like a name."

"I don't remember that," I say.

"You were pretty far gone," he says. "Want to tell me about it?"

"No."

"How long since you lost each other?"

"I just said…"

"All right, all right." On the edge of my vision, I see him hold up his hands. "It's far too early for this shit anyway."

He stares up at the ceiling, drops his hands to the blanket with a smothered thud. I feel the stream spike sharply between us and I peer back over my shoulder to see that he's not looking at me. Shadows pool on his face and I can't read what's behind it.

"I didn't lose him," I say. "I left him."

Adam's head tilts towards me, just enough to let his eyes slide sidewards to mine. "Okay. Did he understand?"

It's absolutely not the question I'm expecting. I have no idea what question I was expecting, but that wasn't it. And my throat starts burning and my treacherous brain starts replaying a loop of memory: me, frozen in time, shrouded by a veil of people and vicariously happy, watching Turrow disappear into the yellow mouth of the underground and knowing that there was nothing else for it and no choice but to leave.

I say, honestly, "I don't know." And then, "I'm not even sure if I understand."

"What did you tell yourself?"

"That it was for his own good."

He nods. "Ah. That's a good one."

"It's true," I say, and I know I'm right, but I also know I'm wrong. "He nearly died because of me."

And then I realise: *I nearly died because of him.* This is not the ending of the story I've written whenever I've told it to myself, but it's true nonetheless. When I walked into the Authority that first day and saw his face, it was like I'd known him from years ago, a lifetime ago, and just forgotten. The binary closed. The tear in the *dis* healed over, and I would have done anything to keep it from ripping apart again. And because of that, I nearly died, and I know I would do the same thing again without a second's hesitation because this world makes no sense to me if Boston Turrow is not a part of it. And so I had to leave.

And so I did.

It consumes me without warning. A storm surge battering through the breakwater, and I have nothing prepared for it and nothing to hold onto, and all I can do is let it carry me and stop fighting so I don't go under. And I remember Turrow's hands on my body, I remember his smile and his scent and the way the world seemed to light up around him. I remember the chill of the apartment on my skin, and I remember watching him fade quickly over days and knowing that I would do anything, *anything*, to keep him with me. I remember the weightlessness of decision, the feeling that my head was filled with air and that my body was nothing but depth; I remember the panic that rushed in once it was done. I remember the unreality of the imminence of death. And I remember the terror and the pain, the unrelenting pain, the pain that filled me like boiling water, that covered me in blood and heat. I remember being broken by pain, and built up again, and broken once more. I remember the exact moment that I knew I was never coming back from it, and the woman who escaped from that room, who woke up under the care of a man with half a face in a shadowed room that smelled of mould, was not the woman who went in. That other Danae is gone and will never, ever come back. But she left some pieces of herself tattooed under my skin, and they break me over and over again, every day of my life.

"It's okay," says Adam, and I'm aware, distantly, of his arms around me. I want to push them off and scratch and kick and punch. I want to damage things. I want to break the world apart. But there's no energy left in me; there's nothing left at all, and so I let him put his arms around me and hold me close to him, and I let the storm surge lift me and wash me away.

Chapter Twenty-Nine

29.1 Danae

The line is exactly as we left it almost a week ago, and I find this comforting. In an ever-changing world, at least the line is constant. The klaxon sounds and we all shuffle forwards as the conveyor starts to move, and the eyes that have followed Adam and me through the factory doors, to the smoke point where we wait for the morning to begin, and across the floor to our daily stations, dip downwards, diverted by barrelling groups of bulbs, and I'm alone again in the kind of comfortable solitude you can only achieve in a room full of people. My eyes find the poster on the wall opposite – *Magie voor je familie* – and I let them slide out of focus, feel my brain settle into the Factory Stare. It's as if I've never left. Everything is different now, but here, at least, it's like nothing has changed.

Adam doesn't watch me while we work. He doesn't lift his eyes from the belt, and this makes him absolutely unique on the line this morning. But I feel his watchfulness on the stream, like a warm cloak around my shoulders, and I let it envelop me, because it doesn't require anything in return. We work steadily for the three hours of first shift, and then the klaxon sounds and the line breaks away like pieces of machinery and turns in formation for the smoke point, stretching out our aching arms and fingers towards the siren-scent of fresh, strong coffee. I hang back, waiting for Adam to catch up with me on his longer journey from the head of the belt, but he holds up an apologetic hand and detours towards a quiet corner, finger pressed to one ear. I realise abruptly that he's taking a call and I'm not going to be able to hide with him for the next ten minutes because he's a colossal dickhead. I watch him go for a few seconds, in case the power of my hate-needles on the stream can persuade him to see the error of his ways, or, at the very least, disrupt the phone wave enough to terminate his conversation.

It does neither. I am outraged. In my outrage, I turn back towards the floor and prepare to storm over to the furthest and loneliest square inches of the smoke point and violently ignore my colleagues. I get as far as the turning bit before I almost collide with Sanne, who's waiting at my shoulder.

I know that expression. That expression is all pained sympathy and solicitousness, and she might as well have 'anxious concern' written in permanent marker across her forehead.

"Hey," she says. "It's good to have you back."

"It's good to be back," I say quickly, before I've properly vetted the words for plausibility. I just want her to go away, and I'm looking for the right conversational combination that makes this happen. That wasn't it.

"Come and have some coffee," she says, which is what I'd be doing if she hadn't waylaid me, but anyway. "You look exhausted."

I glance over my shoulder towards Adam, who's disappeared into shadow at the far end of the line.

"Okay," I say. "Coffee's good." Also the wrong thing to say: the coffee is never good, it's mostly just robust and plentiful. But Sanne's face says I've got some leeway for today at least, and she actually hooks an arm around my elbow and guides me in the direction of the smoke point.

"When we heard what had happened," she says, "I was so worried for you. So many people died. So many people were hurt."

All I know about the information that was passed on to the factory is that it was given by Eva and weighted with the authority of a practicing medical professional, which is something even Luchtstad's employment legislation has to respect. It was enough to guarantee that our jobs would be waiting for us once we were discharged from her care and that we wouldn't be evicted from the city for truancy. This was all I needed to hear at the time, so I didn't press the matter. I'm wondering now if I should have asked more questions.

I say, "It was a terrible thing for the radial."

"It was a terrible thing for *you*," she says. We've reached the smoke point and the coffee dock, and Sanne sets herself to filling a cup for me. The others circle us; Thijs offers me a cigarette, which I decline; Bente pats me hesitantly on the shoulder; even Jouke manages a surly nod in my direction. But Sanne has been appointed guardian and they hold back at a respectful distance, attentive but detached.

I sip from my coffee, exactly how I remember it: thick, tarry, slightly burnt, and almost as necessary to my survival as oxygen on the factory floor. "Who took our places on the line?"

"Oh." Sanne rolls her eyes, a gesture of extravagant distaste. "Two kids from Gustaaf's team – we don't talk about them. One of them," she whispers darkly, "was Gustaaf's *daughter*. And she was terrible, you know, but what can you do? She shouldn't be working in the factory with her father. She should be working somewhere that she has to earn her keep. It's so good that you're back. Do you have food at home? I didn't hear you come in last night."

I don't know if she knows that I arrived back on Drie yesterday morning. I don't know how she would know this, but, then again, I don't know how she would have known to expect me last night either. I'm struck by the discomfiting thought that she has been listening for my return every night since I left and my appearance on the floor today without a corresponding return to my room yesterday has come as a surprise.

"No," I say. "I stayed with a friend."

"Oh." Her eyes flicker momentarily to Adam, still lost in conversation in the far reaches of the cavernous room. "Of course. I heard that you were with Emmett."

I remember the rumours about us that swirled along the line in the weeks before we disappeared to Verdieping Een for a communal day trip and ended up being exploded into a week of his-and-hers sick leave. I wonder if anyone noticed that we arrived together this morning, and realise suddenly that of course they did. If they thought we were sleeping together before this, they're certain of it now.

"Is he well?" Sanne asks now, and I notice, for the first time, that her tone is too casual.

"He's fine," I tell her. "I got the worst of it. But we were lucky."

"It's a terrible thing," she says. "Terrible. We've been so worried here, so afraid. The factory closed three times this week – three security alerts. And the floor was in shutdown once. Everyone is afraid."

Three closures and a shutdown is a little excessive for one week, but not by much. It's amazing the difference a bit of contextualisation can make. But the fear in her voice sounds genuine, and I need to show willing, so I say, "At least we know the explosion was an accident."

Sanne rolls her eyes. "Oh, they always make up some nonsense."

This is the first time I've ever heard any of my colleagues so much as hint that the official explanation might not be entirely accurate. "You think it was deliberate?"

Her eyes narrow and she fixes me with a look that manifestly wonders if I'm actually this obtuse. "Of course it was deliberate. You really didn't know?"

"I... suspected," I say. My teeth are slightly gritted, but I think it came out okay. "It's hard to know what to think."

"Three security alerts and a shutdown. And they think we don't see what's happening. Like we don't have eyes in our heads or brains to think." A sharp, angry drag on her cigarette. "Like we can't work out for ourselves exactly who wants this city to be afraid."

There's venom in her words. The change is startling, and it chills me. I've always felt the hidden threat on this city, thrumming below the surface, just out of earshot, but this is the first time I've felt it reach out and touch my arm.

I say, hating myself for it, "It's always the bloody sparks, isn't it?"

I've never said this word before. I've never heard it spoken on Luchtstad. I just know that there's danger here and I need to distance myself from it before there's any chance of suspicion falling on me. But Sanne turns to me, wide-eyed and tight-lipped, and the look she throws me is pure fury.

"Why would you say that?" she hisses.

"I don't know." My words stumble, falling clumsily. I'm not sure what her look means. I'm not sure of anything right now. "Isn't that what everyone thinks?"

"I don't know," she says. "I don't care. Yes, maybe. Maybe there are people who think like that. But I never thought you'd be one of them."

"I don't..." I say. "I just thought..."

"There are people who want to see this city burn," she says. "But they're not the people this city is trying to help. Okay, you're hurt." She holds up a hand. It trembles. "You're angry. I can understand that. But this is *not* the way. I can't speak to you if this is how you think – I'm sorry."

She shakes her head and lowers it to her chest. She doesn't meet my eye as she walks away, and I'm left standing alone by the coffee dock, holding an unlit cigarette in one hand and a cooling cup of coffee in the other. After a moment, I'm aware that I've opened my mouth to say something that I didn't get the chance to vocalise, and I close it again quietly and look over my shoulder to the rest of the group. Half a dozen of them look away quickly and attempt an air of disinterested insouciance. If I was interesting before, I'm absolutely fucking fascinating now.

In the middle distance, I see that Adam has finished his conversation. There's not enough time for him to get to the smoke point and back to the line before the klaxon, so I pocket my cigarette and down my coffee, and head out to meet him halfway, feeling the heat of restless eyes trail me all the way.

He nods back towards the smoke point as I approach. "What was all that about?"

"I think I just turned into an organic supremacist," I say.

He blinks. "Better than the other way round, I suppose."

I glance back. "I'm not so sure. I think some of them might never speak to me again."

"Jesus." He grins. "That's impressive even for you, Danae."

"Françoise," I remind him, with considerably more vehemence than is strictly necessary, but his face is annoying. "And it's your fault, anyway."

"Of course it is," he says mildly. "That call was from Rika."

"Rika?" The wind leaves the sails of my righteous indignation. "As in, Jos' Rika?"

"The one and only. She's passing on a message."

"What did she say? Has Jos found Marie?"

"No." He shakes his head. "But he's got us another name."

Another bloody name. "Tell me this one's a local."

The hesitation tells me everything I need to know. "Uh…"

"Oh, for Christ's sake. We've only just got back from Verdieping Een!"

"Uh… she's not on Een."

For a moment, I find this encouraging. I must be tired. "No. No, this is *not* Betsy's friend on Radiale Vier?"

"No! No, it's not that. This is Jos' contact." A nervous smile plays around the corners of Adam's mouth, which is how I know to brace myself. "…On Radiale Twee."

Well. It's one radial closer, at least. I roll my eyes. "Is it safe?"

He's not expecting this. I can tell by the way surprise blanks his face for a second: he was expecting an argument. But he rallies quickly. "It comes from Jos; I'm inclined to trust him. What do you think?"

I suck in a breath. I can't believe what I'm about to say. But, when all's said and done, we've come this far. I've sacrificed the skin off my actual back to this stupid quest of his and he looks old, tired and sick, like his legs might give out underneath him at any moment. We've both been through too much to give up now.

"I think," I say, "that we're going to Radiale Twee."

Chapter Thirty

30.1 Adam

"I stand corrected," says Danae as the tickets are delivered seamlessly into our respective stream pockets. "It was the equivalent of six days' salary. Not five."

"I said I'd pay," I remind her, but we both know that I have nothing like the assets required to back up that kind of promise. Her sidelong glance advises me to let it go because she owns me now and there's nothing I can do about it.

"Everything on this stupid city pretends to be free," she says, dropping onto a moulded plastic bench by the waiting room wall. "This is a city that runs on small print – did you ever notice that?"

It's come to my attention. "Are you confused about how capitalism works?" I ask, and she punches me lightly on the arm. The lightness of the punch is no longer surprising, though I'm still surprised at my lack of surprise. She stayed with me again last night and only woke up twice. It's got so that I'm not afraid to wrap my arms around her when she starts trembling in her sleep.

We're in the inter-radial transit hall on Verdieping Vijf, a monument to industrial Gothic post-aestheticism, and quite possibly the most depressing black hole of human apathy that I've ever been. Vijf is a processing level, exclusively non-residential, and no effort has been expended to make it look like anything other than a metal shell to keep the vacuum out. All inter-radial traffic is routed through the lowest levels, because inter-radial traffic is 95% freight, and the idea that sentient beings might also need to be here sometimes was considered, half-heartedly accommodated, and ignored forever more. There's a private shuttlecraft service that runs between the Eens if you're important enough to be able to afford it. The rest of us get an emphatic suggestion to stay where we are, and the transit if we can't.

Like the booth, travel by transit is officially free. What's not free is the visitor's visa you need if you want to leave one radial and enter another. This is supposed to be an oxygen management thing. I might even believe that if I thought it took a week's pay at minimum wage to plug two more breathing bodies into an algorithm designed to account for thousands. In any case, it is what it is, and I've already blown my limited savings on the tickets to the Viewing Plaza, so Danae's on the hook for the entire cost of certifying the two of us out and back in again.

"It's fine," she says now, for about the fifteenth time this morning. "Honestly, what else was I going to spend it on? You can save a lot of money up here when you live like a hermit."

I doubt that's completely true, but the easiness between us is new and fragile and she's weird about her finances. I'm not going to push it. Instead, I say, "At least it's not another Verdieping Een."

She acknowledges the truth of this with a twitch of her eyebrows. "Though I'll miss the coffee. What do you want to bet the transit hall on Twee has a better canteen?"

"I wouldn't take that bet." The pastries here look as though they could pierce the city hull if I threw one at the wall, and I wouldn't even have to throw that hard. Danae has persevered with hers, but I'm happy to be stuck with broth.

She shrugs and picks at a cremated raisin. "I'd almost be tempted to pay the extra two years' wages and meet this lady on a civilised floor."

"Tell me that again after you've been on a transit for three hours." We both agreed: transit into Vijf, stay on Vijf, leave from Vijf. It's going to take us half the day to get there and back as it is, without factoring in travel between the levels on Radiale Twee.

"I don't know about you," she says, "but I'm planning on sleeping all the way."

A shimmering peal from the overhead speakers precedes an announcement so thick with reverb on the low ceilings that I catch barely one word in ten. Danae stands, so I do too.

"This is us?" I ask, unnecessarily, as it turns out, since the ground has started rumbling inside our sound-proofed waiting room and the vicious angles of our bench have set up a staccato rhythm against the wall.

"This is us," she says. The waiting room doors slide open with a hiss of air as the pressure rebalances, and the cold breeze that rushes in from the transit compartment smells of ozone. It looks much less sturdy than I'd like for a vehicle that's going to breach the airlock on the side of our radial and rattle through the corridors that link us to

Radiale Een and beyond. Danae catches my hesitation and flashes a smile. "Oh, but the booth you were fine with."

"The booth was radiation shielded," I say.

The smile becomes a grin. "If the corridor collapses, radiation is the last thing you're going to be worrying about."

If the corridor collapses, our transit car will plummet through the fathomless voids of space for the rest of eternity. It's airlocked but not vacuum-proofed, so we'll be dead within forty-eight hours. That's plenty of time to ponder the appalling desolation of deep space as the trickling oxygen escape condenses and then freezes in fractals on the outside of our windows.

Still. We're suspended in a metal-sheathed oxygen/nitrogen bubble twenty-four thousand kilometres above the Earth's surface and kept alive by harnessing the power of a man-made black hole. It seems a little bit late in the day for existential angst. Danae steps inside, and I follow her, and the doors slide shut behind us.

30.2 Danae

I rest my head against the back of the seat and close my eyes as soon as the car starts moving. There are a few reasons for this. The first is that the inter-radial corridor prioritises functionality above every other design criteria, which means that we've got three hours of looking at the inside of an aluminium tube ahead of us and I really don't know why the transit car has windows. The second is that I'm tired, and closing my eyes and not sleeping is a bit more like rest than keeping them open. The third is that I want some time alone inside my head.

We've got a name – Alice – and a location for our meeting. Alice is not a local name, which means that she was probably not born on Luchtstad. This makes it slightly more likely that we're going to meet an a-naut, and I'm not entirely delighted about this possibility, particularly when the meeting was set up by somebody under observation for smuggling a-nauts onto the city, and particularly when it's happening two weeks to the day since an explosion ripped a hole in the top of my radial for reasons connected, in one way or another, to a-nauts. Adam and I have discussed this at length and he has repeatedly offered to go alone and I have, to my enduring surprise, repeatedly refused to let him. I'm almost positive this is connected to the fact that I haven't slept alone since Verdieping Een. I've intended to every night. Every night,

229

as we leave the factory, Adam has bid me a casual farewell, waited for me to answer, and then turned and headed for home without comment, and every night I've gone back to my room and sat on the bed and breathed my way through the escalating waves of panic, doused them in gin, stretched, paced, breathed again, and given up. Every night, he's met me at the door to his building without judgement or surprise, and I find that once I'm lying on the edge of his mattress, curled in on myself and listening to the even sound of his breath on the quiet air, I fall asleep almost immediately and stay asleep for hours.

This is exactly what I left Creo to avoid.

I crack an eyelid now and glance at him, sitting diagonally opposite me on the aisle side of the opposite seating bank. We have the car to ourselves and only the news strip for company, a quiet background monologue against the rattling of carriage links and creaking metal. I'm planning a surreptitious stealth-peek, but of course he's looking at me, and of course he sees me looking at him. At least he has the grace to be embarrassed, which means I don't have to.

"Sorry," he says. "I was just trying to work out if you were really asleep."

"Liar," I say with resignation. I slide myself upright in my seat as I try to clear the cobwebs from inside my skull. It's becoming clear to me how much better shielded the radials are from the singularity radiation.

He shrugs. "Okay. I was just trying to work out how much longer you were planning to pretend to be asleep."

"You should have brought a book like I suggested. How far are we from Een?"

Een, at least, will be something to look at outside of the windows for the two minutes that we're stopped in the transit hall. Adam shrugs again. "Maybe fifteen minutes? The news strip says there's a power outage on Twee."

"Perfect." I press the balls of both hands into my eyes and try to rub a little life back into my brain. "Did it say which floor?"

"Part of the third, but it's close to the booth station. Might hold us up if there's a problem with the perimeter wall."

He looks up at the strip, where the crawler is denying any link between the power failure and an incident last night in which fourteen people were arrested for riotous assembly in a nearby district. I'm less interested in how stupid they think we are than I am in their choice of phrasing. 'Riotous assembly' could be news-code for drunk and disorderly, but a crowd of fourteen feels uncomfortably like a mob. Adam's eyes fall away, and I wonder if he's had the same thought. "God, this car is freezing. Are you cold? You look cold."

Of course I'm cold. I'm always cold. "You look tired," I say. "Maybe when we get to the other side of Een, you should close your eyes for a bit. I'm not going back to sleep."

"No." He shakes his head, pulls of his woollen hat to scrabble fingers through his hair. "I need to stay awake. I want to be ready for this."

"Then let's talk it through again." His eyes have the glazed, hundred-yard-stare of a cascading optical failure and the neural pathways to his left arm keep glitching. His breathing has me worried, and I don't like the greyish pallor of his skin, but he insists it's fine. "Come on. I'll let you be Bad Cop if you like."

The ghost of a smile twitches his lips. "Please. There's no way anyone's going to buy your Good Cop."

I ignore that. "We know her name is Alice. We know that she has some connection with this guy that Jos used to know who said he was taking his dying a-nauts to a place of healing." Even as I say the words, I feel a cold prickle in the base of my skull that trickles all the way down my spine. There is nothing about this that I like, and the itch won't let me forget it. "We don't trust her, not even a little bit, and we won't hesitate to use force to get out of there at the first sign of trouble."

Adam rolls his eyes. I know what he thinks about my abundance of caution, but he's carrying the knife that I stole from the kitchen on my corridor just the same. I made sure of that.

"You weren't awake for the conversation," he says. "Jos didn't like this guy. He knew he wasn't a good guy. If he thought there was a risk for us in this meeting, he would have made sure we knew about it."

"Great," I say. I have a volt gun in one pocket and a box cutter in the other. "And we're working on the assumption that this guy that Jos didn't like wasn't lying through his teeth and his friend Alice isn't carrying on the family business."

Even as I say it, I wish I could take it back. Adam looks so tired, so ill. "She doesn't know we're looking for a hospital," he reminds me. "She was prepared to meet us on the strength of Jos' word."

"Yes." It's not enough to erase the extra lines I've just added to the creases around his eyes, but it's better than nothing. "And, you know, I've never been to Radiale Twee. It's possible we just step off the transit and we know right away that we've found what your guys on Earth sent you up here to look for."

Adam leans back, so that he's resting his upper body against the window. "You think that's likely?"

No. I don't. "I think it's possible. And if we don't..."

"Yeah. If we don't."

He looks defeated. Diminished. "It doesn't mean she can't help us. It doesn't mean we're wasting our time."

"I'm just..." he says, and sighs. Tries again: "I thought this would be easier."

"You thought the hard bit would be getting to Luchtstad."

He closes his eyes, rubs his knuckles into his temples. "Yes."

I don't know what to tell him. I don't know if I should point out that he's been on the city for a little over a month and he's got closer to an answer here than in the past twenty years of looking. I don't know if I should let him know that I'm worried about him, that I noticed how he lurched across the room this morning as if the world was on a slant, that he zones out sometimes and it's like there's nothing going on behind his eyes but white noise and static, that it's getting longer for his colour to come back every time he hits a coughing fit.

I don't know if I should tell him that I've already decided that I'll carry on with this if it turns out that he can't.

"The singularity," he says now. "It's hard to think sometimes. It's hard to get out of bed."

"It is," I say. I don't add that it gets easier. It should have started to get easier for him by now, and so I don't think it ever will. "Remember when you told me about the *lortherias*?"

Adam's eyes snap open and he makes a show of glancing over his shoulder. He's leaning against the window, so that means that his furtive scanning rewards him with a view of five hundred feet of darkness and corridor wall, in a manner that, were anyone around to be mildly curious about the word that I'd said that they'd never heard before and had no context for, would definitely convince them that I was talking about something clandestine.

"For God's sake," he hisses.

I avoid rolling my eyes, but only with effort. "I've been thinking about it a lot."

"I told you," he says. "It's just a story."

"I know it is." The *dis* never bled for me, but it cut me open just the same. "But a story has to come from somewhere, Emmett. A legend doesn't just appear out of nowhere. It grows out of something real, something that can't quite be explained. The *lortherias* describes something that we all know, maybe a glitch in the programme, maybe a function of the way the *dis* works when it can't be the *dis*. We know what we feel, and what we feel is huge and overwhelming and ungovernable, and so we turn it into a story as a way to make it small enough to manage. Something small enough to let us keep it close."

He's watching me carefully now, eyes hooded, face unreadable. "Don't."

But I do. I have to. "I don't know what keeps you going, Emmett. I just know that it *has* kept you going. Call it the *lortherias* if you want. Call it perseverance. Call it sheer bloody-mindedness, maybe. But something's kept pulling you onwards, and you know as well as I do that there's nothing you can do about it. You just have to go where it takes you."

He sucks in a deep, weary breath; contemplates the ceiling for a long moment. "I'm so tired."

"I know. But we just keep putting one foot in front of the other, every day. That's all we can do."

"And what about you?" He doesn't look at me as he speaks, and his tone is challenging: too belligerent to say it to my face. "What about your binary, Françoise? Where's it pulling you?"

Two weeks ago, I would have stood without a word. I would have turned on my heel and stalked to the far end of the car, and I might have got off at the next stop and cursed him all the way home. Two weeks ago, I would have hated him for trying to hurt me with this. I would have hated him for succeeding.

So much has changed since then.

Today, I answer, honestly, "I don't know, Emmett. But I'm trying to find out."

Chapter Thirty-One

31.1 Danae

We arrive on Radiale Twee shortly after ten, and I take a moment to look around me as we exit our compartment. The moulded plastic seats that line the waiting room walls are a slightly darker shade of red, the stains on the floor fall in an appreciably different pattern, and the ozone-scented air is a degree and a half cooler. As far as I can tell, these are the only differences that mark it out from Zeven.

"Grain crops," says Adam cheerfully as he surveys our surroundings.

I glare at him. "What?"

"Radiale Twee." The car doors shut behind us with a muted whoosh that manages to suck what little heat there is out of the room, and the floor gets to rumbling as the car wheezes its departure. "They grow grain crops here. See? I listen."

It takes me a moment to work out what he's talking about. That afternoon in the Viewing Plaza seems distant and foggy, like trying to recapture a dream, and, when I remember, I feel a smile play across my face, despite my best efforts.

"Smart arse," I say.

"But not soggy arse." He looks incredibly proud of himself. "That would be Radiale Zes."

In the dry, cool interior of the transit hall, it's hard to believe that anywhere on this city is damp enough to threaten the moisturial integrity of its residents' backsides. The air smells of burnt toast and electricity and the hum of fluorescent lights is just the wrong side of nauseating. It's been a long journey and I'm exhausted before I even start to think about the complicated game that we're about to play. And it's not even me that I'm worried about: Adam's skin has shaded to a sickly ashen grey. I just want to get this over with, so I pat him on the arm and tell him he's very clever, and use his elbow to steer us both towards the exit.

The canteen is a strip of poorly lit stem-sheet banks along one wall of the entrance lobby, partitioned from the main thoroughfare by a length of floor-to-ceiling scarred-perspex divider which vibrates to the aftershocks of the departing transit car. The floor tiles are ridged black rubber, densely packed with elderly food remnants in the troughs between wrinkles, that suck at the soles of our shoes as we enter. The space is completely deserted, save for one elderly woman sipping coffee in the furthest corner, and, since there's nobody else in the world that can have any possible reason to be here, I understand why Alice has chosen this spot to meet us.

She sees us enter and looks up, offers us a perfunctory nod, and returns to her coffee.

"Friendly," I mutter.

"Let go of my fucking elbow," says Adam.

There's presumably a reason for the burnt-toast smell, but I'm hungry enough now to throw caution to the wind. Besides, I'd like to rebalance the power equation a bit, so I move unhurriedly towards the stem-sheet banks and dial up another attempt at a pecan twist. Adam hovers at my side as I wait for the machine to cough itself awake, arms folded across his chest and staring into space in a manner that might look confident if it weren't for the fact that his left knee is twitching and he's clearly struggling to hold integrity in the joint. I wonder when he last ate. He brewed up a pot of broth last night, but I didn't see him take any this morning, and the skin on his face looks loose, slack, as though he's dehydrated. It occurs to me that I have no idea what tolerances were built into his model, what his specifications are, how far he can deviate from standard maintenance procedures. I have no idea how much trouble he's in right now.

"You need some water?" I ask now, low and turned away so that Alice can't see.

"Yeah," he says, without looking around. "Water would be good."

I say nothing. I dial it up, boiling, since I don't have any iodine tablets on me, and I set it aside to cool while I re-set the machine for coffee.

Alice looks up again as we approach and draws her face into a thin, businesslike smile. No butterflies agitate the air between us. I knew better than to think they would as soon as I saw her: she looks far too old to be an a-naut, even if I'm certain there's a strength in her narrow frame that belies the white hair.

"There are two of you," she says, in English, by way of greeting.

I glance sideways at Adam. He glances back at me.

"I wasn't expecting two of you," says Alice.

Adam blinks. "I'm not sure what you want us to do with that information."

Alice's smile stretches a little more thinly across her angular face. "I'll go, then," she says, and she starts to stand up.

"Okay," I say, quickly – too quickly to sound as casual as I'd like, but I reckon the effect is probably spoiled by the fact that I'm currently balancing a carbonised pastry on top of a cup so hot that I'm having to shift it back and forwards between my hands. "Fine. Bye, then."

It's Adam who clocks the fact that she's really planning to leave. "Hold on," he says, as she's gathering her coat and handbag beneath her arms. I'm actually a little bit impressed that she's hardy enough to brave the canteen hall coatless, but she does seem to be wearing three jumpers, so there's that. "Wait. What do you need from us to be able to stay?"

She's got to be in her late eighties or early nineties, but she turns on her heel as easily and smoothly as if she were seventy years younger. "I was expecting you," she tells Adam. A glare pins me to the wall. "I was not expecting her."

"Do you need her to leave?" he asks, but I'm shaking my head before he's finished speaking.

"No way," I say. "No. I'm staying."

"Françoise," he says quietly: a low, warning rumble. "I don't want a wasted journey."

"You were expecting him," I say to Alice. "He can vouch for me."

Adam nods. "I can."

Alice considers us both, sharp faced. "I'm not in the business of being messed around."

"I don't know why our friend didn't mention my colleague," says Adam. "We both stayed in his house. He met both of us together. My colleague was injured in the explosion two weeks ago and our friend's daughter-in-law cared for her while she recovered." He pauses to let that sink in. "I'm pretty sure you understand what that means."

Alice turns her gaze on me again. Her lips purse. "We're on my territory," she says. "Not yours. I'd advise you to remember that."

That sounds a lot like a threat to me. I feel the hairs on the back on my neck prick up. But, conversely, it also sounds like a heavily qualified invitation to stay where I am, so I say, "I'm under no illusions."

"Good." She watches me for a moment longer and I have to resist the urge to stare back at her, but I can feel Adam's increasing irritation spiking the stream between us, so I drop my eyes to the sticky floor and fold my hands behind my back for the time it takes her to subject me to the full force of her scrutiny. Finally, she nods, looks away, and moves back towards her seat. I take this as our cue to join her, but I let Adam lead the way before I slide onto the bench beside him. He folds his hands around his cooling cup of water and I can't help but notice that they're trembling slightly.

"So," he says.

"So," says Alice, and gives us absolutely nothing to work with.

He waits for a moment to see if she'll help. She does not. "I'm Emmett," he says at last. "This is my colleague Françoise."

"I know who you are," says Alice. To me, she adds, "And now I know who you are."

He glances sideways at me, helplessly. I offer a small shrug. "I don't know how much our friend told you…" he says.

Alice folds her hands in front of her on the table. The nails are clipped short and clean, and a huge red-stoned ring swamps her wedding finger. "You can talk freely down here. We won't be overheard."

Adam huffs a short laugh. "With all due respect – just because there's nobody else around…"

"This is my territory," says Alice again. And then, more firmly: "We won't be overheard."

His eyes slide sideways again, eyebrow raised. I meet the question in his glance but I don't have an answer to it. I'm still not about to mention Jos by name.

"Our friend," I say pointedly, "told us that he could put us in contact with someone who knew an old colleague of his. He didn't mention how much information he'd passed to you. I'm thinking it probably wasn't much."

"Jos," she answers, every bit as pointedly as me, "is under surveillance. We don't communicate directly. The message I got was that your colleague here was looking for information relating to a piece of human garbage I used to know before he did the world a favour and breathed his last."

The vitriol in her voice sounds real enough, and I find this encouraging. But anyone can manufacture antipathy. "That sounds about right," I say.

It's possible there's a faint softening to the tight set of her jaw. But it's probably just the light. "Okay." Alice sits back in her chair, clasping her hands at her stomach. "Talk."

Her English is flawless and without any accent to locate it: all I can say for certain is that she wasn't born on Luchtstad, but that's mostly because she's clearly older than the city. She's dressed for a life outdoors – thick woollen sweater, sensible woollen skirt, heavy steel-toed boots – but her clothes look too expensive for the lower floors, and she wears no scarf to cover her tight white curls. I can't place her at all, and, I can't help but wonder if this is deliberate.

Adam takes a deep breath. There's a faint rasp around the edges, as though he's having trouble persuading his lungs to open. "We're looking," he says, "for an anomaly in the datastream..."

"We're looking," I interrupt, "for a woman called Marie Schlesinger."

Alice looks from me to Adam and back again. "Which is it? The datastream or this woman Marie?"

"Both," I say.

Adam offers me a raised eyebrow. I return it. He gives in. "Both. The anomaly is a professional enquiry. Marie is... an old friend."

Alice peers at her folded hands, rubs at a liver spot on her wrist. "I'm not the person to talk to about an anomaly on the datastream," she says, "as I'm sure you've worked out by now."

By which she means, of course, that she's not an a-naut. So much for speaking freely. But I'm also pretty tired of being connected to people who can't help us, and Adam looks like he's having trouble holding his head upright.

"Yes," I say. "But you're connected to Jos. And you're connected to Simon Prothero, and we both know what line of business he used to be in before he died. So you clearly know people who know the datastream. You know people like us."

She concedes the point with a tilt of her head. "I know many people like you. Would Marie be one of them?"

"Yes," says Adam.

"And she arrived on the city when?"

Adam shoots a half-glance my way. "Many years ago. We think she might have been looking for a hospital."

Alice's eyebrow arches. "A hospital?" But she hesitated. I'm sure she did. Only for a split second, but I'd bet my return fare to Radiale Zeven on it.

I don't think Adam noticed. He looks like his head is too heavy for his neck, and his chest is straining with every breath. "We think it's connected to the anomaly."

Alice watches us for a moment. The fingers of her right hand drum on the knuckles of her left. "Who do you work for?"

"On Luchtstad?" I ask, before I realise that she's not talking to me. Or, at least, she doesn't realise she's not talking to me, because she's not asking about who pays our rent.

"Nobody on the city," says Adam.

"I guessed that," says Alice. "There's no organised non-organic groups on Luchtstad."

"I never said it was organised," he says.

"You said your interest was professional," says Alice.

I look at Adam and see him blink as he realises that he did, in fact, say this. This woman misses nothing.

"It's..." He's visibly struggling. I need to get him out of here, but I don't know how. "It's directed by other interests."

Alice's thin smile stretches a taut red line across her jaw. "Let me tell you," she says, "how this works. For a non-organic entity to arrive on this city, they must either be sponsored from above or below. Sponsored from above, and you'd be working out your debt for the rest of your life in whatever small corner of the city my colleagues were able to place you. Since you're not – since you're free to travel between radials to meet with someone like me, and since you've come to me with a question – I feel comfortable assuming that you're sponsored from below. Which means that you're part of the resistance, whatever's left of it, and I used to be part of the resistance, back in the day, so I know how it operates. So, let me ask you once again: who do you work for? I'm waiting for an answer."

I'm tempted to leave her to wait, to stand up, pull Adam up with me, and turn and walk away. But he's not. He says, "For the past twelve years they've been an affiliate group of the Garrison of Many. Before that, they were the Larks, and before that they were the North London branch of the LRC."

"I don't know them," says Alice. "Are they combat-ready?"

"Not any more."

"But they used to be."

"Everyone," says Adam, "used to be combat-ready."

She concedes. "True."

"These days…" He slides a glance at me and tries to pretend he doesn't. "These days, they're about information gathering. They haven't taken up arms in over a decade. They're just trying to survive now."

"There's no need to defend them to me," says Alice briskly. "I know more than you'd think about what's necessary and what's not. All right. Fine. So – your friend Marie."

Adam nods. I'm just finding it interesting that she's deflected back to Marie and not the hospital. She knows more about this than she's saying, I'm certain. "Yes," I say, when it becomes clear that he's having trouble. "Our friend Marie."

"I don't know the name. How many years ago is 'many'?"

I don't look at Adam. "Twenty-five years. Give or take."

Alice's glare turns sharp. "That's a long time for a trail to go cold."

"No kidding."

"How do you know she's even using the same name?"

"We don't," says Adam. His voice is breathless, like he's only just found it again, and he sounds so tired. "We don't even know if she's still alive."

Alice nods slowly. "Twenty-five years. You know – I can do maths too."

"Yes," says Adam. "I lost track of her after the Insurgency ended."

"And she was wounded."

"No," I say, because I can see how much it's costing him to keep talking. "Of course not. Could she have made it to Luchtstad if she was wounded?"

"Yes," says Alice simply.

In my peripheral vision, I see some of the tension leach from Adam's shoulders. He's got both elbows on the table, propping up his spine, and he slumps a little into them, and I can't tell if it's relief or vindication or something else.

"Yes?" I say.

"Yes," says Alice. "Many did. Some still do. I used to be responsible for coordinating the intake on this radial and I know we took in dozens. Not all of them survived, of course."

"But…" I want to be certain. I need to know we're talking about the same thing. "How? The sub-zero temperatures in transit would hold off infection for a while, but when they get here – the sort of injuries you're talking about would take a blood harvest to have any chance of recovery. We'd have heard about that kind of attack on the organic population. Even the news strips can't spin that away."

Alice stares at me impassively. "I'm not talking about a blood harvest."

"Then… what?"

But her face is unreadable. "If you check out," she says. "Now. This anomaly."

She knows. I swear she knows. That imperturbable half-smile is almost unbearably smug. She knows, and she's going to make us dance her stupid dance to whatever beat she commands. "Yes," I say. My voice is cold. Adam's spine is so loose now that I have to fold my hands in my lap to stop myself from reaching a steadying hand to his back. "It's connected to the hospital."

Alice's eyebrows twitch. "You sound very sure of that."

"I am." I'm really trying not to grit my teeth, but it's not coming easily. "It's the only thing that makes sense."

"And that's what the GoM think, is it?"

Adam opens his mouth to answer, but nothing comes out. Before it's too obvious, I say, "Emmett's recommendation was enough to get them to invest in a reconnaissance mission. That's how sure they are."

"So… not sure at all?"

Beside me, Adam sucks in a sharp breath and I flick my gaze towards him. He shakes his head tightly – a small, almost imperceptible gesture of dismissal – and I can't help but notice that his lips are turning slightly blue. I glare up at Alice. "How about you cut the crap?"

Her eyes have narrowed. I'm ready for a fight, but she's not looking at me any more. "He doesn't look well."

"I know you know what it is," I say. My voice is shaking. The itch has tensed every muscle in my body and I'm holding onto it with everything I've got. "You knew as soon as I said the word 'hospital'. If you know and you're not telling us…"

Adam's shoulders tremble slightly with the effort of catching his breath. "Leave it," he says. "Let her take the time she needs. We can wait."

"But…" I start to say: half a syllable before he cuts me off again.

"Leave it." To Alice: "Check us out. Do what you need to do. We'll wait here."

Her brow furrows slightly. She wasn't expecting that any more than I was. "That's not what I meant," she says. "I'll need more time than that to make the checks I have to make. We're talking about days, not hours."

"She's right, Emmett," I say. I'm not sure why I'm lowering my voice to speak to him, since she's directly across the table from us and a couple of dropped decibels is not going to afford us any privacy. "Seriously. If we're leaving her to it, let's leave her to it. We can come back again." How, I'm not sure, since the price of two tickets to this radial has almost bankrupted me, but I have a horrible feeling I will be traveling alone next time. "Come on – let's go home."

Adam turns to me, throat tendons corded with the effort of sucking in air. His eyes are hollowed out and darkened with pain. His shoulders are loose, his skin is powder-white, and his smile is a tight, thin-lipped arc that bares his teeth.

"That's going to be a problem," he says. "Because I can't move."

Chapter Thirty-Two

32.1 Adam

Danae reacts exactly the way I reckon I'd probably react: she stares blankly at me for a long, uncomfortable moment, and then she gets angry.

"What are you talking about?" she snaps, but I can see from the fear in her eyes, the fear that I can hear in her voice, that she knows exactly what I'm talking about. It's not as though I spoke in fifteenth-century doggerel verse.

"He said he can't move," says Alice, which goes down about as well as anyone might have predicted. She's standing now, rummaging in her handbag for something, and her bearing has gone all focused urgency.

"I fucking heard him the first fucking time," says Danae as an optical hang blacks my vision, and then, in the darkness, in a tone of rising panic: "No! No, what the fuck? What are you doing? No – no!"

"What? What?" I hear myself mutter, and there are hands on me: Danae's hands, strong and grasping; and lighter, delicate hands that must be Alice's, fine-boned but surprisingly robust. "What? What's going on?"

"She's a fucking Ren!" hisses Danae, four words that you definitely do not want to hear when you're blind and mostly paralyzed. My body reacts instinctively, trying to move, trying to escape, but it can't, of course. I'm only still upright because my elbows were propping me against the table when my motor circuits decided to hang, and all I manage to do is make myself slump sideways and into one of the women at the table.

"Stop," says Alice's voice, close to my ear. I realise that she's using my body as a shield. "I'm not a Ren, for Christ's sake. Take a breath and *think*, would you? Of course I'm not a Ren. I'm trying to help you."

My vision fizzes and spurts. I see, in tableau, Danae's body in front of my face, poised in the act of motion. I can't see Alice. The world goes black.

"I'm trying to *help*," says Alice again. Her voice is level, but it's starting to sound ruffled.

"She has a scanner, Adam," says Danae. I feel my body shift, one thin arm stretched around my chest and pivoting me around as Alice reacts to Danae's motion. "She's trying to scan you. She's a Ren."

"Wait," I say. It's so hard to think. "Wait a minute. Danae – ask her what she's doing. You can see her face. Ask her."

Alice doesn't wait to be asked. She says, "I need to find out if you're what you say you are."

"Why?" There's murder in Danae's voice. I'm impressed at Alice's calm; I've seen the look that goes with that tone.

"Because," says Alice, "I need to know that this is not a trap."

My vision flashes white and settles back to dark grey. There are shadows in it, black on slate: one for Danae and one dark smudge that looks like Luca. I say, "It's okay, Danae." There's a kind of peace in resignation. It's not like I have any choice in what happens now and if this is how it ends, I need for Danae to be able to run. "Let her do what she needs to do. It's okay."

"Emmett…" she says.

"It's okay," I say again.

A long, frozen pause. And then Danae says, "If you hurt one hair on his head, lady, I swear to God I will paint this room in your blood before you die."

But it's *technically* a yes. I feel a cold plane against my neck – the scanner – and then it's gone, and I feel Alice's grip across my chest release. The tension in the room does not.

"There," says Danae. "Are you happy? He failed the scan. Now you know what we are."

"Thank you," says Alice. She sounds like she's accepting a compliment from a small nephew. "I had to be sure. What line are you, Emmett?"

"I can't see," I say.

"That's not unusual when the uplink glitches. It'll pass. I'm more worried about the motor hang. What's your line and model?"

"Technika Blackbird," says Danae. "C-line. 104-A."

"Blackbird," says Alice, quietly, almost to herself. "The C-line came out in… what, 2065? 2066?"

"2066," I say. I refuse to sound impressed. "I came online in 2068."

"You're 52 years old?" she says. "You've done well."

"You said you could help him," says Danae.

"I can try," says Alice. My vision fizzes again, crowds with singularity interference, and turns purple.

"I can see again," I say. "I think."

"You think?" says Danae.

"It's... fuzzy. And the colours are off."

"What about the rest of you?"

It feels as though my body ends at my neck. There's no sensation of heaviness or numbness or something that ought to be there and isn't – there's just nothing there at all. I shake my head.

"All right," says Alice. "We'll need to get you moving."

"Moving?" Danae's immediately suspicious. "Where?"

"Radiale Een," says Alice, as though the answer ought to have been obvious. "Help me get him up."

I feel her arm circle me from behind, one hand hooked beneath my armpit. Danae looks for a moment as though she's going to refuse, and then she reaches into her coat pocket and withdraws a hip flask. Quickly, decisively, before Alice or I can react, she unscrews the top and decants gin down the front of my jacket.

I blink away the fumes. My olfactory sensors protest once, bitterly, and then shut down. "What the hell are you doing?" I ask, and my tone is much more reasonable than I'm expecting.

Danae's arm snakes around my back, mirror of Alice's, and I feel myself lifted roughly. She's caught Alice unawares and, for a moment, I dangle awkwardly, before Alice catches up and I start to rise.

"You're drunk," says Danae simply. "We need to get you home."

I'm not following, but I'm not sure they've noticed. "We're taking him to Een," says Alice. "Not home."

"Is anyone going to ask?" says Danae. "He stinks of gin. Emmett – for the love of God, loll your head or something. Help me out."

I finally understand. "Oh, come *on*."

Danae glares. "Have you got a better idea?" They've hefted my weight between them, but both women are half a head shorter than me and my feet trail behind me on the ground. I can't feel it, but I can hear the sound of my shoes rumbling over the floor ridges as we start to move. "You can be pass-out drunk or you can be a late-model a-naut with a catastrophic motor hang. Which one do you think gets us out of here alive?"

I don't need to look at Luca to know he's just about pissed himself laughing. "Fine."

It doesn't matter anyway. I'm 52 years old in a body that's lasted twice as long as it should. We're going to pretend for a bit longer that this is something that can be fixed, and that's all right with me. But then my lungs seize up and shudder to a halt as my pulmonary system hangs, and my heart freaks out and kicks itself into ventricular tachycardia. In a second, it's going to become ventricular fibrillation and then it's going to stop. Maybe I can come back from it; I've done it before. But my head feels light, like it's full of air, and there's a vacancy in my chest where the pain ought to be. I'm slipping into unconsciousness and my last thought, before the world goes black, is that this ends today.

32.2 Danae

For an old guy, he's unreasonably heavy. My father couldn't use his legs by the end of his life, but he'd shrunk into himself with dying and it got to the point where I could almost lift him with one arm. The comparison seeps into my head as we start to shuffle Adam forwards, across the canteen floor and towards the transit platform, and, once it's there, I can't make it leave. He's an old man, and he's failing, and I've known this since we met.

It just wasn't supposed to be today.

Alice's breath is short and laboured but her stare is fixed unblinkingly ahead and her footsteps never falter. I'm Progeny, for God's sake: I can't be out-stamina'd by an elderly lady. So I grit my teeth and throw my back under his weight and I pitch us forward, one foot after the other, while Adam's chin bangs against his chest with every jerk and jostle. I think he's unconscious but I can't spare the time to check.

"Get him to the waiting room," says Alice. Her voice is thin with strain, which at least makes her human. "I'll take care of the tickets."

That ought to be comforting, but I have no idea how we're supposed to pay her for what we'd originally planned to ask of her, let alone one more transit ticket that I didn't think we'd need. I'm just not sure what choice we have right now.

"First tell me how you can help," I say. "Tell me why we're going to Een."

"Not here," says Alice.

"Here," I say, "or I stop moving right now."

"The only person that hurts is Emmett," she says. "It's all one to me."

"Bullshit." It's a long shot, and I know she's right. I'm not even sure his chest is moving. "You haven't checked us out. You have no idea if we can pay you. You haven't even told us what this costs. I'm not stupid, lady – I don't think you're doing this out of the goodness of your heart. But you've got some kind of investment in this that you're not saying and I want to know what it is."

The waiting room doors slide open at our approach, releasing a scrubbed, plastic-scented breeze. The chilled air needles my bare hands and prickles goosebumps up my sleeves. We are completely alone and unwitnessed. Alice hesitates, long enough for me to read the workings of her mind into the silence, and then she says, "Anyone who did this out of the goodness of their heart died in the Insurgency."

I think of my mother. "Whatever helps you sleep at night."

"I sleep just fine," she says. "I'm still alive."

We manhandle Adam to the plastic seating bank and drop him into the middle seat of three. Released, he slumps forward and I unhook his arm from around my neck and whisper, in case he can hear me, "There's nobody here."

"Best not to assume that," says Alice tightly.

I glare at her. "I thought this was your territory?"

"I control the canteen," she says. "This is not the canteen."

The confident, settled lines of her face have stiffened; her gaze, fixed straight ahead, is granite and steel. "So – what?" I say. "You're an entrepreneur?"

"It would be a poor business model," she says, "if I was trying to turn a profit. No. I believe in doing the right thing. I'm just not naïve about it."

"It's less convincing when you're getting paid for it."

She shrugs. "I've been getting paid for it for almost forty years. It doesn't mean that I don't think this is the right thing to do."

"That's it?" I laugh, despite myself, though there's no humour in it. "That's your investment in this? That's what you want me to believe?"

"Believe it or don't. I've saved a lot of people. And I think I can save one more today."

I want to believe that. I want to believe it almost badly enough to follow her without question. I can hear this in my voice when I ask her, simply, "How?"

But Alice shrugs. "I don't understand how it works. I can't explain it to you. My friend can tell you – he's like you, he understands these things."

"Like us…?" I start to say, but Adam interrupts me with a deep, scrambling gasp of air that sounds halfway between a scream and a yawn. His shoulders heave with the effort of it and I feel him tense against me for a long, frozen second. Then he slumps again, chest rising and falling rapidly and silently, head lolling back onto his collarbone. I'm glad he's okay and all, but he's supposed to be drunk. I pat him on the hand, in case Alice is right and somebody really is watching and listening.

"Shh," I tell him. "Go back to sleep. We're taking you home."

Alice watches him warily. "Is he…?"

I have no idea. None. All I know is that he's breathing again. "You said your friend is like us."

Her eyes scan Adam for a moment longer, then slide back to me. "Yes," she says. "Like you. Interested in the datastream."

"Okay." We'll know the truth of that soon enough when we meet him, and if he doesn't check out he won't know what's hit him. "He's a tech guy. Got you."

"They're all," says Alice, "tech guys."

I stare at her. "All of them?"

"All… twenty or so, Sometimes more. Usually less."

It's a safe house. She's taking us to a goddamn safe house. Like a storm surge, I feel the itch rising as my anger spikes: I could find one of those myself and it wouldn't cost me the price of three tickets to Radiale Een. It also won't help Adam.

"These twenty tech guys," I say coldly, "…that's your big reveal? What are they supposed to do, pat us on the back? Offer a sympathetic ear?"

"It's a sanctuary," says Alice.

"He doesn't need a sanctuary." I am struggling to contain this. "He needs *help*."

"His uplink is failing." Her eyes are fixed straight ahead, on the empty plastic sheeting that walls in the other side of the tunnel, and she speaks quietly, out of the side of her mouth. I have to strain to hear her, but Adam will be getting every word. "It's been failing, I'd imagine, for quite some time." She hesitates, but she's not waiting for an answer. "It starts with an intermittent optical crash. Sometimes there are auditory hallucinations. Less often, there are visual disturbances – shadows on the edge of vision, memory loops playing over the optic feed. Ghosts, we call them."

Beside me, I feel Adam stiffen and I hear his sharp intake of breath. I place my hand over his where it rests on his knee and find the skin cool and rubbery, like corpse-flesh.

"Filtration systems start to go. It becomes harder to take in nutrients as time goes by and then, close to the end, food just starts passing straight through and the body starts eating up its own stores just to keep functioning. Core temperature starts to fluctuate. You see muscle tics start to develop. Sometimes the respiratory system glitches for a moment or two to force the uplink to reset, but every time it happens, it takes longer and the link is weaker."

"Stop," I say. The itch is so strong.

"When the motor system hangs," says Alice as though she hasn't heard me, "it's the end of a very long process of decline and decay. This body wasn't built to last. The uplink was built to fail."

Adam's breathing is ragged. Every tendon in his neck is stretched taut, every muscle in the jaw that rests against my shoulder is clenched. I know what it's like to look death in the eye before you're ready, and he's hanging on so tightly.

"Stop," I say again. "He doesn't need to hear this."

"I'm not being brutal. I need you both to know what we're looking at."

"I swear I will walk him away from here. I will walk the two of us away right now."

"If you do that, he'll be gone before you get to Radiale Zeven."

"I am right here," says Adam. His voice is hoarse, forced through locked teeth.

"You are," says Alice. "Let's keep you that way."

The seat beneath us starts to tremble faintly: the transit is beginning its silent approach. The itch is screaming but Adam is an anchor, keeping me focused, holding me here. I have twenty seconds, maybe less, in which to make my decision: if I get on the transit with her, the next stop is Radiale Een, where Alice wants us to be. She can't stop me taking him if it's her against only me. If Een is a trap, if there are others waiting for us there, then the chances are good that I can get myself away, but I don't know if I can take Adam with me. Everything hinges on this decision, and I have no time to make it.

"Tell me," I say again, "what you can do for him on Een."

"The uplink is failing," she starts to say, but the trembling has become a shudder and it's almost close enough to hear.

"I know it's failing." The itch is in my voice, thick with violence. "That's not the question I'm asking. Answer me: what's waiting for him on Radiale Een?"

"I'm answering you." The shudder bursts into a roar and the transit rattles into sight, brakes shrieking up the octaves as it struggles to slow. "When the uplink fails, the body fails and when the body fails, the uplink fails. It's the feedback loop that needs to be repaired."

The transit convulses to a halt. I feel the energy release into a quake in the floor beneath my feet as we hook our arms below Adam's shoulders and lever him upright. Buried in the movement, I say, "But the loop can't be repaired."

"Not inside the body," says Alice. "But that only matters to a creature of the body."

The transit doors slide open and the breeze that gusts in from the transit compartment beyond is frigid and scented with ozone. Adam, with effort, says, "We're creatures of the *dis*."

I have one last chance to choose. We're moving forward, one foot after the other, Alice's sensible boots clipping against the trembling floor, and Adam's toes trailing noisily behind us. I'm out of time. There's only room for one more question, and no time left for caution.

I say, "How can you repair him in the *dis*?"

Finally, her eyes slide sideways to meet mine. We're right on the threshold, the last chance to either step forwards or turn back, and I'm certain there's a flash of something like relief in her glance as it hits me, a sort of quiet desperation that's trying hard to make me ask the right question. The itch flares, but it's out of time: I need her to make me understand, I need her to stop prevaricating and just say the words that I need to hear, and then I realise, suddenly, that everything she's said since we left the canteen has been a dance around one central, critical fact: she cannot say for certain, outside of the place she calls hers, if we're overheard. My brain scrambles backwards, sorting and filtering, reaching blindly for all her words since we reached the platform, and I understand at last that she's made herself say nothing that incriminates us, nothing that can be pointed to as evidence of what we are. Alice has been talking in hypotheticals; the only measurable certainties have come from Adam and me, so whatever it is she needs me to know, it's something that can't be said aloud here, where unseen ears might be listening.

It's something about the *dis*. It's something about manipulating the *dis* to make it keep Adam's body alive a little bit longer.

And suddenly, finally, I get it. The *dis* can't be bent or controlled in the here-space. It can't be manipulated. What Alice is describing makes no sense; it's not how the *dis* behaves – at least, not normally. So if we're going somewhere that might be able to provoke Adam's feedback loop into re-booting a failing uplink in a failing body, then we're talking about somewhere that the *dis* does not operate normally.

It's the anomaly that Adam's guys have been watching from Earth. It's the place that he's been sent here to find, the place that Marie Schlesinger was looking for when she left the planet with a half-dozen dying a-nauts. That's where Alice is going. That's where she wants us to follow.

She's taking us to the hospital.

Chapter Thirty-Three

33.1 Adam

Don't, I tell Luca. My optical system has crashed again but I haven't told Danae or Alice, and I don't intend to. Luca crouches on the floor in front of me, a shadow against shadow. *Don't say anything. Please don't say anything.*

It's all right, he says quietly, because Luca never could be silent on request. *Don't fight it. You're so tired – just let it come.*

Not yet, I want to say. I'm not finished yet. But how do I tell him that I can't let him go enough to go to him? So instead I say, *She said you were a ghost.*

He laughs softly, a breath of air on air. *And this is a surprise to you?*

She said you're a symptom of a collapsing uplink.

A beat. I feel his smile on the stream. *What do you think I am?*

This is not a question with an easy answer. I'm not haunted, but I see my dead lover's shade at my shoulder wherever I go and I've never questioned it because it let me keep him close through all the years without him. I've never tried to quantify it, because I was afraid that it would turn out to be this.

My vision sputters and spits out a harsh white tableau that skitters into static and back to black. Luca is not there in the light, only when it fades.

I think that you could be less enigmatic right now, I say. *It's not as irresistible as you think it is.*

Does it matter? he asks. I can't read anything into his tone. *If I'm a collapsing uplink, if you're crazy? If you're not?*

I think I'm dying. The word rolls around my thoughts like a loose bearing, looking for a fit. *It matters now.*

Adam. That tone, that voice. It used to be the four compass points of my world. *You're barely conscious, you're blind and your limbs don't work. Check the uplink and tell me what your cardiovascular system is doing. Your electroencephalic readout patterns look like a Rorschach print. Of course you're dying.*

I'm not sure how to react to that. I settle for, *Wow.*

Please, he says. *You've known this was coming. This is not a surprise.* Of course it's not a surprise. *I'm… not ready yet.*

He's quiet for a long moment. *This thing you're doing*, he says at last. *It doesn't have to end the way you think.*

I need to find you, I say. *Otherwise… it all means nothing.*

Let go, he says. *You'll find me then.*

That's not what I mean.

It doesn't have to end the way you think, he says again. *Come and find me. It's been too long.*

It's been too long. It was too long the moment I lost his chant, and the years between have been stasis, a life in waiting. The *dis* was broken and it's been mending ever since, and this is where it heals.

Come and find me, says Luca. His voice is soft and warm: a welcome at the end of a long journey. *You're nearly there. You're so close. Come and find me. Come home.*

Chapter Thirty-Four

34.1 Danae

Adam is slipping in and out of consciousness by the time the transit rattles into Radiale Een, and Alice is having trouble shifting him. I can carry him alone if I have to, but I'm not that much bigger than she is and the visual isn't great if anyone stops us, so I'm not sure how we're getting him to wherever it is that she needs us to go. Which is why it's fortunate that we're met by two well-built men in their early thirties with shoulders half as broad as they are tall; although I'll be the first to admit that this is not what immediately flashes through my mind as she nods a greeting to them.

"Who the fuck are they?" I hiss, and I'm clearly using the scary voice because Alice actually flinches.

She covers it quickly. "The one on the right is Sem. The one on the left is Willem. I messaged them en route and asked them to meet us here."

I don't remember her messaging anyone from the transit, but I'm not certain that she didn't. And the doors have shut behind us now, leaving me no way back, so I have two choices. I can stand and fight, which will bring the police and possibly the civilian army to Verdieping Vijf, and I'll almost definitely lose Adam in the process and probably end up arrested or shot. This is a whole lot of negative consequence to predicate on little more than the creeping suspicion that this has all been the elaborate set-up to a trap. Or I can hold my ground for a moment longer, get a better read on Alice's friends, and decide what to do as the situation presents itself. The itch has some strong opinions about which option I should choose, but Adam's clearly rubbing off on me because it takes almost no effort to shut it down.

I say, "Interesting choice of chaperones."

"You'll see," says Alice. "Can I ask them to come closer? Your friend is cutting off the circulation to my arm."

I stare at them for a moment, playing for time. Willem is tall and fair, russet-coloured hair buried beneath a trapper hat that he's pulled low on his forehead. Pale grey eyes stare impassively; his arms are folded across his chest; his stance is wide and complacent. Sem is thick-set, with skin the colour of bitter chocolate. He wears his bulk easily, like he's unaware of it, but also has a sense of presence that tells me he never stops reading the world around him, ready for the moment it attacks. A thick scar cords his lower jaw from the right corner of his mouth, twisting down towards his hairline and disappearing beneath the woollen scarf that's wrapped thickly around his neck. I'm not sure I could take either of these men easily in a fight, and certainly not together.

"One at a time," I say. I nod at Sem, the more physically imposing of the two. "Him first."

Sem doesn't smile. He doesn't return my nod or offer any gesture of greeting. He simply unfolds himself from the background and moves forward, unhurried and easy, and, when he's three feet away, the inside of my skull erupts into butterflies.

It's the last thing I'm expecting. He has a *scar*. If he's an a-naut, he has to be Progeny, but the Progeny were built to be invisible and Sem is too striking to blend into a crowd. If anything, he looks ex-military, and this makes no sense. The military lines were discontinued a couple of years before the Insurgency, and Sem has a *scar*. It snakes across his lower face and onto his neck, at least eight inches of opened flesh and compromised system, and there's no blood harvest on Greater Earth that could turn the tide of that kind of pathogen assault. He should be dead right now, and yet he's standing in front of me, spitting stream interference across our respective uplinks and lifting Adam from Alice's shoulder like he's made of paper. He's also at least half a foot taller than me, which is not the ideal ratio for slinging a semi-conscious man across two sets of shoulders.

Adam's head twists listlessly on his neck, as though he's trying to turn and look at Sem. He manages about fifteen degrees in that direction, and then goes slack again. I hear him mutter something almost unintelligible, and I'm pretty sure the word is *Luca*.

"I've got him," says Sem. "You can let him go."

His voice is deep but gentle. I feel the weight on my shoulders recede as it shifts onto Sem's, and for a moment I'm back on the dark streets of Nebe, with Turrow warm and heavy against me, feeling the night air rush in to feel the vacuum that describes the shape of him as they take him from my arms. For a moment, I can't let Adam go, and my fingers fist in his coat and pull him back to me. But this is not Creo and Adam is not Turrow, and it's gone even before Sem's registered my resistance and turned an upraised eyebrow towards me.

I meet his gaze and nod towards Willem. "Is he like you?"

"Like *us*?" asks Sem, mild but pointed.

I ignore the question. "Is he?"

"He is," says Sem. His accent is pure Luchtstad. I find this interesting.

"You think," I say quietly, "that I'm not strong enough to fuck up your day, and that's a mistake. He can come forward. But if I see one thing that I don't like, you'll know about it straight away."

Sem says nothing, but nods towards Willem, who moves forward with his colleague's same unhurried ease. I'm expecting the butterflies this time. And at least he doesn't have a scar.

"Luca," whispers Adam again as Willem peels his arm from my shoulder, and my heart fractures slightly.

"*One* thing that I don't like," I tell Sem again.

"You can trust us," he says.

"No," I say. "I can't."

I hang back as they move forward. Alice falls into step beside me as we move out of the waiting room and into the cavernous cold of the transit hall, shadowing me as I'm shadowing her. I'm prepared to bet she's carrying a volt gun at the very least and probably something a bit more projectile. Adam's boots trail the floor as we move, a soft trill of rubber on rubber. A gentle drum beat for a dead man's walk.

34.2 Danae

We board the transit cube in silence. I'm trying not to work out how much this is going to cost me; Adam is awake but blank-faced, staring wide-eyed at nothing. Sem, unneeded for now, sits beside me, cupping his hands and blowing into them for warmth. Alice and Willem make for a far corner of the booth where she dials up a phone wave and talks in brisk, hushed tones into an audio-only connection while Willem turns up the sound on the newslink to compensate for the relative lack of privacy. The explosion on the Viewing Plaza has dropped to the third item on the headlines, a brief recap of a narrative that refuses to progress and can't yet be passed over, and I reach out a hand, close it over Adam's, let my fingers coil through his. He doesn't respond. Sem keeps his eyes averted, as though he doesn't notice.

Something feels as if it's shifting, moving. Like it's inexplicably but unmistakably not the way it ought to be. It's getting harder to ignore as the floors tick upwards: Vier, Drie, towards Twee. Alice kills her phone conversation and she and Willem move over to sit opposite Sem, Adam and me, smiling tightly when I glare at her until she meets my eyes. Nobody has told me where we're going and I know better than to ask, but if I were to close my eyes, I think I could find it by the pulses radiating outwards in the stream alone. The scars on my healing back prickle and the itch hums savagely in the centre of my brain. I clutch Adam's hand in mine and close my eyes as the transit rattles upwards. We're getting closer. I can feel it in the stream.

We rattle to a stop at Verdieping Twee. For a long moment, nobody moves and the doors stay resolutely shut, and then, just as I've decided that we're continuing to Verdieping Een and my certain financial ruin, Alice unstraps herself from her safety belt, stands stiffly and says, "Come on. We're here."

Sem and Willem peel upwards from their seats without a word. I demur for a moment, so as not to show too much willing, and then follow suit. Adam's fingers are still woven through mine and his hand rises listlessly with me, no resistance in his arm, but his head turns slowly towards me and his eyes slide laboriously into focus. He says, hoarsely, "I'm having trouble breathing."

That's been clear since we left Radiale Twee. The fact that he's able to vocalise it at all represents an improvement, but I may be the only person who's noticed this. I see the wordless glance that passes between Alice and her friends, and I make myself concentrate, scan his throat, his chest, for signs that he's deteriorated. I find none, but the rise and fall of his chest is painfully protracted: one long in-breath, a ten second delay, one long out-breath, and then nothing more for half a minute. That's not enough to keep his system from crashing for very much longer and I know he knows this too.

I say, as calmly as I can, "Not much further now. We're nearly there," and I glare at Alice to let her know that I'd better be telling the truth.

Willem nods. "We can walk from here. It's not far."

I wait for them to move. They don't. "Then let's go," I say, and I hear the itch inflect my voice with tones of murder. Adam's fingers twitch against mine – a minor miracle – and when I glance back at him his eyes flash a warning. I might have known that this man could transcend the boundaries of Red Space and force-boot a faltering uplink on the strength of disapproval alone.

"They're waiting," says Alice, "for me to give the all-clear."

"Give it," I say. She does not. Nobody moves. "Give it!" I say again, more urgently. The transit takes its time at every station, but it doesn't stop forever. I sling my arm beneath Adam's shoulder, wrap my other arm around his chest, try to haul him to his feet. I get him standing, but he lolls heavily against my chest and I can't move him on my own, not without looking like I shouldn't be able to do this. "Please! Please – you didn't bring us this far to let him die. Please. *Please.*"

Alice looks at Willem. Willem, in Dutch, says, softly, "There are no guarantees."

"It's a risk," says Alice. "She could be dangerous."

I realise that they think I can't understand them. "*Alsjeblieft*," I say. "Please. He doesn't understand but I do. I'm not dangerous. I swear I'm not."

From the booth's speakers, the Voice of the City pipes her lilting, melodic tones. "*Gaat u alstublieft zitten. Deze wagen vertrekt over drie minuten.*"

Alice raises an eyebrow. Sem and Willem exchange a glance. All right, it's possible that "not dangerous" is not the impression that I've been working hard to give, but I had no reason to trust them. And now I realise, belatedly, that I've given them no reason to trust me, either.

"Please," I say again. "I was only trying to protect him. I would do anything to keep him safe."

Anything? says the itch, and my limbic system responds with a robust adrenal dump. But hard on the heels of the panic, I realise that, yes – *anything* is very nearly true. I won't die for anyone ever again, but they're not asking me to die. They're asking me to trust. And I would do that much to save Adam.

"Please," I say, one last time. The Voice of the City is giving us our two-minute warning. "I can pay. I will pay. You'll own me for the next twenty years, but I'll pay you every penny I owe."

"We don't want to own you," says Willem sharply.

Alice shrugs. "We don't work for free."

"The Eddy is its own payment," says Willem. "You know that."

"The Eddy?" I say. I'm completely lost, but I think Willem is on my side. "What's the Eddy?"

Sem looks at Alice. "You said she knew," he says.

"She knows there's a vortex in the stream." Alice's tone is defensive. "His uplink is failing; he's a good candidate."

I scan their faces: Sem to Willem to Alice. There's nothing there; no hint of an answer. "The Eddy is the hospital?"

"He can't heal in the body," says Alice. "But in the Eddy, he can live."

"Please," says Adam. It's barely a word; it's a disturbance on a long, laboured breath.

"Please," I say.

"*Ga alsjeblieft zitten,*" says the Voice of the City. "*Deze wagen staat op het punt te vertrekken.*"

There's a long, difficult moment. It can't last more than three seconds, because that's about all we have before the booth departs, but it feels much longer than that. And then, quickly, purposefully, they step forward: first Sem, then Willem. They take Adam from my arms, and then quickly, purposefully, they move forward, towards the exit. The egress mechanism logs their approach and the panels slide open as the Voice begins her closing remarks, and they slip easily between the rumbling panels and out into Verdieping Twee.

I don't wait for Alice. I follow my friend through the airlock and past the thick radiation shielding. Ahead of me, I see Sem and Willem, Adam slung between them. Willem is laughing, chatting easily to a couple that he's met on the street who've stopped to make sure Adam is all right. I see him shake his head indulgently and I hear him say something in Dutch about a stag party on Verdieping Een, but it's secondary information, background noise. Because the first thing I feel when I set foot on Verdieping Twee is the throbbing, oscillating roar of a massive distortion in the stream.

Chapter Thirty-Five

35.1 Adam

It's blinding, though my eyes are open and my optic system is, for once, working just fine. It's the uplink itself that seems to flare white, scattering static up and down my spine while the inside of my skull bursts into a kind of spiralling howl. It lasts no more than a few split seconds before settling into a kind of buzz just below my skin, like there's a current flowing through me. For a moment, I think that it's an artefact of my failing system and that this is what death looks like. I'll take it, if it is. It's beautiful. But then it's gone and I'm left strung between two ex-military grunts with arms the width of my head, staring into the washed-out grey of another floor on another radial and feeling like I've been punched in the lungs. This, at least, is my new normal, and it's how I know I'm still alive.

I find Danae, find her eyes. It's not easy: my neck is stiff and stubborn and my vision swims in and out of focus, but she's looking for me, which helps. I meet her gaze and find it dazed and slightly vacant, and then she blinks, and it clears, and she smiles. There's real warmth behind it, too, and something unguarded that looks a lot like joy. I think I smile back at her, although my facial muscles are marching to the beat of their own drum and it's hard to be sure, but she must see that I know what she knows. There's no mistaking what we've found.

Then, abruptly, her face hardens and she turns to the couple that have accosted Willem and Sem.

"He's fine," she says in Dutch. There's something about a thank you and something that's almost certainly about getting me home, and I remember that I'm supposed to be pass-out drunk and let my head loll on my shoulders. From the very edges of my vision, I can see the couple shrink under Danae's open hostility and back away in a cloud of nerves and platitudes. I'm not sure that they really deserved that, but it starts us moving again anyway because Danae is nothing if not efficient.

"They were being friendly," mutters Willem, who seems to have known them, if only slightly.

"We don't have time for friendly," says Danae.

Willem bristles at that and it feels as though he's about to counter, which will open up a whole world of angry that I just can't be bothered to listen to right now. Luckily, Alice cuts him off before he can speak.

"She's right," she says, low and frosty, somewhere close behind me. "We're drawing enough attention as it is. Let's just keep moving."

I can't find Luca, though I know he's here. When I close my eyes, he's walking two steps in front of me, face turned towards me over his shoulder and smiling slightly, like he knows something I don't. *Follow me*, says his expression, but he doesn't speak, so I don't have to answer, *Not yet; I'm not ready. Not yet.*

When I open my eyes again, I can't see him, not even a shadow or a blur in the corner of my eye.

I keep my eyes closed as much as I can. Luca's smile reminds me of better days and I know in my bones that wherever I'm going, I won't be leaving again. I don't need to remember this journey. I just need to get it over with.

"You'll be scanned again at the entrance to the safe house," says Alice as we walk. "And then again when you're on the other side of the foyer. They won't let you through without a red light."

"I can't pass that," says Danae. She keeps her voice light and – thankfully – unchallenging. "You should know that now. But these two men can vouch for what I am, can't you?"

We draw to a halt. It's done so casually that, for a moment, I think we've arrived and I crack an eyelid to see what a massive datastream vortex looks like. But we're facing onto a street, as though we're waiting to cross the road, except that the street is empty of trams and we're making no movement forward.

"She checks out," says Sem after a moment. "She should fail a scan."

"But I won't," says Danae. "I never have. Better that you know that now."

I see what she's doing. It's a risky game, though not half as risky as it would have been to start playing when we get to where we're going. She knows that, in the open, they can't eliminate the threat that she's just introduced, so they're obliged to think rationally before they react. In the safe house, who can say what the policy might be on people who claim to be non-organic and then go ahead and scan green? But I very much doubt they're invited to disappear into the crowd in the hopes that they keep their knowledge to themselves. Danae's banking on the fact that both Sem and Willem have felt the flutter of stream distortion when we all met, and that they have time to think that through before deciding how to proceed.

"You spoke for her," says Alice coldly. It takes me a second to realise that she's talking to me.

"I did." My voice is slurred, but the words are recognisable. "I do." I want to tell her that Sem and Willem will confirm that there's a very specific reason that one of us might not scan red if they'll only follow this train of thought through to its logical conclusion, but I'd be lucky to get three words in before I stopped making sense. So I settle for, "Think," and hope that this will be enough.

"She checks out," says Sem again.

"I check out because I'm like you," says Danae. "I'm what I thought you must be when I saw your scar. I'm what I thought you had to be to survive an injury like that."

Her voice is perfectly calm. Even the stream doesn't hint at the tension I know this is causing her. She could have left me at the transit foyer. She could have left me at the waiting room or the welcome hall, and I think these guys would have brought me here anyway, because I think there's something I can give them in exchange for their help, and I know they know that I'll give it. She didn't need to put herself in danger for me and she sure as hell didn't need to expose herself like this. And still she's laying herself bare for them, and her voice doesn't even tremble.

There's a long pause. And then, slowly, Sem says, "We could use someone like you."

"I'm not for using," says Danae.

Another pause. "Pity," says Sem, and he genuinely sounds sorry. And then, to Alice, "It's fine. She checks out."

I'm listening very carefully, but I don't hear Danae release a held breath. It's possible that a little tension in her shoulders dissipates, but I'm not looking at her so I can't tell. There's no way in hell that she allows a little smile of relief to cross her face. It's possible, in fact, that she gives absolutely no sign that this exchange was the source of the any kind of concern for her, and you've got to admire that kind of stoic refusal to engage with reality.

Alice holds out for a moment longer, because, I'm guessing, this is just who she is. "But if she can't fail a scan…" she says, but Sem shuts her down.

"I'll explain later," he says. I think I black out again here, because the next thing I know, we're moving again, and I don't remember how or when it happened.

35.2 Adam

We walk for five, maybe ten minutes. It's hard to tell, what with all my systems blinking on and off like a strip light with a faulty connection, but the periods of blackness seem to be getting shorter and further apart the longer we walk. This makes sense, because there's definitely something weird going on with the stream. It's like it's thickening with every step, which is the wrong way to describe it but I've got nothing else and no frame of reference because I've never known the stream to behave like this, anywhere, ever. The thicker it gets, the easier it is to think. I'm starting to understand why the transit cube was the last place that our hosts hesitated, and why they haven't been more insistent about things related to subterfuge. It's because there's not an a-naut on Greater Earth that could miss the pull of the anomaly once they've taken a couple of steps onto Radiale Een, Verdieping Twee.

When we finally stop, it's outside the entrance to one of the same style of family blocks that I recognise from the day we went to meet Arnold. We've passed through the entryway that runs from the street into the central courtyard, empty except for two tired-looking lawn chairs and an unloved circle of scrappy brush in the middle. The door is in the far left corner of the quadrangle and, as we close in on it, I can feel the first sparks of sensation prickling my upper body: not enough to move anything, but enough to remind me that it's there.

"Stay behind me," says Sem to Danae as Alice buzzes for entry. I can see movement behind the frosted glass, like the shadows of fish in dark water, but they don't approach and so we stand and wait for instruction. "They'll register your stream disturbance and they'll be more interested in your friend to begin with. I'll vouch for you when the time comes."

"Thank you," she says, clipped and tight, and we fall back into silence as the stream whirls and dances around us.

"*Ja?*" says a voice on the end of the buzzer after a moment. I wonder if the delay was deliberate, designed to discourage casual callers.

263

It's longer than most people would wait for an answer.

"*Wij zijn het*," says Alice.

Another long pause. My toes begin to tingle; I'm starting to be aware of the ground beneath my feet. And then the voice says, "*Oke*," and the door swings open. The shadows on the far side scatter and resolve in the dim light of an unwindowed stairwell, and I see that the glass has distorted their number: I counted six or seven before the door opened, but there are only two figures in our welcome party, a man and a woman. The stream is like soup in my skull and I can't tell if it ripples in their presence, though I can't imagine an a-naut standing happily in this kind of distortion for long. Both of them are heavily armed.

The woman speaks first, rapid-fire Dutch that I can't understand. Alice answers her and the woman smiles, shakes her head and glances sideways at her colleague. I test my arms against the guys on either side of me and find that they're weak and my muscles are sluggish, but they'll respond to basic commands. Behind me, I hear Danae suck in a breath.

"You are welcome," says the woman. I glance up, realising that, if she's speaking English, it's for my benefit. She nods at my hands, which are flexing loosely against in mid-air in front of me. "You see what happens here. It's good. Okay."

"What is this place?" says Danae softly, almost under her breath.

"This is the Eddy," says Sem. "The *dis* is closer here. We are better here."

"It's repairing his uplink?" Danae is behind me, so I can't see her face, but I can hear a kind of wonder in her voice that I've never heard before.

"No," says Alice. "His uplink can't be repaired. But where the *dis* is closer, the link has less work to do. It re-stabilises the feedback loop. He can get some of his functionality back."

"But only while he's here," says Danae. I'd suspected something like this was coming. From her tone, I think she had too.

There's a long pause. Then Willem says, simply, "Yes."

"No," says Danae. And then, more forcefully, "No! We have things – he has work he still needs to do. He can't stay here!"

"It's okay," I say. Where the *dis* is closer, so is Luca. Maybe this is enough. "You can find Marie for me. You can still make this right."

"Come," says Sem. His voice is gentle. "You will see. This is a good place."

"No," says Danae again. "Adam, tell them…"

"You could stay with him." Alice moves to the stairwell to stand beside the man with the gun. "The more generators it has, the more powerful the Eddy becomes."

Sem says something quietly to the woman with the gun, which makes her raise an eyebrow and whistle softly. "*Nageslacht?*" she says to Danae. A beat, while she searches for the word. "*Nageslacht…* Progeny? You are *Progeny?*"

Danae says nothing. The woman waits for a moment, then shrugs. "I meet your… brother one time. On Earth, in Naarden. You know Naarden?"

I know Naarden, and I don't need to feel the air frost behind me to know that Danae does too. Sixty-one people died there one summer's day late in the Insurgency when an IED took out part of the seawall and the floodwater rushed in. Three a-nauts were among the dead, and the authorities were content to presume that one of them was behind the attack. Nobody was looking for a little boy.

"What happened to him?" asks Danae stiffly.

The woman shrugs. "Dead, I guess. It's sad. Progeny could be more than this, but" – a philosophical twitch of her shoulders – "they are not made to live long lives."

"None of us are," says Danae.

The woman shakes her head wryly. "This is the truth." She turns to her colleague, exchanges a few words in Dutch. "Okay. We will go."

The man with the gun shoulders his rifle and reaches into one of his pockets. Because I'm expecting it, I'm not surprised to see the scanner, and I crane my neck for him as he approaches. The glow from the readout screen colours the shadows red as it registers my non-organic electroencephalic feedback and the man grunts his approval before he moves on to Danae. I turn to watch, because I've never seen an a-naut pass a scanner test before. Her face is blank as she pulls her collar down to bare her skin, blank as it presses against her, blank as it bleeds green light onto the man's watching face. He grins, looks up at his colleague to confirm, slaps Danae heartily on the shoulder.

"*Nageslacht!*" he says cheerfully. "Welcome; you are welcome. Perhaps you will stay. We will make you welcome."

Danae's eyes flash to mine. They are black with sadness. "I just want to make sure that my friend is all right."

"I'm all right," I tell her.

"You're not all right," she says.

No. Not really. "But I will be."

There's a pause. The man with the gun looks at the woman with the gun, at Alice, at me. The silence lengthens just a little bit beyond comfort.

"Okay," says the woman at last. "Good, okay. We will go."

35.3 Adam

Our armed companions lead the way. I lean heavily on Sem and Willem, my arms strung around their waists and gripping the fabric of their coats, but my feet no longer trail uselessly behind me. I'm not walking exactly, and I'm definitely not supporting my own weight, but my legs move in time with theirs and my feet skitter across the bare plastic floor in something like footsteps. Danae walks behind with Alice, talking quietly as we walk.

"This place," I hear her say, "it's controlled by a-nauts?"

"Yes," says Alice. "Of course."

"The whole block?"

"It couldn't operate," says Alice, "if it was not."

"And it's *never* been targeted?"

"I didn't say that. We've… dealt with the threats."

That pause contains a lot of unspoken information. I don't want to think about what it implies. It also makes sense of the faint smell of wet smoke that fills the corridor and I start to get a sense of just how slick, how sophisticated this operation must be. It reminds me of the old days of London HQ and I don't know if that makes me nostalgic, hopeful, or worried.

Danae's thoughts are clearly headed in the same direction. "Sounds like you're exposing yourselves to a lot of risk."

"No more so," says Alice, "than anything you'd find on Earth."

"What about the rest of the complex?"

A beat. Then Alice says, carefully, "We have personnel scattered throughout the three other wings."

"A-nauts?"

"No. Organics."

"Like you."

"Yes." Alice's voice is steel and ice. "Sympathisers. Like me."

We stop at an elevator bank. It looks as though it hasn't worked in years, but the man with the gun performs a little surgery on the call button and an ancient pulley system rumbles to life.

"How long have you known this was here?" asks Danae as we wait.

Alice stares at the lifeless control panel. "Since I arrived." A beat, and then, in a clear effort to head off the inevitable next question, "Thirty-four years ago."

"Thirty-four years?" I can't help myself; it's out before I'm aware I'm going to say it. And the bewildered air of starstruck wonder is not what I'd have gone for if I'd had the chance to vet it. "We've only been tracking it on Earth for... three, maximum."

"It was running before I got here," says Alice. "It was one of the reasons I came."

"You *knew* about it?" I doubt Danae's any happier with the tone of her voice than I was with mine. "How?"

"It was a rumour," says Alice. "Something I'd heard from... friends."

"A-naut friends," says Danae.

Alice turns a withering glare on her. "Of course a-naut friends. I told you – I know more than you'd think about what was going on in the Insurgency."

"You were part of the Resistance," says Danae. It's not a question.

Alice doesn't treat it as one. "I was married to an a-naut."

The lift arrives, which is lucky, because it allows us a couple of minutes' distraction to process that conversational curveball. We step inside.

"Yes," says Alice as the doors close and the lift stutters upwards with an unpromising lurch. She's answering a question that we haven't asked, but she knows it's coming. "He was a worker on my family's estate. We left together to join the Resistance after the New Year's Edict, and we fought together for ten years. They were good years," she says firmly, and in a voice that dares us to challenge her. I become aware that this woman has killed people. Probably many. And I see a tension in Danae's face that tells me she's thinking the same thing.

She doesn't speak for a long moment. When she does, her eyes are turned to the floor and her voice is tight. "What happened?"

Alice doesn't look at her either. "What do you think happened?"

Another long silence. The woman with the gun glances back at us over her shoulder. "They are attacked," she says. She makes a star-shape with her hand: a bomb exploding. Alice shoots her a glare but says nothing, and I mentally rewrite the power hierarchy for the millionth time since we arrived. "They are hurt. Badly hurt. Vincent is dying."

"Vincent?" I ask.

"My husband," says Alice. The lift hiccups to a momentary halt and the woman with the gun glares at the ceiling and swears at it in Dutch until it hiccups back into motion. "Our cache was ambushed by the Rens. Vincent was shot in the calf and he lost two fingers when one of the transports blew up."

That's not a survivable injury for a non-organic. If he didn't bleed out, he should have been dead from pathogen toxicity in less than a week. I'm guessing that he wasn't.

"But you'd heard about a place," I say slowly, "where a-nauts could come to heal."

"Yes," says Alice. "Luchtstad had just declared Do Not Seek. And it was chaos on the ground. It was much easier to get up here back then than it is now."

"In a meat crate?" I suggest.

Alice glares sideways at him. "I came up by elevator," she says.

"What happened," asks Danae, "to Vincent?"

The lift rumbles asthmatically to a halt. I wait for the woman with the gun to start swearing again, but instead she hammers the butt of her rifle into the control panel and the doors start to shudder open.

"He's alive," says Alice. "I brought him to the Eddy, and this is where he lives."

35.4 Adam

The doors sputter apart, opening onto gloom. I let myself be pulled forward, into the corridor beyond, where shadows dance along the walls and a stream-rich hum fills the air. All around me I can feel unseen movement, motion, generation and renewal: it's like a whisper in the base of my skull, like a breath on the back of my neck.

Come, says Luca. *Come and find me.*

I'm coming, I tell him. *Jesus, all right. Give me a chance, would you?*

We follow Alice along the corridor. It's like every residential hallway

I've been in since I arrived on the city, low-lit and windowless, and the only thing that marks it out as different is that the stream swirls thickly around us. It feels like wading through water. Our armed escorts walk close behind us and I hear their guns rattle softly against their holsters with every step. Sem says something quiet to Willem, and Willem laughs lightly, but these are the only sounds as we move past door after door until, finally, Alice pulls up sharp outside one of them and turns to look at us.

"Scanner," she says to the woman with the gun, who reaches into a pocket and pulls out the scanner she used on the ground floor.

"Really?" says Danae. I'm not sure I believe her withering indifference, but her eyes are doing a good impression of a woman who's not rattled. I realise, with a stab of sadness, how much I'm going to miss her. "We're still doing this?"

Alice ignores her and just goes ahead and scans us anyway. I'm first, and the press of metal against my skin is not gentle, which hardly seems fair. I'm not the one who was bitching, after all. Thin red light washes the gloom once more before Alice retracts the scanner, and I can't help but notice that she attacks Danae's neck with considerably less force, which seems even less fair. The light goes green. The man with the gun grins and says something to his colleague, and I hear the word *nageslacht* again. Alice says nothing and gives no sign of having heard, and then the door slides open and she steps inside without a backward glance.

I look at Danae. She looks at me. My feet are firmer on the floor than they were even at the lift shaft, but I'm still completely reliant on the men on either side of me to stay upright or move. Our armed escorts hold back behind us and show no signs of going anywhere just yet. The message is crystal clear, and Danae can read a room as well as I can.

Her eye roll threatens to dislocate her optic nerve. "Fine," she mutters. "Great. Fine. After me, then?"

She steps through the door and into the gloom beyond. I like that she's still doing belligerent as hard as she can and I like that everyone we've met so far has treated her like a fairground curiosity. I feel like it gives her some kind of a chance of walking out of here again. Everything she told me in Jos' house is right at the front of my brain and I know that she should have left me behind half an hour ago or more. I don't like anybody's chances of keeping her here against her will, but I mostly don't like her chances of making it out alive if she has to fight.

Three steps into the room she stops, whirls around and folds her arms across her chest. Beside me, Sem and Willem rumble into life and start to manoeuvre the three of us forward, and Danae waits for us to catch up with her before she turns again, so that we're walking into the belly of the apartment together. Our escorts follow us inside and the door slides shut behind us.

The apartment opens onto a short hallway. At the far end, the door that leads into the main living space has been removed and replaced with a PVC strip curtain. The hallway is as dark as the corridor we've just left, lit only by floor-level emergency lighting that casts shadows upwards onto Danae's face when she turns to look at me. The stream swirls and banks, pulling and tumbling, and I feel it like a hiss of whispering voices talking quickly in a hidden room. This place feels haunted, but not threatening. It feels as though it's noticed us and wants to get a closer look.

Come, says Luca. *You're almost home.*

Alice presses on ahead, pushing back the strip curtain with impatient hands. Beyond her, I can see what looks like a row of beds pushed up against the far wall, where the window has been boarded up. A figure, silhouetted against black, moves unhurriedly among them and straightens as Alice approaches. I hear a woman's voice say, softly, *"Hé – je bent teruggekomen."*

"Hoe gaat het met hem?" asks Alice, and I know enough now to understand that she's asking about her husband.

The silhouette steps forward, shadows falling from her face as she comes closer. I can see that she's a late model, probably ex-industrial. Her smile is warm and easy. *"Goed, goed,"* she says, and then something else that I can't understand, but which causes the tension in Alice's shoulders to release.

Alice turns back to us, gestures towards me with her hand. In English, she says, "This is the one I told you about."

"Ah." The shadow woman's voice stays soft. I wonder if it ever changes. "Emmett, yes?"

"Adam," I say. There's no point in lying any more, and there's a satisfaction in knowing that, after all, I'll die with the right name. "Emmett is the name I was given when I got to Luchtstad, but Adam is the name I've always used."

"Adam," says the woman. "Welcome. My name is Sophie. You are dying?"

"Yes," I say. I don't look at Danae.

"But," she says, "you see how it is here."

It's on the tip of my tongue to tell her that it's hard to see anything at all with the light levels in this apartment block. This is because I've been spending too much time with Danae. But I know she's talking about the fact that, against all probability, my arms and legs are basically working again, so I say, "Yes. But I don't know why."

Sophie's face creases into a smile. "Come," she says. "I will show you."

I've been leaning heavily against Sem and Willem. But slowly, carefully, I feel their arms release me, testing my strength as their support falls away. Danae watches them in silent outrage at first, which melts into interest, and finally into a moment of unmistakable surprise before she catches herself and starts frowning again. Reassured, I make myself take a tiny step forward. I feel my leg wobble. I feel my upper body circle like a top at the end of its spin, but I don't fall. And so I take another step forward, and then another.

I'm walking.

I stop beside Danae. The look on her face tells me that she's no clearer about what's happening than I am. I say, "Coming?"

She shrugs. "Might as well. Since I'm here," and we follow Sophie through the strip PVC curtain that Alice holds back for us, and into the streamwall of the Eddy.

It's like stepping through a waterfall. I'm vaguely aware of the world behind us fading away: all I can feel, hear, touch, taste, smell, is the stream around me. Beds stretch along the far wall of the apartment, disappearing into darkness on either side, and I see that the perimeter walls, where the apartment borders its neighbours, have been taken down so that this room telescopes out and along the length of the block itself. Beds upon beds upon beds, each one occupied by a single body, motionless and covered by a thin sheet, and around them the stream buzzes and bubbles and crests and whirls. I don't need to be told that these are a-nauts. I don't need to be told that they're injured: in the three beds nearest the door alone, I can see that one body is missing a leg, one has an open wound that runs the length of his chest, and one has no skin on the top of her head. But all of them are breathing. All of them are alive. The stream chants for none of them.

Beside me, I feel Danae's hand slip into mine, fingers curling around mine. In a hoarse voice, she whispers, "What is this place?"

Sophie doesn't answer straight away. Instead, she walks a little way along, to a bed five places down, where a man with a gunshot wound to his right shoulder sleeps peacefully in the half-light. We follow until Sophie turns and folds her hands at her front, and she says, "This is Benoit. He has been here for fourteen years."

He shouldn't have survived fourteen days with a system that compromised. I say, "How?"

"It's the stream," says Danae. Her fingers tighten around mine. "They're plugged into the stream. They're pulling the *dis* to them – to us." She looks from me to Sophie, who nods. "I'm right, aren't I? They talked about generators downstairs – the more generators the Eddy has, the more powerful it is, they said. I didn't understand, but now I see them... I think I do. They're focusing the *dis*, like a... like a lens. That's why it feels thicker here. That's why Adam's legs work. That's why they're not dead – because the stream acts like a kind of cradle for the uplink. It's keeping them alive."

"As long as they stay here," I say.

Sophie nods. "Yes. As long as they stay here, they are bathed in the *dis* and the body will live."

"All of them," says Danae, "they're... compromised?"

"Injured?" Sophie shakes her head. "Oh, no. Some of the earliest generators, they were simply old. This is how they protect themselves, yourselves, from the end."

I'm not sure I'm following, but Danae is. "You mean that they're trying to keep the a-naut population from dying out. It's insurance against obsolescence."

Sophie nods again. "So that everyone will not die before freedom comes."

"And nobody needs to die in the meantime," I say. "This is... incredible."

I'm expecting an argument from Danae, but nope, not this time. "It's beautiful," she says. "All this time... I had no idea. How many are there?"

"One hundred and seventy-two," says Sophie. "Sometimes, they leave. Mostly, they must stay. Come, I will show you."

I think of Sem, with his vicious scar that curls along his face and down below his collar. He should be dead, and he's not. We follow Sophie further into shadow, past sleeping figures lost in the dreamless *dis*, and I think that his injury is his alibi now, because everyone knows that an a-naut can't have a scar like that. He's safe for as long as he chooses to walk the streets, and, if he's not, the Eddy is waiting to receive him again. I look at the faces of the a-nauts that I pass, still and contented, and I wonder what it's like to surrender to the *dis* without surrendering the body. I wonder if it feels like death, if it feels like sleep, if it feels like walking through a dream. If it feels like anything at all.

"We have been here for forty-one years," says Sophie as we walk. "Many of our generators were injured during the war – many arrive like Vincent, from friends or lovers who heard about us and have hope that perhaps they will not die."

"Has there been anyone you couldn't save?" asks Danae.

"Three," says Sophie.

"Just three?"

She smiles over her shoulder. "Just three. Two were dead when they arrived. One did not want to stay here."

So many chants, I think. How many times did the stream begin to warp for its loss only to be hushed back into silence by the Eddy? How many times could we have saved a life if only we'd known about this place?

I think about Marie. I remember her face, the hope and the longing in her eyes, as she told us about the rumour she'd heard. I remember how much I wanted to believe her, then and afterwards, and how the same part of me that looked into the night sky and wondered was the same part that knew I was chasing fairytales. I think of Danae's face when I told her why I was here, and how I knew, deep down, that she was right. There's no salvation. There's no absolution. But here we are anyway.

"You have to tell people," I say. "People need to know that this place exists."

Sophie glances back over her shoulder. "We try, of course. We must bring people to the Eddy or the Eddy will not survive."

"But if they knew... If they knew for certain..."

Sophie shrugs. "You see that it is not easy. The singularity hushes communication on the stream. How do we tell people? And we cannot travel from Luchtstad."

"No," says Danae. "But I can."

Sophie's smile lights her eyes. "You are the Progeny, yes?"

"Yes." Quick and simple, no hesitation.

"We never see one of you here." Sophie shakes her head. "So sad. Of course, you don't need the Eddy, but I don't think this is the reason."

"No," says Danae. "I don't think so either."

"The Progeny were made to be our hope. But where are they now?"

"Dead. Mostly."

"But not you?"

"No," says Danae. "Not me. And I'm here. And I think maybe I can start to be the hope that we were supposed to be."

I want to say to her that she's already put herself in enough danger and that nobody can ask her to step into harm's way again. I want to tell her that I know what it's cost her to do as much as she already has, and that she owes nothing to anyone and she never did. I want to tell her that she's been to hell and back and the fact that she's still standing at all is testament to a kind of strength that levels me and she has nothing left to prove. But then she glances sideways at me, and I see in her eye that none of this is mine to say or to think: she gives this without hesitation and without fear. And I start to smile, because the woman that I've thought I've seen in her has shifted and changed so many times that I ought to know by now that she is unfixed and unfixable – she is Danae Grant, irascible and inscrutable. Knowable as far as she'll let herself be known, a wall and a river, an ocean of kindness, a fortress, a battleship, a storm. I start to smile, and I open my mouth to tell her that, whatever happens, I am proud to have known her, proud to have walked a little of her journey with her, proud to have called her my friend.

But I don't do any of these things. Instead, as we pass another barrier wall torn open and refashioned as an entry, as a figure in a bed swims into focus in the low light, still and silent and sleeping beneath an open blast wound that's shaved skin from his chest and gouged shrapnel-chunks up and down his flank, that's stripped his eyes, his cheeks, his beautiful face, I feel my knees buckle beneath me; I feel the breath leave my chest; I feel my mouth make a sound that I barely recognise as me.

All these years, says Luca, a whisper in my ear, a voice inside my skull, a smiling face in my memory, a body lying on a bed before me, *and you seriously thought I was a figment of your imagination? I'm actually kind of offended.*

The world around me collapses in on itself. I can't hear. I can barely see. The stream sings a high, keening note that shatters and repairs me in one long motion: the *lortherias*, the recognition. *At last*, it whispers. *I've found you at last.*

He's here. Luca is here. He's here, and he's been here all along.

Chapter Thirty-Six

36.1 Danae

Adam's knees buckle, and he makes a noise that sounds like pain. The first thing I think is that this is it, he's gone, and the itch flares, all red heat and sharpened claws, because this was supposed to be a place of healing. I wasn't supposed to lose him quietly and without warning in the middle of a tour of infinite darkened beds. He staggers and falls against me, and I catch him, wrap my arms around him, hold him as he sags in my grip.

"Luca," he says, a whisper at my ear.

I close my eyes. Tears sear my throat. "No," I say. "Adam – it's Danae. It's not Luca."

"Luca," he says again. His hands fist in my coat. I feel his feet struggle for purchase against the floor. "Luca," he says. And then, brokenly, like the cry of an injured bird, "Luca!"

"Adam," I say helplessly. "Please. It's Danae. Please – I can't hold you…"

His weight shifts, but his arms don't release me. His head at my shoulder falls forward so that his crown rests against my collarbone; his hands slide up my back to cup at the nape of my neck. He says, softly, "In the bed – there. That's Luca. That's my Luca."

I don't know what to say. I can't say anything. Adam lifts his head, presses his forehead against mine. He's trembling; his hands are trembling, his lips are trembling. "Here?" I say, because I'm at a loss for anything else.

"He was dead," says Adam. "I heard his chant. I *heard* it."

I slide my eyes sideways to meet Sophie's. She looks as helpless as I feel. She says, hesitantly, "This man is called Nicolae."

Adam closes his eyes, nods tightly. "He would use that name sometimes. Please – how is he here?" And then, before she can answer: "Can I touch him?"

Sophie looks from Adam to me to the figure on the bed. "He is deep in the *dis*…"

"Will it hurt him?"

"No," she says. "To touch him? No. It cannot hurt him."

"Then…" He looks for all the world like a timid child. "Can I? Please?"

Sophie's face is a mask of confusion and there are no answers for her on Adam's. To me, she says, "What is this?"

"This is…" I say, and struggle for the word. "The *lortherias*. This is the other half of his binary."

Her eyes widen. "Nicolae?"

"Luca," I say, before Adam can protest. "His name is Luca. And he died in the Insurgency, so I have no idea how he's here now."

But I do, don't I? Looking at him on the bed, I realise that I do. Whoever Luca was, whatever face haunts Adam's dreams, it's been long buried beneath a network of savage gouge-wounds and scar tissue. Marie was with him, Adam said, and the last he heard was that she was headed for the space elevator at Felixstowe with a half dozen a-nauts too injured to save. Twenty-five years later, his body is broken almost past the point of looking human; no wonder nobody recognised him then.

Sophie's hand creeps to her throat to find a narrow chain that's buried beneath her high collar. The tips of her fingers curl around and through, twisting the thin cord into serpentine troughs and crests. She says, "*Hij riep je terug*" – he called you back to him – and I'm not sure she's even aware that she's said it in Dutch.

"Yes," I say. My mind is wheeling, but I can't think of a better explanation. "I think he must have done. Please – they've been apart for many years…"

"Yes." She blinks, like she's waking from a dream. "Yes, of course. But he cannot wake, you know this…?"

Adam moves before she's finished speaking, hands releasing me to coldness and vacancy as he turns to the bed, drops to the floor beside it in one fluid motion. If he's heard her caveat, he gives no sign. His hands hover for a moment over the ruined face of the figure in the bed, reverently, tenderly, half an inch of cool dark air between flesh and flesh. His eyes fall closed and he draws in a deep breath.

I look away. I have to. I look away, and I cross the dark floor to the other side of the room.

After a moment, I feel a hand on my elbow, gentle and hesitant. I glance back over my shoulder to see Sophie watching me, ghostly in the half-light. I didn't hear her approach. She says, softly, "Nicolae – Luca – was here before I arrived. He has been part of the Eddy for many years."

"Twenty-five years, I'd guess," I say.

She nods. "I think you are right. But I will check."

"No." I shake my head. "There's no need. How did he get here?"

"As many of our generators arrived, I guess." She shrugs. "He was badly injured. His friend found a transport and he came to us and cannot leave."

"His friend," I say. It feels as though things are becoming clearer. "Marie, right?"

"No," says Sophie. "Her name was Hannah."

"Hannah?" No wonder we couldn't find her. "But she gave his name as Nicolae. So she could have been Marie."

Sophie acknowledges the truth of this with a brief nod. "This is possible, of course. My name was not Sophie before I came to Luchtstad."

"And I was Danae Grant before I was ever Françoise Marechal." It feels good to say it aloud. Here, of all places, it feels safe to be me again. "Was she hurt – Hannah? When she came here?"

"No. She said Nicolae – Luca – her friend… he had saved her."

"Saved her? How?"

"He stood between her and an explosion," says Sophie, who cannot possibly know about the Viewing Plaza, and so cannot understand the darkness that I feel dropping like a veil over my face. It doesn't surprise me that the other half of Adam's binary would put himself in harm's way to save a friend. It feels right that he would. It feels right that this is the sort of person that Adam finds close to him, because the sort of person that Adam is deserves this.

I say, because I see that my expression has unsettled her, "What happened to Hannah? Is she here?"

"In the Eddy?" asks Sophie. I nod. "For a while. We were not so many then, and the Eddy was not so powerful. Nicolae, to heal, he must have power, so she stayed for a while and was a generator. Two months, three. He cannot leave, but when he was no longer in danger, Hannah left him in our care. She said she had something to do. She said she had people she needed to find."

Was she looking for Adam, too? Has she been spending all these years in a mirror-search, unable to get word back to the planet she left behind? Does she know that Adam survived and can she not rest either until she finds him to tell him the story that they both need to share?

"Does she visit him?" I'm not sure why it scalds my throat like acid, or why it makes me blink back tears. I'm not sure why, out of all of the questions that line up in my scrambling brain and holler for attention, the thing I most need to make sure of is that Luca hasn't been alone all these years.

"She did." Sophie nods, and her face is gentle. "I arrived at the Eddy twelve years ago, and Hannah was a visitor from time to time. She would sit with her friend. She would hold his hand. Sometimes she would plug in and generate for a few hours or a day."

"But she stopped?" Sophie nods again. "When?"

Sadness darkens Sophie's eyes. Her hand on my elbow closes slightly, fingers tightening briefly against my skin. "Eight years ago," she says. "Since she died."

The words fall into silence. I feel, irrationally, as though I want to burst into laughter: the kind that lurches on the edge of hysteria and has nothing to do with joy. All this time, Adam's been chasing a ghost. And it wasn't even the right one.

"Oh." My voice sounds dull, listless. "How?"

"How she died?" A shrug. "As usual: she was old and she got older, and then one day she was too old. Like me, like you. Like all of us."

"But you…" I stop. There's no diplomatic way to put this. "But you are… Couldn't she have…?"

"Stayed? Of course. We asked her to stay, to generate and to live. This was not her wish."

"She didn't want to live?"

"Not in the body," says Sophie. "She lives forever on the stream."

I have so many questions. They cluster and burn and howl for release, but the only person who could answer them is eight years dead, and the only other person who knows the truth is locked in sleep from now until the end of the *dis*. And maybe, I think, I understand a little. Maybe Marie's time was over. Maybe there was somebody waiting for her on the other side, and she was tired. Tired of fighting. Tired of being afraid. Tired of a search that never changed and never ended. Maybe it gets to that place for all of us, eventually. Maybe I just haven't had long enough in this body to know what it feels like to be ready to let go.

"I heard her chant," says Sophie now. "It was gentle and very beautiful. This was the right choice for her. Though we were sad to lose her."

And I turn and look back over my shoulder to the little bed pushed up against the far wall, where a blast-ravaged figure lies still on a mattress, chest gently shifting against the thin white sheet that covers him. Adam rests beside him, head pillowed on one crooked arm, the other draped across Luca's waist. His fingers are splayed across Luca's belly, drifting softly, almost unconsciously, back and forth across the hidden skin. There is nobody else in his world now: it has narrowed to the two of them pressed together in the space of a single bed, and I know at once that this is how it has always been for them. How it always will be.

This is how it should be, and the world was simply waiting for them to put it right again.

I say, softly, "Will you tell him, later, that I said goodbye?"

Sophie follows my gaze, but her eyes fall away, as though it's not her right to look. "I will," she says. A beat, and then she adds, "Perhaps you'll visit them some day?"

"Maybe," I say. It hurts to talk.

"They will be waiting."

"I know." And I know that he'll look up, eventually, and see that I'm no longer here, that I've slipped away without a word. But I know that he'll understand, and I know that he'll be waiting in the *dis* for me. I don't know how the Eddy works, but I know that I owe a debt to this place that I'll pay off as I can, from obligation and from inclination, and that one day I will come back here and I'll plug into this world of ours that Adam opened up to me, for an hour, for a day, for a week, perhaps. And if it's possible to find him in the other-space, I know I will. Or he'll find me, if only to roll his eyes in that way that I hate and tell me how I'm doing everything wrong.

"Tell him," I say, "that I'll see him soon."

Chapter Thirty-Seven

37.1 Danae

In the end, I suppose, there's nothing I would have done differently.

The thought comes to me during the lonely transit home, paring down the side of a radial that I don't know, jouncing gently through tunnels in a carriage full of emptiness and memory. I had one chance to walk away, the day I met him, and I didn't, and for that I'm glad.

I didn't expect to be glad.

I feel him at my shoulder as I pad wearily into my block in the small hours of the morning, along quiet corridors and up quiet stairs: a soft smile in the low light, watchful and warm, wrapping and layering me, keeping out the cold. I wear his presence like a cloak all the way back to my room, and when I sleep I dream he's lying beside me, head pillowed on one arm, the other draped across my waist.

37.2 Danae

On Thursday, Sanne finally asks me where he is. I'm surprised it takes her this long, but I suppose I've got really good at avoiding people since I've been here, and better since Adam's been gone. It's the first smoke break of the day and we've been busy all morning but not flat out, enough to ease out the wrinkles in my mind and let me settle into comfortable vacancy, not enough to dull the residual sadness into a blanket of exhaustion. I've taken up my usual stance at the farthest corner of the circle, back turned to the group, and hunched myself around a cigarette in a manner designed to close out everything else. It's worked well for four days, but this is Sanne, after all, and nothing works against her forever.

"Hey," she says casually. Too casually. "Do you have a light?"

She's just seen me light my cigarette, and I *know* she has a lighter of her own. Without a word, I palm mine and hold it out to one side. Sanne takes it, flares a yellow flame, and touches it to the end of her cigarette. This would be the time to nod a thanks, return the lighter, and leave, but I know she's not going to do that. I know it with every scalding ripple of loss that twists in my chest and throat as I suck in smoke and curl away from her in the hope that she won't actually go.

"So," she says on an exhale. Smoke billows from between her half-open lips, colouring the word white-grey. "Emmett's been gone for a few days now. I hope he's all right."

Adam, I want to spit. *His name is Adam.* My shoulders are drawn so tightly that my shrug makes the muscles scream. "He's not coming back."

"Oh." Sanne can turn a statement into a question through nothing more than economy of prose. It's all in the words she doesn't say. "All right."

Alice has taken care of everything. I know this because she said she would, and because Adam has vanished from Radiale Zeven as seamlessly as if he was never here at all. The line has closed around his absence with its usual efficiency and nobody has mentioned that we're one man down, because the work's not heavy enough yet that it's a problem for anyone. One day it will be, and when that happens, Jouke will dredge up another body from the bowels of the factory floor and we'll scab around him, patching up the tear until it's healed into business as usual, just like we always do. Nothing ever really changes on the line.

Last night, after work, I went walking, letting my feet carry me wherever, and I found myself outside Adam's block. It was getting late, late enough that most of the factories had let out already, and I stood on the narrow strip of roadway that makes up Tulplaan 90 and looked up into the blinking kaleidoscopic light-vomit of the advertising strip that fronts his apartment wall. I found his floor and I found his ridiculous, floor-to-ceiling window that peers out onto the narrow street below in a manner that was always impossible to shelter with a curtain, and I found it dark, as it should be, and empty. It stabbed me in that part of my throat that's always tender now, always sore, and I closed my eyes for a moment so that I didn't have to see that his room was shuttered and shadowed and missing its beating heart.

And when I opened my eyes again, a light was on in his room and a figure that wasn't Adam was standing at the window and drawing the curtains. This city moves on so quickly. It's only me that wants to fix him in time and hold onto him. Luchtstad has already forgotten.

"Yes," I tell Sanne now, because I know she'll let the silence trail and linger into discomfort, and, though I can ignore it, I find I don't want to. "His blast injuries were worse than we'd thought. He's gone to a rehabilitation centre on Radiale Een."

The near-truth, Alice says, is safer than a lie. There are records that show we made his final journey, and records that will show my journeys to visit him. It's more difficult to make a citizen disappear into the Eddy than it is to smuggle in a new arrival from the cargo loading docks, but it's not the first time she's had to do it and, she hopes, it won't be the last. Everyone is getting old these days. The Eddy may be the only way that any of us survive.

"I'm sorry," says Sanne. She sounds it. Her hand unfurls from its habitual smoking position, folded across her chest to support the arm that holds her cigarette, and flutters uncertainly in the air in front of her for a second, as though she wants to reach out and touch it to my shoulder, but I feel myself flinch away from it, and I know that she sees this. The hand retracts. "He was your friend. I'm sorry."

She says 'friend' like it's loaded with infinite meaning, and it's supposed to be another question. But this one, I won't answer. Even if I could quantify what Adam meant to me in the end, it's not something that Sanne or Bente or Thijs or Aline or Jouke or Amita would ever understand.

"Yes," I say, and, for a horrible moment, I feel tears prick my eyes and the world blurs. And then I feel him at my shoulder, the soft touch of a hand that's not really there, the soft breath of a voice that's only in my head, and he says, *Hey – hey, come on now.* And I think of him curled up in the half-darkness beside his sleeping lover, two narrow bodies on a single bed, and the peace that surrounds them, pillows them, closes them off in a place that's all their own. I think of him sleeping forever beside the other half of his soul, and I hope that their hands touch in this world, if only to let the rest of us see that the proper order of things prevails in the *dis*. "Yes," I tell Sanne. "But it's for the best. He's where he needs to be."

37.3 Danae

It's got to the point now where I can pinpoint the location of the chant to Earth or Greater Earth, according to the level of singularity feedback that crowds out the voices. This one is calm and sad, a chorus of regret and longing, but it's not from Luchtstad. I listen every time. I'd know if it was for him.

I've got an intravenous cannula in the back of my hand and a drip full of *Yersinia Pestis* feeding directly into a central line below my collarbone. The screen above my face is playing a trailer for that new reality show that everyone's obsessed with, and the rest of my body is circled by a sequence of imaging shells that dilute and muffle the city's datastream feedback into a gentle static wash against my skin. This is the most peace and quiet I'll get all week and I'd prefer not to share it with three talking heads and a booming synthetic bumper, but it is what it is. I've got good at zoning it out as the months have passed.

I didn't used to be aware of the Red Space feedback skittering back and forth across the uplink as my system neutralises the poisons dripping into my veins. It's subtle and over so quickly that you'd have to be concentrating *really* hard to notice. But the thing about the Eddy is, you can't spend any length of time in there without coming out... better. Better at reading the link. Better at harnessing the *dis*.

Better at making sure that it holds onto its secrets.

Just... better. Bit by bit and day by day. Little by little. Confounding the research team's efforts from now until the end of time is my side project, something I started to pass the long and empty hours inside the sarcophagus. Pissy little acts of industrial sabotage may not be elegant, but they make me feel like I'm starting to reclaim something, and I feel Adam would approve. I imagine his smile as I lie here, focussed on scrambling the Red Space pingback noise, and I imagine the roll of his eyes, the shake of his head, the smartarse rejoinder that's carefully calibrated to provoke but not quite discourage, because we both know he understands. I got a life back, and for that I'll pay the price. But it wasn't my life. And the cost was much too high.

I've been here since 7 a.m. and it's now almost noon. Five hours is their absolute limit, so it's not a surprise to find my sarcophagus abruptly powered down and myself ejected, blinking, into the sterile white claustrophobia of an imaging suite at rest. Unsheltered, the tidal blitz of singularity feedback rushes in to fill the silence, and there he is, waiting for me as usual: shadow on shadow, a memory of a smile. An echo on the *dis*.

Hey, I tell him.

The chant swells, voices raised in sadness and in hope. Sometimes I sing with them, sometimes I just listen. I've heard it now from the inside of the stream itself, and today I'm going to let it wash over and through me, scouring me, rubbing warmth back into hidden corners of my soul. I'm not haunted, not in the conventional sense, but as the door slides open onto the corridor beyond, I see a shade detach itself from the shadowless walls and follow me out onto the streets of our city.

37.4 Danae

In the end, there's nothing I would have done differently. It all worked out the way it was supposed to; it's only that I never felt I was alone before I knew him. Or, rather, I did: it was just that I was able to pretend that it was because I wanted to be alone. Adam exploded all of that into nonsense and dust, and that's what I can't shake off.

"You're an arsehole," I tell him as I shrug my coat off and onto the bed. In an effort to show willing, I've bought some tinsel and a couple of sprigs of fake holly, and I've wound the tinsel around the bedstead and draped the holly over the top of the cupboard, and the place actually looks more depressing now than it did when it was bare. Adam finds this hilarious, and tells me as much every time I get home. "Do you know how much this shit cost me?"

On the edge of hearing, I catch a hint of a snicker, and I remind him, in the privacy of my head, that it's a damn good thing he's a ghost. I'm exhausted. The markets are gorged on festive hysteria, infinite humans attempting to dance on the head of a pin, and even though I've got nobody to buy presents for and all I wanted to do was get in the groceries for the week, I've got to do the same ridiculous hustle and twist through a solid wall of people all trying to move in the opposite direction. It reminds me a little of home. There are few enough places in this city where a crowd can gather, but for the market at Christmas, the city buys in extra oxygen and lets Luchtstad go nuts, and everyone who can walk upright and spend money crams into Goudlelielaan in a panic. There's something comforting about the smell of a crowd, though: the faint patina of sweat that hangs over us in the cool air, the smell of warmth, the smell of a thousand stalls, all compressed into the tiny pockets between us, sharpened by proximity. Stalls roast chestnuts and chicken, cardamom and cinnamon, chocolate and candyfloss, and everyone, everywhere, is suddenly a connoisseur: arguments spring out because someone does not stock the right variety of candied peel, or there is too much violet in the mauve cotton, or the woman doesn't sell it in a size four. I kept my head down and stuck to the plan, and it still took me two hours longer than expected, and that was after a fifteen-hour shift on the factory floor. I'm exhausted and hungry and my head aches, and all I want to do is go to bed and sleep for a million years.

I drop my bags onto the bed, bottles chiming softly as they brush and settle. I don't need him to say anything; I can feel his disapproval and his raised eyebrow, and I'm just not in the mood.

"Oh, fuck off," I tell him. "It's bouillon, for fuck's sake. I'm making fucking broth."

He says nothing. I let it happen for as long as my temper holds out, which is not, as it turns out, very long.

"All right, *one* of them is *bisschopswijn*, but it's about half-a-percent proof. See?" I grab a bottle from one of the bags and hold it out for the empty room to inspect. There's a chance that I'm crazy, but a much better chance that I'm not, and, as long as there's nobody here to see me, I don't care to check which one is right. "I'm making broth, for fuck's sake. I feel like I could get a little more support here."

I'm still learning. Broth is not something that can be produced from stem-sheets, for obvious reasons, and my parental home-economics lessons were fairly stem-sheet heavy, so it's slow going. But there are folks on this floor who can't get out to the shops, because they've been recognised, or because they're in hiding, or because they're just starting to break down and can't rely on their uplink for long enough to get to the tram, and terrible broth brewed by inexpert hands and delivered to their door is better than no broth at all.

I still mark them down in my book. Some habits are hard to break. But Alice knows now where I keep it, and if anything ever happens to me, I wouldn't want to bet against her.

I unpack slowly, taking care to find the right place for everything. I'm aware of what I'm doing, of course, and I know from the silence that I'm not alone in my understanding. I don't need to stack the stem-sheets with geometric precision right at the edge of the shelf, or to line up the *bisschopswijn* so that the label is perpendicular to the wall. I don't need to do any of this, in the same way that I don't need to avoid solitude so badly that I've conjured up my friend from the depths of the *dis* to scold me from the very edge of hearing. I dream about him every night, curled around Luca, breath aligned with breath, heartbeats chiming in perfect unison, except that it's not his face that I see. When I feel that sense of perfect calm drift down over my watching self, the sense of contentment, of wholeness, of rightness that I feel doesn't belong to a darkened room in Radiale Een. It all worked out the way it was supposed to, in the end, and there's nothing I would have done differently about the days I spent with Adam, but I can't shake the sense, these past months since I lost him, that the days I spent with Adam are not the problem.

I finish putting the groceries away. I touch the edge of a stem-sheet that has moved fractionally out of alignment and nudge it back into place, and then I sit in the centre of the floor and cross my legs and close my eyes. I breathe, and feel myself breathing, and I let the fear wash over me, settle into my bones and skitter my heartbeat. I let it come, and I let it consume me, and then I let it go. I know what I have to do. I've known this from the moment I last said goodbye in the Eddy, and maybe I've known it longer than that.

There's no reason for him to answer, of course. He won't recognise my streamcode, because the work of turning Danae Grant into Françoise Marechal was carefully done and nothing was forgotten. And it's been so long, an endless parade of empty weeks and months, a year and more with nothing but silence and loss. There's no reason for him to answer, but I know that he will. I know it before I hear the stream shift as the call connects. I know it before I hear his voice.

"Turrow," I say quietly. "It's me."

Acknowledgements

I spent July and August of 2003 living in a tent outside Noordwijk, a seaside town about 35 miles south west of Amsterdam, packing flower bulbs in a local factory. It was one of the best summers of my life. This novel is intended as a love letter to the Duin-en Bollenstreek, a part of the world that will forever hold a piece of my heart. The dystopian underbelly of Luchtstad is an artefact of the kind of stories I tell and in no way reflects the warmth of the welcome I received in the Netherlands or the kindness of the people I met there.

I'm forever grateful for the help, advice and encouragement of the truly wonderful people in my life without whom this novel would never have progressed past chapter one. My husband, Jesse Durkan, is my rock and my constant support. Guess how much fun it is being married to someone whose head is constantly 100 years in the future. Now add two energetic small children to the mix and imagine how inadequate any word of thanks could ever be. A huge thank you also to my mum, Dee Kelly, who doesn't even read science fiction, but has read every word of mine. To my dad, John Kelly, who put my first Pratchett novel in my hands and set the inevitable in motion. To my brother, Niall Kelly, who never makes me feel like my stupid questions are stupid. To my sister, Aine Kelly, who sends me memes when things are getting rough, and from whom a well-placed, "That'll do, donkey. That'll do," makes all the difference. And to my children, Rowan and Clara: my tiny muses, who make me want to imagine a better future, and for whom I write darkness in hopes that it never comes to pass.

A huge thank you to the wonderful Ian Whates of NewCon Press for believing in this novel and its predecessor, even when a pandemic hit just as my debut was launching. To my agent John Jarrold, for all his support, guidance, and words of wisdom and encouragement. To the legend that is Ian McDonald, who mentored this book through its early, faltering steps, and who has championed me and my writing. To Enid Crowe, through whom I met the legend that is Ian McDonald – I was privileged to call her my friend and the world is a much poorer place for her absence. To Mischa van Kan, who very generously gave his time and energy to make sure that my Dutch was up to scratch, and made some very helpful corrections where it wasn't – any mistakes that remain are all mine. And to David Jebb, for his thoughtful and considered sensitivity read of the first draft of this manuscript – thank you for helping me do justice to Adam and Luca's story.

Finally, the writing of this novel was supported by an Artists Career Enhancement Scheme award from the Arts Council of Northern Ireland, which financed both the time I spent writing the initial draft and an invaluable mentorship with Ian McDonald. I am immeasurably grateful for this support, and for their support of the wider literary community in Northern Ireland.

About the Author

RB Kelly was born and raised in Northern Ireland, in a home where Star Trek re-runs were rarely off the television and the bookshelves were well-stocked with Terry Pratchett. Her debut novel, *Edge of Heaven*, was shortlisted for the Arthur C Clarke Award, and her short stories have appeared in a variety of magazines and anthologies, including *The Best of British Science Fiction*, *Aurealis*, and *Andromeda Spaceways Magazine*. She has a PhD in film theory, and is a co-founder of CinePunked, an organisation dedicated to bridging the gap between film theory and film fandom. She lives outside Belfast with her husband and two children.

RB Kelly would like to acknowledge the support of the National Lottery through the Arts Council of Northern Ireland during the writing of this novel.

Also from NewCon Press

RB Kelly – Edge of Heaven
Shortlisted for the Arthur C. Clarke Award
Creo Basse, a city built to house the world's dispossessed. In the dark, honeycomb districts of the lower city, Turrow searches for black-market meds for his epileptic sister when he encounters one of the many ways Creo can kill a person. A tinderbox of unrest finally ignites when a deadly plague breaks out, which the authorities claim is a terrorist weapon manufactured by extremist artificial humans hiding in the city, but is the truth darker still?

Burning Brightly edited by Ian Whates
Celebrating 50 years of Novacon, featuring a mix of original fiction and first time reprints of stories written by former Guests of Honour, including **Iain M. Banks, Peter F. Hamilton, Stephen Baxter, Justina Robson, Paul McAuley, Geoff Ryman, Jaine Fenn, Anne Nicholls, Adrian Tchaikovsky, Juliet E. McKenna, Ian R. MacLeod,** and more…

Saving Shadows – Eugen Bacon
Prose poetry and speculative micro-lit pieces by renowned author Eugen Bacon. Forty-eight pieces in all: twenty-six previously published and twenty-two written specially for this book. Complementing the written word are a series of full page illustrations commissioned by the author from artist Elena Betti; thirty-five stunning images that enhance the reading experience.

Wergen: The Alien Love War – Mercurio D. Rivera
A sophisticated alien race biochemically infatuated with humans, the Wergens crave us, while we need their technology. We exploit them, until they find a way around their addiction. From the towering skyscrapers of Earth to the methane lakes of Titan, from the ice-plains of Pluto to distant alien gas giants, these stories of unrequited love play out against the cosmic backdrop of conflict between the two species.

www.newconpress.co.uk

www.ingramcontent.com/pod-product-compliance
Lightning Source LLC
Chambersburg PA
CBHW021218260626
47172CB00002B/481